SHIFTING SANDS RESORT OMNIBUS

VOLUME 4

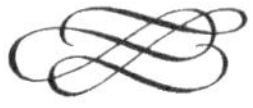

ZOE CHANT

ELVA BIRCH

Copyright © 2019-2021 by Zoe Chant, Elva Birch, and Ellen Million Graphics

PO Box 82851
Fairbanks Alaska 99708

ISBN: 978-1-933603-70-4

All rights reserved.

No part of this book may be reproduced in any form or by any electronic or mechanical means, including information storage and retrieval systems, without written permission from the author, except for the use of brief quotations in a book review.

Cover design © 2019-2021 by Ellen Million. Visit ellenmillion.com for signed paperbacks and other swag!

No generative AI was used in any part of this publication.

For my parents, who believed I could do anything I set my heart to.

SHIFTING SANDS RESORT

Sun, surf, shifters, and secrets!

Escape to a shifters-only resort on a hot tropical island full of secrets and sizzling romance.

Shifting Sands Resort is a complete paranormal romance series with self-standing novels that interconnect in an intriguing mystery.

This omnibus edition is in the author's preferred reading order, with short stories and novellas mixed in with the novels.

CONTENTS

TROPICAL LION'S LEGACY

CHAPTER 1

"You've got a visitor," the secretary told Alice Anders as she waltzed in the office to check her inbox. "I just paged you. He's waiting for you in the principal's office."

"Am I in trouble?" Alice asked archly.

To her surprise, the secretary only shook her head, looking flustered, and gestured at the principal's door even more anxiously.

Leafing through her pile of fundraiser fliers and dress code memos, Alice opened the door absently, and drew up short.

Sitting in Principal Wetch's seat was an undeniably impressive figure.

At six foot four inches tall, Alice was used to towering over other women, and even many men. But when this man stood politely when she entered the room, she had to look up to meet his eyes, and his shoulders were proportionally broad. His suit, probably worth twice Alice's middle-school gym teacher salary, did nothing to hide the fact that he was incredibly ripped. His brisk handshake was strong and he was dead handsome, with a strong, clean-shaven jaw and an artistic touch of gray in his short, dark hair.

Alice would have eaten her dirty gym socks if he wasn't a shifter and her bear rumbled in cautious agreement.

"Can I help you?" Alice asked, sitting across from him at his imperious gesture. She started to sit gingerly, then slouched deliberately.

"I think you can," he said in a silky voice, settling into the principal's seat and leaning back. "I understand you'll be traveling just after the end of the semester for your coworker's wedding."

"Yeeeeees," Alice said, drawing out the word. "Is there some problem with that? I should have my grades done in plenty of time. I'm only a gym teacher." She could not quite keep the challenge out of her voice; she never backed down from a fight and she sensed that this would shortly become one.

He smiled at her. "You're a bear shifter." It wasn't a question.

Alice froze, and could not help glancing at the door, still barely ajar. Shifters were a well-kept secret in this area.

Before she could formulate a response to his statement, he went on. "You have a brother in Oregon, and two aging parents here in Lakefield."

He gave her a conspiratorial look. "Such a shame that they'll be losing the house."

He continued before Alice could so much as blink at him.

"You teach gym at Lakefield Middle and have been the wrestling coach here for seven years. You've taken them to regionals three years running, which is very impressive for a school of this size. You never returned your last rental to Blockbuster before they went out of business five years ago. Your bank account has seven hundred and twenty-three dollars in it and you have lined up an under-the-table summer job at a construction firm laying concrete forms."

Alice wasn't the sort to stare. Glare maybe, if a student needed to be intimidated, but staring was for women who were easily shocked, or let themselves be surprised.

She was staring now.

"Interesting, that your last visit to Shifting Sands Resort ended up being canceled due to… what was it? Chicken pox?"

Alice didn't believe for a moment that his hesitation was anything but feigned for effect.

"It's rare for adults to contract chicken pox," the strange shifter observed. "Rarer still for shifters to get it."

"You need a note from my doctor?" Alice asked mockingly. She made herself keep her casual posture, even though she and her bear were both bristling in alarm.

"I already have it," the man said casually. "But it's a little odd that it was from a doctor in Portland. And that your airline tickets were changed at the last minute to Oregon, rather than Costa Rica. Took a bit of a hit on that, didn't you?"

Alice was done pretending. "What do you want?" she asked outright, sitting forward and planting her feet.

The stranger smiled slowly. "I have a matter of interest at the resort, a problem that has proved unexpectedly challenging."

Alice immediately distrusted his tone. "What *kind* of interest?" she demanded. "And what does this have to do with me?"

"I have an offer for you," the man said smoothly, not answering any of her questions. "One that will more than cover your time and any inconvenience. One that will more than cover the medical costs your brother needs."

Alice felt her heart drop out of her chest. "What do you know about that?" she asked fiercely, not even trying to pretend ignorance.

"I know that a million dollars will go a long way towards his care and comfort. With plenty left over to buy your parents a lovely retirement home."

Alice forced herself to act like she wasn't intimidated, though her stomach and her heart seemed to be having a wrestling match in her belly. "Oh, a million dollars," she said mockingly. "Is that all?"

"Very well," the shifter across the desk said, his mouth curving up in a smile that indicated he knew she was bluffing. "*Fifty* million. Money is no object to me."

Alice had always thought that breaking into a sweat from anything but exertion was just literary nonsense, but she did now. "Fifty million?" she murmured, in a very un-Alice way. "What exactly do you want me to do?"

He laughed, and it was a surprisingly warm laugh. "Don't look so shocked, Alice. I'm not going to have you *murder* anyone."

That had been the only thing Alice could imagine for that kind of money, but she somehow didn't feel relieved. "What is it you want me to do?" she repeated.

"The owner of the resort is a woman named Scarlet Stanson."

You don't have to murder her, Alice had to remind herself.

The man slid a business card across the desk. "All you have to do is find out what kind of shifter she is."

CHAPTER 2

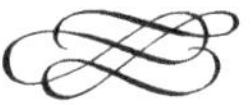

"Conall says Gizelle's been in her animal form for nearly the whole day, the poor dear," Laura said, sidling up beside Graham Long at the open door of the refrigerator. The wolf shifter wasn't talking to him, but to her identical twin sister Jenny, the otter shifter sitting at the kitchen bar.

"She's a little shaken by the idea of Neal coming back to Shifting Sands," Jenny explained. "He's the one who coaxed her back to human form and she was pretty broken up when he left with Mary."

"Was she in love with him?" Laura asked, slipping under Graham's arm to take a plate of leftover Alaska salmon filet and a bottle of orange juice.

"Nothing like that," Tex, Laura's bear shifter mate, was quick to assure her. "But he was the first one she really trusted. I think she's worried that Neal won't like who she is now. She's changed so much since they last saw each other."

Laura, having poured them all glasses of orange juice, ducked back under Graham's arm to return the bottle.

Graham was still standing in front of the open fridge, eyeing the contents without interest. Nothing looked appealing, but he still felt oddly hungry and his lion was pacing restlessly in his head. Finally, he snagged two cold breakfast sausages and a croissant and took a cluster of apple bananas from the fruit bowl.

The others nodded at him as Graham took the stool at the end of the bar where Laura had left him a glass of cold juice and he nodded back. That was as much conversation as they generally expected from him.

"I'm sure Gizelle will be fine once he's here and they've had a chance to reconnect," Tex said. "I'm more worried about how Conall is going to react to Neal."

Conall, Gizelle's mate, was a deaf Irish elk shifter. Losing his hearing had been devastating to his soaring music career and he had been unfriendly and prickly when he first arrived at Shifting Sands.

Gizelle's love had mellowed him considerably, and her touch allowed him to hear, but he was still cool and grim around strangers, and he was intensely protective of his mate.

Maned red wolf shifter Neal, once a prisoner in the same shifter zoo that Gizelle had grown up in, had been a hardened Marine before his capture. He had been key in helping Gizelle find her way back to her human form when they were freed, but he was not overly friendly or easy to get to know.

Now, after more than a year, he was returning to wed his mate, Mary, and would see the young woman that Gizelle had blossomed into for the first time.

"Even if Conall and Neal can't stand each other, *this* wedding should still go much more smoothly than our last one," Laura laughed. They were still picking up the pieces of the last wedding that Shifting Sands had hosted, one that had ended in a bloody duel, a happily jilted groom, and the establishment of a small shifter retirement home on the island.

"Well, Neal probably won't sue the resort, at least," Tex agreed. "And Mary isn't going to leave him at the altar to marry a waiter like Darla did. Probably."

They all laughed, except Graham, who caught his face before it could smile.

Jenny, who worked as Scarlet's lawyer, grimaced as the laughter faded.

Her mate Travis, the resort handyman, caught her expression and asked, "Any word from Darla's dreadful mother on that lawsuit she threatened?"

"Not yet," Jenny said. "But we're expecting the worst."

"Horray," Laura said humorlessly.

Jenny frowned. "What I really don't understand is why Scarlet isn't trying harder to find Aaric Lyons' heir. My firm found some really promising leads, but she's actually told me to *stop* pursuing them."

Graham hunched over his food, feeling his ears heat.

Benedict Beehag, the heir to the shifter zoo that Gizelle and Neal had been trapped in, owned the entire island and had been trying to sell it out from underneath Scarlet and dissolve their contract since he had inherited. The unfortunate part was that he seemed to be going out of his way to market it to the very worst kind of underworld characters and he had even tried to hire away Scarlet's most trusted staff in a hostile takeover.

Scarlet, with the help of Jenny, had been able to thwart his efforts at every turn, but Beehag had proved unpleasant as a landlord and had not given up trying to sell the property, though each prospective buyer seemed more unsavory than the last.

Jenny had recently discovered an obscure clause in the lengthy contract that required Beehag to give the heir of the original owner, Rupert Beehag's partner Aaric Lyons, first right of refusal on any subsequent sales of the property. Everyone had assumed the line had died out, but Jenny uncovered records for a grandson, Grant Lyons, who had moved to America and presumably changed his name.

"Money?" Laura suggested. "Even if Darla's mother *doesn't* sue, there's no way she's paying off the remainder of her bill for that wedding, and Scarlet went all out on the expenses for it. The resort can't be doing well, financially. Maybe she figures she doesn't have the funds to buy the resort, so why bother? Maybe she doesn't want to risk the funds on hiring detectives?"

Jenny shook her head. "This would be calling in favors from people I've worked for; it wouldn't even cost her. And there's a possibility—even if it's slim—that when we find him, we'll find that *Lyons'* got the money for the sale. He can't be a more unappealing landlord than our current one."

"Do you have any idea why she's balking?" Tex asked Travis. "You've been here longer than anyone but Graham."

Travis shook his head.

Graham had been studiously peeling his apple bananas, keeping his head down and hoping he didn't look guilty, and he was startled into looking up at the sound of his name.

His *fake* name.

"Do *you* have any ideas?" Laura had been looking his way and Graham scowled to cover his confusion.

He only grunted and shrugged one shoulder in answer. He was relieved when no one seemed to expect anything else. They turned the conversation to happier plans for the upcoming wedding.

He finished his breakfast as quickly as he could, cursing the tiny, challenging peels of the miniature bananas and his own instinct to crush them rather than disrobe them.

Then he escaped, dumping his peels in the trash and leaving his plate in the sink.

He scowled to himself as he stalked to the kitchen to get Chef's request for produce from the garden.

He'd gotten used to being Graham. He *felt* like Graham.

Graham was someone who had friends, however reluctantly. Friends who trusted him, included him in their jokes, and even asked him for favors. Friends he actually wanted to do favors *for*.

Graham was hard working and quiet. He was dependable and steady. He was solid.

Graham was a good guy.

But he wasn't really Graham.

And Grant Lyons wasn't any of those things.

CHAPTER 3

"Wouldn't it be hilarious if you met your mate here, too?"

Alice pretended to laugh. "Har har," she offered, hoping it sounded less bitter to them than it did to her.

Her co-worker and best friend Mary meant well, of course. And Amber, who was snickering as she climbed out of the poorly-sprung resort van, didn't have a mean bone in her body. (She also looked almost exactly like she had when she and Alice were rooming together, which was terribly unfair.) Neither of them realized how much the idea of *mates* hurt Alice.

"Oh my gosh, the entrance looks exactly the same as it did," Amber exclaimed. "Wow, the memories! The smells! The flowers! Oh my gosh, the flowers on that hyacinth!"

Mary had her nose in the air as well. "What amazing surprise has Chef concocted?" she wondered out loud.

"Pot roast," Amber deduced. "With a garlicky marinade and a side of fresh roasted radishes and some kind of onion soup, and I think chocolate for dessert."

Alice stared at her as her own bear confirmed every one of those smells in turn. "Pregnancy nose is so weird," she said in awe.

"You couldn't even smell the difference between dish soap and toilet cleaner when we were rooming together."

Amber, who was not quite to the stage of waddling, but well past the dangerous-to-ask 'plump or pregnant?' phase, smiled. "It's not entirely a blessing! I had to kick the cat off the bed because she smelled like cat spit," she confided. "And if I weren't already banned from scooping the catbox, I would be incapable of it for the stench."

She reached for her bag, but Tony, coming around from the other side of the van where he'd been talking with a man he had greeted as Travis, stopped her. "You aren't supposed to carry heavy things!" he insisted, grabbing it first.

"It's not heavy," Amber protested.

Tony gave a harrumph of disbelief and shouldered the bag anyway.

"You know, women have been giving birth and carrying their own luggage for thousands of years," Amber reminded him.

"Be glad I'm not insisting on carrying *you*," Tony said, ignoring the laughing protests of Travis as he scooped up half of their luggage and sailed into the resort entrance. "I know where our cottages are, you girls check in!"

Neal, Mary's mate, grinned and silently took another load of luggage in his wake.

There were other guests already queued to check in at the desk in the glorious little courtyard and while Amber and Mary chattered about weddings and babies, Alice found herself scrutinizing the woman behind the desk.

Her movements were brisk and efficient as she handed out keys and ran credit cards and shuffled forms, and Alice guessed even before she heard her introduce herself that this must be Scarlet. The brilliant red color of her hair suggested the origin of her name, though Alice kept second guessing whether or not it was dyed. It looked too bright to be natural, but too natural to be from a bottle.

Maybe the spa was *really* exceptional.

She wondered wistfully if they could do anything for her own limp, short, brown hair, then dismissed the thought. Even if they could, they couldn't do anything about the towering height or the linebacker physique, and even less about the aggressive forward nature and short temper. She wasn't the pretty, pleasing type like Amber and Mary. And she certainly wasn't here to snag a mate to marry.

It was their turn at the desk.

"Welcome back, and congratulations!" Scarlet greeted their party with a warm smile. "Please consider yourself at home and let me know if you need anything while you're here."

Though Alice thought Scarlet probably said something like that to everyone who came through, it felt particularly sincere and even grateful. Her smile included Alice, who felt uncomfortable, remembering the business card that was burning a hole in her pocket.

At least you don't have to kill her, she reminded herself.

Which was good, because Alice was pretty sure she wouldn't be able to do that. Not even for fifty million dollars.

Forms were spread out over the counter. "Please inspect these for accuracy, initial here and here, and sign on the last page. You received copies of the rules and requirements, but I do want to remind you that our foremost rule is no predation."

She was looking at Alice when she said that, which made sense, as the newcomer, and a scary bear shifter, but Alice wondered if there was more significance to Scarlet's glance than that.

Alice met her gaze without wavering, trying to guess her shifter type just from her characteristics; she'd been able to tell Mary was a deer shifter the first day they'd met as new teachers in middle school, and she knew that Amber was a cat shifter immediately from her feline grace, even if she never in a hundred years would have guessed Andean mountain cat, an obscure wild cat like a tiny snow leopard.

The sense of power around Scarlet was without question, but for some reason, she didn't feel like any of the large predators that Alice could think of. Something mythical? There was supposed to be a dragon lifeguard, which opened up a whole box of 'I didn't know they were real' possibilities. A gryphon? A unicorn? An… angel?

Scarlet was still looking at her, and Alice finally decided that a direct approach was a good as any.

"So, what's *your* shift form?" she asked casually.

Mary and Amber both went still beside her and she could feel their surprise without turning to look at them.

Alice grinned. "I mean, you've got all our information," she said casually, indicating the form as she scrawled her initials boldly and flipped the page over. "It's a fair question."

Scarlet only smiled coldly and kept her secrets.

"The restaurant is open for breakfast and dinner only, but the buffet is available around the clock." She pushed brochures over the counter. "The bar and spa hours are listed here, as well as yoga sessions, meditation, and dance lessons."

Oh well. Alice would have been surprised if it had been that easy.

CHAPTER 4

Graham arrived at the kitchens still scowling, but no one was surprised by that.

"Morning, Grumpy," Breck called to him as he waltzed past with a tray of fruit cups. "Chef's got the list on the fridge. Let him know what you've got so we can put the rest in on the mainland order. Travis is leaving in an hour."

The resort produce garden was not all that large; it couldn't possibly provide all of the vegetables the kitchens used. But it could add a little splash of incredibly fresh produce when called upon and Graham's tomatoes were generally accepted as ambrosia from heaven.

Graham frowned over the list hung on the gleaming fridge with a heart-shaped magnet.

"Morning, Graham," Breck's mate Darla said shyly at his elbow. The snow leopard shifter was the newest addition to Chef's kitchen and still seemed timid around Graham.

Grant would have liked frightening her. Graham tried to scowl a little less and nodded in greeting.

He stepped aside to let her open the fridge and pull out a gallon jar of milk, then vanish back down one of the shining kitchen aisles to where she was mixing some mysterious dough; her failed baking lessons were commonly available in The Den, the manor where most of the senior staff lived. Most of them were perfectly edible, if too ugly for guest consumption.

Chef's progress through the noisy kitchen was made obvious by the opera he was singing at the top of his considerable lungs. "Ah, Graham," he greeted in his booming voice. "I'm not sure about the status of your tomato crop, but if you could perform a miracle and have four dozen of about this size, you would be the answer to a prayer."

Graham frowned at the example tomato Chef was holding. "I'll have to check," he hedged. Truth was he knew off the top of his head that he only had about half of that ripe now, but he might be able to cheat a little.

"And basil," Chef said, looking at the list.

"Got plenty."

"Any hot peppers ripe?"

"Few handfuls of jalapeños, a couple of chocolate habaneros." Graham had been eyeing the ripening habaneros avidly; it was a strain he'd never grown before and the plants had been reluctant to bloom in the tropical heat.

"Perfect! I'll take any you'll part with. I've got a spicy Moroccan dish that is perfect to try out on our current crowd."

Chef wandered back to check on a simmering pot and correct Darla's kneading technique. The two of them did a lilting duet from a show tune together.

Graham tucked the list into his pocket and left out the back door.

The resort was steep and non-shifters would have found the terrain challenging, but Graham climbed the steps two at a time, head down, shoulders rolled forward, face scowling, so no one would be tempted to talk to him or ask for directions.

The last of the guests from the latest flight were checking in, two of them familiar, while the third was a stranger. The two figures he recognized would be the mates of Neal and Tony, who had both been key in bringing down the shifter zoo on the opposite side of the island.

But it was the third one who caught his attention.

She was an amazon, towering over the two slighter women with her, and she had short, dark brown hair in a practical bob. She stood at easy attention, with a fit, powerful body not the slightest bit masked by her simple t-shirt and jeans. She had the barest swell of hips from behind, and a small, firm ass.

Graham forgot about talking to Scarlet, forgot about tomatoes and secret identities.

His world had narrowed to this woman and his lion was growling at his ear, intent and focused.

He could not have said how long he stood and stared as the strange woman finished signing her forms and turned at last.

Hazel-green eyes met his and every breathless suspicion was confirmed: this *was* his mate.

Others on the staff sometimes talked about how it felt to meet their mate and how they fought their instincts when they met for various reasons.

Graham was a fighter. Down at the very bones of whatever name he wore, he was a fighter, and he felt now like he did when he was preparing for battle: calm and ready and focused.

But it wasn't his instincts he was ready to fight. He crossed to the middle of the courtyard in just a few steps and she met him there.

For a long moment they stood, silently sizing each other up.

Then she growled at him, and he was lost.

CHAPTER 5

Alice appreciated the need for rules. Without rules, there were no games. Without games, there was no competition. Without competition, there was no growth.

But she still resented being read rules like she was some kind of errant kid who didn't understand that she shouldn't eat other guests.

Scarlet must have had a lawyer go over her agreement; every i was dotted and every t was crossed. And Scarlet herself… Alice knew it was too much to hope that the woman would prove to be friendly and forthcoming, but she hadn't expected the sharp, judgmental scrutiny that she got, or the intimidating power that the woman exuded.

Fifty million dollars, she reminded herself. Fifty million dollars to snoop out just one tiny detail. So Alice was so forward and friendly that she feared she was being flirtatious, asking about the resort and Scarlet's role until she was aware of Mary giving her suspicious sideways looks.

Scarlet seemed nothing but cool and professional in reply, her veneer unbroken until a leggy, cream-colored young cat leapt up onto the counter between them.

"This is Tyrant," Scarlet introduced with a tolerant smile that cracked her cool facade, scooping the kitten off the paperwork. "She doesn't understand boundaries."

Alice wondered if that was a dig at her for being nosy, but Scarlet let the three women coo over the affectionate feline and trade chin scratches for purrs, explaining that this was a real cat, not a shifter. "Though Gizelle does seem to hold out hope," she chuckled, releasing Tyrant back to the floor with a swift stroke from ears to tailtip.

Mary laughed knowingly and Amber said, "I'm looking forward to meeting Gizelle in human form at last."

Alice had heard all the stories about the shifter zoo and Gizelle's captivity. "I'm looking forward to meeting her, too," she said more boisterously than she intended.

That earned her an actual frown from Scarlet and Alice remembered that Gizelle was shy and afraid of more than Mary was. She grinned winningly back at Scarlet. Sometimes the timid students surprised her by responding well to a little encouragement. One of her best wrestling kids had been soft-spoken and terrified before joining the team.

Scarlet only looked at her more dubiously, and handed them each a key. "Let me know if you have any questions or problems," she said dismissively.

Fifty million dollars, Alice reminded herself, taking hers.

Then she turned away to go with Mary and Amber to their cottages… and even fifty million dollars was nothing.

He was standing at the entrance to the resort, wearing a green polo shirt with the Shifting Sands logo and khaki pants like the rest of the staff. His big hands were in fists at his side and his thick blond hair was wild around his face. He had a jaw like a brick and blue eyes like holes to the sky, and a dozen other romantic notions that meant absolutely nothing as he started to stride towards her.

Alice was in motion before she was aware of giving her feet the command, her bear roaring urgently to her as she crossed the distance to her mate.

Damn Mary for being prophetic, Alice thought fiercely. And damn her for feeling like she had a net of butterflies instead of a stomach, for the weakness and need that was burning inside her. She didn't want to swoon at his feet, and at the same time, she desperately did. It made her teeth clench, the way she wanted to give herself to him. She belonged to no one.

They were standing in the middle of the courtyard, staring at each other, and Alice was distantly aware of the surprised scrutiny of her friends, and of Scarlet.

But mostly she was aware of his strength and the height of him—he had an inch or two on her—the smell of him, and her own rising desire.

Without considering, she peeled her lips back, and growled at him wordlessly in challenge.

What are you going to do? she taunted him with her eyes, half-hoping he would run and prove all her fears right.

He didn't run.

He reached over and put one hand at the back of her neck and pulled her in for a bruising kiss. It wasn't a kiss that asked permission, and it wasn't a kiss that pretended to be gentle or courtly, and at some point Alice realized that she was the one kissing *him*, her arms around his broad shoulders and her mouth fierce against his.

The sound of a throat clearing made her stop at last, her mouth throbbing, and draw back.

Mary and Amber must be staring, and probably Scarlet was too, but Alice had no interest in looking away from the strange, gorgeous man's intense gaze to find out.

She wanted to ask who he was, find out why he looked so grim, hear the sound of the voice that must come from those lips, from that chest.

She wanted to know where he came from, what he'd been like as a child, what he was afraid of, what he did for fun, where those big hands had been that made them smell like dirt and grass.

She wanted to know why *him*, why *her*, what *now*…

But most of all, she needed to know, "*Where?*"

His smile was so slow, so hopeful, so utterly beautiful that it gave Alice a little unwelcome jolt in the center of her chest.

Then he was taking her hand and she was following him out of the courtyard as Mary and Amber fell into delighted laughter behind them.

CHAPTER 6

The touch of her hand in his was electric and Graham had to struggle to remember which of the cottages would be empty now… fourteen had just been vacated, but wouldn't be made up yet... eleven wouldn't be occupied for another few days.

And it was close, which was his primary concern now.

She smelled like a long day of travel and, beneath that, like simple soap and sunshine. Her hand was strong in his, long-fingered and rough-finished.

They made it to the intersection to the first tier of cottages before Graham had to kiss her again, to taste those wild lips and feel those hands around his shoulders.

It was with great difficulty that he managed to draw away again and get them both down the white gravel path to a cottage he hoped would be empty.

He nearly broke the door, wrenching it open, and was grateful to see that there was no luggage or personal affects within. He didn't pause in his beeline to the bed in the room beyond, and then they were wrestling down together.

She was so *strong*.

It was nearly a battle, each testing the other's strength, pushing for dominance, growling, stripping off clothing without care for seams or stitches.

This was no fainting daisy, there was no place for shyness; she knew what she wanted, what they both wanted, and she would take it if he didn't give it.

And oh, he wanted to give it to her.

As Graham kicked off his pants, she drew her nails along the length of his cock. He drew in his breath with a hiss, then pressed her down into the bed.

For a moment, she struggled with him, trying to tip him over on his back instead, and for that moment, Graham actually thought she might win the contest. Then she gave a little sigh of surrender and need and spread her legs and he was driving into her at last.

She was so wet and ready that he buried himself into her in one clean stroke and they held there a heartbeat before erupting into a frenzy of clawing and growling and thrusting.

It was like fencing, or dancing—advance, retreat, test boundaries, withdraw—and then there was a delicious moment of surrender when the woman in his arms gave a helpless noise of pleasure and went limp in his arms, giving herself completely to the release that washed over her.

That, even more than her lush, fierce, scrambling need, broke something in Graham… and he was helplessly coming with her, utterly lost to her heat and the soft, sweet noises she was making.

They lay apart at last, gasping for breath and desperate for the kiss of cool air on sweaty skin.

His mate.

He'd met his mate, and she was *perfect.*

She was strong and beautiful and fearless and there was a secret vulnerability to her that made Graham want to wrap her up in his arms and hold her safe forever.

"So, I'm Alice," she gasped in introduction, when she finally had breath for it. "Hi."

For a moment, Graham could only revel in the beauty of the name. Then he realized he needed to give his own in return and froze in indecision. Did he continue the lie he was living or start with the truth and go into the lengthy explanation his real name would require? Was he Graham, or was he Grant? Who did he want to be for his *mate*?

The window for answering politely was stretched and growing uncomfortable, and Graham felt panic rise in his throat. He needed to be cool, he needed to keep things under control. He needed to come up with something to say before she thought he was some kind of moron who didn't have a grasp of basic social skills.

"I love you," he blurted.

CHAPTER 7

Alice lay in a haze of comfortable bliss, her whole body feeling deeply satisfied.

Whoever this man was, he knew his way around her parts like he had a map, and he was strong and forward and *beautiful.*

She knew that a mate wasn't going to be the same happy ever after for her that Amber and Mary had found, but it was wonderful to revel in the sated animal need for a moment. She had the impression from her bear of rolling in sunlit flowers and having every itchy place scratched.

She supposed she should introduce herself and did, once she had breath. "So, I'm Alice," she said, staring up at the cottage rafters. "Hi."

"I love you," he replied after a moment, and Alice felt all of her contentment vanish at his words.

"Nope," Alice said firmly. "Nope, nope, nope." She sat up and supposed she should find her clothing, but whatever scraps of dignity she'd started with had been left in Scarlet's courtyard anyway.

"Look," she said, trying to find a tone that was firm but still kind, because whatever else she wanted to do, it made her chest squeeze to think of hurting him. But she couldn't string him along, either.

That would only be worse.

And she had her own life, her own troubles. She wasn't going to drag him back to that and she wasn't going to run away from what she had—her family, a job she loved—to pursue a *relationship*. She couldn't see a way that would end in anything but resentment.

"This was… great," she said. "And I know that Amber and Mary found something amazing with their mates, and that's awesome for them, but this is just sex and animal instinct, it's not destiny or nonsense like that. There's this romantic notion about mates, but it's just leftover evolutionary crap or something, it's not… fate."

He was sitting up on one elbow now, his whole face scrunched up in a glower.

Alice found his chest incredibly distracting and had to look somewhere else in order to continue forming complete sentences.

His thick arms were just as bad, and his hard jaw, and his tousled mane of hair.

He was a minefield of places she didn't dare look.

And he wasn't helping the conversation much, scowling at her like she was babbling nonsense.

Which she might have been doing, since she caught herself staring at his word-gobbling chest again.

"You don't love me," she insisted, wrenching her eyes away again. "I'm a gym teacher from the Midwest and I love my job, and you work at a fancy island resort in the tropics, and you've said three whole words to me, and none of them were your name."

"I'm Gra—Graham," he said, reluctantly.

His rumbling growl of a voice did nothing to still Alice's jangling nerves.

"Alice," she repeated and she thrust out a hand as if a formal handshake could possibly undo the sweaty, desperate sex they'd just had. "I'm glad to meet you. I am. But that's out of the way now, so don't expect a wedding date or anything, okay? We should be *honest* about this."

He continued to gaze at her, a piercing look that Alice was sure saw right through her attempt to keep him at arm's length. Whatever she said out loud, her sated body still hummed for him and her bear was still insisting that this was theirs, *forever*.

But her body was *wrong*, her bear was just an *animal* at the end of the day, and Alice was where she belonged, back in control of things.

When Graham reluctantly shook her hand, she feared she'd made another mistake, because the feel of his fingers against her palm sent shudders down her spine and made her bear… purr.

Bears don't purr, she told her animal crossly.

Neither do lions, her bear said smugly.

But clearly, until she'd shattered the moment with her declaration of nope, Graham, and the lion who obviously shared his body, had been deep in purr territory.

He wasn't now, of course, still scowling at her darkly like he was trying to figure out a puzzle.

Alice hastily reclaimed her hand.

"Oh look, there's my jeans. I'll just… ah… get dressed and go see if I can catch up with Mary and Amber." Alice crawled gracelessly off the bed, wondering how he had ever made her feel like her cumbersome body was something to be worshiped. She tugged her pants up with effort, nearly unbalanced, and finally managed to wrench them on.

"Alice," he started, and it made the hairs at the back of her neck lift.

"Thank you," she said brightly. "This was great fun. Maybe we'll hook up again later, if I've got time. Wedding stuff, you know. Not mine. Mary's. Mary's wedding."

Her shirt was in a heap on the floor and her bra was nowhere in sight. Well, she wasn't so amply endowed that it mattered much.

She pulled the shirt over her head, discovered it was backwards, and stuffed her arms through anyway. "*Ciao*!" she called, as merrily as she could, then she was fleeing in a random direction out of the door.

CHAPTER 8

Graham felt like the sun had gone out with Alice's flight, though the room was still infused with golden light through the filmy curtains. Part of him wanted to roll on the rumpled bedcovers and inhale her scent on the pillows.

The rest of him wanted to hit something.

This is not fate.

His lion wanted to pursue her, of course, but Graham tamped down that with a growl of his own. *Ciao* indeed. If she wanted to keep this casual, *fine.*

He was glad he hadn't told her his real name, even while he felt like he was a bottle under unbearable pressure, desperate to tell someone, anyone, especially her, who he really was, and beg for forgiveness.

One of the pillows tore apart under his hands before he could stop himself and Graham rose with a snarl to take a shower and wash her from his skin.

Her key found the bottom of his foot and he growled in pain before he picked it up and was sorry he looked at the cottage number because now he'd know where she was staying. Dammit.

He put the key on the bedside table, vowing to return it to the lost and found, and stomped to the shower.

He left the cottage in utter disarray, knowing that he'd hear about it later and not caring.

Still damp, still stung, he threw himself at his garden until afternoon, tying up the bean vines that were unfurling wildly across the beds, gently thinning the new lettuce, turning fresh dirt to plant a new batch of cucumbers.

By the time the staff meeting came around, he had buried everything again and felt the familiar layer of indifference settle around him. As long as he didn't *think* about her, he wasn't angry.

And Graham was *good* at not thinking about things.

He was still carefully not thinking about anything when he arrived early at the staff meeting and he was sorry that he wasn't in a better mood, because Neal and Tony were there, grinning and catching up on all the gossip and adventure that had happened at Shifting Sands since they'd been there.

"... Which is when the boat blew sky-high and Laura and I were left adrift in the middle of the ocean," Tex was explaining.

"The fireworks were nice," Laura said, laughing. "And he sang to me!"

"Sounds romantic," Neal said with a grin.

Neal hadn't done much grinning before Mary, Graham observed, and he scowled harder than ever. Wasn't that how mates were supposed to work? His own experience was proving vastly different.

Tex went on to talk about the otter who saved them.

"That was me," Jenny explained. "Not dead after all!"

That was when Neal realized that Graham was there and he interrupted the story to rise and shake hands with a smile.

Graham shook the offered hand, but gave no reply to Neal's cheerful greeting, wondering if there were layers of meaning in his knowing grin. Would Mary have already had a chance to tell him about his unorthodox introduction to her bridesmaid?

Fortunately, Breck arrived just then and Neal turned his greeting to him, letting Graham edge into the room and find an out of the way chair to sit on. "I hear you got married? Can this be? Is it *possible*? Did she drag you kicking and screaming?"

"There was screaming and a lot of clawing," Breck conceded. "But not so much of the dragging." He was grinning broadly, his eyes soft the way they always were when he spoke of Darla. "Wait until you meet her," he added adoringly. "She's so amazing."

Graham caught himself before he could growl out loud.

Lydia came in then and gave Neal and Tony each a warm, affectionate hug, Wrench glaring over her shoulder at the strangers protectively. "You've done so much for us," she told Tony appreciatively.

"Oh, it's not so much," Tony said, abashed. "Just doing my job."

Lydia wasn't the only one who made a skeptical noise. As an agent in the Shifter Affairs department, Tony had been instrumental in getting all the shifters who had been rescued from the zoo the paperwork and legal documents to return to their lives after a period of long absence and, in many cases, presumed death. Following that, he had been extremely useful in stopping a mob boss that had been hounding Jenny, Laura, and Wrench.

Congratulations were still being exchanged, for Neal's upcoming nuptials and Tony's impending fatherhood, when Scarlet arrived to start the meeting at one o'clock on the dot.

Graham stared fixedly at the floor, refusing to look at her.

The meeting was lighthearted, centering around the details of the upcoming wedding and the day-to-day considerations of the resort. The lawsuit from Darla's mother had not materialized and, if money was tight, it appeared that they were at least fairly well set to meet the coming weeks. Scarlet was glad to report that they were going to have a steady stream of guests; the debacle of Darla's wedding had not only *not* hurt their guest list, the publicity seemed to have been largely in the resort's favor.

As Scarlet concluded the meeting and left, nearly everyone else remained and the conversation dissolved into further gossip and talk about the wedding.

"How long are you staying?" Lydia asked.

"Three glorious weeks," Amber said in delight. "The wedding is the end of next week, and we'll have a week afterwards."

"We'll be leaving the same time," Tony added. "This is our last chance for a vacation before the baby comes."

That led to excited speculation about the baby, its gender, and what its shift form might be.

Laura shyly confessed her own pregnancy news to Tony and Neal. "We haven't told Scarlet yet," she said, her hand in a beaming Tex's. "We're… not really sure what our plans are next."

Graham squirmed and looked for a way to leave that wouldn't be obvious; choosing a chair in the corner had kept him out of the conversation, but it had also trapped him in the back of the room with no polite way of slinking out.

Babies, weddings, mates, and *secrets*.

He was in hell.

Then Neal turned around in his chair to look directly at Graham and said pointedly, "Speaking of honeymoons…"

And everyone looked at him curiously.

"I hear you and Alice didn't waste any time," Neal ribbed.

Graham had liked Neal much better when he said much less.

"Alice?" Breck said, puzzled. "Mary's friend? The maid of honor?"

"Honeymoon?" Laura said curiously.

There was a moment of silence, Graham wishing he could actually make someone burst into flames with a glare.

Then Neal, oblivious to his efforts at directed spontaneous combustion, laughed. "Mary says you looked like someone had slapped you with a fish. And apparently the kiss was enough to sizzle the plants in the courtyard."

The staff erupted into congratulations and speculation.

"The last bachelor tumbles!" Travis crowed.

"I'm so happy for you," Lydia said warmly.

Wrench was sitting close enough to Graham to give him an approving punch in the shoulder and Graham turned on him with a growl.

Now that the attention was on him anyway, there was no point in trying to get out quietly. He stood and shoved through Wrench and Lydia, then plowed through the room, chairs crashing aside to a chorus of surprise.

He slammed the door so hard behind him that it rattled the artwork on the walls outside and stalked away to find something to drink.

CHAPTER 9

Alice reeked of sex to her own over-sensitive nose.

Sex and strength and sun-warmed dirt and some kind of plant she didn't know.

Part of her wanted to savor it, simply revel in the heady flavor of it and enjoy the hum of satisfaction her body still clung to.

But it also made her remember his words, *I love you*, and the way her heart had responded to them.

She turned the wrong way out of the cottage when she fled and ended up dead-ending at another cottage where a pair of mountain lions were sunning on a little porch.

"Sorry, wrong turn!" She waved apologetically and turned around to creep back past the cottage she and Graham had just defiled, crossing her fingers that he wouldn't appear in the doorway.

Then she was wandering down white gravel paths at random, not sure what cottage she was in; the key that Scarlet had given her was apparently wherever her bra had gone.

Downhill took her to the beach and Alice spent an hour or more walking the length of it back and forth with her shoes in her hands, trying to make sense of the thoughts tumbling through her head. Secrets. Her family. Fifty million dollars. Mates. *Love.*

It *wasn't* love.

She turned her t-shirt around the right way, but it didn't help her head.

She finally found her way back up to the bar deck overlooking the pool. The bar itself was unmanned, but there were tempting bottles of beers in a glass-doored cooler and Alice considered taking one. Probably something stronger was called for. Probably water was smarter.

Before she could decide, a voice from behind the bar startled her. "It looks like it would taste good, but it's mostly bubbles and regret."

A woman was sitting on a milk crate behind the bar, her head just below the level of the counter. Her knees were tucked up close in front of her and clutched in skinny arms. She had long, messy brown and white braids on either side of her head and her brown eyes were big in her thin face.

"That sounds about right," Alice said dryly. She opened the door and took one, pulling the cap off without a bottle opener and taking a large gulp. "You must be Gizelle."

"We've met before," Gizelle said dreamily. "You were there the day it rains blood."

Alice raised an eyebrow at her and Gizelle shook her head firmly and stood. She was taller than Alice would have guessed from her crouched form.

"I'm Gizelle," the woman agreed, lifting her chin. "You came with Neal." She didn't offer to shake hands and stayed an almost-uncomfortable distance away.

Alice nodded. "Have you run into him yet? He was eager to see you again."

A dozen conflicted expressions passed over Gizelle's face and she shook her head. "I'm trying not to run," she explained cryptically.

"How's that working for you?" Alice asked dryly, thinking of her own flight from Graham's bed.

"Dubious results," Gizelle admitted.

Something occurred to Alice. "They say you can hear other shifters' animals, is that true?"

Gizelle blinked at her. "Yes, sometimes," she said trustingly.

"What does Scarlet's animal sound like?" Alice tried to sound casual.

Gizelle considered. "It's a whisper, even when I touch her, like wind in leaves, like a far-off song I can't understand."

Alice frowned. That wasn't much to work with. "Like… birdsong?"

"Rustling feathers…" Gizelle said in sudden alarm.

For a moment, Alice thought the beer was hitting her rather harder than she was accustomed to and she wondered if the bartender stocked shifter-strength alcohol. Then she realized that the earth beneath her feet was actually moving, shaking back and forth in a gentle rumble that subsided almost as soon as she recognized it.

An earthquake. Mary had warned her that the resort had been having little flurries of minor quakes. Cluster quakes, they were called, nothing to worry about at all.

Gizelle did not seem to share that opinion.

She dropped to the ground with a shriek of terror, curling into a tiny ball and weeping.

As Alice bent to try to comfort her, alarmed by the woman's trembling, a large figure materialized from the far side of the bar and charged at her.

"Don't you touch her!" the man roared and Alice had only a moment to register the attack before he was driving into her.

Instinct and training drove her body and without thinking, Alice was twisting and lifting and using all of his own forward momentum to throw him aside. Her beer bottle went flying across the floor, but didn't break.

He was shifter strong and fast, if not a fighter, and it was only a heartbeat before he had rolled to his feet and was facing her, snarling.

Gizelle's mate, Alice realized, from his protective defense of her. What was his name? Connor?

Before Alice could explain that she wasn't harming the gazelle shifter, another figure joined the fray, and she recognized Graham at once from his scent and his broad shoulders.

He went straight for Gizelle's mate, an animal challenge rumbling from his chest as he inserted himself between Alice and her perceived threat.

Alice was moving before his fist could land, driving into him shoulder-first, so that his blow passed harmlessly through the air to one side of the other man's face.

"Would you both stop being idiots?" she roared.

Graham lowered his fists and Gizelle's mate paused, looking between the two of them, watching their mouths rather than looking at their eyes. Gizelle herself had shifted at some point and was a tiny, trembling gazelle pressed up against the bar.

"Goddamn alpha *morons*," Alice said between clenched teeth, planting her feet. "Take a moment to assess, will you? I'm not hurting Gizelle, and he's not hurting me. Even if he wanted to, I am perfectly capable of defending myself. I don't *want* your help."

She didn't want to admit how it felt, seeing Graham streak to her defense. Even as she protested it out loud, it had struck some unexpected nerve in her chest, knowing that someone would do that for her. It struck her that he *could* protect her, if she let him, and Alice wasn't sure what to do with that idea.

She only knew that it frightened her, and made something uncomfortable happen beneath her breastbone.

CHAPTER 10

Graham let his hands fall to his side as Alice berated the two of them. Conall, frowning at her mouth as he lip read her tirade, relaxed. When Gizelle timidly put her muzzle into his hand, he gave a little shudder.

"I… apologize," he said formally. "She was afraid and I reacted badly." He knelt beside the gazelle, and she seamlessly shifted into her human form, arms around his neck as she sighed into the comfort of his embrace.

Graham realized he owed an apology as well, but scowling at Alice, he couldn't find the words.

She didn't want his protection.

She didn't want anything from him.

And why should she? He didn't have anything to offer her.

"S'okay," Alice told Conall, after giving Graham a return scowl. "I think the earthquake scared her."

Gizelle looked out from the shelter of Conall's arms with big, frightened eyes. "They woke it up," she said anxiously.

"Who, sweetheart?"

"The bad people without voices," Gizelle said, then she buried her face in his chest and refused to speak.

Alice looked quizzically at them, then shook her head and went to collect her beer bottle, frowning at the wasted beer. "Okay then," she said dismissively. "It was nice to meet you, I'm going to go find Mary and Amber and take a shower as soon as I've figured out what cottage I'm in."

"Twenty-two," Graham growled, grabbing a towel from behind the bar.

Alice gave him a hard look.

"You left your key," he explained shortly as he went to mop up the spilled beer.

"Did you find my bra?" Alice asked, standing in his way with her hand outstretched for the towel.

Was it a joke? Was he supposed to laugh? Graham felt like he was on the spot, and attempted a chuckle. "Huh. Huh."

It didn't sound like a chuckle, and he felt like a fool. He wasn't even sure why he was *trying*. She'd made it perfectly clear that she had no interest in anything more than sex, and he should be *glad* for that.

"You didn't happen to *bring* the key?" Alice asked him, not impressed by his terrible attempt to laugh.

Graham shrugged. He'd forgotten the key in the cottage after his shower. "It won't be locked." He gave her the towel.

"Great." Alice turned away dismissively to clean up the mess and Graham turned and left the bar rather than watch her bend over the way he desperately wanted to.

Jenny caught him as he walked into The Den, excited and bubbling over with news. "We got a lead!" she said, grinning.

Graham stared at her, not sure of the topic or an appropriate response. He was pretty sure she wasn't talking about Alice.

"Tony was able to get a little more information on Grant Lyons for us," Jenny explained in answer to his confused glare. "Most of it is in a sealed plea deal, but we found out where he did time, and why."

Graham's blood turned to ice. They knew. They *knew* what Grant Lyons had done.

"Did Scarlet change her mind about trying to find him?" Bastian asked, flipping through the mail on the counter.

Jenny shook her head, dark curls bouncing. "We're just going to keep looking quietly," she said, her eyes dancing. "Think about it! What if we could find him? What if he's still rich and could buy the island? Beehag and his asshole lawyer wouldn't be able to stop the sale and we wouldn't be wondering week to week if they were going to be able to find a way to break the resort lease just to spite Scarlet."

"What does Benedict Beehag have against Scarlet anyway?" Saina asked, reaching over Bastian to pick a fashion magazine out of the pile.

"Well, Scarlet was there when they broke up the zoo and his uncle died," Bastian suggested. "Maybe he blames her for his uncle's death?"

"I never got the idea that Allistair and Benedict were close," Jenny said thoughtfully. "I just get the feeling that Benedict doesn't like the *resort.* Maybe he's got something against shifters. I mean, his uncle did keep them in cages; maybe the whole family has some grudge against them."

Graham's limbs had thawed enough to consider creeping past for his room when Breck and Darla came laughing down the hallway, arms around each other.

"We got more information on Grant Lyons," Jenny told them, excited, and Graham stalked past, then stopped just far enough down the hallway that he could listen, heart at the bottom of his stomach, but not be seen shamelessly eavesdropping.

"Do tell!" Breck was always up for gossip and news.

"We found out why he was in prison, and where," Jenny said avidly. "Which gives us more clues about friends from his past who might know where he is."

Graham leaned against the wall, feeling the tiniest shiver of relief. They wouldn't have any luck pursuing friends. Grant Lyons didn't have *friends.*

"What did he do?" Darla asked softly. "To be put in jail, I mean?"

Any relief Graham had been reveling in vanished into despair at Jenny's words. "He killed some guy. Most of the details were obscured as part of his plea deal."

Darla made a little noise of dismay.

Graham closed his eyes against the memories that still kept him awake most nights.

"Are we sure we want a *murderer* to own the resort?" Bastian asked skeptically.

You don't, Graham wanted to tell him.

"It sounds like an improvement to me," Breck said. "Besides, it's not like all of us have shiny clean slates. *Graham* was in jail for manslaughter, and we trust him. Laura worked for the mob. Wrench's hands aren't particularly clean..."

Graham held his breath, waiting for them to put the pieces together.

He wanted them to, he realized. He wanted them to figure it out, so he didn't have to tell them or suffocate under the weight of the secret.

Instead, Saina changed the subject, perhaps worried that she would be next in Breck's list; she had not always been scrupulous about the use of her siren magic. "Amber's asked us to help throw a bachelorette party for Mary. Should we have it here, or at the bar?"

"Let's do it here," Jenny said eagerly. "We can kick the boys out and do daiquiris!"

"You don't have to kick *all* the boys out," Breck suggested slyly. "It's traditional to have a stripper at these affairs and I will reluctantly let you demean me in this manner."

"*Reluctantly*," Bastian scoffed, as the others laughed.

"Only if it's hands-off," Darla said possessively. "And I get to watch!"

From the giggles, Breck must have tickled or poked her. There was the sound of a kiss, murmurs about a private show, and more laughter.

The conversation flowed to the party, and the wedding, and Graham trudged on to his room, feeling ashamed and angry and aching.

He wanted to be someone different, someone better. He wanted to deserve his friends' trust. He wanted his past to stop haunting him.

Graham closed the door quietly behind him and leaned on it with a groan.

He *wanted* Alice.

CHAPTER 11

Dinner with Mary, Amber, and their mates was straight-up torture.

They all knew that Graham was Alice's mate, and that she had slept with him, and if they didn't know the details of their parting, they at least knew that it hadn't exactly ended with pledges of devotion.

I love you, he'd said.

Well, *she* hadn't ended it with pledges of devotion.

If her dinner partners didn't say anything directly, their careful choice of topics and thoughtful sideways glances sent the message quite clearly: they thought she was being crazy.

She *felt* crazy.

She felt as loony as the gazelle shifter and she desperately wished she could get away with shifting and running away to escape the awkward dinner and her own awkward self.

But being shy and eccentric as a small, delicate antelope was a lot different than it was as a giant, clumsy brown bear and Alice knew it would only be ridiculous if she tried. To say nothing of destructive.

So she plowed through the meal and the conversation with

bullish cheer, praising the food, making observations about the weather, and expressing gratitude that Mary had chosen not to put the bridesmaids in heels—in part because of Amber's advancing pregnancy and in part because Alice already towered over most of the wedding party.

It occurred to her rather suddenly that Tony had been investigating Scarlet when he first came to the resort; she had been near the top of his list of suspects for the disappearing shifters that Beehag had been kidnapping. Had he figured out what her animal shift form was in that time?

It was far preferable to think about the uncomfortable topic of her real mission on the island than it was to think about Graham.

Alice steered the conversation to ask about their original visits to the island.

Mary and Neal laughed about his attempts to avoid her when they met.

"I couldn't figure it out," Mary chuckled. "I'd catch sight of him and it was like I was wearing roadkill perfume—he was suddenly fleeing in the opposite direction."

"Not my finest hour," Neal agreed, smiling fondly at her. "But sometimes, it's a rocky path to true love."

Everyone very carefully did not quite look at Alice.

"What about you, Tony?" Alice asked brightly. "You were actually here investigating Scarlet, weren't you? Did you find out any juicy secrets about her before you got distracted by meeting Amber and breaking up Beehag's zoo? Everyone's dying to know what her shift form is."

She did her best to sound casual, but the looks she got suggested she had not moved past *crazy* in their minds.

"Most of what came up in the investigation is classified," Tony said apologetically. "But no, we never did find out what she is."

Then the dessert tray was brought by Chef himself, the cook with arms like barrels and a warm, friendly smile in his handsome, graying face.

"Strawberry cheesecake," Alice selected from the tray.

"An excellent choice," Chef said, as he set the artful little plate in front of her. They were small strawberries, but a generous portion of them, deep red and drizzled with a matching sauce. "These strawberries are grown here on the island by our very own Graham and were picked this morning. He's a masterful gardener, and we're lucky to have a selection of his fresh fruit and produce."

Of course Graham had grown the strawberries. Alice gave the chef a suspicious sideways look, not sure if the mention of Graham was deliberate or not. Probably everyone knew about them by now. It wasn't that big an island.

It was too late to change her mind, so Alice smiled. "Sounds great!" she squeaked.

"That looks amazing!" Amber agreed with a sly sideways look. "I'll have one, too."

"I couldn't eat another bite," Mary groaned, while their mates picked out their own desserts.

"Eating for two," Amber said merrily.

Alice didn't want to start eating before they were all served, so while the others talked about pregnancy and joked about having to roll Amber to their cottage, she stared at her strawberries—strawberries that Graham had planted, nurtured… plucked with those big, strong hands…

Damn it.

Her bear's fire had only been dampened and now it rose again in her, swamping logical thought.

Amber's cheesecake was swiftly brought out and Alice finally took a tentative bite: creamy cake of a perfect consistency, just the right amount of sweet and deliciously cool in the hot tropical evening... and one flawless strawberry.

It was an amazing flavor combination and Alice closed her eyes and savored it, until she realized she was remembering the taste of Graham's kiss.

She ate the rest with mechanical efficiency, trying to keep up with the dinner small talk and not sound like she was thinking about a splendidly shirtless Graham feeding her strawberries.

As they gathered up to leave the restaurant at last, Amber said firmly, "You boys go on ahead! We'll catch up!"

Alice knew what they were planning and was not surprised when Amber and Mary each took an arm and steered her to the bar rather than to the paths that led to the rental cottages.

She could have shaken them off; despite being shifters, both of them together did not have the strength to make her do anything she didn't really want to. But they were her friends and she knew that if she didn't have this conversation now, it would be an even more awkward one later.

She shoved images of Graham and strawberries firmly from her head as Mary ordered drinks for all of them, and met their appraising gazes with her chin up.

"So, what's going on with you and Graham?" Amber finally asked.

Mary added, "We didn't actually expect you to join us for dinner tonight. Or to see you much at all the next few days, to be honest."

"We've got a wedding to get ready for," Alice said innocently. "I couldn't just leave you guys hanging."

Mary and Amber exchanged looks that could only be described as deeply skeptical.

"That doesn't answer the question," Mary said firmly.

Alice sighed, noisy and unladylike. "Look, I'm really happy for both of you. But that's not how mates always work out. The sex was great and that's all there was. We both have our own lives already. He doesn't fit into mine and I'm not going to give up my job to move here. You know how much I love my job! I took our team to state three years running! Anyway, a mate isn't true love or any nonsense like that."

Mary and Amber looked confused.

"You like him, don't you?" Mary asked.

"What's to like?" Alice said as carelessly as she could. "He's hot and he's built, but he's said maybe two complete sentences to me, under duress. That's not much to build a friendship on, let alone a relationship."

One of the sentences had been *I love you*, she remembered, and she was painfully grateful when the cowboy bartender brought them drinks: a fancy fruit thing with an umbrella for Mary, a virgin version of the same for Amber, and a stout glass of whiskey on the rocks for Alice.

Real girly, she thought with a grimace. *A catch like me, it's a wonder I'm not beating off the men.* She toasted Amber and Mary and downed half of it in a swallow.

She was rewarded with a burn down her throat that held no candle to the burning in her belly.

CHAPTER 12

Graham had forgotten all about the tomatoes Chef had requested the day before and he didn't think about them again until he received a text from Scarlet asking him to see her in her office 'at your convenience.'

At your convenience generally meant *drop what you're doing and get here right now*, so Graham aborted the morning workout that he'd been planning on and hiked immediately to the top of the resort, not even bothering to change into his staff uniform first.

He wondered if that gave the wrong impression when Scarlet raked him with her glance and frowned. "Should I be expecting your resignation?"

For a moment, Graham was deeply confused. Then he remembered. *Alice.*

Not that he'd forgotten her for a single moment since he had laid eyes on her—her intoxicating hazel eyes, the defiant tilt of her chin, the waves of her sensible, short hair—but he hadn't considered that Scarlet might not know that Alice didn't want him.

Oh, she had *wanted* him, had answered his desire with her own passion and heat, but she hadn't wanted *him*.

It's not fate, she'd said flatly. *Just leftover evolutionary crap or something.*

And who could blame her? Graham was no prize. He offered her nothing.

Graham realized he was scowling at Scarlet and hadn't answered her. "I'm not going anywhere," he growled.

Scarlet raised an eyebrow at him. "Should I be finding a position here for Alice?" she prompted. "What are her qualifications?"

Graham gave a defiant shrug. "Don't think she's interested in moving here." Hearing the words out loud was like a punch to the gut. He thought he'd made peace with it, but no part of him actually had.

Scarlet's eyes went soft, which was the last thing Graham wanted or needed. "I'm… sorry to hear that," she said gently.

Graham refused to lower his gaze, despite the discomfort hers always caused and, for once, she looked away first.

"What did you need?" he asked gruffly.

If he had not been staring at her, he would have missed the little sigh she gave and the fall to her shoulders. "I wanted to know what your plans for the future were," she said neutrally. "Because I am considering closing the resort and filing for bankruptcy, and if you were leaving that would simplify the decision."

The defiance went out of Graham in a shocked, sympathetic rush. "You… can't do that."

"I don't have a lot of choices," Scarlet snapped.

"The lawsuit," Graham guessed.

Scarlet picked up a heavy stack of paperwork and let it drop back to the desk with a thump. "The anticipated gift from the generous and benevolent Jubilee Grant."

Graham frowned. "As bad as you thought?"

"Four hundred and fifty thousand for cancellations, loss and damages. Eight hundred and twenty thousand for *mental anguish*. As a bonus, a copy of a report to the Costa Rican government that we should be investigated for food sanitation violations."

She moved that aside and picked up a manila envelope with a familiar logo on it. "As if that weren't enough, Beehag's asshole lawyer is trying to use the lawsuit as a reason to break our lease."

Graham grunted. None of this was good news. "Can you fight it? Have you shown it to Jenny?"

"I haven't told her yet," Scarlet said, with a shake of her head. "It only came in this morning, and we have some time to formulate our responses. Let everyone enjoy the wedding without this hanging over their heads. I'm sorry to burden you with it."

"It's not a—" Graham broke off with a grunt of surprise as a small form bumped against the back of his calf and gave his ankle an affectionate rub. He didn't bother to finished the sentence as the leggy, cream-colored cat walked into the room like she owned it and launched herself up onto Scarlet's desk.

"Tyrant," Scarlet greeted, as gravely as if she was a shifter and not a normal cat.

Tyrant had been a gift intended for Gizelle, but she had clearly chosen Scarlet as her primary companion, to the amusement of everyone at the resort... except Scarlet.

Tyrant gave a mrrr of greeting and tried to investigate the paperwork, reaching a paw for the shining closure on the manila envelope. Scarlet scooped her up from the desk and cuddled her in a brief, unexpected display of warmth, rubbing her cheeks and coaxing a whisker-quivering purr from the half-grown cat before setting her down on the wide window sill behind her. Several potted plants had been replaced by a cushion, and Tyrant blinked happily at the sunlight pouring in and began to groom herself, still purring.

When Scarlet turned back to Graham, her face was cool and serene again. "Please don't say anything to anyone," she said firmly, not really making it a request. "I haven't made any firm decisions yet, and there's no reason to put a pall over everything."

"I won't say anything," Graham agreed, keenly aware of the growing weight of the secrets he was keeping.

He felt Alice's presence a split-second before Scarlet frowned. "Can I help you?"

CHAPTER 13

Alice had a keen sense for 'interrupting something awkward.' Teaching middle school students was basically made of those moments.

The door to Scarlet's office was open and Alice was drifting in before she realized that the warm, welcoming sensation she was feeling was only from her bear, recognizing Graham's broad back before Alice even registered it.

"I won't say anything," he was growling, in that voice that made her shiver despite her best efforts.

"Can I help you?" Scarlet asked sharply.

For a moment, Alice completely forgot why she had come, her senses swamped with Graham. *Down girl*, she told her bear firmly. She smiled resolutely, ignoring the tension in the room and pretending her own entrance hadn't been its own special form of awkward. "Yes, actually!" she said cheerfully. "I'm putting together the scrapbook for Mary's wedding, and I had some questions I was hoping you could help me answer…"

Graham glanced at her once and looked away so quickly that Alice wondered if eyeballs could get whiplash.

Then he turned and walked out without a single word more, leaving her feeling irrationally bereft.

I don't need him, she reminded herself.

Her bear had strong alternate opinions.

She looked back to find Scarlet giving her an unreadable look and laughed inelegantly. "He doesn't say much, does he?"

Scarlet looked at her without saying anything for a long moment, then smiled rather stiffly and moved the pile of paperwork before her on the desk off to the side. "Was there something specific you were looking for?" she asked politely, gesturing to the chair opposite. "For your… scrapbook?"

Alice wondered if there was sympathy in Scarlet's eyes and decided she would take a conversation out of pity if it would help her find more clues. She sat down in the chair and made a show of opening the notebook that she had taped a few photos of Mary and Neal to.

"I was hoping you had some photographs of their visit here, or maybe some stories."

"I'm afraid I don't," Scarlet said simply.

Alice didn't really have a plan, other than to try to get Scarlet to open up and start chatting.

"Well, I was thinking about doing a bit about the resort itself, since that's where they met. Can you tell me a little about how it got started and when you took it over?"

Scarlet regarded her for a moment, and then said, with suspicious neutrality, "The resort was designed and nearly entirely built by Aaric Lyons in the early 80s. Upon his disappearance, his wife sold this half of the island to Beehag. Four years ago, I secured a lease to restart the resort and got it into operation."

"That must have been a lot of work," Alice said encouragingly.

"Yes," Scarlet answered briefly. Then, reluctantly, "I have an excellent staff."

"Graham and Travis were among the first people working here, right?" Dammit, how had the topic gotten around to Graham? Alice stumbled on. "It was almost forty years—the jungle must have really grown everything over in that time. I bet it took a long time to cut back the overgrowth."

Scarlet was silent.

"So, um, okay…" Alice looked down at her pathetic scrapbook, trying not to think about Graham with a machete, beating back jungle vines. Shirtless.

"You're not really here looking for information about Mary and Neal," Scarlet observed.

Alice blushed. She was *terrible* at this spy stuff. She thought about her brother, and her parents, and had to make an effort to draw herself together. Scarlet made her feel like she'd been called to the principal's office. Did she know about the man with the business card who had sent Alice? N. Padrikanth Moore, the pretentious name had been, no business name, or logo, or any hints as to what kind of person he was. But good people didn't generally make offers of fifty million dollars to snoop shifter types out.

"I'm sorry to pry," she said hastily. "I really was hoping to put something nice together for them, but I've kind of run into a dead end." She gave the most natural smile she could manage. "I didn't mean to be a bother."

Scarlet's expression became… complicated. It wasn't disgust and it wasn't anger, but it also wasn't quite pity, or anything else Alice could put her finger on.

"Graham," Scarlet said quietly.

Alice stared at her in consternation. If there was anything worse than Scarlet knowing that Alice was a spy, it was Scarlet thinking Alice was pining over the gorgeous gardener who had upended her life by turning out to be her mate.

Even if she sort of *was*.

Scarlet's gaze was unsettling, even when she was clearly trying to be gentle. "Graham is a good man," she said evenly. "He's quiet, but clever, and he works very hard. He is kind. He would treat you well."

This was a hundred times worse.

Alice tried to laugh and failed spectacularly. "I'm sure he is. Er, I'm sure he would. Ah, thank you," she squeaked. "I don't think it's going anywhere, though. I've got… a job, you know. He… has a job. Jobs we love. Jobs we need. Good jobs." She clamped her mouth shut, knowing she had said job entirely too many times in a row… and now she could only think about blowjobs, because her traitor bear was feeding her memories of Graham's naked splendor and she was helpless in the rush of desires that had come with talking about him at all.

If Scarlet had a clue what was going on in her head, Alice didn't want to know. "I'm really sorry I bothered you," she said desperately, rising to her feet. She knew which battles to concede. "Thank you for your time. Lovely resort. Great food."

And she fled out into the courtyard, shutting the door behind her out of habit.

She didn't get far, only as far as the bench in the courtyard, where she collapsed and tried to get her tangled mind in order.

She shoved Graham—and his glorious cock—from her mind with effort. She had to make some progress with Scarlet's shift form. She had to, or she could kiss her only hope for saving her family goodbye.

Alice drew in deep breaths, searching for her usual calm and carefree attitude. She wasn't going to get much out of Scarlet directly, she was sure. But she could use her senses.

With each breath came smells.

Usually, it was just a wild symphony of scents, all tangled together in an overwhelming disharmony that no one else seemed to notice. But if she concentrated, she could pick them out… a wolf shifter had been here… maybe Laura? No, a different wolf. Another bear, as well, perhaps Tex, but just as likely a guest.

Most shifters came through the courtyard in human shape; she could smell soap and sweat and alcohol, leather and plastic from luggage, the tang of grease from their wheels, tantalizing whiffs of the breakfast Chef must be finishing up at the restaurant, the undertone of saltwater on the breeze.

She could smell the little cream-colored cat with Siamese points in orange and its deodorizing cat litter. She could smell the paper of the mail on Scarlet's desk, the distinct musty old book smell; all of Scarlet's books appeared to be older, well-used books.

And muffling it all were the flowers and vines and potted plants throughout the courtyard. Over the vivid, pushy jungle smells, Alice couldn't pick out any animal scent that was strong enough to be someone who lived here. The strongest of the animal scents was actually lion—Graham's lion, specifically—musky and earthy and irresistible. Alice gritted her teeth and pushed to her feet.

She was getting nowhere, fast, and she could feel her chance slipping through her fingers. She realized she'd been crying as the tears started to dry on her cheeks, and scrubbed them away defiantly.

She *had* to find out what Scarlet was.

There was no other choice.

CHAPTER 14

Graham peeled off his gardening gloves at the end of the row and sat back on his heels. Did she have to be so hot?

Alice was relentlessly disturbing to him, with the proud lift to her jaw and the soft mane of her short hair. Even the way she stood, alert and poised on those long, long legs… and worst of all were her hazel eyes, glittering and full of challenge.

Graham wasn't sure if he wanted to answer that challenge or simply sink to his knees at her feet in surrender the way his lion was sure they should.

He had no interest in running into Alice by accident, so even though he was hungry after a morning of work, Graham gave the buffet a wide berth and found himself sitting behind the hotel at the picnic table he had gotten in the habit of eating at with Breck and Neal before the latter had moved away from the island with his mate.

It somehow didn't surprise him when Neal appeared, carrying a tray from the buffet.

"How the tables have turned," the red-maned wolf shifter said wryly. "Sandwich?" When Neal had first come to Shifting Sands, it had been hard for him to accept Scarlet's generosity. Breck and

Graham had taken to discreetly bringing extra food to share at the picnic table so he didn't have to select his own food from the buffet.

Graham shrugged, then nodded. "Thanks."

Even a second-rate sandwich from the buffet was something you didn't turn down. Scarlet insisted on the highest quality of everything; the bread was fresh and fluffy, the meat was cold and flavorful, paired with a creamy cheese, lettuce from Graham's garden, and a spicy mustard.

"I didn't mean to embarrass you in front of everyone," Neal said, after a few moments of eating in silence. "It sounded like you… hadn't wasted time."

Graham hunched miserably over his meal and didn't respond.

No, she hadn't wasted any time explaining exactly how there was nothing between them but *leftover evolutionary crap*.

"The gang's all here!" Breck's bright voice was the last thing that Graham wanted to hear, but the waiter appeared around the corner of the hotel, carrying his own tray. "Brought an extra sandwich for old time's sake," he said with relish. "But if you guys are all set, I can throw myself on that bomb."

Without waiting for an invitation, he scooted in next to Graham on the bench. "Shove those big muscles over, flower-boy."

The waiter made a production of enjoying his first bites with relish. "Scarlet may be a terrible harpy, but she lays a good spread," he said approvingly.

"She's not so much of a harpy as all that," Neal protested. "I think it's an act; she's always been bighearted by action. Even if she constantly swears she isn't running a…"

"Charity!" Breck finished with Neal. They chuckled.

Graham thought about Scarlet's dismal news and the defeat in her face that she had tried so hard to mask and could dredge up no humor, taking a vicious bite of his sandwich.

"All we need to complete this reunion is Gizelle," Breck observed. "Grazing off over there, pretending we don't exist. Have you seen her yet?"

Neal frowned and shook his head. "I figured I'd let her find me herself, so I haven't gone looking."

"You won't believe how she's bloomed," Breck said warmly. "She's usually human now, brushes her hair—or lets Conall do it—wears clothes most of the time. She helps out at the bar sometimes, hasn't broken any glasses in weeks."

"Conall, he's good for her?" Neal asked cautiously.

"So good," Breck assured him. "I thought he was a giant, angry jerk when we first met, but he loves that young woman more than anything and she adores him right back. He spoils her rotten, and fortunately she's too naive to take advantage."

"He threw a guy who was harassing her into the swimming pool," Graham added, though he had intended to stay out of the conversation.

"Oh yeah, that was a sight," Breck laughed. "A deer the size of a mammoth and this mangy, wet bully of a big-mouthed bear. Scarlet marched that jackass straight off the island, you'd better believe it."

"Good," Neal said with satisfaction. "I'm glad she's safe here."

It suddenly occurred to Graham to wonder what would happen to Gizelle if Scarlet closed the resort. As far as she'd come, as remarkable as her progression had been, she would have a hard time adjusting to a place with normal humans, and she still lacked understanding of many social norms. No one at Shifting Sands cared that she wasn't polite or didn't remember to wear clothing, but she still reacted to new things with fear and had a habit of shifting to her gazelle form and fleeing if there were loud noises.

Neal was wrong. She wasn't safe here. None of them were.

Guilt swamped Graham.

"Speaking of safe," Neal said leadingly.

"What's up with you and Alice?" Breck asked more bluntly, when Graham didn't look up.

Graham shrugged one shoulder and stuffed as much sandwich in his mouth as he could manage. "Nothing."

"What do you mean nothing?" Breck demanded. "She's your mate!"

Graham shrugged the other shoulder and knew that both of them were staring at him without having to look up.

"Was it a problem in bed?" Breck asked drolly.

Graham almost choked on his sandwich. "No!" *A hundred times no.*

"Did you… insult her?" Neal guessed.

"No," Graham said shortly. Not unless *I love you* was an insult.

Maybe it was, from someone like him.

"Did you say *anything*?" Breck asked suspiciously.

Graham shrugged.

"Did you at *least* tell her your name?" Neal demanded.

That earned them a grunt that might have been a laugh. He'd told her *a* name.

Graham still wondered if it had been the wrong name. He put the rest of the sandwich in his mouth and swallowed.

"Look," he said gruffly. "I appreciate that you're trying to help, but she's got a job. At the end of her vacation, she's going back to it. *I've* got a job, too, and I'm going back to it now."

He rose from the bench and stalked off, wondering dismally exactly how long his own job was going to last… and what he would do after that.

CHAPTER 15

Alice lay in her bed, listening to the night sounds around her little cottage, wishing she could sleep.

A sheet wasn't warm enough. A blanket was too warm. The pillow was too flat, but two were too much. No position was comfortable.

And she couldn't stop thinking of Graham.

It wasn't just the sex, as mind-blowing as that had been. It was the hurt and longing in his eyes that he couldn't quite hide, it was the way he'd smiled at her when they first met, slow and full of depth. It was all the questions she wanted to ask him, all the stories she wanted to tell him.

By the time dawn's light started to creep around the curtains, she was gritty-eyed and grouchy, and tired of trying to sleep.

Alice got up and yanked her clothing on, then wandered quietly out of her cottage, up the white gravel paths towards the restaurant. Singing voices, light, and laughter spilled out of the closed doors of the kitchen, but the restaurant was as empty as she had expected for the hour of the day.

She wandered along the buffet for a moment because she felt restlessly hungry, but the food offered was no more satisfying than her bed had been. She took a piece of rolled lunch meat out of a sense of obligation and munched it as she left the restaurant.

At the door, she turned right, up the steep resort, towards the spa and the office. If she was canny, could she surprise Scarlet shifting? Maybe she was some kind of alien and Alice could catch her coming out of a cocoon...

She tripped over the corner of a potted plant at the corner of the courtyard; it didn't fall, but it rattled in the plant stand, and Alice turned and fled, cursing her uselessness as an investigator.

"You're up early," a gentle voice greeted her and she turned to find a beautiful Latina woman holding a yoga mat coming from the spa.

"Jet lag!" Alice said with false brightness. "My internal clock is all out of whack! Traveling would be so much easier without the traveling part, you know."

"I'm about to go start a sunrise yoga class," the woman said kindly. "Would you care to join me?"

"I… er…" Alice couldn't think of a good reason not to. "I don't have a mat?"

The other woman laughed. "Most guests don't. We can stop by the activity center and get one there. I'm Lydia." She offered a slight, gentle hand and Alice tried not to crush it.

"I'm Alice."

That earned her a second, thoughtful look. Alice could only imagine what she'd heard.

But Lydia didn't bring Graham up, only asked how Alice was liking her stay so far and chatted sweetly about the resort and the weather as they picked out a mat for her to use and walked past the pool to a wide lawn overlooking cliffs past the beach.

Apparently, Alice was the only one to show up for the class and she was keenly aware of her clumsy, over-sized body as Lydia, lithe and impossibly bendy, took her through a challenging series of poses.

They talked casually as they stretched and Lydia mildly corrected her posture.

"About Graham…" she finally said, exactly as Alice had been dreading.

Alice groaned, letting her head fall limp. Lydia had picked a moment when it would be challenging and graceless to storm off; she was leaning on her hands, with her butt in the air.

"Graham is a bighearted man. He doesn't have a lot to say, but he's clever and he's kind. You should give him a chance."

It was eerily similar to what Scarlet had said. Alice gave up her pose and sat down with a thump. "I'm sure he's a great guy," she said, and she was alarmed at the longing she heard in her own voice. She cleared her throat. "But I have a job back home, and he has a job here, and I just don't see a life where either one of us is willing to throw what we already have away."

Lydia looked at her thoughtfully. "Do you know a lot of mated couples?"

Alice snorted. "Not one, until Mary brought hers home."

"When I met Wrench, I knew he was for me, but… I had this idea of what he ought to be that he wasn't. I wasn't disappointed, but it took some adjustment. I had to get past his rough exterior and street speech and swearing, and once I did I found this amazing man who I needed to spend the rest of my life with. It could be the same, for you. Don't be put off by the fact that Graham was in jail, or that he can seem distant."

Was Wrench really a name? Alice wondered. Then the rest of Lydia's soft-spoken statement caught up with her.

"Graham was in jail?" Alice exclaimed. "For what?"

For the first time, Lydia looked flustered. "Oh, I'm sorry. I assumed you knew. It's not really a secret. But it's not such a bad thing. My own mate was in jail for a while. And I was alarmed when I found out, too."

"What was he in jail for?" Alice repeated. "Graham, I mean."

Lydia hesitated, then said, "Manslaughter. None of us know the details, but manslaughter is usually just an accident."

"Huh," Alice replied.

"But Graham is more than his rapsheet," Lydia was quick to say. "Just like Wrench is. And don't be put off by fact that he is so cool and reserved. He'll take patience to get through to, but he has a warm heart under that gruff exterior. It might take a long time to get him to open up, but he deserves that chance."

"Cool and reserved?" Alice scoffed. "Good god, the man declared his love for me before I found out his name."

Lydia blinked at her, but seemed to have reclaimed her calm. "Then why aren't you with him?"

"This isn't the basis for a *relationship*," Alice insisted. "I'm glad it worked out for you and… Wrench? Really? Okay… but I'm not looking for a man and I don't have room in my life for one. And Graham wouldn't be happy there anyway."

Lydia continued to gaze at her, not judgmentally, but patiently.

"I'm six foot four and turn into a bear that could eat his face off," Alice said desperately. "I live in a tiny apartment and have a high-stress job teaching ungrateful middle school students. I'm constantly traveling for sports events. I'm just... not girlfriend material."

"Graham doesn't care about that," Lydia assured her confidently. "Let's end our session in five minutes of child's pose, to lengthen our backs, open our hips, and ease our stress."

Alice obediently knelt and leaned her head forward onto the mat. She sighed into the stretch.

Graham *didn't* care about any of that, she thought achingly. She actually believed him when he said he loved her. He would go back to Minnesota with her in a hot minute, if she asked him to. He would give up his perfect life here, with his friends, doing something he enjoyed in paradise, and he would follow her to… what?

To her hardscrabble life in a snowy state with strangers? He wouldn't fit in her tiny apartment in Lakefield and she could barely afford it already. She couldn't possibly put food on their table, and as far as she knew, jobs for landscaper *felons* were not available in any abundance. She couldn't take care of Graham… she couldn't even take care of the family she *had*.

Before she could stop herself, tears leaked out of her eyes and she was glad that her forehead was down on the mat.

She was trying so hard not to think about her family, because it only made her feel helpless and despairing.

Why couldn't her mate have been a billionaire, like Gizelle's deaf musician? she wanted to wail… but the brief, ungrateful thought made her chest squeeze with guilt and regret. The sad fact was, Graham was everything she wanted in one sexy package and the more she reluctantly learned about him, the more she wanted to comfort him, to pull him into her arms and kiss him and show him that she knew who he really was beneath that quiet facade and checkered past.

Yoga, she decided, let her think too much. Once Lydia finally released her from this torture, she was going to go find the workout room that Neal and Tony had talked about and do something that would distract her more thoroughly. Maybe they had a punching bag, because she really felt like hitting something.

CHAPTER 16

"You'll hurt yourself, hitting the bag that way," Graham had to say.

He didn't want to say anything, he wanted to slink out of the staff gym before Alice noticed him. But he couldn't let her continue to batter at the bag that way, couldn't bear to think of her in pain if he could do anything to stop it.

Alice was panting and sweaty, and the strong, gorgeous lines of her long body were fierce and graceful. "I suppose you're some kind of fighter?" she said angrily, giving the heavy bag another furious, flawed hit.

Some kind of fighter, Graham thought.

"You'll fracture your wrist," he growled. "Hold it straight, like this, and step back a little, so the force goes all the way up to your shoulder when you make the hit. Those are the big muscles that can take it. Wrists are weak."

He'd broken enough of them to know, he thought regretfully.

Alice gave the bag another hit, a better hit, and the bag shuddered on its chain. "Hot damn," she said, pleased. "Thanks."

Graham turned to go, but Alice stopped him with a word, "Wait…"

Graham stared at the door jamb.

"We're grownups," Alice said. "If you want to use the workout room at the same time, we… should be able to do that. If you want to lift, I can spot you. Or, whatever."

Bench presses, with her curves above him, shining with sweat? Graham wasn't that stupid.

But the only excuse he could think of to retreat from his workout involved admitting that he didn't think he'd be able to concentrate with the distraction of having her in the same room. And that sounded weak.

He grunted and went to do sit-ups on the inclined bench.

Predictably, he lost count, listening to Alice continue to punch at the bag, and then start arm curls. After he guessed he'd done a few hundred, he realized in a panic that he should probably switch, or it would look like he was incapable of doing anything else.

Pull-ups on the bars would have been his next stop, but Graham became aware that he probably should only do things that involved sitting; he was irresistibly aroused, and it was going to be obvious if he wasn't careful.

He made the mistake of glancing over at her, and she was looking away swiftly. Her color was high, but Graham told himself that might have been due to exertion. The day was hot and the fan in the workout room was not helping much.

What he really wanted to do was punch something, and the heavy bag was tempting. If he put his back to her… Graham was moving before he could reconsider, wrapping his hands with efficient motions to save his knuckles.

Crack.

The hit was always satisfying, and the chains groaned. If Travis hadn't reinforced the equipment—the whole room—to shifter specifications, it probably would have fallen.

The bag swung back and Graham met it with all of his frustration and a fist; not as hard as the first time, because that kind of hit was sloppy. No opponent would wait around for a fighter to regain their balance after committing all their energy into a punch that way.

He lay into the bag with all of his focus he could muster, dancing on the balls of his feet, feinting, hitting. But he couldn't shake his awareness of Alice behind him.

She was this tantalizing presence, like a source of heat, like magnetic north to his compass. It took all of his willpower to keep his attention on the bag before him.

Did he draw her that same way? Or did her bear have the same indifference to him that she seemed to? Graham reminded himself that her cool practicality really was the best practice. He didn't have anything to offer a mate.

A fist slipped and only shifter reflexes kept Graham from taking the heavy bag in the face. He lowered his hands, forcing his fingers to relax, and only then felt the sweat he'd worked up. The bag slowed in its pendulum motion and as the creak of the chains and the support beam stilled, he became aware that Alice was silent behind him.

"You're good," she said into the quiet, as if she felt compelled to fill it. "I teach wrestling, but it's a really different sport, of course. All about holds and takedowns and grapples, not so much on the hitting." She laughed nervously. "You don't want to teach middle school students how to hit. At that age, all they want to do is strike out already. They're swimming in a sea of puberty and haven't quite figured out how not to be self-centered jerks enslaved by their hormones."

Graham couldn't speak, too busy picturing what grappling Alice would be like. Those long limbs, that beautiful neck, strong fingers twined with his…

He grunted, unwrapping his hands.

"Graham…" The bench that Alice had been sitting on gave a creak as she stood.

He ought to turn and face her. It would be polite. He willed himself under control, and failed.

She was standing too close; he could feel her right behind him.

"Graham," she said again.

Graham gritted his teeth and turned. If she wanted to see what she was doing to him, then fine.

"No kissing," she said, and for a moment, Graham didn't understand. Then she was tugging his shirt up, and when he helped her get it over his head and throw it across the room, everything was clear and uncomplicated. He bent to her neck... not to kiss, but to bite, gently, then harder as she made a noise that was no part pain.

CHAPTER 17

Alice had no delusions that she was any part Pretty Woman or Julia Roberts, but keeping kissing out of things seemed a sensible way to remind herself that this wasn't about romance or love.

So Graham did not kiss her.

He bit and nibbled and dragged his teeth along her skin, and licked and growled. His hands were gentle and strong, and his chest—that glorious chest—was even more beautiful than she remembered. He effortlessly raised her to a fever-pitch of need and hunger.

Her clothing followed his, and they were both touching and growling in desire. His cock was hard in her hand, his fingers were wet in her folds and played her clit like an instrument, until she was crying and begging for him.

They tried the workout bench—too narrow, the wrong height, too awkward for more than a few desperate strokes. They tried up against the wall, nearly knocking over the weights rack, then finally he was bending her over on the floor itself and entering her from behind, spreading her and biting at her neck until she gave a cry of release and he was joining her in the ecstasy with a roar of his own.

She shuddered through aftershocks as he slowed his thrusts and fell through the pulses of pleasure with her.

They collapsed to the floor and for a blissful moment, Graham cradled her in his strong arms, holding her close as their heartbeats returned to normal.

Finally he rolled away to lie beside her and Alice had to fight down her own instinct to snuggle back into his sweaty embrace.

"Where'd you learn to fight?" Alice asked, when she could form words again. "I didn't recognize your style." Mostly his style had been 'destroy the bag,' but the control and skill had been unmistakable.

The answer surprised her. "Prep school in England."

"Bullshit," Alice said, rolling her head to look at him. That was *always* a mistake, and he was still naked. "You did *not* go to prep school. And I thought you were *American*." She sat up, looking for her clothing instead of staring.

"Not bloody likely," Graham answered in a breath-taking accent, reaching for his own shirt. "Or at least, not always." His American accent was good, but now that Alice knew what she was listening for, she could hear the British beneath it.

"Well, that didn't look like proper British boxing," Alice said, in her own terrible 'I've watched a little BBC' accent as they dressed.

"It's not." That was a more Graham-like growl, too clipped to reveal any dialect. But to her surprise, he went on. "I… when I was eleven, my father died and it turned out he was badly in debt. I went from king of the school to charity case in a week, and there were a lot of kids—older kids—who were desperate to remind me what an ass I'd been and how far I'd fallen. I got good at hitting back."

Alice looked at him again, really looked at *him*, and when he accidentally looked up and met her gaze, he flinched but didn't look away.

It was a *confession*, hard-given. Alice blinked in surprise, guessing that Graham had probably never told anyone that.

I love you, he'd told her. And now, more than that, he was telling her he *trusted* her.

His blue eyes were so full of longing and regret. Alice wanted to reach out, to brush back the mane of his hair and feel his jaw in the palm of her hand.

But that was as dangerous as kissing and Alice could feel her defenses crumbling already.

"Why are you telling me this?" she asked quietly.

"I want…" he paused, and Alice could see him wrestling with the words. He wanted *her*, she knew with bone-deep certainty. He wanted more than he could ask. "I want to be *honest.*"

We should be honest, she'd told him. Her own words, thrust back at her.

But she was afraid of honest. Honest terrified her.

Honest meant admitting she was falling in love with him.

CHAPTER 18

Graham wasn't sure what made him tell Alice about school, about losing his father. He hadn't intended to, not really.

He was just… so tired of trying to hide it all.

Her hazel eyes were a safe place, a haven forever.

Even if she said she didn't want *forever.*

They gazed at each other a long moment and Alice looked down first. Graham waited for her to make an excuse and flee, and was surprised when she didn't. She sat backwards on a beat-up chair and Graham settled opposite from her on a workout bench.

"My brother and I went to public school," Alice said quietly. "But kids are kids, and they can be pretty cruel. No one messed with me, but I had to bloody a few noses for my brother. I never learned… real fighting. Just a little schoolyard scrapping. But I was bigger and stronger than other kids, even before I could shift, and I didn't have to do it much."

Graham wondered if this was the place normal people made conversational noises and was glad when Alice went on without prompting.

"My brother, Andy… he's not a shifter. If he had been…" Alice's face was complicated.

Everything about Alice was complicated, however hard she tried to deny it.

After a moment, she lifted her chin. "We're being honest. My brother is sick. Really sick. He hasn't been able to work, doesn't have insurance to cover treatment, doesn't want my parents to know, even if they had any money. My parents are about to lose their house. And they don't want Andy to know. So… I'm stuck in the middle and a teacher's salary barely covers my food and the rent for my crappy apartment, so there's nothing I can do to help either of them."

Graham wasn't sure what the right response was, but "Shit," seemed as appropriate as anything.

"Sorry," she said, blinking hard to pretend she wasn't crying. "That's probably a little too much honesty for what we have. I just… haven't had anyone I could tell."

"Can I... help?" Graham had to ask, resisting the desire to pull her into his arms without asking.

Alice's mouth quirked into a wry smile; even crying, she was impossibly good looking, her face all proud planes and sun-kissed skin.

"I don't suppose you know what Scarlet's shift is?" she said, clearly expecting him to take it as a joke.

It *wasn't* a joke. Graham knew he was scowling, and hoped he had gotten the expression in place before Alice saw the underlying surprise and fear.

"How would that help?" he asked curtly, forcing his body to stay relaxed.

Alice didn't seem to notice the effect of her unexpected words, busy wiping her face and pulling herself back together. "It's crazy. Right before I left to come here, this… guy came to see me. Some big shot in an amazing suit. Mob, maybe? I don't know. No Godfather accent or anything. He gave me a business card with a number and a name, nothing else. He knew every tiny detail of my life and he offered to pay me fifty million to find out what Scarlet was. And craziest of all, I actually believe he would." She gave a wry chuckle. "Not that I have a chance in hell of cracking that egg. It's been dead-end after dead-end, and Scarlet probably thinks I'm stalking her. Or maybe flirting with her. It's been awkward."

Graham gave a gruff laugh a little too late to sound completely natural.

He was alarmed.

Deeply alarmed.

He needed to warn Scarlet…

"Don't tell anyone, okay? It's not the kind of thing I really want to explain."

Graham felt his stomach churn as his loyalties clashed. He couldn't refuse his mate's request; the weight of his lion's insistence that they honor her trust was like having the heavy bag on his shoulders, but with claws. But Scarlet should know… he *owed* her, and that weight felt equal, but with claws of guilt.

Alice was looking at him again, that way that she got, that Graham sometimes felt in his own face, like she couldn't help looking at him, like she wanted to look away but couldn't.

He couldn't deny his mate.

"Yeah," he said shortly, sealing his fate.

The relief on her face was the barest salve to the fire of his guilt.

He stood up abruptly and wasn't sure what to say. To his gratitude, Alice stood too. "Thanks," she said shyly. "I mean… for that, and… I'm glad we're being honest, you know. It's nice to have someone… I trust."

Shy gave Alice a whole level of appeal. She usually blustered through things with a cow-catcher of confidence that Graham was beginning to understand was just a facade.

And while her strength and competence was incredibly sexy and hot, it was her vulnerability, her weakness, that did something unexpected to Graham's insides.

"I… want to be," Graham said, then got himself tangled around the grammar. "Be someone you trust, I mean…."

But don't, he wanted to add. *Don't trust me. Don't have faith in me. Don't believe the best of me, because it's all a lie. You were right to run…*

He should tell her the rest of *his* story, he thought, but he couldn't get the words from his mouth. He knew what she would do, and he wouldn't be able to bear her reaction. She'd be horrified. She'd be disgusted.

She'd be *afraid.*

Right now, she wasn't afraid, she was looking at him with unexpected softness and thoughtfulness.

Before Graham could figure out how to tell her the rest of what he wanted to, Alice cleared her throat uncomfortably, balled up a fist and punched him in the arm. "Anyway, thanks," she said cheerfully, not quite looking at him. "Good workout."

And just like that, she was gone.

Graham rubbed his face and threaded his fingers through his unruly hair.

For someone who wanted to keep things uncomplicated, she certainly set him on a roller coaster of emotions.

He wasn't sure how long he sat there before the phone in his pocket buzzed. Scarlet had given it to him so that she had a legitimate way to contact him, and he took it out expecting a text from her.

The number was unknown, but Graham knew who it was immediately by the content of the text:

PEOPLE ARE SNIFFING. $1000 TO KEEP QUIET.

CHAPTER 19

Alice hated how socially inept she could be, hanging behind Mary and Neal, Amber and Tony.

When they had invited her to join them on a trip across the island, she had been so eager to get out of the sleepy resort and *do* something other than think about all the things she couldn't control that she undoubtedly missed all the cues that they wouldn't really want her along. It didn't even occur to her to put together all the pieces and realize what a personal journey this was going to be.

The ride itself had started well; Neal drove the resort Jeep down the ridiculously winding, bumpy road to the airstrip they'd flow into, and they all laughed and talked about the state of the track and the incredible heat, and the island, and the wedding, and their plans to go snorkeling. From the airstrip, it was still a merry trip, over a road that was nearly but not quite as bad as the resort road, to the compound on the other side of the island.

But as they drew closer, the mood dampened, even if the sunny day did not.

When they pulled into the overgrown drive, the party was sober and quiet.

And now she was the most awkward fifth wheel since the wheel itself was invented, watching the two couples wander hand-in-hand through the abandoned compound and the charred remains of the zoo where Neal and Tony had been tortured.

The jungle was starting to spill in over the lawn around the compound. Alice could tell that it had once been neatly groomed and sharp-edged, but now it was almost blurry as brush crept in from the forest, sending tendrils of vines and shoots of roots across the unkempt grass.

The arboretum they walked solemnly through was still mostly standing, but Amber exclaimed over how damaged it was and even Alice could see that neglect had not been kind to the more delicate plants within.

"There were so many birds when I was here," Amber said thoughtfully. "Hummingbirds, and orioles, I remember."

They all stopped and listened.

"I don't hear any birds at all," Alice observed. There were insects, and frogs, but no birdsong.

The compound was even more eerie after that realization.

The house itself was largely undamaged, but had clearly been stripped and stood empty, with gaping dark windows. Here, too, jungle had started to take over. Green vines trailed up over the walls, and skinny saplings spotted the lawns and choked the gardens.

Rain had washed the worst of the soot and ash away, but the bones of the zoo behind the house were still black, twisted and warped. The wall around it looked like it had been burned to the foundations by impossible heat. No cage was whole, but some were half-standing, at least one wall ripped open and burned down on each of them.

It was a stunning display of power and Alice was awed by the sheer scope of the damage.

This was the act of someone who clearly had no intention of being caged again.

She wished she had a hand of her own to hold, watching the others cling to each other. Even though she hadn't been imprisoned or abused in this place, she could imagine what it had been like, how horrifying it would be to be caged and forced to stay in her animal form.

No offense, she told her bear.

Her bear was as bothered as she was. *No one is meant to be in a cage*, she said gruffly.

They found, picking through the rubble, the cell where Tony had been held.

"It wasn't that long for me," he said, with a sympathetic sidelong look at Neal, who had spent ten years in his own enclosure.

Amber clung to his arm. "I remember how it hurt you," she said fiercely. "I *remember*."

Mary said nothing, her fingers twined tight with her mate's.

They found Neal's cage next; it was little more than a few black bars striking up through concrete, and some crumbling steps.

"I tore the lock off the door when I was finally free," Neal said thoughtfully, crouching at what must have been a doorway once. "I gave it to Gizelle. I wonder if she still has it."

He spoke mechanically, like it was something distant and half-forgotten, but when Mary knelt and put her arms around him, he hunched over as if he still felt pain.

Alice retreated swiftly, knowing she was unwelcome in the moment of comfort. Amber and Tony had already returned to the arboretum and Amber was sitting on an unbroken portion of bench while Tony made her drink water and fussed about her health.

Alice wandered to the back of the zoo, over the scar of the wall, to the shaggy lawn that overlooked the sea. They were so high here that the waves were barely wrinkles below them, and the noise of surf was a distant hum. A road, half-washed out, led steeply down to a long dock and a half-moon of beach.

There were burned bars and chunks of rubble even here, as if they had been thrown from the zoo in a fiery explosion. Alice tested one of the dark concrete slabs with her hand, expecting the black to rub off on her like fresh soot, and was surprised when it came away clean. She sat on it, pulled her knees up against her chest, and wished she weren't thinking of Graham.

He might not say much, she thought, but his solid presence beside her would have been comforting.

She glanced back at the zoo, where Mary and Neal were sitting together in the bones of his cage. He had his arms wrapped around her and she was murmuring in his ear as she held him.

She could have that, it suddenly occurred to Alice.

She could have that unwavering support, that true bond, that unflinching comfort.

Graham loved her.

It was more than his blurted first words, it was more than the way he had rushed to protect her from Gizelle's mate. It was the way he gazed at her when he couldn't help it. It was the trust he cautiously extended her, like he was afraid of being pushed away… with good reason considering her insistence that there was nothing between them but animal need.

She could have the same security and partnership that Mary and Amber had found, that same happiness.

All she had to do was accept that she loved him in return.

CHAPTER 20

"We've got him," Jenny said triumphantly, pulling her phone from her ear. "We've got Grant Lyons!"

Graham, who had been planning to sneak straight past the kitchen and go to bed hungry rather than face the smirks and pity and questions that the rest of the staff would have, froze in the doorway.

He wished, not for the first time, that he'd fought harder to get the servants quarters that Breck had claimed when they first moved into The Den. At the time, Breck had needed the private entrance much more than Graham did.

Now, every eye from the living room and kitchen was on Jenny—and because Graham was right behind her, his entrance was at the edge of the spotlight.

"I've got a contact who has Lyons' current name and location, and he's agreed to sell it to us. I'm wiring him the money right now." Jenny had her phone in her hands and was clearly starting the transaction.

The rest of the staff murmured in excitement and interest.

"I wonder if this is what Tony feels like doing spy work," Jenny said gleefully. "I can hear the James Bond theme in my head."

"Stop."

Graham's voice surprised even him and if he had been at the edge of a metaphorical spotlight before, he was now in the blinding center of it. Breck and Darla were standing at the sink still holding the dishes they had been washing and drying together. Saina and Bastian were sitting at the kitchen bar, Travis leaning at the end of it. Wrench and Lydia were in the living room sitting together on the couch near Laura, and Tex had been closing the windows. Someone had muted the television at Jenny's exclamation.

"He's not, you know, a shining example of morality," Jenny said apologetically, looking at Graham. "But I understand he's good for his word. I got his information from a guy Tony knows, so it should be pretty safe."

Graham laughed humorlessly. "Johnny Ace *is* good for his word… unless someone else is willing to pay more."

Jenny blinked at him. "How did you know his name?" she asked slowly. "I only got this information this afternoon."

Graham looked around the room.

These were his friends.

These were *Graham's* friends.

They trusted *Graham*. They thought he was a good guy.

If he was honest with them, if he told them the truth, they'd know better. He'd destroy every fragile thing he'd found here, salting the earth of their friendship.

Secrets rose up in his throat, threatening to suffocate him, and he hated the taste of them.

He fingered the phone in his pocket and pulled it out. "Because the rat bastard asked me for money *not* to tell you."

They all stared at him, not daring to put the pieces together.

"I… don't understand," Jenny finally said.

She didn't *want* to understand, Graham knew.

Darla gave a little inhale of revelation, loud in the quiet room, and Graham closed his eyes.

"I'm Grant Lyons," he growled. "I'm Grant Lyons," he said louder.

It was one of the worst moments of his life.

"Why didn't you tell us?" Travis asked quietly.

"Does Scarlet know?" Bastian demanded.

"Oh, *Graham*." That was Lydia, sounding shocked and sorrowed.

Wrench gave a low growl.

"Do we have to call you m'lord?" Breck asked.

Graham opened his eyes in time to see Darla elbow the waiter in the side.

"It's a valid question," Breck protested. "Weren't the Lyons landed lords?"

"Why didn't you say something when you realized you could buy the resort?" Jenny demanded, sounding understandably put out.

"With what money?" Graham countered, angry. "I don't have a penny. And yes, Scarlet knows. She's known all along. She's in no position to come up with three hundred and fifty *million*. She's facing pretty certain bankruptcy already. Jubilee Grant's lawsuit came through, and she… didn't want to spoil Neal and Mary's wedding by letting them know."

Apparently, coming clean meant coming *completely* clean. Graham made himself snap his mouth shut before he said even more.

"Little late for that, *Grant*," Travis muttered sympathetically.

Graham turned, to find that the wedding party had come quietly through the open door behind him, and they were staring at him with the looks of shock and betrayal that he had expected.

He had eyes only for Alice, who was standing behind the others, the disillusionment in her face like a blade.

"So much for honesty," she said coldly, and she turned on her heel and stomped out.

Then it really was the worst moment of Graham's life.

CHAPTER 21

Alice turned blindly on the path and ran, grinding her teeth and wishing herself anywhere else.

She'd told him everything, and he'd told her half-truths.

I want to be honest, he'd said. *It's nice to have someone to trust,* she'd told him.

And he wasn't even Graham Long.

Alice came to another fork in the path and jogged uphill, because it was harder, because she wanted the clean sweat of hard work to wash away the ugly anger and resentment and betrayal that she was feeling.

What could she trust of what he'd told her? What part of it was real and what part was the mask that he'd shown everyone?

It didn't make her feel any better that he'd been lying to everyone.

Everyone except Scarlet. *Scarlet* knew. And if Scarlet knew about Graham...

The path ended in a high wall and a closed gate marked "KEEP OUT" in red letters. Alice snarled, and turned to find somewhere else to run, then caught a whiff of Graham and knew he'd followed her.

She waited.

He wasn't running, he was walking slowly, and by the time he got to the gate, Alice had worked herself into a fury.

"You know what Scarlet is," she accused him, when he finally rounded the last corner and wearily approached.

"You knew what she was the whole time, and you knew what it would mean for me, that I could save my family. You *lied* to me. I *trusted* you."

Did he understand how rare her trust was?

Graham didn't answer, only went to the gate, opened it and went in without saying a word.

Alice hesitated a moment, then followed him.

For a moment, her anger was washed away in surprise. They walked into a garden, a beautiful, riotous, protected little area of green glory. An open greenhouse lay in one direction, uncovered beds, groaning in flowers and fruit, in the other. Jungle towered above it on the island side, open fields to the ocean side. Even in the darkness, it was gorgeous.

And it smelled… like home.

This was Graham's haven, she realized. The forbidden garden, his secret place.

But she wasn't ready to forgive him, or accept this gift as any kind of compensation for his lies and deception.

"Why didn't you tell me about Scarlet?" she demanded, only a few steps into the garden. She turned and glared at Graham, not letting herself drink in the peacefulness of the plants around them. She didn't want peacefulness, she wanted Graham to suffer some fraction of the agony she was feeling.

"Her secrets aren't mine to tell," Graham growled, in that low voice that masked accents.

"I might have accepted that," Alice snarled. "But you let me believe you didn't *know*."

Graham was silent. Insufferably silent.

"You lied about who you are," she went on, hating the silence worse than the lies. "You lied to me and talked about trust and honesty, and I don't know how I'm supposed to ever believe you about anything again."

"I'm sorry..." Graham started to say.

But Alice didn't want an apology any more than she wanted peace.

She was angry, and hurting, and she wanted to *fight* him, because she didn't know what else to do.

"You're only sorry you got *caught*," Alice hurled back at him. "You would have cheerfully continued to deceive me... for how long? Until I left after Mary and Neal's wedding? What if I'd decided to quit my job and stay here with you? Would you have let me sacrifice my whole *world* for a complete fiction?"

"I wouldn't have..."

"How can I believe anything you say!" Alice snapped, hating his gentleness, resenting his calm. "I don't know what you would have, what you might have, I only know what you *did*. What you *said*. How you *lied*. I told you everything. You let me believe you were being honest with me."

She was being impossible, she knew, and that was the very worst part. She was the one who had pushed him away, held him at arm's length. She was the one who had tried to deny that their bond was anything more than sexual need. *No kissing*, she'd told him, as if that had protected her heart in the slightest.

"I actually fell in love with you!" she railed at him, the pain in her chest like a band being tightened. "Until ten minutes ago, I thought maybe we could make something work, that there really was something here! Something *real*!"

"Don't," Graham said, sounding angry at last. "Don't love me!"

Alice was out of words, out of breath, out of the fury that had carried her this far; it was leaking out of her with the tears on her face.

Graham seemed to have absorbed all of it. "You want *my* secrets? You want to know the whole truth, who I really am?" he threatened.

Alice stared at him, not sure what to do with the emptiness in her chest or the silence in her throat.

"I'm a fighter, I'm a killer. I told you the truth about school, and I got recruited soon after to fight in an underground cage fighting ring. It was all shifters, and it was a fight in human form until one of the fighters shifted in sheer survival instinct. You know how you get shifters to take animal form? You hurt them. You hurt them so bad, they have to shift, they can't help themselves. Ask Tony, or Neal. Beehag had it down to an art."

Graham was speaking between gritted teeth, his sides heaving like he'd just run the length of the resort.

"I was *good* at hurting people. Really good at it."

Alice didn't doubt it.

Then Graham stepped forward, a sharp, aggressive move designed to frighten her.

"And I liked it," Graham hissed, close to her face. "I liked to hurt them."

CHAPTER 22

It was out there. It couldn't be taken back. She knew who he really was now, and that was it.

Graham couldn't hold his angry facade for long, not in the face of Alice's foolish bravery as she gazed back at him wordlessly. She was too beautiful to bear, too courageous to endure.

"You should go," he said, stepping back and turning away. "I won't bother you again."

But she didn't go. "Why did you go to prison?" Her voice was quiet and firm.

Graham was done with lies and secrets. He would answer any question she asked.

"I killed a man."

He could have stopped there. He could have let her assume it was just an accident, could have stuck to half-truths like he always did. He could have forced her to ask the questions. Instead, he went on, continuing to stand looking away.

"He was a good fighter, strong and fast, light on his feet and well-trained. Not the best I'd ever been up against, but... good. I... thought he might have been a big cat shifter."

Had he really? Had he really had no doubts at the beginning of the fight?

"He fought hard, snapped my wrist before I got his collar bone broken and turned the tide of the fight. But he never gave up, never… never begged for mercy… never asked..."

Grant had begged.

Shift, he'd hissed, hearing the man's rib break at his hit. *Shift and concede the fight.*

Give up, he'd pleaded, when he dislocated his opponent's shoulder. How much abuse could he take?

Shift, he'd shouted, over the crowd's cheers and jeers.

Shift! he'd beseeched, holding the man's broken body in his arms, not sure how he hadn't surrendered to his animal instinct long before.

Then Graham finally realized why he hadn't, as the light in the man's blazing eyes slowly flickered out.

"He wasn't a shifter," Graham said. He was not sure when he had dropped to his knees, hands making fists in the gravel. "He was just a human that they'd put in a cage with me."

Behind him, Alice gave a hiss of dismay.

"I *tortured* him," Graham admitted to the strawberries before him. "I begged him to shift… but he *couldn't*. The stuff they classified in my file? It was what I did to him. How badly I hurt him. It was slaughter, it wasn't manslaughter."

"What did you do then?" Alice asked quietly. She must be horrified. It was a wonder she was still there.

"The fight coordinator was a lovely bloke by the name of Cyrus Angres. He'd been setting these fights up for a couple of years, and he was afraid that the usual show was getting… stale. I realized he'd done it knowingly, set me up to kill that man for money, and it took six guys to pull me off him. I got away, went straight to a bobby I knew in London who was a shifter and told him everything. It went to the top of International Shifter Affairs. The whole ring went under, I got a reduced sentence for manslaughter, all the details of the guy's death marked out with black pen… and afterwards I got a new identity from Johnny Ace to start over in America with."

“As Graham Long, gardener.”

“Gardening ran in my family,” Graham said numbly. “When Scarlet found me, she was just like Jenny, hoping I had money to restart the resort; she only had about half of what she needed raised. All she found was a broke, broken, bottom-of-the-barrel groundskeeper at a half-rate golf course in Florida. She… could have left me where she found me, it would have been a lot easier. But she made me come here, gave me purpose, showed me how to start over.”

Alice’s feet crunched over the gravel and she sat down on the rock edge of the strawberry bed facing Graham. “I can’t picture Scarlet in Florida,” she said thoughtfully, as if *that* was the surprising part of the whole sordid story.

“She wasn’t,” Graham said quietly. “She can’t leave the island. She got my phone number, wired me a plane ticket, convinced me to use it.”

“Graham…”

“Grant,” he corrected. “Grant Lyons. Murderer.”

“*Graham*,” Alice insisted. “You are Graham Long now, and it was Graham Long that I fell in love with.”

He put his forehead down on the rock edge of the strawberry bed next to her. “Grant is still who I am,” he said plaintively. “And you don’t understand. I liked to hurt people. I *liked* it.”

“Bullshit,” Alice said flatly, to his surprise.

She didn’t get it, Graham thought in despair. “You don’t know…”

CHAPTER 23

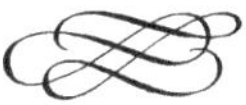

Alice had not believed that there could be anything more devastating and distracting than Graham's—Grant's—bare chest.

She was wrong.

When Graham spoke—really spoke, in a confessional rush of words—he had the sexiest British accent that Alice had ever heard. The extra 'r's, the clear 't's, the drawn out 'oo's… move over Tom Hiddleston.

She had to force herself to listen to his words, and not just drown in his voice.

He believed he was a monster, she realized as he spoke. A terrible person who did terrible things and liked them.

But Alice knew better. She knew Graham from the bottom of his soul to each gentle fingertip. She knew his heart.

"You don't know…" he said softly.

"I *do*. I watch this happen to kids in sports all the time. They don't love the sport, they only love being good at it," Alice said firmly. "They get so wrapped up in what people expect them to do with a talent that they start thinking of themselves only in terms of that skill. They define themselves by what they're good at, and they think that they enjoy it because it's the only time they feel worth anything. That's not enjoyment, that's *entrapment*."

She knelt beside him, putting a hand hesitantly on his shoulder. "Enjoying a fight where you get to be good at something, and there are people cheering you on, and you know that all your injuries and theirs will heal up in a couple of days… that's not the same as liking to *hurt* people. You *knew* the difference, and you went out there and flipped tables because you were tricked into an unfair fight that only had one ending."

Her arm slid around him and Graham turned in her embrace to lay his head on her shoulder. She tangled her fingers in his hair and rested her head on his.

It was so comfortable, so natural, to hold him like that; Alice didn't even mind the sharp gravel pressing into her knees.

"Graham," she started.

"Grant," he corrected firmly into her collarbone. His arms had crept around her, and he was pressed up close against her for comfort.

"I'll call you what you want," Alice said just as firmly. "But you are not the Grant you've convinced yourself you are."

"Who am I, then?" he asked, drawing back to look her in the eyes.

Mine, Alice wanted to say.

Ours, her bear was growling.

Alice couldn't say either of those things out loud, so she simply leaned forward and kissed him.

After a split second of surprise, Graham opened his mouth and kissed her back desperately, taking her face in his hands.

She'd been right not to kiss him before, Alice decided. It was like baring her soul to him; it undid her. She was helpless in his hands, utterly lost to his taste and his tongue and his hungry mouth.

Every inch of him was irresistible. Both of them rose to their feet, still kissing, as Graham lifted her shirt from her. She tried to get his shirt off while he was trying to unclip her bra, and they quickly realized they were working to cross-purposes and stripped off their own clothing.

For a moment, they simply stood close, not touching, just gazing at each other. But not for long; Alice couldn't keep her eyes, or her fingers, from his beautiful shoulders, or his broad chest, or his amazing jaw, and she gave a little gasp as Graham stepped forward, his cock pressing just where it should as he kissed her again.

Alice didn't think that he could unravel her more, but the second kiss was deeper, and there was no clothing to keep his intoxicating skin from her starving fingers.

She gave a gasp of surprise as he suddenly wrapped his arms around her and lifted her to lay her back, directly into one of the beds of strawberries.

Then his weight was over her like a shield and he was pressing into her as Alice spread her legs in invitation. She was impossibly wet, he was impossibly hard, and when he slid into her there was a moment of pleasure so intense and intimate that Alice had to cry out in surrender.

For a heartbeat, he held there, buried inside her, then he bent to kiss her, and began to thrust, slowly, gently, deeper every stroke, and Alice felt like he was drawing her up on an unbreakable thread.

She kissed him back, arching up, wrapping her legs around him because there was no such thing as close enough, no place inside of her that didn't want him.

When she found shuddering release, crying out in pleasure she didn't want to deny, she opened her eyes and found him gazing at her in wonder and need.

Impulsively, she wrapped one leg around his and turned him onto his back, barely staying coupled as they rolled. She lifted his arms above his head and leaned on his forearms, pinning him, riding him, taking him deeper than she'd ever thought was possible. He let her hold him down, hips rising to meet her strokes, until she was falling into a second whirlpool of pleasure.

He broke free of her hands then and wrapped his arms tight around her, holding her closer and closer, until he was spilling his ecstasy into her, groaning and growling near her ear.

Neither one of them let go this time, continuing to embrace as their heartbeats finally slowed and they could catch their breath again.

She was never going to be able to eat the berries again without evoking the memories of Graham. The scent of bruised leaves and squashed berries and disturbed earth was heady and strong; Alice felt like she'd just made love in a dessert.

"Poor, crushed strawberries," Alice finally said.

She giggled. "The gardener is going to be so pissed…"

Below her, Graham made a rumbling noise. For a moment, Alice wondered if she was too heavy to keep lying on him, then realized he was laughing. It was the most beautiful sound she'd ever heard, vibrating through her entire body and she chortled with him helplessly.

"Alice," he said, sitting up with his arms still around her. His laughter stilled. "Alice…"

If his voice in confession was disturbing, his voice saying her name struck some raw nerve inside of her and Alice suddenly felt like her world was dropping away. "I don't know," she said to the question he wasn't asking. "I don't know what this means. I don't know what it changes." She plucked a flattened strawberry from her shoulder blade and shook it off her fingers.

"Scarlet…" he started to say.

"Don't tell me what she is," Alice stopped him. "I can't ask you to do that. You were right that it's not your secret to give, and I shouldn't have asked you."

Graham gave a little shudder. "*You* were right that I know what she is, though. She's been a friend of my family for decades. She was my grandfather's... partner."

"Don't tell me what she is," Alice repeated. "Not like this." Then, as if she was compelled to ask, "Partner, like... lovers?"

"No, though I think that she may have loved him. She was technically his secretary, but she was much more to our family than that. The resort was supposed to be hers, when he built it."

"Where did she get the rest of the money?" Alice asked, when he was quiet for a moment.

"She didn't," Graham explained. "This *is* only half of what the resort was meant to be. She scrapped the plans for a little community that was meant to be located over on this corner of the island, hoping that if the resort took off, she'd be able to add it on later."

"And now?"

Graham sighed. "Now she's going to lose it all."

Alice shivered in the cooling evening breeze and stood up to find her clothes. She tossed Graham's pants at him. "She doesn't have to…" she said thoughtfully, pulling her shirt on without a bra.

Graham, as appealing shimmying into his pants as he'd been getting out of them, scowled at her. "What do you mean?"

"You've got some flush clients who love this place," Alice suggested. "Isn't Gizelle's mate a billionaire? Hasn't royalty stayed here? What if Scarlet ran a crowdfunding thing? Like, a timeshare program, but without the vulture salespeople, to raise enough money to buy it outright. They'd *have* to sell it to you if you came up with the cash, right?"

Graham stared at her. "They'd have to sell it to me, but they're listing the island as a whole; we'd have to buy the entire thing. They want three hundred and fifty *million* dollars."

Alice tried not to choke on the very idea of that kind of money

"That would be… a lot of crowdfunding," Alice conceded. "And I think I have a squashed strawberry in my underwear."

CHAPTER 24

When Graham and Alice returned to The Den, there was no real way to get back in to his room privately, or sneak to the shower, or pretend that nothing had happened, so they didn't try. The rest of the staff was already gathered in the living area, and the hum of conversation that they'd heard through the open windows came to a stop when Graham cracked the door.

Everyone politely pretended they weren't craning to see if it was Graham alone, or if Alice was with him, except Breck, who turned completely around on the couch, propped his chin on both hands, and greeted them cheerfully.

"Welcome back, your lordship!"

Darla gave a chiding murmur that couldn't hide her amusement and Laura threw a pillow at him.

"There's a bottle of wine on the counter," Mary pointed out.

"Oh, good," Alice said, opening cabinets at random until she found the glasses. "You want one?"

Graham shook his head.

While Alice filled her tumbler, the others discretely rearranged themselves on the chairs and couches so that the only free spots were together.

Graham stalked to take one of them, Alice following. He settled gingerly into place, wishing he had taken a glass of wine simply to have something to do with his hands. Alice flopped down beside him, pushing her sandals off with each opposite foot and tucking her legs up under her. They weren't quite touching.

Everyone *grinned*.

"We've been talking about how we might save the resort," Jenny said quickly. "We're thinking about trying to raise the money ourselves. If we can, they have to sell it to you."

"If you're in," Laura added.

Graham grunted.

"Great minds think alike," Alice said. "We were just talking about that."

Jenny had her computer in her lap. "We're definitely going to ask Conall, and Magnolia. Laura and I are still fighting legal battles over the life insurance policy that Fred stole when our parents died, but Fred's estate is running out of appeals to make, so we should get it soon. It will be a pretty good drop in the bucket."

"I… have a few things of value," Bastian said uncomfortably.

"You can't sell your hoard," Saina said to him, dismayed.

Bastian took her hands in his. "It's not worth a lot," he said, looking embarrassed. "But this is greater treasure." He looked around at the others in The Den. "If the resort isn't here, I don't have a hoard worth having."

Saina kissed him. "I know people who can fence anything we need."

"I have some jewelry," Lydia said thoughtfully. "Nothing spectacular, but some of it is gold."

"I've got a watch," Tex said. "It might have some value as an antique."

Jenny was busily tapping onto her keyboard as everyone volunteered what they could and guessed prices that seemed pathetic compared to the monstrous number they were aiming for.

"What about Scarlet?" Alice asked. "She must know some well-to-do people to ask." Graham wondered if she was thinking about the mysterious offer for the information on Scarlet, and her own dire straits. Fifty million would go a long ways.

Lydia, sitting nearly in Wrench's lap on the crowded couch, shook her head. "Scarlet told us not to look for Grant Lyons."

"To protect Graham," Alice reminded them. "But you all know now."

"Your…" Darla smothered Breck with the throw pillow before he could finish the *lordship* part.

"We were thinking we would try to do it quietly and surprise her," Laura said. "She's so private and proud, I think she might try to stop us."

Graham knew she would, and his nod caught Laura's attention.

"Are you in?" Laura asked him.

"I've got nothing of value," Graham apologized.

"The sale has to be in your name," Laura pointed out. "You'd be the owner."

"Do I have to be?" Graham asked with a scowl. "Can't I sign it away to Scarlet?"

"Yeah, you can do that," Jenny said confidently, to his relief. "That's quite straight-forward."

"Good," Travis said with a grin. "I don't want Graham the Grouch calculating my bonuses."

"Are you bleeding?" Lydia asked suddenly, leaning over to Alice.

Alice looked down at her leg. "Nope," she said, peeling the red spot off. "Strawberry."

"I thought I smelled strawberries!" Amber laughed. "I couldn't figure out why."

"I think there's one in your hair, Graham," Mary observed shyly.

"Hypocrite!" Breck exclaimed in outrage. "All the grief you give us for damaging your precious flower gardens and you're off rolling in the strawberry beds! Flowers are one thing, but we *eat* those."

Everyone stared in wonder at Graham and it took him a long moment to realize that it was because he was laughing.

CHAPTER 25

Alice spent a long moment after she woke with her eyes closed, too comfortable to move, clinging to sweet, peaceful sleep.

Graham had an arm draped over her and one foot hooked around her ankle. A single sheet was more than enough warmth for the morning; already the temperature was rising as the sun came up over the island.

Despite a shower, Alice could still smell strawberries, and it filled her with unexpected contentment.

This was where she belonged, she thought, and the idea was so unexpected that her eyes flew open in alarm and her peace shattered.

Graham stirred as she sat up and, in a smooth, practiced way, rolled out of bed and began getting dressed as if on autopilot. Alice was watching him as he woke up enough to realize what was different, turning back to look at her in amazement and confusion.

She gave him a crooked smile as he stood there, frozen with one leg in his pants.

"Morning," she said wryly.

He scowled at her; clearly this was his reaction to any surprise. "Good morning," he growled, stuffing the other leg into his khakis.

Alice pushed off the sheet and was delighted to watch Graham nearly fall over staring at her. "So… ah… I told the girls I'd work on the bachelorette party with them today."

Graham managed to save his balance and, still shirtless, he walked around the bed as she stood up. "Alice…" he started.

Guessing his train of thought, Alice was swift to say, "I don't know what this all means long term, okay? I have a job I love, and problems I can't solve living here at Shifting Sands." Damn his chest… even with her body humming and satiated, Alice wanted nothing more than to lay her hands over those gorgeous muscles and push him back down on the bed. Instead, she reached for her clothing and began to get dressed.

Did he look hurt? Alice couldn't guess behind the frown on his face or his stony silence, but just the idea of it made her stomach clench. "It's not that I don't…" she wasn't going to say that she loved him again. That would only make it harder to leave. "I'm really… I don't want you to think…"

She didn't want to leave.

Graham and his naked chest closed the distance between them and he put his hand gently on either side of her face. This made it very challenging to continue getting dressed and Alice stopped trying.

"You don't have to know," Graham said softly. "We can take it a day at a time."

Alice surprised herself with a rush of warmth and desire. "Yeah," she agreed breathlessly. And that was as long as she could resist his shirtless self, slipping her arms up around his broad shoulders to kiss him. In short order, they had peeled each other out of the clothing they'd just put on and he was showing her how to make the most of those days that they were taking one at a time.

Hours later, freshly showered and *still* somehow smelling of strawberries, Alice found herself at the buffet.

She took a second baked chicken leg from the buffet, considered putting it back, and then took a third one out of spite.

Spite, or appetite, she thought; she'd skipped breakfast to shamelessly make Graham late for work.

She considered a fourth chicken leg and decided that she should save room for dessert instead. Graham had mentioned a fresh crop of strawberries…

Mary and Amber had their heads together with Laura and Jenny at one of the larger tables and Alice thought they were waving her over until she realized they were trying to catch the attention of the woman behind her.

"Magnolia," Laura called. "Could we talk to you a moment?"

Magnolia looked like she had never turned down a fourth chicken leg in her life. Or possibly a tenth.

They sat down opposite from each other at the table, Magnolia with a tray heaping with fine cheeses and fruit and fluffy sweetbread, Alice with her pile of chicken legs and a four-inch-high sandwich. Jenny had her laptop open in front of her and was busily typing.

"I'm Alice." Alice was never sure how long to wait for someone else to introduce her, and generally did so herself.

"Magnolia," the other woman greeted with a gracious smile and an elegant fingershake. "You're Graham's mate."

Alice blinked at her, momentarily speechless. No one else had said as much aloud after the first terrible day, and it felt weird to hear it. "Yeah," she agreed. *Mate* was as good a classification as anything, she decided. She didn't feel like a *girlfriend*.

Magnolia smiled at her and Alice thought dazedly that she'd never been at the receiving end of a smile that lovely and sincere before. "I'm delighted to meet you," the woman said. "Graham needs a little goodness in his life like you."

No one had ever called Alice 'a little goodness' before, but she supposed that if anyone could, it was Magnolia, who probably outweighed her by two hundred pounds.

"What did you need, darling?" Magnolia asked Jenny.

Jenny lowered her voice and they all leaned into the table when she did. "It's a bit of a delicate question," she confessed. "But we're trying to raise money to buy the island. We've recently found out that Graham is Grant Lyons, and he gets first refusal of a sale by contract. If we can get enough people together, we'd be able to buy it outright and we'd never have to worry about Beehag breaking the lease or selling it out from under us."

She went on hastily. "I'm drawing up contracts that would give investors a stake in the resort, and we can talk about terms and such, but… is that something you'd be interested in? Something you could help with?"

Magnolia looked thoughtful, but not entirely happy.

"Is there a reason that it isn't Scarlet herself telling me this?" she asked suspiciously.

"She doesn't know," Laura admitted. "It's a long shot, but we're trying to surprise her."

Magnolia laughed in delight. "I love a good surprise," she said eagerly. Then she sobered. "But I'm afraid there's very little I can pledge. My money comes from a trust that I have limited access to. I don't have any savings I can reach, and my lease payment here is almost my entire monthly payout."

Everyone at the table gave a sigh of regret. "I understand," Jenny said. "We'll keep looking."

Magnolia inspected a be-ringed hand thoughtfully. "I have some jewelry. It won't be much compared to the asking price of the island, but it's yours, no contract needed. Scarlet *should* own the island."

"Saina's offered to fence anything we can get together," Laura said gratefully. "Bastian's got her looking for buyers for part of his hoard. We'll put our insurance settlement in, if we can ever get it litigated. Fred managed to get a fancy law firm in New York to defend his estate, so there have been problems."

"We're also writing to all the survivors of Beehag's zoo," Mary explained. "They all owe Scarlet for her hospitality, and this would be a great way to repay it."

"Tony is taking a bit of a risk giving us their contact information, but I don't think any of them will mind. It's not likely that any of them are sitting on millions of dollars," Amber said wryly, "but there's always some hope."

"And little pledges *will* add up," Jenny added optimistically.

Fifty million would add a lot, too, Alice thought wryly. But she didn't like to think about that, or the fact that Graham had the key to that payout… or the fact that even if she knew it, she wasn't sure she could betray Scarlet's secret.

Even for fifty million dollars.

Even to save her brother and her parents.

Her chicken legs were suddenly looking a lot less appealing.

Alice thought about the pathetic scrap book she'd tried to use as a cover for asking Scarlet questions. "Scarlet's pretty private and proud. She's probably not going to be really happy that you're sending her business failures to everyone she's ever helped."

The others looked at her with expressions of mixed guilt, skepticism, and curiosity and Alice wished she hadn't said anything at all. She took a fierce bite of chicken leg.

"I mean… not that I know her well," she said uncomfortably around her food. "But I guess *I'd* be pretty embarrassed."

"That's why she wouldn't do it herself," Jenny said thoughtfully. "But if we can buy the island, it would be worth it. I think she'd understand."

Alice nodded. "Yeah, you're probably right."

"Besides," Laura added, "it's not like this is actually a failure of *Scarlet's*. She was kind enough to take all those shifters in, knowing that it was her bottom line that would pay for it. It was... a failure of kindness, not business."

"Oo," Jenny said. "Failure of kindness. I like that. I'm stealing it." She typed feverishly into her laptop.

"This is a lovely thing you're doing," Magnolia said, eating gracefully. "I'll help out any way I can."

Alice finished her meal as quickly as she could, wishing she had an ounce of the other woman's grace.

CHAPTER 26

Graham politely averted his eyes when Gizelle opened her door naked.

"Is Conall here?" he asked gruffly.

Gizelle cocked her head at him. "He's always somewhere," she said, not offering to get her mate or put on clothing.

"Can I talk to him? I might need your help."

A smile bloomed over Gizelle's face. "I like to help."

She scampered away into the bedroom, leaving the cottage door open behind her.

Graham hung at the doorway for a moment, not sure if it was an invitation to enter or not, and finally went in and gingerly took a seat in one of the plush chairs.

When Gizelle reappeared, Graham was relieved to see that she was dressed. He stood as Conall came into the little living room and they briefly shook hands before sitting opposite each other. Gizelle curled up beside the Irish elk shifter, a hand casually resting on his bare arm so that he could hear and didn't have to rely on lip reading.

"Is there a problem?" Conall asked, eyeing the folder that Graham was holding.

"I hope this is actually a solution," Graham said. He leaned forward to hand Conall the folder over the sturdy wooden coffee table. "Jenny is working out the finer details, but we're hoping you're interested in buying an interest in the island and saving Shifting Sands Resort."

Conall took the folder and opened it with a frown. "I'm surprised that Scarlet isn't approaching me with this herself."

Graham grimaced. "Scarlet doesn't know. We're only in the early stages of trying to figure out if this is even feasible."

"You look like you drew the short straw," Conall observed, glancing up from the paperwork in the folder with a hint of a smile.

Graham chuckled. He and Conall had quietly become good friends. Others joked that it was because Conall, deaf, didn't have to worry about lip reading Graham because he never said anything.

Graham had volunteered to come talk to the Irish elk shifter, mostly because he wanted to confess who he was personally, rather than letting the information get to Conall by the grapevine.

"My real name is Grant Lyons," he admitted. "I am the blood heir of Aaric Lyons, the man who started the resort forty years ago. It's in the lease contract that I get first right of refusal on a purchase of the island. If we can raise the funds, we can buy the island at their public asking price, even if there are other buyers."

Conall looked at him quizzically, but didn't question the revelation of Graham's true identity.

Gizelle, on the other hand, was nodding sagely. "You're from the lion who came before," she said, as if it made perfect sense. Then she added, "I will still call you Graham."

"I would like that," Graham told her gravely.

Conall nodded thoughtfully as he flipped through the paperwork that Jenny had sent with Graham. "I'll have to consult with my financial advisor, of course. I'm quite interested, but… this is the asking price? Three hundred and fifty million?"

Graham nodded. It was a stunning amount of money. "The sale is for the entire island as a package, almost twenty thousand acres, including Beehag's compound, the dock, the airstrip, and the resort. That's the price set by an independent auditor. On top of that,

Darla's mother has filed the lawsuit we were expecting. More than a million."

Conall closed the folder. "I am only a paper billionaire," he said frankly. "I have some assets I could liquidate, but most of my wealth is tied up in my business, which is still on the market. We've had two buyers now who seemed interested, got as far as earnest money, and then bailed out under mysterious circumstances. If I were a superstitious man, I might suspect a conspiracy."

"But you're interested," Graham said in relief.

Conall looked at Gizelle, who had her legs up the back of the couch, leaning her head backwards off the seat staring upside down at Graham, hand still carefully on Conall so that he could hear.

"We belong here," he said soberly. "I don't relish the idea of anyone else getting their hands on the resort with the ability to throw us out or disrupt our peace. I've seen some of the prospective buyers that Beehag has brought through, and it's clear that he's working to uproot Scarlet from the island. He's involved with someone subtle and clever, who is willing to use unorthodox methods. My interest in the resort is selfish and personal, but no less sincere. I'll make some phone calls and get you a concrete pledge. If I could do the full amount, I would, and I genuinely hope you are able to raise the rest."

Graham bowed his head. "Thank you," he said, rising and shaking Conall's hand. "I appreciate it."

Gizelle let go of Conall as he stood to shake Graham's hand and Graham caught the brief flinch when she did. "Wait!" she said suddenly, and she vaulted over the couch and disappeared into the bedroom.

"Has she seen Neal yet?" Graham thought to ask, making sure Conall was watching him.

Conall shook his head. "She does things in her own time," he said patiently. "I've had a chance to talk with him a little, though. Good man."

Gizelle came back out of the bedroom. She was holding a tablet and a pair of earphones. "Can these save Scarlet?" she asked shyly.

Graham exchanged a look with Conall, not sure how to answer.

She hadn't been touching him, and had been facing Graham, so she had to turn and repeat herself to her mate, adding, "It's my fault."

"What's your fault, sweetheart?" Conall asked, concerned.

"When it rains," Gizelle answered calmly. "And the cage breaks."

Conall frowned and shook his head. "You don't need to give up your tablet," he assured her, ignoring the rest of her nonsense. "It is kind of you to offer, but you can help me talk with my accountant—that will be a big help."

"You could help us distract Scarlet," Graham suggested, inspiration striking. "It's a secret, that we're trying to raise the money. Could you help keep her from finding out?"

Gizelle smiled like the moon. "I'm good at keeping secrets!" she said enthusiastically. "Oh! Secrets! We haven't finished reading *The Secret Garden*! I will ask her to!"

"She'd like that," Graham said sincerely to her back as she fled from the house, still clutching her tablet.

Conall smiled fondly after her, then scowled self-consciously when he caught Graham watching him.

"I didn't mean this exact moment," Graham said, with an apologetic shrug.

"Like I said, she does things in her own time," Conall said briefly.

They shook hands again and Graham went to take the news to the rest of the staff.

CHAPTER 27

"Hey, handsome!" Alice called as she approached.

Graham stopped raking and leaned on the handle like a Greek statue, his mane of hair golden in the sunlight.

"I keep making you late for work, so I brought you lunch from the buffet," she said cheerfully.

Graham smiled slowly. "Thanks," he said gratefully. "Scarlet read us the riot act at the staff meeting today. She had a lot to say about how romance and weddings shouldn't be keeping us from doing our jobs, and how she can't run a business if we insist on treating it like a summer camp."

Alice gave a laughing groan as she handed Graham the plates with the sandwich she'd put together. "She's probably in a terrible mood."

"Everyone who can is avoiding her," Graham agreed.

It wasn't only the upcoming wedding that was distracting everyone, of course… everyone was doing what they could to get money towards the purchase of the resort, and if the outstanding balance was still intimidating, it was encouraging to watch the total slowly rising as they got in touch with more of Scarlet's previous guests. Alice had been flabbergasted when Jenny gleefully announced that the Empress of Atlantis had dropped a cool five million into the pot. She wasn't sure which part of the statement astonished her the most: Empress, Atlantis, or *five million*.

"Next you're going to tell me a royal *unicorn* family is making a donation," Alice had scoffed in disbelief, trying to think of anything more unbelievable.

"Already did," Jenny had laughed, pointing to a respectable pledge in the ledger. "Not royalty, quite, but English nobility."

In ten days, they had raised more than half of the impossible goal.

She and Graham sat together on the bench overlooking the cliffs, the ocean crawling beneath them and beating on the rocks.

There were moments when Alice thought her life was in a perfect, fragile balance.

She was… when she was honest with herself… absolutely head-over-heels in love with a sexy, tenderhearted man with madly talented fingers and fabulous hair.

Graham didn't ask what they were now and he never *called* her his girlfriend—not that he would waste any syllables for extraneous things like titles anyway—but she was visiting his room every night. And each afternoon that he could be coaxed away from the gardens. And every morning when she caught him on break, and when they passed on the paths…

Her bear, apparently, was insatiable, and fortunately, his lion was, too; however he protested that he wasn't going to be able to keep up this pace, every time she kissed him, he was more than capable of laying her down and making her bones turn to jelly.

They never talked about love, or the future. But Alice thought about a lot.

Love...

...and secrets.

There were also moments when Alice knew keenly that it was all temporary, that soon enough, she would be returning to her grubby real life, helpless to help her parents or her brother, unable to do anything to save either of them.

And Scarlet's shift form hung between them like a giant white elephant.

Alice was sure that Graham would tell her what it was if she asked, but she knew just as certainly that she couldn't ask. Forcing him to betray someone else's trust in him seemed like the cruelest thing she could do to him.

So Alice never mentioned how much help even a portion of fifty million dollars would be in their slow fundraising efforts, and she never brought up Scarlet if he didn't first, and she tried hard not to think about her life back home and the solution-less problems that she would return to.

Graham made it easy.

He told her stories about growing up in England, and she told him about growing up in the rural Midwest with her brother. He talked about his father, and learning how to garden on their estate when he was young. Alice told him about learning sports with her father, and fishing and boating in the rivers and lakes. He even told her, hesitantly, a little about his fighting days, and showed her a many-times-folded flier.

"King of the Jungle!" Alice chortled. "Look how short your hair is!"

"I could cut it again," he offered at once.

"Don't you dare," Alice said. "I think a guy with longer hair than mine is the sexiest thing ever."

He even let her work with him in the gardens at the top of the resort, showing her how to twist ripe strawberries off the plants without bruising them, and how to harvest herbs, and which weeds to pull. He told her what all the jungle plants were, and how they grew.

Evenings were often spent in The Den, sitting cozily with the rest of the staff in the living room, and over the course of the week no fewer than seven people later commented to her that they'd never seen Graham talk so much. Two of them had marveled over the fact that they'd never realized he was British before.

The glorious tropical days spilled one into another and Alice trembled, thinking how short their time left was.

"What's wrong?" Graham asked, taking a bite of his sandwich and giving her a sidelong look.

"I'm not ready for this to be over," she confessed quietly.

Graham was quiet. "Does it have to be?"

It was as close as he'd come to asking what they were going to do with the future.

"I don't know," Alice said miserably. "I wish I did."

Before them, the ocean wrinkled away to the horizon, dotted with a dozen small boats.

"I haven't seen boats out there before," Alice observed.

Graham squinted out at them curiously. "We don't often see a lot like that," he said, letting her change the subject without argument. "Must be some kind of fishing competition or something."

Alice might have tried taking the conversation to the topic of fish, but Graham's pocket abruptly buzzed and he withdrew his phone curiously.

The screen made him frown and stand. "I have to go," he said apologetically. "Scarlet said immediately, and she *never* says that."

He paused only long enough to kiss Alice—one of those kisses that left no sense in her head to worry with.

But the worry came rushing back as Graham disappeared in the direction of Scarlet's office and Alice gazed out at boats with her chest aching.

CHAPTER 28

There were five guests waiting in the courtyard outside of Scarlet's office next to a pile of gigantic suitcases. They looked sweaty and winded and Scarlet was giving them a smile that Graham knew entirely too well: she was furious and frustrated and fighting very hard to give absolutely no impression of it.

"Please wait here a moment," she said with a polite nod of her head, and she clicked her way across the courtyard to meet Graham and draw him out of earshot.

"There a problem?" Graham asked with a growl. "You said you needed me immediately." He eyed the guests; they didn't look like the kind of threat that he had anticipated when he got Scarlet's text.

Two of the women were fanning themselves and one of the men, slightly overweight, was sitting on a suitcase like his legs had given out in the heat. The second man was the only one who was slightly menacing, and he was frowning thoughtfully at labels on the potted plants.

"I wish there was *only* one problem," Scarlet hissed. "But this is the most urgent. They aren't shifters."

Graham scowled across the courtyard. "Friends of shifters?"

Scarlet had talked about relaxing the shifter restriction for friends of guests, especially for events like weddings.

"No," Scarlet said with a humorless laugh. "They don't even *know* about shifters. They are *furries*."

"Furries?" Graham repeated, confused.

"Humans that dress up like anthropomorphic animals. Those suitcases are entirely costumes. *Fur*suits."

Graham almost laughed.

"It was a last-minute reservation," Scarlet said defensively. "The charter has already left, and I can't send them back to the mainland on the boat until morning. We're going to have to put them up for the night. I need you to get the word out to the entire staff, and every single guest, that we cannot have anyone shifting in public, or talking about shifting, or doing anything only shifters can do, until we get rid of them. No magic."

She groaned then, though her posture remained perfect and to the guests she undoubtedly looked like she was simply having a nice, casual conversation. "And oh, Gizelle… will you find Conall, see if he can keep her out of the way. She's already on edge, the last thing I need is her getting scared. Make sure that Liam keeps the elders off the common grounds. We need to avoid a scene."

"What's our story?" Graham asked.

"That we're fumigating the hotel for an infestation of *cloth-eating* bugs and have no other openings. We're moving the existing hotel guests to cottages, and I'm having Travis quarantine the building. The humans will be put up on the beach for the night in a tent. In the morning, we'll have Travis take them in the boat to that new all-inclusive hotel on the mainland. On my dime, of course."

Graham winced. This was not a good thing for a resort already in dire financial straits.

But if there was one thing Scarlet was good at, it was guarding secrets, and Graham knew that she would bend over backwards to protect the trust of her clients.

CHAPTER 29

Not knowing how long Graham's summons would keep him busy, Alice took the empty sandwich plate back to the buffet and wandered around the center of the resort.

Amber and Mary were laughing and sunning at the pool while Neal and Tony were racing laps. Alice watched them a moment from the bar deck, considered joining them, and decided that she couldn't muster up the appropriate feeling of vacation for the moment.

"Get you a drink?" Tex invited, as Alice took a seat at the bar. He was sitting behind the bar tuning a battered guitar.

"It's probably a little early," Alice decided. "I'll take a ginger ale." Bubbles, she thought, but less regret. She had enough regrets.

Tex poured her a ginger ale from the tap into a glass of ice and resumed tuning his guitar. "Got a request?" he asked.

"Something happy," Alice suggested, eyeing his cowboy hat skeptically.

Tex laughed, touching the brim of his hat with a nod, and launched into a ridiculous song about faithful dogs and faithless women that had a fast, upbeat tempo, even if the topic wasn't entirely happy.

As he finished with a flourish, Alice's phone rang. She gave the bartender a thumbs-up and fished her phone from her pocket.

A glance at the number had her blood running cold.

"Are you okay?" she blurted, answering.

Tex busily turned away to do something at the far end of the bar to give her privacy.

"Jeez, Alice, you sound just like Mom." Andy's voice was reassuringly strong.

Alice gripped the edge of the bar. "You don't call unless something is wrong," she reminded her brother crossly. "What's going on?"

"You sound like you're a million miles away," Andy observed.

"I'm in Costa Rica," Alice reminded him.

"Oh, crap, I forgot. Is this costing too much? I wasn't calling for anything that important." Andy's voice was thick with guilt.

"No, it's fine," Alice said swiftly. "I have an international plan for the month. What's up?"

"I… I just got off the phone with Mom and Dad, and it's really hard to talk to them without really talking, you know. I can't tell them what's really going on with me, and it's all weird silences and waiting for the other person to talk."

Because they were keeping secrets from each other, Alice thought achingly. "Have you thought more about just *telling* them?" she prodded. If she could get one of them to break down, maybe the other side would cave, too.

They had one of the weird silences that Andy had described. "I don't know," he said miserably. "What if they freak out? What if they…"

"Spit it out," Alice told him.

"What if they think I… I don't know… deserved this?"

"Give them some credit," Alice said in exasperation. "They aren't jerks and they would never blame you for *getting sick*."

"They might not say it," Andy sulked. "But I'd always wonder."

Alice made a rude noise of exasperation that was probably lost in the long distance connection.

"Alice," Andy said hesitantly. "Alice, I know you've already done so much. You missed your last trip to Costa Rica because of me."

"My choice, Pipsqueak," Alice reminded him. "You don't get to make me a martyr, thank you."

"You said before you left that you might have a chance to get some money… there's a treatment I could qualify for, but I can't get the tests I need to see if I'm eligible without a down payment." Alice could hear the desperation in Andy's voice. "It's… about a grand."

Alice's heart dropped in her chest. "I don't have it," she said quietly. She wouldn't get it, either, she reminded herself. Scarlet's shift form, and the fifty million dollars it could bring her, was tantalizingly close—and impossibly out of reach. Her bank account was tapped. Her credit card was maxed. She wouldn't even have been able to come on this trip if her friends hadn't paid for most of it.

"Yeah, I knew that was probably the case," Andy said, trying to sound brave. Alice had a sudden image of him as a kid, chin quivering. She'd have done anything to protect him. She still would.

"So, what have you been up to?" Andy asked, in that determinedly cheerful voice he was so good at. "Meet any cute guys on your tropical vacation?"

Alice smiled despite herself, thinking about how far beyond 'cute guy' Graham was. "Oh, yeah," she said lightly. "I met my mate."

This silence was more shocked than weird. "What?!" Andy demanded. "Mates are a real thing? Who is this guy? What do you mean?"

Alice turned to see Mary and Amber walking up the stairs from the pool deck, waving as they approached.

"Mates are real," she told Andy. "He's a great guy, you'd love him, sorry, got to go! Losing the signal, whoops!"

She hung up on him, thinking with amusement that she'd just given him a great deal to fill the weird silences with the next time he called their parents.

"You ready for your big moment tomorrow evening?" she asked Mary as they came up to the bar with her and asked for water from Tex.

"It still feels utterly unreal," Mary confessed to her. "I can't even keep track of the days here, and suddenly, it's going to be tomorrow."

"The last guests are coming in on the morning flight," Amber said. "So, we'll do the spa tomorrow after lunch and everything else is already in place. Tony swears he has not lost the rings and checks on them every hour on the dot," she promised.

"It's weird not having anything else to do," Mary said. "I don't know what to do with myself. My last day being unmarried!"

Alice yawned. "I was thinking about a nap, myself," she offered.

"Were you busy last night?" Mary teased.

Alice grinned sheepishly.

"I could use a siesta before dinner," Amber agreed, rubbing her belly.

Mary threw up her hands. "Fine! Naps it is."

They finished their drinks and wandered through the cultivated greenery back to their cottages, Alice careful not to think of anything but how pleasant things were *now*.

She didn't need to borrow trouble from the future.

CHAPTER 30

"Oh, Graham, those are *gorgeous*. Even better than last week's! You've outdone yourself."

Graham grunted, knowing it was the truth as Chef picked up one of the tomatoes he'd just brought to the kitchens and admired its perfect, unblemished skin and bright color.

"These will be the crown of the meal," the cook said in delight. "Scarlet said there was an extremely important guest arriving in time for dinner tonight."

Breck, laying out the ingredients to stuff them with, gave Graham a suspicious look. "You wouldn't happen to know who, would you? She was very mysterious about it."

"Scarlet is good at mysterious," Graham said with a shrug.

Chef gave a booming laugh. "There's an understatement."

"Chet."

Magnolia was standing in the back of the kitchen, her violet silk dress swirling around her.

Graham might have thought he had simply misheard the cook's name, but Chef's face sobered instantly. Magnolia always had his attention in some measure, but now she had it completely.

"He's here," she said simply.

If Graham had not been looking directly at Chef, he would not have believed the number of emotions that could cross a single person's face in such a short time. It settled into something determined and apprehensive—a perfect match to Magnolia's.

The precious box of tomatoes was set down on the counter without a single second thought and Chef, in an unprecedented move, stripped his apron off and left it on the counter as he abandoned his work and went to Magnolia.

"You… spoke to him?" Chef asked quietly.

"I wrote," Magnolia said gravely. "When we were first trying to raise the money for the resort."

Chef bowed his head, slowly, as if he was fighting a great weight.

Graham was wild with curiosity by now, but trying to hide it. Breck had no such self-restraint. "Who are you talking about?" he demanded. "He, who?"

Chef and Magnolia ignored him. "Now?"

"He's out in the restaurant," Magnolia said softly.

"Have you seen him?"

Magnolia shook her head.

Chef rarely touched Magnolia in public, though his adoration was never exactly hidden and nearly everyone knew that they were mates. Now, however, he gathered her into his big arms and held her close. Graham could not have said if it was for his comfort or hers.

Graham could barely hear her fierce whispered words in reply, "He can't separate us now. He *can't*."

Then Chef was marching down the kitchen aisle, Magnolia gliding behind him. He left the kitchen, holding the door for Magnolia's regal exit, and the two together went out into the restaurant, hands laced together.

"I am mad with curiosity!" Breck admitted, and he dashed after them.

Graham considered staying behind out of respect for their privacy... for about three seconds before following Breck.

By the time they got to the restaurant, there was a small crowd gathered. Magnolia and Chef stood together, facing a strange man in a sharp suit who was flanked by a pair of uniformed bodyguards.

"Your Majesty," Magnolia said coolly.

"It's Your Highness again, Cousin," he replied, his voice equally chilly. "I stepped down from the throne." He paused, then said, "You look... well fed."

"I can still put you in a headlock, Einar," Magnolia said crossly.

"I don't doubt that you could," Einar replied, and Graham thought that the corner of his mouth twitched a little in humor.

Breck squeezed Graham's elbow. "Royalty!" he hissed in delight. "I knew Magnolia wasn't just anyone..."

"Royalty?" Graham hissed back in amazement.

"Valtyra," Darla said, appearing beside Breck. "That's Einar, he was the king of Valtyra. He recently abdicated in favor of his granddaughter and her new husband."

Einar's gaze turned to Chef, who was standing ramrod straight at Magnolia's side, looking grim and determined.

"Guard Chet," he said mildly.

"Your Highness," Chef replied, bowing his head stiffly.

"Oh!" Darla exclaimed quietly. "*Oh!* Chef is *Royal Guard*! This explains so much."

"What?" Breck demanded in a whisper. "What does it explain?"

"Royal Guard can't marry or have relationships. They forsake even their families and renounce their own happiness to serve the royal family." Darla's voice was pitched to carry no further than the three of them, and was full of compassion. She slipped her hand into Breck's.

"You're out of uniform," Einar finally said mildly. "To say nothing of delinquent of your post for twenty-five years."

Chef's face got very red and his mouth grew thin, but he didn't move.

Magnolia stepped closer to him, glaring at Einar protectively. "I didn't write to you because anything has changed. I'm not coming back, and I'm not leaving my mate."

Einar looked at her thoughtfully. "I wouldn't ask you to," he said gently. "I was wrong to, before."

That was clearly not the answer Chef and Magnolia were expecting; they exchanged wary glances.

"I was a young king at the time," Einar continued. "I thought I needed to toe the line, play by all the rules. You were supposed to honor the marriage contract and Chet was supposed to honor his duty. I took it personally when you chose instead to honor each other."

He held out an envelope, sealed with gold and red wax. "A gift from Their Majesties Signy and Kai Natt och Dag af Leijona, Chet. A full pardon of your absence without leave, a commendation for your service to the crown for the long and loyal protection of our cousin, and a complete and honorable release of your vows."

Chef took the envelope mechanically, looking dazed as his color washed away. Magnolia gave a little noise of surprise and covered her mouth, her violet eyes wide above her hand.

Then Chef was letting the envelope fall carelessly to the tile floor as he turned and crashed to his knees at Magnolia's feet as if he could not bear to wait another moment. "Agneta Annika Margareta Solberg af Bjorn, will you marry me?"

"I will," Magnolia wept. "I will!"

Chef surged back up to his feet, crushing her into his embrace and kissing her with less restraint than Graham had ever witnessed in him.

Einar grinned like a boy. If the bodyguards on either side of him were the slightest bit surprised by the sight of a giant cook kissing the king's large cousin passionately, they didn't betray a bit of it, stone-faced behind their sunglasses.

Magnolia was the happiest person that Graham had ever known.

She never met a day without a smile and her cheerful optimism had buoyed many people out of blue days. She enjoyed herself without limits, took pleasure in everything, and spread her joy like a small—or not-so-small—celestial body casting light into the darkness.

But Graham thought now that he had never seen her *truly* happy before.

Tears ran down her smiling cheeks as she kissed Chef—Chet—and laughed in delight and hugged first him, and then her cousin who had been king, and then, to their great discomfort, both of his guards.

Chef, smiling and crying, and not caring who saw, shook everyone's hands, including Breck's, Darla's—she stood on her toes and kissed him on the cheek—and Graham's.

Chef's happiness was only quieter than Magnolia's, no less.

Graham, watching them embrace again, suddenly found purpose, in a life that had been adrift of it.

He wanted to make Alice that happy.

It didn't matter where, or how, but he wanted to bring that kind of joy to Alice, if he could. He wanted—he needed—to make her smile like that, to weep in happiness. He would spend his entire life in pursuit of that moment, and if it were ever possible to achieve, he'd spend the rest of his life trying to do it again.

He slipped out of the restaurant through the empty kitchen—the rest of the staff had emptied onto the deck to congratulate Chef and Magnolia and ogle the visiting royalty.

As Graham took the white gravel path back to The Den, he stewed over his options… move to Minnesota, find a job… tell Alice what Scarlet was. He was willing to do all of it.

He was chewing over that last idea in particular when his lion growled near his ear and he looked up to see a figure standing outlined in the light of The Den beyond.

It was one of the human furries, he realized, just a moment before he registered the gun in the man's hands.

There was a sharp bite at Graham's neck that confused him a moment.

A dart, he realized, and he growled and clenched his fists. The man fired again as Graham charged him.

Graham's swing went wide as his blood seemed to turn to sludge in his veins. All his limbs were heavy. Too heavy. His second swing hit, but had no force behind it.

The man shrugged it off. "Save your fight for the cage, Grant," he sneered.

Graham was confused that he was somehow leaning on the man rather than hitting him. "Not… Grant…" he managed. Alice loved *Graham*. That was who he wanted to be.

Then darkness took him.

CHAPTER 31

Alice woke up from her nap thinking of Graham.

This was not unusual. She couldn't seem to *stop* thinking about Graham: his hands on her skin, his growl, that devastating accent when he spoke, the pain and guilt in his gorgeous blue eyes, those moments when he softened and let his guard down and she wanted to crawl into his lap and kiss him… It felt like she was never not thinking about him.

What was unusual this time was the anxiousness that was coursing through her. Something was wrong.

Her bear was as bothered as she was. *He's not here*, she growled. *He's* gone.

Alice realized that she'd gotten used to a sense of him in her head, a comfortable feeling of Graham like a familiar scent on a favorite sweater.

Rather than letting herself linger in bed a few moments, touching herself and thinking about his hands, Alice rolled out of bed and pulled her jeans on, swiftly stuffing her feet into her sneakers.

"Have you seen Graham?" she asked the first person she saw.

Tex, at the bar loading a tray full of champagne glasses, grinned at her, but kindly didn't tease. "Last I saw, he was headed for the kitchen with a crate of tomatoes," he offered.

"Gotcha."

Alice took the stairs to the restaurant deck two at a time, the worry she'd woken to blooming in her chest.

The restaurant was in celebration mode; everyone was cheering and toasting and laughing.

At first, Alice thought it was just Mary and Neal's upcoming wedding, but she realized that it was far more widespread than that; the entire restaurant deck was centering their attention on a cluster of tables in the middle, where Magnolia and Chef were sitting together with a stranger in a fine quality suit. Dinner seemed to be an afterthought to drinking and talking, and most of the staff were mingling with the guests and drinking rather than serving them.

It looked like fun, and Alice was usually up for a foot-loose, impromptu party… but Graham was still missing from her head.

She lifted her chin at Mary, across the room, and turned away.

Graham wasn't here. Even if this had been his kind of gathering, which Alice doubted, she knew without hesitation that he was nowhere near.

She walked behind the restaurant, past the bizarrely-draped hotel; she had been warned about the fumigation deception to protect the shifters' secrets and knew about the accidental human tourists who were being put up on the beach. Travis had even fabricated something foul-smelling to give the ploy extra depth, and Alice covered her nose uselessly as she passed it.

The Den was empty, quiet and dark on the cliffs; no one answered her knock, and when she went in anyway, Graham's room gave the same answer.

If she thought he was in there, she might have opened the door and gone in without invitation. But her bear assured her he wasn't, so Alice left The Den feeling more mystified and worried.

Her feet took her next to the upper gardens, and Graham's close-guarded greenhouse.

She stood at the entrance of the garden a long moment, more

hesitant to violate this space than she had The Den. This was Graham's place, his sacred space.

Alice breathed deeply, inhaling the scent of green things, fruit, and freshly-turned dirt. It was evening, and somewhere nearby a frog was trying to tempt a mate as the chorus of night insects began to swell.

Graham was not here, either.

She left the garden, closing the door behind her solemnly and stood for a moment.

The view from here was breathtaking. Alice could see down over the entire resort: The Den, the cliffs, the tented hotel, the festive restaurant, the cottages. The beach was a silver crescent in the falling twilight, and the waves wrinkled and flung themselves at the shore.

Alice squinted. There was movement at the dock and it took her a moment to realize that two figures were walking towards the resort's boat. No, one figure was walking, half-dragging the other. Someone had imbibed a little too much at Tex's bar, Alice thought, but after watching them for only a moment she knew she was wrong: the second figure was clearly unconscious.

Graham, she thought in panic as the first man dumped him unceremoniously into the back of the boat.

If he was unconscious, did that explain why she couldn't feel him in her head? She still knew he was there when he was sleeping.

Alice was already moving, running down the white gravel paths as fast as she could manage.

She had glimpses of the boat as she wove her way down through the resort and saw it slipping quietly away from the dock as she desperately ran.

By the time she got to the dock, the boat had already passed the reef and she could barely hear the roar of the engine over the sound of the surf. It didn't pull south and round the tip of the island, but headed north, and she stared after it in consternation.

Alice forced herself to think logically. If the boat had been going for the mainland, it would have gone the other direction. The only other place it could go was the abandoned installation on the other side of the island.

She set her jaw and bolted for the top of the resort, taking the steps two at a stride.

Scarlet was not in her office, but Alice went in anyway. Her bear's hackles rose at once; this was risky and they both knew it. She stepped behind the desk, wondering if she dared to actually ransack it for the keys she was after.

Before she could work up the nerve, a silhouette appeared in the doorway, tall and ominous.

"Can I help you?" Scarlet sounded as serene as if she hadn't just caught Alice creeping around in her office.

Alice braced herself for a fight. "I need the Jeep," she said, balling her fists at her side. She didn't phrase it as a request.

"Graham," Scarlet said, eyes narrowing. "He's… not here."

"The boat," Alice said shortly. "I saw someone dump him in the boat and go north."

Scarlet gave a sound that was half growl and half a sigh of great wind. "I can't go there," she said, sounding frustrated.

"I can," Alice said fiercely.

"You'll need help," Scarlet said, pulling a key down from a hook beside the door.

"There's no time," Alice said, reaching out her hand. The sense of urgency, of loss, was rising like a storm in her chest.

Scarlet was standing between her and her exit, the key closed in her fingers, and Alice started to bristle. "I have to go," she snarled.

Scarlet's green eyes drilled into her and for a moment Alice had to wonder what it was that kept the woman from the other side of the island, what could possibly be strong enough to resist that will and the terrible power behind it.

Before she could gather herself to fight the woman who was standing between Alice and her mate—however helpless a fight it might be—Scarlet dropped the key into her outstretched palm. "I care about him, too," she said simply, and stepped aside.

Alice was bolting before she could make any sense of that, key cutting into the palm of her hand.

The drive across the island was considerably less enjoyable than the same trip had been a week before. Gone was the cheerful comradery and the leisurely pace. Gone was the sunlight, and there was no laughter at Alice's lips as she pushed the Jeep as fast as she dared over the pitted road.

It took what felt like an eternity to get there and Alice could only stew over the memory of Graham's limp body being dropped into the boat and mourn the comfortable feeling of him in her head that she hadn't realized was her new normal.

The open gate to the compound caught her entirely by surprise and she drove in with more speed than she meant to; only afterwards thinking that she ought to have pulled the Jeep over and attempted some kind of stealth. There were lights past the house and Alice could hear unexpected music and crowd noise over the Jeep's engine.

Two guards suddenly loomed into the light of her headlights, bearing rifles.

"Ah, hi!" she called cheerfully, wishing she'd thought her plan through a little more thoroughly. She climbed out the Jeep, not wanting to shift and damage Scarlet's vehicle if she didn't have to.

Only then did she notice the two guards behind her, armed with nightsticks, and a chill went down her back; four guards was a lot even for her bear. "I was out driving around and got turned around in the dark," she bluffed. "I'm a guest at Shifting Sands, do you know how I get back there?"

They didn't look particularly convinced by her air-headed speech and one of the guards behind her suddenly said, "That's the girlfriend of the guy I collected from the resort earlier today. Cyrus is going to want this one for leverage."

One of the men raised his rifle and shot her.

For a split-second, Alice thought they'd shot her with a bullet and this was the end of her ill-considered heroism as well as her life. Then she realized that it had made a whooshing sound rather than a gunshot crack, and it was only a tiny sting of pain.

There was a small dart in her shoulder and Alice rationalized that it must be a knock-out drug. She was briefly amused at the idea of a dart meant for a human having any effect on her bear.

But when she reached for her bear, ready to unleash an angry, five-hundred pound animal on the unsuspecting guards, nothing was there.

She was still reeling from the realization when they closed in on her and her late attempt to defend herself was cut short with a staggering blow to the head from one of the nightstick-wielding guards. Before she could regain her balance, she was being bound and marched into the compound.

CHAPTER 32

Graham woke to the familiar sound of a distant, hungry crowd… and the loud growl of a nearby generator. He was lying on his side, darkened concrete before him, broken earth below him. It was bright, but after a moment, staring at his shadow, he realized it wasn't daylight; a brilliant worklight was trained on him. He lay still, trying to make sense of things, to figure out what felt so terribly wrong.

Alice, was his first thought, but he had no sense of her nearby. She was simply gone from inside of him, and the hollow place she'd been felt like a gaping hole.

He glanced down without moving and found that he'd been bound, at wrist and ankle, both anchored to the wall he was looking at. He might be able to break the chains as a man, but he could definitely break them as a lion… which was when he realized that his lion was as gone as Alice.

He must have made some kind of noise of alarm at the realization, because a boot found the small of his back.

"You awake yet, your lordship?"

Graham felt the hollow place inside fill with rage and recognition.

He rolled to the wall and brought himself up to a seated position. He was in a battered, three-sided concrete room. Bars had once enclosed the fourth side, but they had been burned and wrenched away. An extension cord snaked to a bright worklight on a tripod, focused on him. He felt like his limbs were heavy, and his bones were humming out of tune. "Cyrus," he growled.

"Surprise!" Cyrus gave him a toothy smile, standing well outside of the range of Graham's chains. One scruffy looking bodyguard stood just past him with a rifle in his hands. Graham couldn't be sure if it had more sedative or real bullets.

"You were a hard shifter to track down, Grant Lyons. Or Graham Long, as they call you now. Long time no see, *Long*." Cyrus laughed at his own joke. "Johnny Ace was very put out that you didn't want to pay his hush money. It didn't take him long to find another bidder."

Graham only grunted.

Cyrus narrowed his eyes. "I owe you, Lyons, I owe you a lot. You busted up my business real good, didn't you. And it's been real hard to get it started again. Have to keep moving around, doing shows in new places, building new audiences. I had a good thing in London, and so did you."

"There was nothing *good* about it," Graham had to protest.

"*You* were good," Cyrus reminded him. "Best fighter I ever had. Gave the crowd a real show, took a beating like a heavy bag and kept swinging. I would have made you rich beyond your wildest dreams. And you threw it away… for what? To be a gardener at a fancy resort where they treat you like trash?"

Graham nearly smiled. His life at Shifting Sands had been idyllic. He should have known it wouldn't last.

There was a chorus of cheers from somewhere not far from them and Cyrus grinned. "We're warming them up for you, Grant."

Graham got to his feet at last and could feel the sedative slowly leaving his limbs. There was still no whisper of his lion's presence or the slightest hint of his mate-bond. "I'm not fighting for you again," he said firmly.

"Oh, I think you are," Cyrus laughed. "You've gotten soft over the years, Grant, and you're weak."

"Unchain me and see how soft I've gotten," Graham challenged.

"Oh, you're still a fighter," Cyrus smirked. "But that's not what I meant by soft."

He snapped his fingers and a second, larger, bodyguard came from around the corner, a familiar figure stalking beside him.

Alice.

Her hands were bound, but only with rope. Her hazel eyes were blazing. "Graham? Graham, are you alright?"

"Does she even know your real name, *Grant*? I wouldn't have guessed that *girls* would be your weakness," Cyrus said thoughtfully, moving to brush her brunette hair back behind one ear. Alice jerked her head out of reach and glared at him.

Cyrus clearly decided that his fingers were worth more than making the point and turned back to Graham. "You never seemed particularly interested in the tail we offered you in London. Maybe they just weren't… large enough for your taste."

Alice went redder than she had been, seething.

Graham could feel the sedative burning off in the heat of his fury, but he held himself stone still, not wanting to tip Cyrus off.

A weaselly-looking man darted in from the opposite direction, a clipboard in hand. "How long, boss?"

"Not much longer," Cyrus said thoughtfully. "I'm not putting him into the cage until the sedative has worn off. That wouldn't be the show they've come for."

"We adding *her* to the roster?" the man asked with a raking glance at Alice. "She's tall and strong, she'd probably start a lot of betting."

"That depends on Grant here," Cyrus said, voice silky. "He fights… or she does."

It took every ounce of Graham's willpower not to betray the rage and agony his words woke. Alice, in a cage. Alice, defending herself against one of Cyrus' fighters. Alice, *hurting*.

"I'll fight."

The man scurried away again.

Was it the sedative that was keeping him from reaching his lion? Graham felt more himself with every moment… as much himself as he could be without the voice that had shared his head for so much of his life.

"Who are you people?" Alice demanded as they pushed her to the opposite side of the enclosure from Graham. "Why can't I hear my..?" She didn't finish, as if it suddenly occurred to her that they may not *know* about her bear.

"Can't hear your animal? Isn't that a nice trick?" Cyrus said smugly. "As well as providing us with this charming, isolated arena, Alistair Beehag had a whole arsenal of wonderful treasures that his nephew has quietly been selling on the black market. Oh, some run of the mill sedatives, poisons, hallucinogens, truth serums. But I was also able to snap up a good quantity of this particular drug—it forces a shifter to remain in their human form. You can mix it with a sedative, or administer it straight."

Cyrus grinned as Graham finally realized what he intended to do.

It was going to be a do-over of his last fateful fight.

Only this time, he was going to be the one who couldn't shift.

CHAPTER 33

Alice wriggled against the ropes holding her wrists, not exactly trying to hide her efforts, but trying not to be obvious. People in movies got out of stuff like this all the time. And if she'd had her bear…

She was so stupid, thinking she could just drive right up and save Graham single-handedly.

"One of these charming gentlemen was in the party of furries at the resort," she told him. "He recognized me."

"Yeah," Graham grunted briefly.

"I see that whatever they gave you hasn't made you more talkative," Alice said wryly.

"Alice," Graham said under his breath. "I'm…"

"I swear to God, if you apologize for getting me into this, I will kick you in the shins." She eyed the guards. "I bet they'd let me, too." Her voice gentled. "Graham…"

"I'll give you lovebirds a moment," Cyrus said, as there was a roar from a distant crowd and loud distorted music began to play. To the guards, he said, "Don't take your eyes off of them."

Alice eyed the guards, who were both holding rifles. More darts? Sedatives like Graham had been given? Real bullets? The lighting wasn't good; it was fully dark by now, and the blinding worklight was pointed at them, making it hard to see anything outside of their puddle of light.

"Alice…" Graham said again. "I love you."

It was a salve on the empty place inside her where her bear and the mate-bond had been. They weren't gone, Alice reminded herself, just silenced. She'd heard about the drug that made shifters stay human from Neal and Tony; it was temporary, it would wear off and they'd be back to normal.

"I love *you*," she replied.

One of the guards snorted in disgust and the other made a gagging sound. "Fucking shifters and their creepy *mates*," one of them muttered.

Alice squinted at them through the blinding light. "They aren't shifters," she said thoughtfully. "Is Cyrus?"

Graham shook his head. "Has kind of a chip on his shoulder about it, too."

"Stop talking," the other guard commanded shifting his rifle suggestively.

Alice subsided to silence, continuing to try to do something with the knots at her wrists without being obvious about it.

Before she could manage to do more than give herself mild ropeburn, Cyrus was back.

He stepped boldly up to Graham—much more boldly than Alice suspected he would if Graham had not been chained—and pulled his head to look directly into the light, checking his pupil reaction. "You're up next, your lordship," he said with satisfaction. "A battle to the shift."

"No…" Alice couldn't stop herself from saying. If Graham, like her, couldn't shift, that meant he had to win to live… and if he won… She remembered how he had looked at his hands, like they were stained with blood. He shouldn't have to do that again, ever.

Cyrus gave her a slow smile. "You'd prefer to fight instead of him, I suppose? Oh, you poor, stupid girl. Don't you understand? He loves this. This is what he was born to do. Has he tried to convince you that he's changed, that he's a better man now, that he's happy growing watermelons and mowing lawns at a luxury resort? He's no different now than he ever was. He still loves to hurt people. You can see it when he fights, how much joy he gets out of it."

Alice watched the guilt and doubt bloom over Graham's face, as hard as he battled to keep it behind his mask of stony anger.

"Don't do this," Alice begged, a note of panic in her voice. "I'll fight instead, if you want. I'm a wrestling coach, and I'm strong and fast. I'll give them a show." Could she actually hurt someone enough to make them shift, she wondered? Was she skilled enough? Did she have the resolve? If she could pin someone long enough, would they call the fight a draw?

Cyrus laughed. "Oh, Graham, isn't that touching. She's willing to take your place, the sweet summer child. Are you chivalrous enough to let her?"

Graham was staring back at Alice, his blue eyes like rocks. "Don't let her watch," he growled at Cyrus.

"You don't get to make requests, your lordship," Cyrus said, a hint of his own underlying anger showing through. "She'll get to see exactly what you are. She'll get to see how much you haven't changed."

Cyrus, Alice was beginning to realize, enjoyed pain the way Graham only thought he did. It was partly that he was seeking revenge for Graham's betrayal, but even more, he wanted the thrill of watching Graham *suffer.* He would enjoy Graham's torture: every bruise, every shame, and every regret.

Even after stories of Beehag's zoo, Alice had not really believed that such people existed. She looked back to Graham. She had not believed someone like him could exist, either: someone willing to draw a line of morality and sacrifice everything in order to prevent further horrors. Graham could have simply walked away with his winnings, and lived a comfortable life of freedom and never looked back. He didn't have to turn himself in to take down the ring, and he had known exactly what he was giving up when he did.

"How can you look at me like that?" Graham asked in a low growl, making Alice realize she was gazing at him with foolish fondness.

"How could I not?" she asked him, and when she smiled at him, his mouth cracked the tiniest bit.

They were not playing appropriately to Cyrus' need to see them miserable and tormented. Miffed, he gestured to the guards. "Unlock him, but keep him close. Bring her, too."

Despite her assurances that she could fight, none of them considered her a threat. Alice recalled her dismal performance with the heavy bag and her easy capture and wasn't sure that they were wrong.

CHAPTER 34

The ruins of Beehag's zoo had been transformed. At first glance, it looked like a creepy pop-up rock concert, with noisy generators running massive lights and huge speakers currently blaring music. In the warm darkness, it was aggressive and challenging, and the audience—not big, but big enough—was cheering and drinking and betting.

The only difference was that instead of a stage, there was a cage.

It wasn't the burn-twisted remains of any of Beehag's enclosures, it was a shining new cage, probably boated in parts and assembled the day before.

While they were still outside of the glitter and spotlight, the guards gave Graham a pair of shimmering gold shorts and an ermine-edged purple robe to put on, and let him wrap his hands.

Alice watched with amusement that didn't quite mask her worry and despair. "I like how they expect you to beat the crap out of each other, but they want to make sure your delicate knuckles don't get hurt," she said mockingly.

She was so brave, so beautiful, so clever. Even dreading what she would think of the show, even knowing how this could destroy everything they had in so many possible ways, Graham was selfishly glad to have her there.

She gave him… hope.

They were in an impossible place. Graham could see no way out of here; even if he won this round, Cyrus would pit him against another shifter, and another; he wasn't going to just let Graham and Alice walk away.

This was the dead end he'd always been ready for.

And somehow, against all reason, she made him feel *hopeful.*

Graham caught Cyrus glaring at him. Then the fight coordinator smiled coldly.

"You wouldn't want to start fighting without warming up first," he said with a smirk. "Boys?" He nodded at the guards, and Graham knew what was coming when someone grabbed him from behind and twisted his arms back.

It wasn't a fight, it was a beating, and a careful beating at that. The audience wouldn't want a rigged fight, they wanted the fantasy of fairness. So the blows were kept from his face, concentrated on his core, places that would cause damage, but not show bruises.

Graham didn't struggle; his only goal was to turn to keep the worst of it from Alice, who gave a wail of agony when it started and then begged Cyrus and swore like a sailor as they held her back. The pain in her voice was the worst of the torture.

When it was over, Graham caught his breath through gritted teeth. He had a broken rib, probably, and was glad it wasn't worse than that. He could still walk, and he could still fight, and that was what mattered.

Someone had a microphone and was shouting loud enough that they could hear it over the noisy roar of the generator. "Ladies and gentlemen… are you ready? He's a seven-time event winner… The muscles with menace... Our very own angus shifter, Cinderblock!"

The shifter who walked into the spotlight, posing and raising his fists, was taller than Graham by a handspan and proportionally wider, built like a mountain. He raised a folding chair over his head and casually twisted it into a pretzel.

The crowd went wild.

Instinctively, Graham measured him as an opponent, feeling the familiar rise of adrenaline. Cinderblock was a big man, but he moved gracefully; his range of movement and speed weren't hindered by his strength, and he would be a tricky opponent even if Graham hadn't already been softened up.

Graham knew he ought to feel afraid, but the emotion welling up in him felt more like excitement. He knew what to do next, down to the very bones. It didn't matter that it wasn't fair, and it wasn't his choice… it was a fight he was ready for.

They were at the edge of the lit area around the cage, standing just in the shadows out of sight, very near the loud generator.

Past the crowd, the nearly-full moon was rising and movement in the sky caught Graham's eye.

"Let him say goodbye to his girlfriend," Cyrus said, loudly to be heard over the generator. He allowed Alice step forward to put her arms around Graham; she had struggled out of her bindings and one of her hands was free. The rope still hung from the other wrist, but the others clearly didn't consider her a risk. They knew that they only had to control him to keep her in line.

"Be… careful," Alice said, softly, as he cradled her face in his hands. She was blinking back tears, clearly trying to keep a brave face for him. "You aren't this," she reminded him near his ear. "You are *Graham*."

Graham kissed her without trying to explain that this was *exactly* what he was and stepped back from her, ignoring the ache in his side that had nothing to do with the broken rib.

One of the guards pulled her back when she might have tried to keep him from going and Graham had to turn away so he didn't try to jump uselessly to her defense.

He eyed Cyrus, who was watching him closely.

The crowd was beginning to tire of Cinderblock's showboating. The announcer, catching their mood, moved on to the introduction of Graham. "Out of the fighting circuit for ten years... the act you've been waiting for... one of the meanest fighters to grace the cage… lion shifter and lady lover… put your hands together for… the King of the Jungle!"

The crowd broke out in jeers and insults; Graham was clearly not the favored fighter.

They were expecting a slaughter, he realized, and he had to wonder if they were expecting it to be literal. The crowd at his last fight had had that same timbre, he thought. That same blood-thirsty lust.

Cyrus smiled slowly, savoring the moment. "Look at you," Cyrus mocked. "You can feel the thrill in your blood. You're still a fighter. You're still *Grant Lyons*, King of the Jungle."

There was another flicker in the sky.

"You're wrong," he said. "I'm Graham Long now."

"You're just the same as you've always been," Cyrus scoffed. "Graham isn't any different than Grant."

Graham smiled slowly.

"Except that *Graham* has *friends*."

Then a flaming dragon appeared above the arena, lighting the grass around the cage on fire and roaring a challenge to the crowd as it swept overhead.

Graham turned on the three guards who had been prepared to escort him to the cage, using their surprise to wrest their weapons from them as chaos erupted around them.

CHAPTER 35

Alice was looking too hard at Graham to notice Bastian's aerial approach, but she was quick to take advantage of the distraction to grab the gun from the guard holding her. She might not be much of a fighter, but she knew he wouldn't be able to shoot anything with her weight hanging from his gun.

A bear, a panther, and a lynx stalked out of the darkness like the start of a bad joke and she cried out in warning, "They have Beehag's anti-shifting drugs!" She wasn't sure if they would hear her bellow over the sound of the generator.

Shots—real shots—scattered off a wall somewhere nearby as one of the guards fired wildly in their direction.

"And real bullets, too, apparently!" Alice added in a panic. She fought harder to get the gun from the guard she was grappling, and it ripped free into her hands. She swung it at the guard like a club, missed and nearly unbalanced. The guard, with more honed reflexes, recovered first and balled up a fist to hit her in the jaw.

Blinking stars of pain aside, Alice saw a charging deer of impossible size, followed by a pair of leopards, one silver and white, one gold and black. They didn't pause to battle any of the guards or shifters in fighting gear who were starting to gather; their goal seemed to be to clear a path for a human figure who was running behind them. Big bears charged after her, one polar bear, one big grizzly, and they bowled over the event staff that briefly attempted to stop them.

Alice wondered if the human figure was Scarlet for a moment, but then she was in the light, and it was the mermaid, Saina, ducking and dashing for the sound system.

Bastian made another sweep over the ruins, flaming above the heads of the fleeing crowd and the members of Cyrus' ring that were starting to muster a defense against the attack. Darts pinged off his hide and fell harmlessly to the ground below. The guard facing Alice was clearly having a crisis of loyalty, and at the massive dragon's second pass, broke off and fled with the audience stampeding towards the dock.

Some of the shifter fighters were taking animal form, meeting this attack with teeth and claws of their own. Was it loyalty to the ring, Alice wondered, or just that they couldn't resist a fight?

Then Saina had the microphone in her hand and the magic of her voice was falling over the crowd, calming them and settling a thrall over them. If they were running, they staggered to a stop. If they were fighting, they lowered their fists and paws and stood in a daze.

Alice felt only the slightest hint of it. At first, she thought it was because she was protected from Saina's magic by her dormant mate-bond. Then she realized that everyone in their immediate vicinity had shaken it off, Saina's siren music half-drowned by the constant noise of the generator and already spread thin over a larger crowd than she usually dealt with. Cyrus was bending to pick up one of the rifles, aiming it at the battle that Graham was fighting with the guards that had been escorting him to the cage.

Alice didn't know much about hitting, and she knew less about shooting, but she did know throwdowns, so that's what she did, driving Cyrus to the ground from behind.

He snarled and fought. Alice wrapped him tighter in her arms.

He headbutted her, smashing her nose.

"Foul!" Alice cried, tasting blood. She got her arm around both of his. "That would be a flagrant misconduct, asshole."

"You still think this is a game, Alice?" Cyrus hissed, trying to squirm out of her grip.

Alice clamped her arms down tighter.

CHAPTER 36

Graham's guards had been expecting a fight. They weren't expecting a dragon, or Saina's siren magic, or the ragtag team of animals that had shown up, but Graham's advantage of surprise still didn't last long.

It was three against one, and they were wearing light armor and carrying weapons; one of them still had a gun, and two of them had nightsticks.

One of those sticks came crashing into his broken rib and another struck his leg, hoping, no doubt, to disable him. Graham pivoted on the other leg and punched one of them in the throat, ducking a nightstick and coming up under the guard's arm at the elbow with his shoulder. The third guard hung back with the gun, trying to find an opening to shoot.

Graham didn't have to think about what he was doing; he simply acted.

Instinct and muscle memory took over, and he merely *was*: dodging blows, looking for openings, trying to keep someone between himself and the man with the gun. He wasn't Grant, and he wasn't Graham, he was just intuition and adrenaline.

Patience paid off; he was able to knock one of the guards into the other and use the ensuing moment of confusion to bring all his weight down onto the other one's wrist, thinking with an unexpected jolt of humor about his advice to Alice as it cracked beneath his assault. The guard howled and was out of the fight cradling his arm long enough for Graham to grab the other and spin, using the man's weight to build enough momentum to hurl him at the guard with the gun.

As they both struggled to keep their balance, Graham wrested the nightstick from the guard with the broken wrist and flew into them, knocking one out with a blow to the head and turning to face the other, just as a black panther materialized from the darkness and tackled him from behind.

Shots cracked out and the sound of Saina's lilting song suddenly went quiet as the generator failed with a sputter and a spray of sparks and all of the lights and sound equipment died.

The people who had been under her thrall shook themselves out, and, nearly as one, they turned to flee down the island for the dock. The guard with the broken wrist joined the flight through the sudden darkness and the guard under the panther cried out for mercy.

The panther shifted into Wrench and exchanged an amused nod with Graham.

"Thanks," Graham said briefly, looking around for a new opponent.

It took a moment for his eyes to adjust to the dim moonlight; apparently his lion's advantages were not all lost with his ability to reach his animal.

"Alice!" Graham cried, sprinting to where she was crouching. Her face was covered in blood and Cyrus, pinned beneath her, was snarling and struggling.

"I'm fine," she reassured him. "He'd be thrown out for poor sportsmanship if this were a real match. But I can't let him up until I have something to *do* with him." She grunted as Cyrus got a lucky elbow in her side, and adjusted her grip on him.

"I have something to do with him," Graham growled and he

stepped on Cyrus' protesting head while Alice carefully let go of him, bending to pull the man to his feet when she was free.

"You going to hurt me?" Cyrus challenged, anger and defeat in his beady eyes.

Graham was more aware of Alice's gaze than he was Cyrus'.

She wouldn't blame him for extracting justice.

But Graham didn't want to.

Of all the people he hated, as much as he desired revenge, here he was with every opportunity to give Cyrus back some small portion of the pain he'd lived with for ten years… and all he wanted was to be done with it.

He had wanted to step into the cage and fight a doomed battle at a disadvantage more than he wanted to inflict pain on this hateful, beaten man.

"No," Graham growled. "I'm not going to hurt you." He frogmarched the man to the dark cage where the Irish elk and the bears had herded most of the guards and fighters who hadn't fled with the audience to the docks below. Some of them were staggering in a daze that Graham recognized as Gizelle's handiwork and he wasn't surprised to see her tiny gazelle shape darting at Conall's heels.

Graham thrust Cyrus into the cage, not exactly gently, but not with the force that he could have. Someone had dragged in the guard he had knocked unconscious.

"You're not worth it," he said disdainfully as Cyrus stumbled into one of his unamused guards.

In the silence following the destruction of the generators, they could hear the distant sound of the boats starting to pull away from the docks below.

Neal, naked and grinning wolfishly, had an armful of chains and locks gathered from equipment boxes around the makeshift arena. "Is this all of them?" he asked.

Graham shrugged.

Tony, in tiger form, came circling around from the back of the cage and shifted back to human. "I checked the perimeter and didn't see any stragglers. These are the only ones that weren't smart enough to run for the boats."

Neal set to work securing the cage.

Bastian was back in human form and he was supporting a very wobbly-looking Saina. "What did you do to them?" he asked anxiously. "Are you alright?"

She had a shallow scratch on her forehead; Bastian frowned and reached for his first aid kit.

"I made them feel guilty," Saina said, with a certain amount of tired satisfaction, letting him fuss over her as she sank to a seat on a fallen speaker. "I reminded them that they were part of something terrible and made them feel bad about it. It probably won't last long—that's a lot more people than I usually try something so complicated with. I doubt it will last long enough for any of them to turn themselves in or rat out the ring; they'll likely forget about the whole thing and the island altogether by the time they get to the mainland."

She hissed as Bastian cleaned her cut.

"Are you hurt?" Graham asked Alice. There was an alarming amount of blood on her face, but it didn't appear to be flowing.

"Nah," Alice said dismissively. "I got a bloody nose and I might chew on the left side until I can shift again and heal up, but nothing that needs stitches." She gave him a suspicious look. "I'm more worried about you," she said softly, for his ears only. "They…"

"I'm fine," Graham said briefly. "Broken rib, maybe." He drew in a deep breath. Definitely a broken rib.

Alice made a little noise of anger and helplessness. "You should have Bastian bind that up."

"Darla's hurt," Breck said, coming out of the darkness with his arm around his mate, saving Graham having to argue about his rib.

"No more hurt than you are," Darla protested. "He got tagged with one of the darts and neither of us can shift now."

They had matching injuries, long slices on their arms. The runes circling their left wrists were gleaming slightly, reflecting the moonlight. Graham suspected that neither of them would have sought medical help for themselves, but Bastian solemnly cleaned the wounds for each of them and declared that they would probably heal with a shift or two once the drug wore off.

"Told you to stay back," Wrench said, frowning and folding his arms. If he'd taken any injury, it wasn't obvious on his scar- and tattoo- marked body.

Gizelle bounded into the space and shifted from gazelle to human in one swift leap. "I helped!" she declared cheerfully.

Conall, who had tossed a number of opponents easily aside in his Irish elk shape, gathered her into his arms. "I told you to stay back, too."

Alice gave Graham a sideways look. "You going to tell me that I should have stayed back, too?" she asked for his ears only.

Graham snorted, and his side protested keenly. "Wouldn't dream of it," he said gruffly.

"Let's see that rib," Bastian said to him without leaving room for argument once he had finished with Darla and Breck. Dragon ears must be as keen as a lion's.

"Great outfit," Breck observed as Graham reluctantly took off the purple satin robe. "Gold lamé suits you! You should add more to your wardrobe, m'lord."

Darla pinched him and said, "Ouch!" as she hurt herself as well.

"So, you're the King of the Jungle." Neal smirked as Bastian dug into his first aid kit.

"Don't they realize that lions don't even usually live in the jungle?" Tony asked drolly.

"King of the Savannah doesn't have quite the same ring," Bastian observed thoughtfully, unwinding a roll of cloth.

"Besides," Alice pointed out, "*this* lion lives in a jungle."

At one time, not so long ago, Graham could have imagined nothing worse than facing the staff with the truth of his past. Now, he gave a gruff laugh that turned to a hiss of pain as Bastian tied off the binding around his chest. Alice's hand in his tightened.

"You're going to have some good bruises," Bastian observed, his look suggesting that he guessed some of the other, less-obvious injuries Graham had taken. "Hope that Beehag's drug wears off soon, because shifting will do more for you than I can."

Tex had been guarding the van and he greeted them with a

grizzly growl from the darkness. Everyone dressed swiftly and piled in.

The Jeep still had the keys in it, to Alice's comic relief. "Can you imagine what Scarlet would have done to me if I'd lost her keys?" she said, clutching her chest dramatically.

Scarlet.

Graham knew what he had to do.

CHAPTER 37

The journey back to the resort was much slower than Alice's breakneck drive had been and the mood was lighter. Most of the staff packed back into the groaning van.

Alice, Graham, Breck, and Darla took the Jeep.

Graham gritted his teeth at every bump and pretended he wasn't hurting, but Alice knew better. She let Breck drive on the way back, content to curl in the back seat next to Graham, trying not to fall into him at the tight curves.

Scarlet was standing at the entrance of the resort, arms crossed, when they pulled in at last. She was frowning, to no one's surprise, but she refrained from quizzing them as they tumbled out of the vehicles and gave her the story in piecemeal bits and vivid, rambling description.

She frowned at a new bullet hole in the van, but to Alice's surprise, did not scold them for damage to resort property when she could have.

"That'll buff right out," Travis assured her with a grin.

Graham hung back, letting the others enthusiastically tell the tale of rescue and revenge with all the details they knew, and Alice stood with him. She felt like her bear was beginning to wake in her head and thought that she'd be able to shift soon. Her bond with Graham was a whisper in the back of her head and she was desperately relieved to feel it again.

"I'll have the Civil Guard collect the trespassers in the morning," Scarlet said dryly as the storytelling devolved into more and more colorful accounts of heroism. "I am sure you are all hungry and tired."

The others all tramped for the buffet and their mates and their beds, leaving Scarlet, Graham, and Alice alone in the courtyard.

"I trust you concluded your business?" Scarlet asked pointedly, not prying for details.

Graham grunted and shrugged one shoulder, then added, "It shouldn't be a problem again."

"I'm glad to have you back in one piece," she said mildly, with a glance at Alice. "Please don't let me keep you from food and rest."

Alice handed the Jeep keys back to her self-consciously. "Thank you," she said awkwardly. "For trusting me."

Scarlet only smiled her cool, distant smile and accepted them without comment.

Alice and Graham, hand in hand, walked through the courtyard and stood at the top of the resort looking down over it for a long moment.

At night, it was subdued, but no less magic, a haven of soft light in the darkness. Alice understood why Graham loved this place.

"Graham," she started to say.

But before she could speak, he was leading her away. Not to the buffet, as her stomach was hoping, nor to the Den, where her tired muscles longed to crawl into his bed again at last.

He led her past the hotel, still in its shroud, and up the path to his garden.

Alice had suspicions about what he had in mind as he opened the gate for her, but when she expected him to kiss her and pull her into his arms, he only sat on one of the ledges and pulled her down next to him.

"Graham," she started again.

"I want to tell you what Scarlet is," he said unexpectedly.

Alice felt her empty stomach clench.

"I… can't ask you to do that," she said mournfully. It was something she hated thinking about; every option was ugly.

"You are my mate," he told her simply. "And I don't want secrets from you. I… can't stand being so close to being able to help you and not doing it."

Alice gazed at him, alarmed and overwhelmed by the depth of what he was offering.

And she wasn't sure she wanted to know, because knowing meant she had to decide what to do with the information.

They were quiet a long time, Alice not sure if she wanted to beg him to tell her… or beg him not to tell her.

Finally Graham raised his gaze. "Scarlet's not a shifter."

He paused, to let that bomb sink in, and Alice stopped him before he could continue. "She's not a shifter? She doesn't have a shift form?"

Graham shook his head. "She's—"

Alice put a finger up firmly. "Don't tell me," she said firmly. "I don't want to know."

Graham blinked. "But…"

"I don't give a damn what Scarlet actually *is*."

"You could save your brother, your parents…"

"The guy with the business card? He didn't ask me what she *was*. He asked me what her *shifted form* was. If she doesn't have one… that's his answer. And it's an answer I feel just fine giving him. I'm not giving away Scarlet's real secrets, and I'm not asking them from you. I can give him the truth, and it doesn't… it doesn't feel like betraying Scarlet."

"He going to accept that answer?" he asked suspiciously.

"I don't know," Alice said merrily. "Let's find out! You have a phone in those gold lamé shorts somewhere? I still have his business card." Cyrus' men had frisked her, but hadn't seen any significance to the card and it had been returned to her pocket. She had memorized the number anyway.

Graham groaned. "Cyrus probably got it. I bet the cost of that comes out of my bonus."

"When was the last time you got a bonus anyway?" Alice scoffed.

They walked down to Alice's cottage to find her phone and disconnect it from the charging cable.

"What time is it there?" Graham thought to ask her before she dialed. It was still dark out, but dawn was starting to color the horizon.

"I don't know what time zone he's in," Alice said frankly. "And frankly, it serves him right to get a call in the middle of the night for being all scary and mysterious."

They sat together on the colorful tropical quilt on her bed, fingers twined, while the call rang through.

This was it, Alice thought. This was her brother's care and her parent's house and her mate's trust, all on the line with a stranger that she didn't know the first thing about. She thought about Jenny's ledger, creeping ever so slowly towards an impossible finish line, and what the money left over could mean to that.

She turned the card over in her hands. N. Padrikanth Moore was the most absurd name she'd ever heard, and she now counted a man named Wrench among her friends.

He picked up on the third ring. "Moore," he said simply, sounding cross but not at all asleep.

"Alice Anders," she said firmly. "You owe me fifty million dollars."

She was expecting to surprise him, but could not tell if she actually had. "You found out what Scarlet's shift form is," he said approvingly.

"Yup," Alice said.

There was a moment of silence. "And…?" the man prompted.

"And you owe me fifty million dollars," Alice said firmly. "I'm sure you know my bank account numbers and probably my passwords."

"What kind of shifter is she?"

"If I tell you, are you going to actually pay me?"

Alice couldn't miss the rich humor in his answer and she

thought that was a good sign. "If you tell me the shift form of Scarlet Stanson, I will wire you fifty million dollars this very day."

"She doesn't have one."

Graham's hand squeezed hers and there was silence on the line.

"What is she?" he finally asked.

"Noooooope," Alice drawled. "That wasn't what you asked. I was sent to find out her shift form. I did that. It's not my fault the answer is 'nothing.'"

There was another silence long enough that Alice actually checked the connection.

She exchanged an anxious look with Graham.

N. Padrikanth Moore began to laugh.

Alice chuckled nervously, but wasn't actually relieved until he stopped laughing and, to her shock, said, "Very well, Alice Anders. You have technically kept your end of the bargain and I will keep mine. What do you want for the remainder of the information I'm seeking?"

"Don't have it, don't want it, won't do it," Alice blurted. "There's no price you can offer me."

"Everything has a price," the mysterious Mr. Moore insisted.

Alice looked at Graham, at the relief she felt mirrored in his face. "I think you're wrong," she said thoughtfully.

Graham slowly smiled and Alice felt her world fall into all the right places.

"It's been a pleasure doing business, Mr. Moore, I look forward to seeing your payment," she said, over whatever the man was trying to say. She hung up the phone and tossed it back onto the bedside table.

Graham's smile was like sunlight and strawberries.

"You want to make love to a millionaire?" Alice asked.

CHAPTER 38

Mary and Neal's wedding was simple and joyous… and completely lacking in battles, supernatural interruptions, and earthquakes.

Scarlet officiated, serene and solemn, with her red hair piled on top of her head, and Graham thought she looked soft and thoughtful, if a little sad, when Neal swept Mary into a passionate kiss at the end of the ceremony.

Alice squeezed Graham's hand, and when he looked at her, her eyes were dancing in anticipation and glee.

They all retired back to the event hall as night began to fall, for a reception where Chef seemed to feel he had something to prove. There was a groaning table of food and a five-tier cake decorated with animal footprints and real fresh flowers, topped with a plastic deer and a timber wolf stained reddish.

"Our supplier didn't have any red-maned wolves available," Darla said apologetically. "I had to improvise."

After the food had been enjoyed and the cake had been cut, Conall and Tex did a hauntingly beautiful guitar duet, and Lydia and Saina gave a salsa-bellydance fusion performance. Saina sang a song that set a glittering feeling of optimism and peace over the crowd.

Then Tony raised his voice and tapped his glass. "Your attention, please!"

Everyone found their drinks, prepared for a toast.

"Tonight is a night to celebrate," Tony said sincerely. "We are gathered here today in a place that has been a happy ending for so many of us… and a happy beginning."

Amber smiled at him foolishly and Graham was appalled to realize he was doing the same to Alice, drawing his mouth back into a more customary scowl with effort.

Alice, her hand in his as naturally as if it belonged there, did not miss this and poked him in the side to make him smile at her again.

Tony continued. "We're here this evening in honor of our good friends Neal"—Neal's former Marine buddies all cheered raucously — "and Mary." Alice gave a cheer for her as if it was some manner of competition and she was single-handedly prepared to take on the entire platoon.

"I want to wish them a lifetime of happiness and love, and a full cup of laughter and joy." Tony raised a glass. "To Neal and Mary! Congratulations!"

Everyone raised their toasts and cheered, with scattered applause and laughter. Neal kissed Mary soundly. Out of the corner of his eye, Graham saw Scarlet rise to start the music for dancing, and gesture Travis and Bastian to start moving the chairs away from edge of the dance floor.

But neither of them moved, grinning back at her, and Tony went on. "We also have one more announcement to share, if you will all give me another moment of your time."

Scarlet turned back curiously, then looked to where Chef sat with Magnolia, perhaps expecting a formal wedding announcement from them. But Chef and Magnolia smiled knowingly back at her, which is when the resort owner seemed to realize that everyone was looking at *her*.

She returned her gaze to Tony suspiciously.

But it was Neal who stood then, grinning briefly at Tony. "I propose a second toast, to Scarlet, who has sacrificed so much for so many of us. She reminds us frequently that she is 'not running a charity,' but time and again, she has put aside her own best interests to give us opportunity, protection, and shelter, at her own expense and considerable trouble."

At his words, many of the staff murmured agreement.

Scarlet frowned. "This isn't necessary…"

Neal waved her protest aside. "Words of appreciation fall short of the thanks we owe, so we have something a little more tangible to offer today. Jenny?"

Jenny was holding a folder as she stood and wove through the tables to where Scarlet was still standing.

"Scarlet," she said simply, "we know that the resort is in trouble, and that it wouldn't be if you hadn't gone out of your way to help us all. You took my sister and I in when you didn't have to."

"And me," Wrench growled from beside Lydia.

"And me," Neal agreed. "All of us from Beehag's zoo."

"It's my fault my mother is suing you," Darla added.

"Our fault," Breck corrected, an arm around her.

"You saved our retirement home," Liam said simply. The elders sitting with him gave murmurs of agreement, except Mr. Danby, who pounded on the table until Darla gently redirected him to folding and re-folding his napkin.

Scarlet gave Graham a brief, betrayed glare, looking conflicted. "I did what I could," she said quietly. "You don't have to—"

Jenny beamed at her. "We *did* have to," she said simply, almost bubbling over with happiness. She handed Scarlet the folder. "Shifting Sands will be yours."

Scarlet looked at her in confusion and slowly opened the folder as Jenny went on. "We gathered the funds from a variety of sources and we have raised the entire asking price of the island. Even if he wants to, Beehag's lawyer can't refuse the sale to Grant Lyons."

Scarlet's alarmed glance at Graham made him realize he was grinning again, and this time he didn't even try to turn it into a scowl. At his side, Alice laughed in delight.

He knew what was in the folder and had gone over Jenny's

careful accounting of every penny: Conall's business had finally sold, and he pledged a massive chunk to the purchase of the island. Magnolia had liquidated a large part of the royal fund she had access to again. Laura and Jenny finally received notification of settlement of their life insurance from Fred's estate. Bastian had sold several of the more valuable pieces from his hoard. The survivors of Beehag's zoo had all wanted to contribute whatever they could, and their modest donations had added up slowly. Some of them had timeshare style contracts or profit shares laid out, but most of the donors had simply given the funds outright.

And Alice herself had promised forty-nine-and-a-half million (less her tax burden), thanks to the mysterious man with the business card. She had already confirmed the stunning sum in her bank account and Jenny had recommended a good accountant to help her handle the paperwork for the windfall and get her family's finances back in order.

Together, they had pooled enough to buy the island, buffer against Darla's mother's lawsuit, and keep operating for at least a few years.

Scarlet's face drained of color.

"All you have to do is sign the offer and express mail it to Beehag's lawyer," Jenny said coaxingly. "Graham—I mean Grant—has already signed his part of the contract, granting you full ownership. Shifting Sands will be yours, free and clear. The whole island."

Scarlet sank slowly backwards into her chair and she put the open folder carefully on the table before her. Then, to everyone's surprise, she put her face in her hands and wept.

There was an awkward moment of silence and Gizelle asked in a stage whisper, "Did you break Scarlet?"

Scarlet looked up at that, her face full of aching happiness behind the tears. "You didn't have to do this," she said again, choked.

"We didn't have to," Graham said, to everyone's surprise. "But we wanted to. You've done a fair bit for us that you never had to." He raised his glass of wine with the hand not holding Alice's. "To Scarlet."

The room raised glasses. "To Scarlet."

She closed her eyes a moment, more tears leaking down her cheeks, then opened them and reached for her own glass. "To Shifting Sands," she replied, and that received a chorus of echoes as everyone toasted the resort they called home.

CHAPTER 39

Graham's bare chest had been distracting, and his accent had been devastating, but Alice was utterly unprepared for the beauty that was Graham in a suit.

It was hard to watch the wedding, even harder to watch Tony's speech, and the emotional reveal to Scarlet that they had colluded to save the resort. Alice wanted to gaze at Graham only, to see the smiles that he kept trying to bury, to see the joy in his eyes, and his satisfaction at Scarlet's surprise and tearful delight.

"You know you could have kept the resort in your name," Alice told him, trying not to stare at the way his suit spread over his muscular shoulders as he stood to help move tables and chairs back from the dance floor. "It would be like being a landed lord again."

"I don't want to be a lord and I don't want to own a resort," Graham said with a shudder. "I just want to grow tomatoes and strawberries and let Scarlet deal with the rest of the nonsense."

Then he looked at Alice, his deep blue eyes intense. "And you," he added. "I want to be with you."

Alice's breath caught in her chest.

She couldn't deny the connection they had any longer, but they hadn't talked about what came next. "Let's go for a walk," she suggested, as the music struck up. This wasn't a conversation to try to have during the wedding chicken dance. Mary was too busy with Neal to even notice her skipping out on the reception.

Graham nodded, and he offered Alice one of his starched arms.

She took it, barely keeping herself from rubbing herself against it inappropriately, and they walked out along the side of the dance floor. Scarlet was circulating among the guests and staff, thanking each of them sincerely for their part, and she caught them at the door.

"My lord," she said to Graham. Alice didn't think that she said it in the slightest bit ironically, certainly not in the mocking fashion that Breck said it. For a moment, Alice thought Scarlet was going to bow or curtsy, but she only tipped her head respectfully. "There aren't words for what you've done for me."

Graham cleared his throat in embarrassment. "Scarlet, you've done more for my family… for this family… more for me... than I could ever repay. But it's not about debt or duty. This is your island. It's always been *your* island."

Scarlet looked between Graham and Alice, her face grave and grateful. "Thank you," she said simply, and she shook both of their hands in turn. Alice wondered afterwards if she imagined the tingling sensation that tickled up her arm.

She wasn't a shifter, Alice reminded herself, and she briefly wondered why someone who *wasn't* a shifter would invest themselves so deeply in a place made for them.

Graham and Alice escaped out the side door, leaving Scarlet to continue her rounds.

They made their way out onto the sprawling lawn, still littered with chairs and flower chains. The dais from the wedding was pale in the moonlight.

Without conferring, they walked towards it and stood looking through the archway at the sparkling ocean beyond.

"Alice," Graham growled, just as Alice cleared her throat and said, "Graham…"

"You first," he insisted.

Alice sighed, not even sure how to say what was bubbling up in her chest. She closed her eyes, and let the sound of the ocean on the rocks wash over her. "Graham, I love you."

Once it was said, it seemed the simplest, most obvious thing in the world. "I love you," she repeated. "I am a part of you, and you are a part of me I can't imagine being without."

Graham let his breath out as if he'd been holding it. "Alice…" he said achingly.

"I'm not done yet," Alice said quickly as she opened her eyes. "Graham, I want to be with you forever. It doesn't matter where, or what else happens."

Graham in a suit was breathtaking, but Graham in a suit sinking to his knees at her feet to gaze up at her in the moonlight was the most romantic thing that Alice had ever seen.

"I love you," he said, and Alice smiled to remember that they were the first words he had said to her. "I pledge myself to you," he went on. "Marry me, or don't, I am yours for all time, in all ways, all places."

She wasn't afraid of the words this time; happiness filled her so completely that there was no room for fear or doubt. "I am yours," she replied simply, and then Graham was flowing to his feet and pulling her into his amazing arms and kissing her with his amazing mouth.

It was several moments before coherent thought was possible. "Graham," she said, pulling away at last. "Graham."

"I will come to Lakefield with you," he said.

"I don't want to ask you to," Alice said. "I want to come here."

"Your job," Graham said reluctantly. "Your wrestling team."

Alice stroked his jaw, enchantingly clean-shaven for the occasion. "Do you remember when I told you that it's easy to be confused about the difference between loving what you do and loving to be good at what you do? That's the truth, and it's my truth, as well as yours. There are things I love about being a gym teacher, and being good at it is right up at the top of that list. But there's a lot I hate, like the administration, and the pay, and watching good students wash out, the parents…" She could have gone on for a while.

"But I'm a millionaire now," she said with a grin. "Or I was for a few minutes anyway. I don't have to teach middle school again if I don't want to. I'm not going to say there won't be parts I'll miss, but there are a lot of parts I won't miss, too… and this is an amazing tropical paradise. I'm sure I can find work to do here. Work that I'll love, even. Scarlet won't kick me out, and… you belong here just as much as she does. This is my home, now."

She wondered how to explain how much the resort was under her skin… she felt like it was the place her feet belonged, like she could do good here, like there was something about the island that called to something inside of her.

Something *good* inside of her.

Graham was smiling, that rare, beautiful, slow smile that he shared only with her.

"This is *our* home," he agreed, and he kissed her again until she was panting and clinging to him desperately.

"I can think of something I love to do," he growled in her ear as she started to work loosening the tie.

Alice chuckled. "Do you love it, or do you love that you're *good* at it?" she teased.

"Let's find out," he suggested.

"Your bed… or a strawberry bed?"

Graham didn't answer, but took her by the hand, and then they were laughing and running over the lawn in the direction of The Den… and the gardens beyond.

A RECIPE FOR HAPPINESS

Chef and Magnolia were two characters I never expected to fall in love with; they were meant to be bit players in the background. But you try telling Magnolia to stay to the background! With every book in the Shifting Sands series, I got to know them a little better, and I was delighted to expand their story in Tropical Lion's Legacy and introduce the crossover with the Shifter Kingdom series.

It was even more fun to go back in time and explore their origin story. A version of this story was available at my webpage briefly during the holidays of 2019, but I added an extra chapter at the request of a reader. This story occurs several years before Tropical Tiger Spy.

Chet had expected the king's cousin to be a spoiled little brat. He was braced for another vain, fashionable princess like all the other nobles he had guarded.

"She's a challenge," the newly-crowned king, Einar, warned the two Royal Guards when they were added to her guard in anticipation of her Christmas Eve engagement party. "You might…you know, you'll see. I'm sure you're up for it. Just try not to let her break any furniture."

Chet had not expected her stunning self-confidence, or her completely disarming charm, or what his bear would do when their eyes met.

She was, in distinct contrast to the thin, self-conscious, diet-crazy courtiers, flagrantly voluptuous. Kind observers might describe her as plump, or courteously call her curvy. Unkind observers would pronounce her fat; she had several chins and rolls of extra flesh. She had a large frame, and it was generously padded.

Chet, from the moment he laid eyes on her, thought she was absolutely perfect.

Her skin, as much of it as there was, was smooth perfection, absolutely roses and cream, and her hair was thick, waist-length auburn waves that other women vainly dyed their hair trying to achieve. Her eyes were violet, her smile stunning. When she moved, her great strength and grace were awe-inspiring.

"I am Agneta Annika Margareta Solberg af Bjorn," she greeted them, and she smiled at Chet's fellow guard, but she *smiled* at Chet. If Chet had not already been pledged to her service, he would have fallen at her feet to do so at once.

"Oh," she said, quietly enough that only Chet could hear. "Oh, this is going to be complicated."

Chet's bear was trying to claw its way to the surface, demanding that this was their one, their true forever mate, and it didn't matter how complicated she thought anything was. It was simple, it was pure, it was everything—*she* was everything.

Chet held onto his self-control through sheer willpower, and it was fortunate that his duties did not include conversation, because he would have been incapable of anything that complex.

Agneta, on the other hand, lost no part of her cognitive abilities and in rather short order had managed to maneuver things so that they were alone, proving only for the first time her talent at getting people to do her will. Chet's fellow Royal Guard gave him a rather skeptical look as he went off on some wild hare chase, leaving them quite alone.

"That's better," Agneta declared with satisfaction, and she rose to her feet and cornered Chet with determination. "Now Chet, my darling, here's what we're going to do…"

Chet shuddered as she took his hands. "Your highness…"

"Oh, no, that will have to go," Agneta assured him. "I won't be *your highness* to you…"

"You will always be *your highness* to me," Chet growled, barely able to think over the feeling of her thumbs making lazy circles on the backs of his hands.

She patted him on the cheek and then let her hand linger there. "We'll go to Einar first thing in the morning. He'll cancel the engagement, release you from your vows, and we'll be able to marry, perhaps next week."

"We're getting married?" Chet said, blinking at her unexpected intensity. Her hand, still on his cheek, was soft and strong all at once.

"Well I'm certainly not marrying some minor noble from Norway when I could have my *mate*," she said archly. "You don't have any objection to marrying me, do you?" It was the first hint of doubt he'd seen in her, a moment of longing and worry that flashed through her soft blue-purple eyes.

She is ours, Chet's bear rumbled.

"No," Chet said. "I can imagine nothing I want more." He felt like breaking into song.

Her smile was electric. "Perfect! There's one more thing for tonight, then."

"Anything," Chet promised her.

"Kiss me," she begged, and nothing could have kept Chet from her then.

He swept her into his arms, kissing her not at all the way a bodyguard should kiss his princess, but in every way that a mate should kiss his destined life partner.

She was so soft, so strong, so intoxicating. Her hair was every bit as silky as it looked, her skin just as smooth, and she kissed him passionately back until they were both panting.

"Merry Christmas to me," she said, giggling in delight, and her hand was on his cock where it was straining against the pants of his uniform. "How far down does this *go*?"

Chet groaned, helpless under her hand. His cock was an embarrassment of riches—he had endured years of porn star jokes (and flat out envy) from fellows in locker rooms. He never wore shorts. He even had a special underwear exception as the standard Royal Guard uniform simply couldn't contain his goods; that had been a stunningly awkward conversation to have with his commander.

It wasn't all the good luck that some might guess. His first kissing girlfriend had fled in terror, and he had generally gotten used to a mixture of doubt and caution in reaction to disrobing in amorous situations, to the point where he had basically given up on amorous situations altogether.

But Agneta had no terror, no doubt, and no caution. "I want it *all*," she murmured near his ear.

Chet was cheerfully prepared to give it to her, *all* of it, when a second door in her chamber, one they hadn't bolted, suddenly opened and the king of Valtyra walked in like he owned it.

Which he probably did.

"Cousin!"

"Guard!"

"Your Majesty!" Chet snapped to attention.

It was hard to pinpoint which of them was most chagrined.

Not Agneta, who simply smoothed her hair and tugged her collar up where it belonged again. "You could knock, cousin," she scolded.

"I didn't know you'd be doing anything like that," King Einar said, mortified. "What is the meaning of this, Royal Guard…er… Chad, is it?"

"Chet," Agneta answered for him. "He's my mate."

"You're engaged to the count from Norway!" Einar reminded her.

"You can break that off," Agneta said carelessly.

"It's a political contract, Agneta, not an appointment for tea."

"My *mate*, Einar," she reiterated.

"We don't get the luxury of choosing our own relationships,"

Einar said firmly. "And you're not a spoiled child, to shirk your duties." He gave Chet a steely-eyed glare. "Speaking of duties."

Chet decided it was a good time for supplication. "Your majesty," he said respectfully, slowly kneeling. "I wish a dispensation from my vows, and the permission to court your cousin's hand honorably."

"Am I talking to a wall here?" Einar snapped. "The answer is no, the answer will always be no. You should both be ashamed of yourselves. I wouldn't expect better of you, Agneta, you've always been spoiled rotten and gotten everything you ever wanted, but *you*, Guard Chet. You came up through our toughest program. You should know how to have self control, how to carry out the duties you've been set. You should be protecting my cousin, not *molesting* her."

"Don't be so dramatic," Agneta scoffed. "He was not molesting me and you *know* it."

"Your majesty…" Chet had returned to his feet, but was uncertain how to proceed. Nothing in guard training or subsequent service had prepared him for this particular situation.

"I've made up my mind!" Einar roared.

"Fine," Agneta snapped back. "Then we're leaving. Enjoy your cold little kingdom and your frozen rock in the north. I'm going somewhere warm, and Chet is coming with me."

"You can't do that," Einar hissed.

"Watch me," Agneta hissed in return.

"Guard Chet!"

Chet, who had been struggling with his instinct to step between them, snapped to attention automatically.

"You will stand down and return to your commander for reassignment immediately. Have a second set of guards sent up immediately and have her highness placed under house arrest."

Chet blinked at him.

He wasn't surprised by the order, and he wasn't conflicted. He knew exactly where his loyalty lay, and exactly what he had to do.

"I'm sorry," he said briefly, and just as Einar started to look smugly at Agneta, he continued. “Her highness has already ordered me to a warmer climate. Can I help your highness pack?”

Agneta laughed. “We really are going to have to work on that, darling. I won’t need to take much.”

Einar sputtered in outrage. “You can’t do this! I’m the *king*!”

“You’ve been king for about a week,” Agneta pointed out. “And I can put you in a headlock.”

“I could cut you off,” Einar threatened. “You’d be out of the succession.”

“I have my own trust money from Grandmama,” Agneta said airily. “And no one wants me in line for the throne, least of all myself.”

“It’s Christmas Eve, Agneta,” Einar pleaded desperately. “Can’t you just stop being stubborn for five minutes and think about the implications?”

“It’s Christmas Eve, Einar,” Agneta countered. “Can’t you just be happy for me?”

There was a moment of quiet between them, each testing the other silently, neither budging.

Then Einar rubbed his face in a thoroughly un-king-like way and gave a noisy sigh. “Go,” he said, resigned. “Just go. I give up.”

Before he left the room, he paused and turned back. “Guard Chet,” he growled.

“Your Majesty?”

“Protect her,” Einar said firmly. “Whatever parts of your vows you feel are worth throwing away with your career, swear you will protect her.”

“I swear it,” Chet said grimly, feeling the cut of his king’s words more deeply than he wanted to admit. “I swear it with my whole heart.”

Twenty-Two Years Later

Chet gazed out of the top floor window, down over the frozen lake.

It was like a photo postcard for the impending Christmas holiday.

Lace-like white mountains spanned the Canadian horizon, and the evergreens were all heavy with brilliant snow. It looked like a train model, with every tree lovingly placed on the picturesque slopes. The sky was a curious variegated blue: rich blue overhead and a pale baby blue where it kissed the mountains, almost indistinguishable from the distant shadows. The lodge windows were clear, triple-paned, and set in great logs from trees that must have been monstrous lords of their forest.

Twenty-two years of traveling, and he and his mate were still finding new kinds of beauty and luxury to enjoy. He wasn't sure how Agneta managed to ferret out something fresh and interesting every time, but every few months, she packed them up and moved somewhere completely different and uniquely wonderful.

"This place is a little chilly," Agneta said thoughtfully, coming to stand by him. "You'd think that as a polar bear, I'd be more interested in this climate, but I am definitely planning somewhere *tropical* next."

"Does it remind you of home?" The sting of their exile was not so keen as it had been at first, gentled by more than two decades, but there were many days that the sight of snow or the smell of saltwater would trigger melancholy.

Agneta shrugged carelessly. "In ways, I suppose."

Chat turned to draw her into his arms. "Regrets?" he asked seriously.

Her smile was slow and sultry. "Not one," she promised, and Chet had to believe her, because whatever grief or guilt he carried, he could not regret his choice to embrace a life of travel with the woman he loved more than the world.

And if her smile made his existence complete, her kiss set it on fire.

She pulled away slowly. "I've already picked our next place," she said, and her eyes were sparkling. "What do you dislike most about all of the places we've lived?"

Chet considered. "The cooking is hit and miss," he said. "But that's not a universal complaint."

Agneta's smile took a hint of mischief. "Do you remember what you said when you first saw that forest?"

"That I wanted to go wander it in bear form, and it was a shame they had so many cameras around the lodge," Chet remembered.

"Good for the wildlife enthusiasts, not so good for the wildlife *guests*," Agneta quoted him, nodding. She looked full of promise and excitement. "I found a place where we can be ourselves."

For a moment, Chet misunderstood, thinking of himself as Royal Guard in an unexpected gulp of hope. But no, she meant— "A place where we can be shifters?"

Agneta showed him a poorly-designed brochure, folded not quite square. "It's so-subtly called Shifting Sands Resort. Read between the lines, or give the owner a call, like I did. She was lovely, though the connection was terrible. It really is a resort for *shifters*, and it sounds amazing. A big pool, a beach, a full-service spa!"

"A kitchen?"

Agneta hesitated. "A restaurant," she said with regret. "I asked for a cottage with a kitchen and was told they had none available for any price."

Chet could see her excitement and wanted no part in dampening that. "I can do without," he promised. "What will your codename be?"

Pretending to be spies had been a harmless diversion when they first went on the run, a fun spin on their new drifting life that gave it a fictional twist to take off some of the sting of leaving their duties and families behind. She always went with a flower name, and he usually picked an obscure spy from screen or page.

"I will be Magnolia," she said firmly. "I quite like it as a name, and it is a lovely flower and a strong tree. For you…James Bond?"

Obscure, it was not, but Chet would do anything for his mate.

Even go to another luxury island where he would never let her know that he was bored to tears.

~

Agneta breathed in deeply as she climbed out of the van, the springs of the vehicle creaking. After more than two decades of moving constantly from place to place, she'd never lost her wonder and delight in each new place they stayed.

"Well, if we can go by smell alone, I am willing to settle down and spend the next twenty years here," she said merrily. It smelled like exotic plants and flowers and saltwater, and the air was just the right amount of hot and humid.

Chet peered around suspiciously as he helped her down, clearly expecting enemies to leap from the looming jungle. But there were no enemies; there had not been enemies for more than twenty years.

"Something's burning," Chet said critically, looking disappointed by the lack of anything to protect her from.

"Something else is blooming," Agneta said mildly, taking his arm. She let the man in the resort uniform hurry forward to take a load of luggage with a grin on his golden-skinned face. He took more at once than a human possibly could, not at all bothered by the weight of her belongings.

"A place where we can openly be shifters," she said with a sigh of delight. "It has been so long since I had a chance to be on four paws. I may never leave, Chet my darling."

Chet, always a harder sell, looked dubious but Agneta knew he would do anything she wanted. She prayed she would never betray that trust.

A red-haired woman with a direct emerald gaze greeted them in her office. "I'm Scarlet. I own the resort and I'll be checking you in today. Please don't hesitate to let me know if there is anything I can do to make your stay more comfortable."

Agneta took the hand she offered and shook it elegantly. "Agneta," she said. "But I prefer to go by Magnolia. This is…Jack Ryan."

Chet also shook Scarlet's hand, and she did not so much as smile at the famous spy name. He gave her a challenging look, clearly assessing her as a threat.

Scarlet didn't ask any questions about their names, only about their requirements as guests and their shift forms. "There is, of course, no predation, anywhere in the resort or in the nearby jungle. The buffet is open 24 hours, with a catered breakfast and dinner at these hours."

They signed a pile of forms and took the keys to one of the upscale cottages.

"Jack Ryan? Really?" Chet asked as they descended the stairs. He walked at her side, though Agneta knew that his instinct was to walk a few steps behind. It had taken many long years to get him to break that habit.

"Well, James Bond seemed too obvious," Agneta teased him. "I like Magnolia, though. I might keep this one."

The game had lost some of its thrill lately, Agneta thought, with a sideways look at Chet as he unlocked the door.

He had lost some of his thrill.

Not to her, of course. Every time she looked at him, it was exactly like the first time she'd seen him. Even without his uniform, he took her breath away with his broad chest and his big arms and his handsome face. They had both aged since then, but Agneta—Magnolia—thought he was only more distinguished now; youth had never been his best feature and silvering hair suited him.

And she was absolutely confident that he was no less thrilled with her now than he'd been the moment they met. He still loved every curve and adored every fold of flesh and looked at her as if she'd hung the stars.

But some of the light had gone out of him. He never sang anymore, and he went through the motions of their life without the skip in his step that he'd once had.

He'd lost his purpose.

She needed protection less now than ever, and while Magnolia would happily spend hours by the pool drinking margaritas and sunbathing, Chet needed something more to do.

Something meaningful.

Shuffleboard and boat tours wouldn't keep him occupied for long; he didn't find being entertained fulfilling. She had persuaded him to take singing lessons in Italy, and cooking classes in Savannah that he'd loved—but they'd had a house with a kitchen there and none of the cottages here had cooking facilities…and he never sang anymore. As isolated as Shifting Sands was, on its own little island in the Pacific off of Costa Rica, classes were limited to a very spare schedule of dancing and yoga.

The cottage was lovely, fully appointed, with two large bedrooms (so that Chet could keep up his personal pretense that he was only her bodyguard), two generous bathrooms, and a private porch screened in greenery sporting a Jacuzzi the size of some swimming pools looking down over the last rows of the resort to the ocean. It had been so freshly renovated that there were still scents of new paint.

Magnolia could have stayed here forever, she thought wistfully, making friends with other travelers. But Chet wouldn't last long. Maybe they could find a college town that was friendly to shifters, somewhere he could take more classes and search for purpose. Perhaps she could persuade him to stay here through the New Year. It was only a week to Christmas, and though they had enjoyed green Christmases, they'd never done a truly tropical Christmas in all their years of travel.

The staff had already been here; their luggage was laid out in the central sitting room.

"I'll get us unpacked," Chet said gruffly, and he went to open the first of Magnolia's trunks. There were beautifully carved solid wood dressers in the bedroom, in an early colonial style.

"Wait," Magnolia said, and he did, of course. "Maybe we should do a structure test of the bed before we get settled in."

"It would be a shame to go to all the work of unpacking if the beds are *insufficient*," Chet agreed with a grin that chased away all of his previous gloom.

Magnolia smiled back in delight and stepped closer. "I reek of airplane," she said apologetically. Bears had excellent senses of smell.

Chet closed the little distance left between them and buried his hands in her loose hair. "All I smell is you," he said, leaning in to kiss her.

~

Nothing felt wrong with Agneta—Magnolia, for now—in his arms. Chet could forget his betrayal, his doubts. More than twenty years with this woman, this amazing, beautiful woman, and he only fell more in love with her as they went.

He still wanted her irresistibly, every time he saw her, still hungered for her kisses and took pleasure in finding new ways to make her gasp and shudder. He was still awed by her courage and her grace.

He still found moments of nirvana, buried deeply in her, making her rise beneath him like a force of nature. The taste of her kiss exceeded any of the gourmet food they had ever enjoyed, and when she cried out in pleasure, Chet thought he might perish from happiness.

The bed survived their test, though it gave many alarming creaks that suggested it might not weather anything more vigorous.

"Oh, my *darling*," Magnolia murmured in his hair as he lay at her generous breast. She called everyone darling, but there was something special about the way that she said it to him.

She made everything wonderful.

He unpacked her clothing while she showered, hanging the fine dresses and arranging the assortment of shoes. The resort was clothing optional, something Magnolia had giggled over like a girl when she read the brochure, but she never arrived anywhere unprepared for formal events. There were already a few packages in wrapping paper neatly tucked away. Magnolia loved to give gifts and Chet refrained from squeezing or shaking them with iron will.

His own clothing required considerably less time: a few good suits, some khaki pants and silk shirts, some nice shoes, a few discrete weapons in holsters that he fingered with regret. He had a few gifts for Magnolia in his own luggage, but he frowned at them, not satisfied. Everything he could find for her seemed insufficient for the happiness she'd brought him. He vowed to spend some time finding something better before Christmas actually arrived. Maybe he could make something.

"There is plenty of hot water," Magnolia told him, emerging from the steaming bathroom. Bath towels would often not reach around her, but the resort had managed to provide two thick terry cloth bathrobes that would actually fit them and Magnolia was snuggled into one of them, nearly purring in delight. "I am already half in love with this place."

She kissed him tenderly and went to riffle through her new closet.

In unpacking, Chet had convinced himself that there was no danger at their cottage and he left her to take his own shower, marveling afterwards in the generous cut of his own bathrobe; he usually had trouble getting his arms into them.

His shower was brief, because his guilt came swimming back with the hot water. He'd broken his vows, he'd betrayed his king…

He dried and dressed swiftly, trying not to dwell. It should seem like it was long ago, but the wound still felt fresh when there was nothing else to occupy his mind.

"I'd like to take a dip in the pool while the sun is high," Magnolia said, when he found her lounging on the porch in a bikini that left nothing to the imagination. "But I'm hungry. Join me at the buffet?"

Chet knew from experience that eating wouldn't ease the emptiness he felt, but he agreed. Magnolia put a sundress on over her bikini.

The restaurant level had a few guests wandering around with trays, a harried-looking waitress who was trying to refill a water dispenser, and a very disappointing buffet indeed. "Hopefully the catered dinner will be better," Magnolia said, nibbling at her mediocre pasta. "Perhaps it would have been good when it was fresh."

Chet frowned at his own plate, not convinced. The sauce was appallingly unbalanced, heavy with garlic and over-salted.

They ate quickly, and wandered down a level to the bar. "I'd love a margarita," Magnolia said, but the bar was unmanned, and the choices in the cooler were less appealing. They each took a bottle of water.

"The heat isn't as bad as Georgia," Magnolia observed, as they took the grand staircase down to the pool deck. "I think it's less humid. The sun feels good here, not as angry."

"It is nice," Chet had to agree. The weather, at least, was perfect. The sun was sizzling hot in a beautiful clear sky, but there was a lovely cooling breeze, and the air felt...fresh.

They found sturdy lounge chairs along the pool with fluffy towels folded neatly at the foot of each one. They were spreading out two of them when Magnolia whispered, "Is that a *dragon*?"

Chet was reaching for one of his knives and turning towards the direction of her alarm before he registered her words.

And sure enough, it *was* a dragon.

It was a jewel-scaled, house-high dragon, curled on the beach around a lifeguard tower, its head swiveled to gaze back over the pool.

"How magical!" Magnolia said in delight. Everything delighted Magnolia.

They lay in the sun for a short while, Chet trying desperately not to fidget in boredom, and then Magnolia sat up. "I'm going for a swim," she said avidly. Watching her strip out of first her sundress, then her bikini, was a delicious torture.

Then she shifted, and if she was lovely as a human, she was no less gorgeous as a snow white polar bear. A few ponderous steps and she was slipping into the sapphire pool, diving and swimming and twisting through the water.

Magnolia swam several lazy laps while Chet watched from the edge of the pool. Then she paddled to the shallow end and padded up the steps. A tremendous shake sprayed water from her thick fur, and then Chet was meeting her with a towel as she shifted back to human.

"Yeah, you *should* cover that," someone called raucously and Chet's blood instantly boiled.

Magnolia took his arm with her iron strength, preventing him from turning to identify the heckler. "Don't you worry about him," she said, as calmly as if she was telling him not to bother with a bug.

Chet made himself focus on her, and she dried her hair as she strode back to her lounge chair with regal confidence. "I don't care what they think," she promised, and Chet honestly thought she meant it.

He cared. He wanted to twist the man into a pretzel and throw him to the dragon.

"They should respect you," he growled, discontent.

"Anyone busy making snap judgments about someone they don't know isn't a person whose respect I would care for anyway," Magnolia countered logically.

Chet sighed. She was right. She was always right. But he still wanted to pound the jerk into something flat.

"I'm going to visit the spa once I've sun-dried a little," Magnolia said, settling onto her chair. "I understand they will even groom you in animal form if you request it. Wouldn't that be lovely?"

Chet sat down on the lounge chair next to hers and stretched out his legs. "Yes," he agreed. In his head, even after more than twenty years, he added, 'Your Highness.'

~

"I simply love the staff here," Magnolia said expansively as a waitress sat them at a table by the edge of the restaurant deck. She was rewarded with a timid smile before the girl scurried away. "The woman, Lydia, who runs the spa is an absolute peach. Have my nails ever looked so lovely?" Her rings sparkled in the low light of the setting sun.

Chet smiled indulgently at her. "I don't think that they have," he said, not looking at her nails at all.

"Did you have as lovely a time while I was busy?"

"I found an interesting-looking book at the exchange shelf,"

Chet said with a dismissive shrug. If this resort went as usual, he would read through the available books in about a week.

He opened his menu and frowned over the choices.

"Oh goodness," Magnolia said, opening her own menu. "These all sound lovely."

Chet shook his head. "It's all over the place," he said disapprovingly. "I like a menu with focus. It's unlikely the chef can do a good job on all of these, every night."

"I've made a food snob out of you," Magnolia teased gently.

"May I start you out with something to drink?" A slight, handsome young man with a winning smile stood at their table with a pitcher of ice water. "I'm Breck, I'll be your server this evening." His tone suggested that he was the one lucky to be serving them. Magnolia liked him immediately.

"A bottle of wine," Magnolia said, though she knew that Chet would nurse a single glass through the entire meal. He still took his vow to protect her terribly seriously, and never let himself get tipsy or lowered his guard. He was sizing Breck up thoughtfully.

"We have a delightful Pinot imported from Brazil I can recommend," Breck suggested.

Magnolia agreed and he filled their water glasses deftly and left the table.

When he returned to pour them the wine, they had narrowed their dinner choices down to just a few. "Which of these looks best?" Magnolia asked. "The Greek pasta plate, or the braised chicken with Brussels sprouts and black lentils?"

Breck looked uncomfortable, but lightly said, "I imagine that would depend on your taste. I'm sure they're…both…great. Very generous portions," he hastened to add.

"You can see *that* part is terribly important to me," Magnolia teased him.

Rather than feeling awkward for bringing attention to her weight, like most people did, Breck grinned. "Lady, I would be *lucky* to have as much woman as you are." He gave her an appreciative look up and down, then he dropped his voice and sidled closer to her. "But I've got to admit, I've got my eye on the big hunk across the table from you. You won't need to order dessert when you've got that much sugar. Mm!"

Magnolia laughed in delight and even Chet chuckled.

"I'll take the chicken," Magnolia decided. Chet chose the pasta.

Breck, not bothering to write anything down, hurried off to take their order to the kitchen.

The sun, on its mad dash for the horizon, was brassy gold and nearly gone already; sunset and sunrise were short this close to the equator. The sky above was dark and subdued. Christmas lights were coming on across the resort, sparkling little stars everywhere. There was muted holiday music coming from the bar below them.

"I just love it here," Magnolia said wistfully.

Chet smiled at her and she knew that he would stay if she asked him to. But he didn't sing with the music like he used to, and his smile was sad.

They talked about the holidays as they waited for the food...and continued to wait for the food. Magnolia might have wondered if their order had simply gotten lost, but no one else was being served either and the other guests were looking unhappy. Breck returned to their table several times to top off their water and refill Magnolia's wineglass, but when they asked how long it would be, he could only apologize and shrug.

Just as they were speculating about whether or not they would have to feed themselves from the buffet, Breck finally brought their meals.

"I'm...*terribly* sorry," he said, and Magnolia knew at once that he wasn't only apologizing for the delay.

Her chicken was cooked dry, and not saved by the salty sauce it was swimming in. The vegetables were all over-cooked and the rice was under-cooked. Even the garnish was limp.

Chet poked at his oily pasta salad distastefully.

"Maybe it tastes better than it looks?" Magnolia said gamely.

But Chet stopped her before she could take a bite. "This," he said firmly, "I *can* protect you from."

He gathered both of their plates and rose to his feet.

Then he vanished into the kitchen, and Magnolia was almost afraid to listen.

~

The kitchen was a disaster. Dirty dishes were piled by the back sink, and half-prepared—*badly* half-prepared—meals were laying out on the counters at various stages of going cold. A sobbing waitress was being raged at by a surly-looking chef, and Breck seemed to be trying in vain to interject with humor to defuse the situation.

"Excuse me," Chet said, in his loudest *listen-up* voice.

For a moment, the only sound was something boiling over, and the waitress' shaky sob.

The cook turned with a wrathful look. "You got a problem?" he challenged. He sounded drunk.

"I now have several," Chet growled. He threw the plates down on an empty space on the counter. "I am not feeding Magnolia that food. I am not standing by while you abuse your staff. And I am not letting you serve that food to anyone else."

"Who the hell do you think you are?" the cook demanded.

"I am Chet." Not Royal Guard Chet, not anymore, but it was a still a name that he could give with pride. It was the only name he had left.

"Well, *Chef*, do you think you could do better?"

"It's…" Chet tried to correct his name.

"I can't work under these conditions! Slovenly help! Substandard ingredients! Constantly being questioned! I'll have you know I've worked in the finest kitchens in Europe!"

"As a dishwasher?" Breck muttered skeptically, earning himself the cook's attention.

"And you, you pervert, with your disgusting simpering ways. It's no wonder no one has an appetite for my food."

"Enough!" Chet roared.

The cook turned several shades of red but was silent.

"I am here to see that my Magnolia gets a dinner worthy of her.

If you can do that," Chet's voice betrayed his skepticism, "do so. If not, get out of my way."

"That fat cow barely needs another meal," the cook muttered.

"What did you say?" Chet asked between gritted teeth. One of his knives was rather suddenly at his fingertips.

The cook, abruptly aware of the danger he was in, looked around for support from his staff…and found none. Breck was actually grinning, and the crying waitress was all eyes and awe. The rest of the kitchen staff was gathered at the back of the kitchen.

"Nothing…" the cook decided to say wisely. Then he tore off his apron. "You know what, this job pays shit. I don't need this kind of abuse. I could get better work than this, at a better place. You people don't know talent when you see it."

He stormed out the back entrance of the kitchen.

Chet took stock of the kitchen thoughtfully. "Do you cook?" he asked Breck.

"Not well," Breck said honestly. "Though possibly better than *he* did."

"Mind if I take over?"

"Can you feed a dozen hungry people from *this*?"

Chet gazed over the kitchen. "I can make something out of this," he decided, opening the refrigerator. "But tell them they only have two choices, neither one of them on the menu. This chicken can't be served like this. A stew would salvage it, but time is an issue. A chicken salad or a…hm…where are the spices? Yes, I could also do a quick curry with this pork. Rice? No, just toss that, it's beyond saving, it's best to start with new. Is there any bread fresher than this? Give me thirty minutes. You, can you clear this counter for me?"

They leapt to do as he bid, and Breck scurried out to let the diners know that there had been a change of power in the kitchen, take their new orders, and keep them plied with drinks.

~

Magnolia could hear the shouting from the kitchen and braced herself for the sound of a brawl.

It didn't come, and after a few nervous glasses of wine, wondering if she should go in and see if her mate had gotten himself into trouble, she heard something that made her heart lift in her chest: Chet. He was *singing*.

Breck appeared at the side of her table.

"Ma'am, your gorgeous hunk of a man has coordinated a coup and is reorganizing our kitchen in order to provide you with your choice of chicken salad or a pork curry."

"He's not making a pest of himself, is he?" Magnolia said in astonishment.

"I can safely say that everyone is very glad to have him there," Breck assured her.

"Well, his curry is not to be missed," Magnolia said, settling herself back into her chair. "Give him my love and tell him to enjoy himself."

"Make love to him, you say?" Breck teased.

Magnolia rapped his knuckles with her napkin-rolled utensils. "Hands off," she scolded laughingly.

"Yes ma'am," Breck laughed in return.

"Just Magnolia," she corrected him. She was warming up to the name. It suited her, she thought.

The waiter winked at her as he went to refill water glasses and flirt his way indiscriminately across the restaurant.

Magnolia closed her eyes and gave a sigh of happiness.

Not only was she pleased to hear the love of her life enjoying himself for the first time in a very long while…she knew she was going to get a dinner worth waiting for.

"That's it," Breck said. "They're all gone." He sounded tired, and happy. He was carrying a last load of dishes back to the sink, where the young lady washing up had been singing a soft counterpart to Chet's opera.

"Magnolia?" Chet said, in sudden concern. He'd forgotten that she must be wondering what had happened. Had the food been worthy? Breck had brought him secondhand praise for the meal, but was that only in comparison to the previous cook's work? He'd been working hard for several hours, unable to take a break and see for himself.

"I had a lovely talk with her," a new voice said, and Chet turned to find the owner of the resort standing across the counter behind him. "She said the meal was exquisite and wanted me to tell you she would be retiring to your cottage, but not to rush if you were having fun."

Chet could not decide if the woman looked disapproving or not, but swiftly bowed his head. "Madame, I have taken great liberties in your kitchen without authority. I apologize if I have overstepped the bounds of propriety."

"Please call me Scarlet," she said, with a slow smile. "It is safe to say that the liberties you took were quite appreciated. Possibly even sorely needed."

Breck gave a snort of laughter. "Sorely indeed," he said, as he took off his coat and began wiping down counters.

"I'd like a word with you, if you're finished here," Scarlet said firmly, ignoring Breck.

"We'll finish the cleanup," Breck said cheerfully. "Hail the conquering hero!"

Chet took off his apron and hung it on a towel rack, then followed Scarlet out to the deserted restaurant deck. It was full night, and most of the illumination was from Christmas lights. Below them, holiday music was drifting up from the bar, where a few last guests were capping their night.

"I understand you witnessed our cook's decision to quit," Scarlet said easily, as they sat across from each other at one of the empty tables.

"I did," Chet said simply, with a frown. He could have been more colorful about it, but chose not to.

"And from there, you were able to take over his duties and serve a meal that my guests were delighted with."

"I did," Chet said again, unable to keep a little of his pride from his voice.

"Do you have formal training in the culinary arts?" she asked mildly.

"A few classes in Savannah," Chet said, equally mildly. He didn't suppose that watching an absurd amount of cooking shows counted for anything; he often entertained himself with them when Magnolia was enjoying other pursuits.

"Have you ever considered a career in cooking?"

Chet's niggling suspicion that she was working up to offering him a job in her kitchen turned into a full-bloomed assumption. But… "My first duty is to my…Magnolia."

Scarlet looked at him seriously. "My staff contracts are generally for room and board, with a share of profits near year's end, but I hope that you understand I could not afford to board my chef in the cottage you are currently renting."

"Of course," Chet said distantly, trying to tamp down the desire that was rising in him. To live here, to settle down, to have work to do—meaningful work!—but it was selfish of him to want that. Magnolia loved to travel. They would stay in one place a week, a month or two, and then she would find some new location with new sights and delights. He couldn't have tied her down even if he wanted to.

"I would happily negotiate for a reduced price on a long-term lease of that cottage if you felt that we could come to an agreement."

It was so tempting…

"I'm afraid we've only talked about staying through New Year's," Chet said regretfully. He couldn't resist adding, "But if you needed some assistance until then…" It was better than sunbathing and yoga. So much better.

"I would be very grateful for it," Scarlet said with a hint of a smile. "As isolated as we are here, it is challenging to replace staff at a moment's notice. I could pay cash wages for a short term; please let me know your required wage."

Chet knew nothing about going rates for self-taught cooks for any terms. "May I have time to consider?" he asked cautiously.

"Certainly." Scarlet seemed to think that this concluded the conversation; she stood and offered Chet her hand as he stood politely with her. "Thank you for your help tonight, Jack."

Chet winced as he shook her strong hand. "It's not Jack. It's..." He thought about the old cook's slip. *Chef.* "Chet," he said rather miserably. Not *Guard Chet.* Just *Chet.*

"Chet," Scarlet repeated warmly. "Thank you."

"I'll let you know what I decide tomorrow in time for dinner preparations," he said firmly. Then he considered. "But... breakfast?"

"We'll pull the menus and have a pancake spread," Scarlet said. "We have several pounds of mix."

She must have seen Chet flinch at the idea of pancake from *mix*, and swiftly added, "Fresh strawberries from our gardens will cover many sins, I hope."

Chet gave her a slight bow, chiding himself for already considering the kitchen his own domain. It wasn't his. They weren't staying.

~

Chet was singing again, something in Italian, and Magnolia found herself smiling up at the sunshine with relief in her heart.

It didn't feel much like Christmas, despite the decorations and the holly. The holidays in Valtyra had been snowy and filled with the smells of pine and cider. Here, it was as blazing hot and sunny as ever, and all the twinkle lights in the world could not transform a palm tree into a Christmas tree.

"I am going to be sad to see you go," Scarlet said frankly and Magnolia squinted at her against the light.

"Oh, sit, darling," Magnolia invited. "I will be devastated to leave. I haven't seen Chet so happy in years as he's been helping you out these last few days."

"I have been hoping he would reconsider my offer for long-term employment," Scarlet said as she sat elegantly across the table from Magnolia. "I am already spoiled for any other cook."

"Long-term?" Magnolia was not used to being caught off guard. "He made it sound as if he was only helping you out for a little while until a new cook came in."

"A new cook I've been unable to find," Scarlet admitted. "I was wondering if I'd be able to sweeten the deal in some way and persuade you to stay."

"What kind of terms did you offer?" Had the deal been that terrible?

"I had hoped to negotiate a long-term lease for your cottage at a stiffly discounted rate," Scarlet said. "I usually pay in room and board, but of course, you are staying in one of our most luxurious cottages, not in the usual staff quarters, and the cost to me is considerably more."

Magnolia looked at her in astonishment. How was this not the perfect arrangement? Chet, so clearly happy with his new work, and the two of them living in this gorgeous paradise indefinitely—it was everything she had longed for.

She had to laugh after a moment, and fan herself with her hat. "Oh, what a fool I've been, darling," she confided to Scarlet. "All these years of moving us along when I saw him getting bored…he would never *ask* me of course, but I could always tell. He must have thought that *I* was the one with wanderlust, that *I* was the one wanting to constantly go somewhere new. Oh, I'll have to scold the dear man."

Then an idea occurred to her. "No, not scold…surprise. Scarlet, my dear, let's talk terms. I won't let you bankrupt yourself for something I would pay every penny I have to buy." She chuckled, and shook her head. "I suppose that is a poor way to start negotiations."

Chet had learned more about food service in the five days since he'd taken over the kitchen than he even knew there was to learn.

He had to scale dishes and time multiple meals at once. He quickly figured out that limiting the menu choices to two was all he could handle. He had to learn which tasks he could pass off, and to whom, before he floundered under the sheer number of things to be done. Hardest of all, he had to accept some level short of perfection, simply in order to serve. He was grateful that the resort was nowhere near capacity; if he'd been thrown into such a job with many more guests, he was humble enough to admit he may have failed.

Breck and the rest of the staff did their best to fill in the gaping holes of his knowledge, and he worked harder than he'd ever worked in his life, and felt more alive. He got to the point where he could wander the restaurant himself during the lulls, and the delight on the faces of the guests was a salve to a wound he didn't even realize he had.

He had given up correcting his name to Chet; they all called him Chef without batting an eye, and he had to admit that he liked it.

Christmas Eve caught him entirely by surprise, and he might not have marked it at all if Scarlet had not come to talk with him about special preparations for the Christmas dinner the following day.

After they had finalized a menu and she had clicked away in her sensible, low heels, Chet stood for a while in the empty kitchen and gazed around it.

It was an ample, modern kitchen, outfitted sensibly in every way, and Scarlet kept it stocked in high-quality ingredients and good tools; it was a cook's dream.

It was *his* dream, Chet admitted to himself, even if he'd never realized it.

Christmas Eve. The anniversary of his desertion from the ranks of Royal Guard.

It was always a bittersweet day.

He couldn't regret his choice; it was impossible to think of any life without Agneta—Magnolia—at his side, and he loved her as deeply and wildly now as he ever had. But he had never entirely made peace with abandoning his duty, and every year, he raised a glass to the guardsmen he'd left behind.

This was the first year he'd ever thought he might find that kind of companionship again, that he could once again have a sense of belonging to a greater whole.

He poured himself a glass of red wine, but hesitated over the toast. His betrayal felt fresh, scraped raw again by hope.

If Magnolia…

"I thought I'd find you here," her voice came merrily behind him. She walked more quietly than a woman of her size was expected to.

Chet turned, the wine still in his hand. "Your Highness," he said unthinkingly.

"Oh, *darling*," she said, the way she said it only for him. "We really have to work on that."

She was holding a manila envelope, and she was smiling. "I brought you your Christmas present early," she said, holding it out to him. It wasn't wrapped.

Chet felt a stab of guilt as he put down his wine. He'd never gotten around to finding her a better present, completely swept up in his unexpected kitchen duties. "Magnolia," he said achingly.

"Open it, Chef," she told him.

Chet was so used to the nickname by now that it didn't register until he'd bent back the clasps and was pulling out the paperwork within.

It was a contract: one part long-term lease, one part employment. His name was at the top, and there were sticky notes at all the places he was expected to initial and sign.

"What is this?" he asked, not daring to hope, as he flipped through the pages skimming section headers.

"Your Christmas present," Magnolia teased. Chet hadn't seen such light in her eyes in a long time. "And mine, I might add."

"This is long-term…we'd stay here?" Chet felt slow and stupid with anticipation. Was it…possible? Was it *right*? "You…"

"I want to stay," she assured him, as if she knew his thoughts—and maybe she did. "I love it here, and I'm tired of traveling. I've never seen you this happy; I *want* you to do this." Then she grinned, and added pointedly, "Chef."

"Your…"

"Magnolia," she said firmly. "I've decided to keep this name."

Chef let the contract fall to the floor as he stepped forward and gathered her into his arms. "Magnolia," he said, kissing her neck and breathing in the sweet scent of her hair. "My love."

"Merry Christmas," she laughed, sliding her strong arms up around his neck. "To both of us."

"I have other gifts for you," Chef murmured.

"I can't wait to unwrap them," Magnolia whispered back.

PICKLED MAGNOLIAS

This flash fiction occurs between Tropical Lion's Legacy and Tropical Dragon's Destiny. I changed my mind about Chef and Magnolia several times while writing the series; I had originally thought that they were not lovers, only cherished friends, and toyed with giving each of them other mates. But the further in I got, the more perfect for each other they were, and I knew that I would eventually have to write their backstory. It was one of my favorite parts of Tropical Lion's Legacy that they were able to make peace with their past and finally plan for a future together.

Magnolia leaned down and looked over Chef's shoulder, letting her hair tickle him as she kissed his cheek. "What's got you up so early?" she asked. Not long ago, this would have been his usual rising time, but Darla and Breck usually took the earliest shift now, baking the bread and pastries for the day together. Magnolia liked the new later schedule and had come to savor lazy mornings with her mate.

Chef turned to draw her into his lap, pushing away the books and papers. "Planning our wedding dinner," he said with a wide grin.

Magnolia drew back. "You aren't going to spend our entire wedding day *cooking* are you?" she teased. There were pages of notes. "I'm going to need a few moments of your time for the ceremony, and at least one dance, and..." she gave a great sigh. "I was hoping you'd join me afterwards..."

Chef gave her a sound kiss. "I intend to make everything ahead that is possible, and plan to make the menu so simple that even Breck could execute it. It is your day, your Highness, and I will serve only you."

Magnolia smiled in delight. "That's what her Highness likes to hear," she teased.

She got back to her feet and went to open her wardrobe, running her finger through the fluttery silks. She was going to have to think about a wedding dress...something that wasn't oppressively hot for the tropical heat. If she were marrying in Valtyra, there would be heavy silks, layers of lace, probably a corset that barely let her breathe and would never make her look any less fat anyway. She was going to insist on something much more comfortable.

"What are you thinking for the menu?" she asked. "Should I wear the blue Persian carpet dress today?"

Chef rose, not tempted by his lists and cookbooks when his mate was waltzing around in filmy sleeping clothing threatening to disrobe.

"I want to try pickled magnolia," he said mysteriously. "And I love the blue Persian carpet dress."

"I do plan to drink," Magnolia said with a laugh. "But I am not sure you should refer to me as pickled in front of the rest of the Royal Guard. They may take offense."

Chef pulled the dress in question from the wardrobe and removed it from the hanger for her, watching appreciatively as she peeled off her flimsy lace garment. She turned to let him pull the dress over her head and tie it behind her.

"Did you know that magnolia was edible?" he asked, bending to nibble at her neck.

"This one is," Magnolia purred. "But I had no idea about the flower."

"Pickled magnolia petals can be used as a salad garnish, similar to ginger slices. Maybe on a bed of arugula…I'll have to try them together. It will probably depend on the pickling spices and the salad dressing."

"I have a better bed we can try," Magnolia said slyly. "And it doesn't involve much dressing at all…"

REUNION

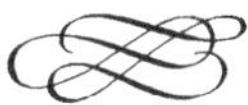

This story was included at the end of Tropical Lion's Legacy; I had originally planned to include these scenes in the novel itself, but swiftly concluded that they couldn't be written from either the hero or the heroine's point of view, and they didn't fit into the pacing of the rest of the novel anyway. Telling this tale as a separate story allowed me to linger over the moments and also to foreshadow a little for the final book…

Neal gazed over the lawn, a slight smile at his mouth as he sat thoughtfully on the picnic table where he and Graham and Breck had shared so many meals.

It hadn't changed a lot in the year he'd been gone; though the hotel was no longer staff housing, it didn't look any different. The jungle still held proud sentry uphill, and the sun, high in the sky, beat down on the sunny lawn.

Neal closed his eyes. The air still had the same green taste and warmth, with just the slightest tang of salty seawater.

But so much was different.

He was different.

He'd found his mate, his reason for happiness. He'd made peace with his estranged red-maned wolf and reclaimed the life that had been stripped from him.

He hadn't returned to the Marines, though he'd reconnected with his teammates. Instead, he and Mary built their own life together, in the small town of Lakefield where she taught math to disinterested middle school students. He took his talents with machinery to a civilian job operating big equipment, and found satisfaction in working for a modest construction company, running excavators and graders.

It was a life he could never have accepted without his time at Shifting Sands, time he had desperately needed to put his ten years of captivity in perspective.

Neal opened his eyes at the sound of unfamiliar footsteps.

A big man, nearly as broad at the shoulder as Neal himself, was approaching the picnic table, stride determined. He was wearing an elegant silk shirt, perfectly pressed khakis, and expensive shoes.

Neal stood up, already guessing who this must be. "You must be Conall," Neal greeted him, remembering to look clearly in the other man's face as he extended his hand for a shake.

Conall was Gizelle's mate, a famous classical musician who had built a small business empire in the wake of an accident that left him deaf. When Neal had first heard about him, he was deeply skeptical that such a man could in any way be a good match for Gizelle.

If Neal had been badly damaged by his years in a madman's menagerie, he could only imagine how it had been for Gizelle, who had been there longer than anyone could remember. For months following their release, she had remained in her gazelle form, and when she had finally shifted to human, she had no memory of her time in her cage, and she continued to be timid and traumatized.

Neal looked at Conall with thoughtful evaluation. He had not believed that a disabled man could possibly be what Gizelle needed, but his friends assured him that she had blossomed with this man's love, and was more calm and centered than anyone had ever imagined she could be.

Scarlet had kept him apprised of Gizelle's status, but her emails were brisk and impersonal, much like she was. Graham and Breck, no surprise, had not proved to be good correspondents. There had been a lot to catch up on in person, and they had been quick to assure him that Gizelle was happy and well.

Neal had to take that on faith, as Gizelle had been avoiding him since his return to the resort.

"You're Neal," Conall replied, and Neal thought his gaze was as suspicious as Neal's had been. "It's good to meet you."

His handshake was strong, his fingers calloused. He had fine clothing and a haughty tilt to his broad jaw.

They assessed each other for a long moment after they reclaimed their hands

"I've heard a lot about you," Neal said, self-conscious about the shape of his mouth as he spoke; Conall had to lip-read his words without Gizelle to help him hear.

"I've heard a lot about you," Conall echoed him with challenge. After a moment, he added, more gently, "Thank you."

Neal was surprised. "For what?"

"For your part in the liberation of the zoo," Conall explained. "For helping Gizelle feel safe again. She is very fond of you, and she missed you when you left." He spoke grimly and matter-of-factly.

He might have been jealous, Neal thought, or protective. Either would be understandable. "I'd like to see her before we leave," Neal said with a neutral nod. "If she wants to."

"She does," Conall said with a similar nod. "It just takes her a little while to work up to things sometimes." He said it with warm patience that put Neal's last reservations to rest. This was a man who understood Gizelle, who was willing to accommodate her quirks and love her for all her unique characteristics, not just in spite of them.

"Whenever she's ready," Neal agreed. "I...missed her, too." The two of them had been the last of the zoo to leave the island; that alone would have given them a bond. The shy gazelle had been Neal's real remaining tie to the resort, and he never would have left if it hadn't been to follow his own mate to another life. He sometimes felt guilty for leaving Gizelle behind, knowing how hard her trust was to win and worrying that he had betrayed it with his departure.

Conall frowned at Neal's mouth and then seemed to understand, giving a crisp nod.

It was tricky ground to navigate; admitting fondness for another man's mate was not particularly straightforward, and it was burdened by social norms that simply didn't apply. Neal had to trust that Conall would realize that their affection was platonic, as Mary did.

"So, ah, how are you liking Shifting Sands?" he asked, recognizing a place for small talk.

"Hard to complain," Conall replied briefly. "Er, looking forward to your wedding?"

"I am," Neal said, and it was true. There was something satisfying about the idea of standing up in front of their friends to make the bond that he and Mary had official. "It would mean a lot if you and Gizelle were there." He was sure that Mary had distributed invitations, but it seemed polite to invite Conall in person since he was there.

Conall looked at him quizzically for long enough that Neal wondered if he would have to repeat himself, then nodded. "I think we will be there, but it's always hard to predict."

Neal laughed, and Conall cracked a smile.

"Thank you," Neal said sincerely. Then he impulsively added, "Thank you for taking care of her."

Their second handshake was considerably more friendly than the first, and Neal caught himself thinking that he could like this man, given time.

It was too bad he was leaving in just two weeks. Time was the one thing they didn't have.

"I haven't been running!" Gizelle blurted, when Neal finally encountered her, nearly a week later, just a day before the wedding.

She was standing at the steps to the beach holding two kittens that didn't want to be held. A fluffy gray half-grown cat with white paws was squirming under one arm, while its sleeker, cream-colored companion had all four paws on Gizelle and was pushing out against her opposite arm with stiff, determined legs.

"It's good to see you," Neal said mildly, walking up the steps with his towel folded under his arm.

She was, as he had been warned, very different looking than the woman who had been a gazelle for so much of their friendship.

She still had wild, white streaks in her wavy dark hair, but it was back in a braid now. It wasn't a particularly tidy braid, but it was out of her face, and she didn't seem uncomfortable in her sundress. She moved less timidly, and she wasn't trembling, or looking for escape. She was still thin, but her cheeks were not as hollow and her brown eyes were less haunted.

The gray kitten had oozed itself out of her arms so that only the back legs were still hooked around Gizelle's elbow, body and head hanging down as she stretched white paws towards freedom. Gizelle shifted her grip, trying to gather both cats together.

The cream-colored kitten had orange Siamese points, and yowled accurately to the breed as it struggled gamely against the indignity.

Gizelle gently tucked paws and tails back into the crook of her elbow. The gray one started purring in defeat. The cream kitten struggled in earnest but Gizelle gently hung on. "These are my Christmas kittens," she explained to Neal. "The angry one is Tyrant and the other is The Sweet One."

"It's nice to meet you," Neal said politely to the put-out, half-grown cats. "Where are you taking them?"

"There are humans on the beach," Gizelle explained. "They don't have animals in them, but Scarlet says that doesn't make them bad people."

"I heard," Neal said; he'd been warned not to shift or do anything in front of the unexpected strangers that might cause them suspicion. He wondered what that had to do with the kittens.

A terrible thought occurred to him, confirmed when Gizelle went on.

"I thought I would see if they wanted voices," she said cheerfully. "Because the kittens don't have humans inside of them, and maybe they are lonely."

Neal blinked at her. "You…can't just mash them together into one body," he said, as gently as he could. "It doesn't work that way."

"Are you sure?" Gizelle asked skeptically.

"Positive," Neal assured her.

Gizelle wilted. "It seems like it *ought* to work that way," she said, sulky.

"Anyway, wouldn't you miss your kittens, if you gave them away?" Neal said, hoping he didn't sound too desperate.

Gizelle snuggled them both closer, to squawks of protest. "Yes," she admitted. "But Tyrant is more Scarlet's than mine anyway. Everyone thinks that's very funny except Scarlet."

She sat down on the steps and pulled Tyrant back down from the shoulder she was trying to scale. "Scarlet also said I shouldn't bother the human people," she said, sounding guilty.

Neal sat beside her. "It's probably not a good idea," he said sympathetically. "They don't know about shifters, and they might be frightened."

"Do you know, when we met, I thought you didn't have a voice at first?" Tyrant was trying to bolt over Gizelle's shoulder again, and was tugged gently back to the young woman's lap. "Your wolf was so far away, so quiet."

That wasn't the case anymore, and Neal's red-maned wolf chuckled in his head.

"He's made up for lost time," Neal said wryly.

As if I was the chatty one in this partnership, his wolf said snidely.

Neal waited to see if Gizelle would have anything to say about the comment; he'd heard from Breck that she could hear shifters' animal voices.

But she only gave him a shy sideways look. "I'm getting better at people," she said hopefully. "People with voices, anyway."

"So I've heard," Neal said warmly. "Everyone is so proud of you."

That seemed to please her.

Tyrant gave a final, frantic squirm for freedom and Gizelle let her go. The kitten bolted away across the broad step, groomed her tail angrily, and then sauntered away as if nothing in the world was wrong. Sweet One remained in Gizelle's arms, purring, and the gazelle shifter stroked her gently and tickled her face.

"I missed you," Gizelle said sheepishly to her lap, but Neal knew she wasn't talking to the cat. "I was lost for a while."

"I was sorry to leave," Neal said gently. "But it was time for me to go. I needed to get back out into the world, take back my life, be with my mate."

"I know," Gizelle said eagerly, looking up at him. "I know now! I have a mate, too. He's so splendid and amazing. Have you met him?"

Neal smiled at her. "I liked him," he said approvingly. "And I'm so happy for you."

Her face unexpectedly fell. "I gave him the lock to your cage," she said anxiously. "It was Christmas, and I hope you aren't angry."

"Of course not," Neal told her swiftly. "It was yours to give."

The relief across her face was like sunlight after a storm.

"I thought you might be mad," she said honestly. "But it was the only thing I had."

"It was a beautiful gift," Neal assured her. "Conall must have appreciated it very much."

"Yes," Gizelle said simply. "Because I gave it to him."

Her eyes were just as Neal had remembered, wise and full of hope, but there was less fear in them now, he thought.

To his surprise and Sweet One's discomfort, Gizelle leaned forward then and wrapped her arms around him for a swift hug, her head for a moment on his collarbone. "I have something else to give you," she said, releasing him almost immediately. Sweet One escaped her lap and groomed herself lazily on the step below them.

"You don't have to give me anything," Neal assured her.

"I do," Gizelle said firmly. "Otherwise you will die."

Then she gazed at him sternly, and he blinked, and she was standing up. "Chef has something delicious for dinner tonight," she said easily, as if she had not just announced Neal's potential death. "But no one will eat it."

"What did you want to give me?" Neal asked, deeply confused as he stood with her. Sweet One was nowhere to be seen.

"I already did," Gizelle said patiently.

"You said I would die," Neal reminded her.

"But you didn't, did you," Gizelle pointed out.

"I…suppose not?"

Then Gizelle hugged him a second time. "Thank you for coming back," she said softly. "I may not need you anymore, but I still missed you. You were my first friend."

Neal carefully put his arms around her in return. "You helped me back every bit as much as I helped you," he said gratefully, giving her a quick squeeze and releasing her. It was a far cry from the first tentative touch of her gazelle's whiskers.

Gizelle stepped back and smiled up at him. "That's what friends do," she said confidently.

"Will you come to our wedding tomorrow?" Neal asked. "Did you get the invitation?"

"It had frosting you couldn't lick," Gizelle said eagerly. "Like sugar, but sharp." Her face went thoughtful. "I don't know if I came to it or not. It isn't long now."

"It's tomorrow," Neal reminded her. "In the evening."

"No, it's a little longer than that," Gizelle insisted. "But not much."

Neal suspected they were not talking about the same thing. "The wedding?" he clarified.

"No," Gizelle said with an oddly sad smile. "The end."

"The end of… what?"

"Of me. Of everything." Her hands were shaking, and as soon as she realized it, Gizelle tucked them into fists and put them behind her, smiling fiercely. "Nevermind," she said swiftly. "It's quiet *now.* I *will* come to your wedding. I *did* carry flowers for Darla."

"Do you want to carry flowers for us?" Neal asked, not at all sure what to make of her doomsaying. He was pretty sure he shouldn't take her literally.

"I'll ask Graham!" Gizelle said enthusiastically, which Neal had to take as a *yes.*

Then she was gone, flying away on fleet, bare feet.

Neal was still shaking his head when he returned to the cottage he was sharing with Mary.

"Did you finally catch up with Gizelle?" she asked at once, perhaps sensing his bemusement as he laid a kiss on her head.

"She's come a long way," Neal said. The Gizelle who had first transformed to save him would never have given willing hugs, let alone two of them.

"She tried to explain to me that Jenny was the one who taught her how to shift when I finally saw her yesterday," Mary said, putting aside her book. "What did you two talk about?"

Neal laughed. "I think she has a skewed sense of causality," he observed. "She also seemed to think she just saved my life."

Mary pulled him down to kiss her. "Then I owe her a great debt of gratitude," she purred in his ear. "Because you've got somewhere to be tomorrow, and I'd hate to have to marry a corpse."

"That could be…messy," Neal agreed with a chuckle. "Depending on the method of death. And we paid a lot for the suit."

They shared a long, lingering kiss that somehow ended up with both of them wedged uncomfortably into a chair that barely held Neal alone.

"I can't wait to share the rest of my life with you," Mary sighed, as they untangled their limbs and pried themselves out the wicker chair.

"Can you wait until we get to the bed?" Neal teased.

Mary kissed him in answer, and they only just made it there.

It was only much later that Neal remembered Gizelle's odd

prediction and wondered what she meant by the end that was coming...

TROPICAL LION'S LEGACY: EPILOGUE

Graham rarely attended the formal dances that Scarlet hosted most weeks; she didn't ask him to, and he didn't offer.

But Alice was adamant. "If I have to stomp around in those goddamn shoes for three awful hours, I'm doing it on *your* toes." It was the last dance before she and Mary and Amber and their mates returned stateside, just a day and a half before their charter flew out, and Graham thought that Alice felt guilty for skipping out on most of Mary's reception.

Alice planned to put in her notice at the school and pack up her things to come back to the resort, but the timeline for her return was still loose. Graham dreaded the weeks without her and would have agreed to worse than a dance to keep her close as long as he could.

It was no surprise to Graham that Alice was significantly lighter on her feet than she had advertised, and the feel of her in his arms more than made up for the snickers of the rest of the staff and the torture of having to wear a nice suit.

And Alice *liked* the suit.

Graham was beginning to suspect she'd only agreed to go to the dance to get him back into it.

"You'll excuse me, *my lord*," Breck said, appearing next to them as they walked off the floor at the end of a song. The waiter held out a hand to Alice. "Chef stole Darla for a turn around the floor, so I'm here to impart some of my wisdom to your lovely lady and show her how a dance floor ought to be used."

"I'll dance with you," Alice said, arching an eyebrow at him. "But if you add any wandering fingers to your words of wisdom, you'll lose them."

"I'm hurt," Breck said, pressing his chest. "You injure me by believing I would be anything but a perfect gentleman. My fingers have never gone *anywhere* they weren't invited."

"Oh, I've heard all about you," Alice said, letting him lead her out onto the dance floor with a smile over her shoulder for Graham. "And I know that Darla will be happier with all your fingers intact, so let's keep them that way, shall we?"

Breck's laughing protests that he was sorely misunderstood—and a faithfully married man at that—faded into the music as he led Alice out through the dancers to a clear spot on the floor.

Graham ducked his head, hoping to avoid eye contact with any forward women who might think this meant he was available for a dance and stalked over to where Tex was pouring drinks at the bar. Tex handed him a beer without being asked and Wrench, who was also clearly trying to dodge an arranged dance while Lydia glided around with one of the guests, clinked bottles with him.

Everything felt… practically perfect.

His mate was safe. His friends were safe.

The resort was solvent and they were going to own it outright, forever. They never had to worry about having it sold out from under them again, or losing the lease.

There were no secrets on his shoulders save one, and that was not his burden. His demons were laid to rest at last, and he finally felt wholehearted. He couldn't imagine loving anyone more than he loved Alice, or trusting anyone more completely.

"Who's that dancing with Scarlet?" Travis asked curiously.

"Haven't seen him before," Tex said. Tex had a bartender's memory for faces and stories.

Graham glanced towards the far entrance. There was a large suitcase and a fancy garment bag sitting by the door. "New guest," he guessed with a shrug. Sometimes dragons or other shifters who could fly chose to come in under their own power rather than taking a boat or charter plane.

"Good dancer," Wrench observed briefly.

Graham didn't have the best view, between the dancers around them and the distance, but Scarlet and the stranger were talking intensely. He couldn't gauge her mood from here, but it was clear that the new guest had *all* of her attention.

That generally wasn't a comfortable position to be in, but the stranger didn't seem to be the slightest bit intimidated, which was unexpected. He was actually smiling at her.

He looked… triumphant.

"Is he going to *kiss* her?" Jenny asked avidly, as the two came close together in a flashy dance pattern—much closer than Scarlet's partners' usually got—and paused longer than the music dictated.

"Does he have a deathwish?" Laura chuckled.

"Graham!" Alice hissed, breaking through the dancers with Breck in tow. "Graham, that's him!" Her hand closed around his elbow and she pointed in alarm at the man they were discussing. "That's the guy who gave me the business card! That's N. Padrikanth Moore!"

"Here?" Graham balled up his fists. If the man had followed Alice with some idea of revenge…

"Did you say *Padrikanth Moore?*" Jenny exclaimed in alarm, nearly choking on her drink. "You're telling me *that's* Beehag's lawyer? *Here? Dancing with Scarlet?*"

TROPICAL DRAGON'S DESTINY

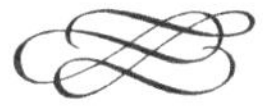

CHAPTER 1

There were several ways to get to Shifting Sands Resort that would have been faster than flying under his own power, but Mal enjoyed the journey and his dragon was grateful for a chance to spread his wings.

It was a long, leisurely flight, letting the world shrink beneath him to model scale. Whole countries were reduced to patchworks of farms and forests and wrinkles of mountains. The hours seemed short and Mal had a pang of regret as first the coast appeared beneath them and then the island that was their goal.

I am not winded, his dragon said wistfully. *I am strong and powerful. I could fly much longer than this.*

But the sun was beginning to set and Mal didn't want to be so rude as to try to check in after full dark.

The island was a brilliant green jewel on an ocean that was beginning to turn gold.

As beautiful as it was, Mal's sense of unease only increased as he approached.

The storms on the way were still distant, past the horizon; the only clouds were fluffy and harmless, stained in sunset colors.

But a swift, high circle of the island confirmed all of his worst fears.

There were weird currents of magic where there ought to be a smooth blanket of it and the tenor of the energy was off-key and unhealthy, like dark poison was running through veins in the earth. Something was very wrong here.

I almost waited too long, he realized in dismay. He'd been too tolerant of the resort owner's resistance to his plans, too interested to see what she would do next. His curiosity had almost been a disaster.

There was a particularly odd hiccup of power some distance from the resort, buried in the jungle, and Mal nearly went to investigate it despite the sinking sun. But his dragon gave a sudden burst of interest. *There*, he said urgently.

Mal folded his wings and dropped from the darkening sky to the sparkling resort below.

There! his dragon repeated, and they angled to land on the lawn downhill of a hall ringed in Greek columns near the top of the resort. Cheerful music and bright light streamed from the grand building.

Mal shifted so seamlessly he might as well have been descending a staircase, his luggage going from being cradled in claws to being carried effortlessly in human hands. He'd dressed in evening best, not wanting to meet the owner of the resort at any disadvantage, and he was glad now that he had; there was clearly a formal dance in progress.

The event hall was elegant and spacious. Couples were dancing and talking and drinking in a warm swirl of cheer and happiness.

Mal walked in slowly, picking out faces from among the many guests that were familiar from his investigations. The shyly laughing blonde would be Mary and the man she was dancing with was her mate and new husband, the former Marine, Neal.

There were two women browsing at the snack table; the towering amazon was Alice, and the brunette woman who would have been tiny even not standing next to her was Amber, her belly round with new life. Their mates, Grant—so recently still hiding under the name of Graham—and Tony respectively, were comparing notes by the bar where Tex, the cowboy bartender, was being distracted by a dark-skinned woman who was kissing his cheek. She had to be Laura and the woman who looked exactly like her was Jenny, the lawyer who had met him in battles of contracts many times... and hadn't always lost. Her mate, Travis, was tightening the connections on a chair nearby.

The reformed thug, Wrench, was dancing around the floor very staidly with flashy, dark-haired Lydia, the swan shifter in charge of the spa. Breck, the leopard shifter in waiter finery, was less restrained as he sashayed around with the strawberry-blonde Darla, spinning and dipping her. He wasted no opportunity to kiss her whenever the dance brought them together. Saina, a bindi sparkling at her brow, was dancing more serenely with Bastian, the lifeguard.

Then the dancers parted for a moment and Mal saw Scarlet.

The owner of the resort, the voice on the phone that brooked no nonsense and had a hundred ways of saying no. The mysterious woman who had reappeared after nearly forty years to restart the resort without a word of explanation.

Every one of his spies had agreed that she was unexpectedly powerful, and unexpectedly shrewd. They didn't have answers for his questions, only more puzzle pieces that didn't fit anywhere: she had great strength, keen intuition, and seemed to show up at the worst possible times.

A mercenary Mal had questioned extensively swore on his grandmother's grave that he'd shot the woman point-blank and hadn't harmed her at all.

And no one had ever seen her shift.

Alice, the last informant he'd sent in, claimed Scarlet had no shift form whatsoever and Mal had no reason to doubt her, even while it raised a whole garden of new questions. If she wasn't a shifter, what was she, and why would someone who *wasn't* a shifter invest so much energy into a resort that was exclusive to them?

She was certainly everything her photographs had promised…

and somehow more. Her profile was elegant, and her up-swept hair was impossibly red in real life. The line of her neck was long and inviting and when she smiled at something, Mal had an unexpected moment of unsteadiness.

Curiosity made him put down his bags and make a swift, subtle gesture with a short murmur of words. Power swam into his vision by command and he was suddenly looking at the room with an overlay of *energy*.

Most humans had a spark of magic, just a hint, hardly worth noting. Normal animal shifters glowed with it; a slight aura all around them that reflected the strength of their animal, and the room was full of those. Saina, a siren, had a sparkling source of enchanted light around her human form and her dragon mate shone just as brightly. All of their mate bonds glimmered like curious flickers at the edge of his vision, connecting each of them no matter where in the room they were. It was unusual to have so many of them in one place, Mal mused.

Mal noticed Gizelle for the first time then. Her curious magic leaked from her in a fractured pattern where she sat next to her mate, Conall, as he played guitar with the band, her touch enabling him to hear. He was an extinct Irish elk and his glow was brighter than most normal shifters, if muted compared to the mythical creatures.

And they all might have been blown-out candles compared to Scarlet.

The light of her power swamped them all, even at this distance, behind the noise of all the dancers. She was intense, brilliant, streaming luminescence. Her energy completely blotted out the physical form beneath it.

So *much* energy.

She was *unimaginably* strong. Mal had never seen anything like it. The information he'd been given barely scratched the surface of what she was.

She had spotted him, he realized, blinking through the radiance. She put down her drink and began to weave her way gracefully through the dancers to greet him as he released the sight spell.

Even as normal sight returned, Mal could still sense the power shimmering from her. She was so potent that it sizzled all the air around her; people retreated from her path without recognizing it.

Of course she is that powerful, Mal's dragon said, his voice rich with desire. *A mate of ours would be no less.*

This complicated *everything*.

CHAPTER 2

Scarlet let herself enjoy the evening without reservation or regret.

The event hall was filled with light and laughter and music. Everything felt simply perfect.

The people she cared about most were all here, safe in the resort she had built to shelter them, and the future stretched out optimistically before her.

She had friends so close she considered them family, security at last… she even had a cat. Scarlet accidentally smiled fondly to think of Tyrant, and the middle-aged guest she was dancing with stumbled and went pale.

She tempered her smile and guided him back into the steps of the dance, careful not to draw him too close.

He was still glad when the music ended and Scarlet politely left him at the bar with a nod to Tex.

She mingled with the others, inquiring about their satisfaction with the accommodations, the food, the entertainment, and she was delighted by their genuine praise. Chef proved himself worth every penny, all over again, and Scarlet was pleased to coax stories of good service from several of the guests. She mentally filed stories to pass on in praise of the spa and the housekeeping.

She felt the new arrival just a moment before he arrived at the far door but took a moment to conclude her conversation with an elderly woman who was giggling with her about Breck's attentions during meals. "Such a *nice* young man," the woman said.

"He is," Scarlet agreed with a chuckle. Finding a mate hadn't stopped Breck from flirting outrageously, even if it meant less now than it ever had. "I'm sure he has saved a dance for you and I will send him over to collect on that in very short order," she promised. "If you will excuse me?"

The newcomer was tall and broad-shouldered, very appropriately dressed in a fine, tailored suit with just a touch of gold embroidery at the wrist. Dragon shifter, Scarlet remembered from the guest list, which made sense given the unscheduled arrival and the extravagant clothing. Mal Moore, her memory provided.

He was also, she thought wryly, rather stunningly good looking and it did unsettling things to her belly when he smiled confidently at her approach.

Down girl, she reminded herself. He was a guest. This was just a standard business meeting.

"Mr. Moore," she greeted with a hand extended politely. "Welcome to Shifting Sands Resort."

He stepped forward to take her hand and they ended up standing rather closer than she had intended. He didn't shake her hand, only held it in his strong fingers and looked down on her with an expression that might have been wonder in his warm brown eyes.

"Mal," he said. "You can call me Mal."

Scarlet tipped her head in acknowledgment. "Mal. My name is..."

"Scarlet. Scarlet Stanson."

The sound of her name from his mouth sent a shiver down her back and his hand, still holding hers, was terribly distracting. "Yes," she said, trying to regain her hand and her composure. She met handsome men all the time and managed to keep herself in control; she wasn't sure why this one should be any different.

"May I have this dance?"

In timing that was either terrible or utterly perfect, the band had just launched into a new song and Scarlet couldn't find—and didn't want to find—an excuse to say no. "Certainly," she said politely, and to her shock, he pulled her into a close dance position rather than open, one hand possessively at her waist, the other clasping hers.

She had to tip her chin up unexpectedly far to keep locked to his gaze and she was baffled that he didn't seem the slightest bit uncomfortable meeting her eyes.

For a few phrases of music, he led her effortlessly through the steps and Scarlet had to resist the urge to close her eyes and simply float blissfully in his strong arms. Her partners were usually more cautious with her, careful and afraid. He guided her out into a flashy spin and back in again.

Scarlet attempted to regain control of the situation when the music slowed. "Mal, is that short for Malcolm?" she asked conversationally, as if she didn't feel the slightest bit giddy.

He laughed, deep and intoxicating, and shook his head. "I should be so lucky," he said. He lowered his head as if he was imparting a great secret. "My given name is Normal."

Scarlet, suspecting a joke, chuckled. "Surely it isn't."

He sighed dramatically. "It is, I swear."

"Did your parents have such high aspirations for you?" Scarlet asked archly.

"They were forced into it. Dragon honor, you know."

He turned her, and for a moment Scarlet held her breath, wondering if he would dip her. He didn't, but there was a pause in the music where he simply held her and Scarlet felt like every nerve in her body was awake for the first time in decades and she was made entirely of all the longing she fought so hard to keep in check.

Then they were dancing a simple back and forth again and he continued. "When my mother was pregnant with me, she was crossing a busy street and tripped in front of an oncoming bus. She would surely have been hit and died if it weren't for a young man who pulled her out of the way. My father asked for his name, because in these cases, the least they were obligated to do was name me after him, but he refused, shrugging and saying that he was just a normal guy, doing the right thing."

"So they named you *Normal*?" Scarlet really did laugh then, and Mal grinned at her in a way that made her tingle to her toes.

She dampened her merriment with determination, but could not quite keep from smiling back at him. "Most people would go with their middle name in such cases," Scarlet observed.

"I assure you, my middle name is even worse," Mal said with a suffering sigh. There was something familiar about his voice...

The music was swelling again and he led her into a turn away from him so that Scarlet was looking away when everything crashed into place and she finally realized who this had to be.

Normal. *Normal* Moore, with an unlikely middle name and a common last name. N. Moore. N. *Padrikanth* Moore, Beehag's vindictive lawyer: the man who had been attempting to roust her from the island for more than a year, trying to woo away her staff and destroy her business.

Scarlet slipped from his grip and had to temper her desire to turn and punch him in the middle of the dance floor. She had stalked halfway across the hall to the far exit when he caught her—or tried to.

"Scarlet," he called. "Wait!" He seemed puzzled when he couldn't catch her arm. She wasn't about to let him touch her again.

She turned and met his eyes with blazing fury.

"Get out," she said quietly between gritted teeth. "Get out of my resort and off my island." It was a growl, and no part of the threat was *veiled*.

He should have backed off. Anyone else would have left his bags and *fled* in the face of her anger.

But Mal, *N. Padrikanth Moore*, only stepped *forward*. "I have a reservation," he said, maddeningly.

And dammit, he did. *Mal* Moore was a registered guest, with a signed contract, and Scarlet was forced to honor that.

"You are a guest," she conceded, furious. "Cottage four. It's unlocked, I'll have a key delivered to you in the morning. If you have *business* with me, you can make an appointment and I will see you with my lawyer. You have her number."

"I need to speak with you about the offer you made," Mal said swiftly.

"You can't stop me," Scarlet snarled and this time she was the one who stepped forward, every inch of her bristling in challenge. "You can try your dirty tricks and your pretty promises on someone else, but you will *never* take this place from me."

The hall was silent. Scarlet wasn't sure if the song had ended or if the musicians had simply stopped playing, but she was suddenly aware that all of the guests and all of the staff were watching from the other end of the hall.

"Scarlet," he said, too quietly for them to hear, "please stop being so *stubborn*."

That was the voice she knew from dozens of staticky phone calls: that infuriatingly superior attitude, that pretense of being reasonable.

"You are a *guest*," Scarlet repeated through clenched teeth. "Please enjoy the amenities we have to offer and contact a member of the staff if you have any problems or questions."

Then she was stalking away, through the door, and gone.

CHAPTER 3

Mal did not sleep well, despite the luxurious bed and its billion thread-count Egyptian cotton sheets, and he lay in them long after the sun rose, trying to make sense of everything.

His thoughts kept returning to the betrayal and anger that had bloomed in Scarlet's face when she realized who he was, and the soft, yearning laughter that fiery look had replaced.

She was so beautiful, so powerful. Those green eyes, that glossy hair that no photograph did justice to… He longed to see if she tasted as potent as she felt, to bury his fingers in her hair, to lay her down and claim her.

She is ours, his dragon rumbled, but Mal remembered the fury in her face and knew that it was more complicated than that.

Mal was not used to second-guessing his methods or questioning his own decisions, but he found himself thinking over every interaction they'd ever had. Had he done her as wrong as she was clearly convinced he had?

He rolled out of the bed and stalked to the desk where he'd left a folder open the night before.

The top photo was a candid, close-up shot of a beautiful woman with candy-red hair wearing a crown of deep green holly.

Scarlet Stanson.

His mate.

She was smiling in this photo, as she was not in so many of her others.

Mal frowned thoughtfully in return.

He understood people, especially shifters. He knew how they worked and what made them tick. After more decades than he cared to admit as a lawyer, he could predict what they would do under pressure with eerie accuracy, and he used that knowledge to his advantage.

But he didn't understand Scarlet Stanson.

He shuffled back to an older photograph, faded with age. It was another Christmas shot; a pine tree in the background was draped in old fashioned lights and tinsel. Scarlet's hair, nut brown, was swept up in exactly the same bun and she looked like someone had surprised her.

Last night hadn't been the first time she'd surprised *him.*

She had failed at every turn to fall into the patterns he had expected of her, bucked his expectations and thwarted his plans.

And she wasn't just a small problem.

The island was never meant to have been developed. Alistair Beehag's private compound was bad enough, but a resort? And not just a quiet, garden variety resort. Beehag's partner, Lord Aaric Lyons, had built a luxury resort designed just for shifters.

Mal had been glad when Lyons vanished and the resort stalled out before he had to interfere. He spent a few years working his way into the Beehag family as their lawyer and was as alarmed as they were when Scarlet Stanson mysteriously reappeared. She had brilliant red hair but didn't look a day older and she pointed out the language in a binding contract for lease that even he could not find loopholes in. Within a year, she had the resort opened for business.

Still, he thought he had time. Decades even, and Mal had always excelled at the long game.

So he waited for her to fail on her own and was surprised when she didn't. She collected a fascinating array of skilled staff, finished the half-built resort in remarkable time, and courted in a chef who could have cooked in the finest restaurants anywhere in the world.

When Alistair Beehag's atrocious shifter collection—a terrible zoo where shifters were forced to remain in their animal form—had been uncovered and the prisoners released, Mal had been furious and had nearly taken the opportunity to rid himself of *all* the problems on the island at once.

But Scarlet unexpectedly took in all the refugees from Beehag's menagerie, before Mal could step in. Mal had been so shocked by the act that he put the rest of his plans on hold, sparing the resort until he saw how the chips fell out.

It was a stunningly poor business move. The resort had barely begun to establish itself, and yet she'd chosen to run her finances—Mal had access to all of them—dangerously into the red in an act of pointless charity. She tied up dozens of rooms that could otherwise have been booked for people who would never be in a position to repay her and hemorrhaged thousands of dollars a day to feed them, clothe them, and send them back to their old lives when they were ready.

None of them were important people, none of them had connections that would serve her. She'd done it, as far as Mal could tell, completely selflessly. She was too smart not to realize how thin she'd stretched herself, even if she appeared to keep the true depths of her debts—already considerable—secret from the staff.

And she didn't give up.

Instead, she hooked a contract for a male shifter beauty pageant, with impressive and flattering media coverage, and business boomed. She even managed to host one of the highest profile shifter weddings in decades.

Mal picked up the newest edition of *Night Shift*, a glossy shifter gossip magazine and had to smile wryly at the splashy cover. A giant cave bear and a leopard were facing off and a distraught bride in the background wearing pounds of jewelry was wringing her hands. Guests were fleeing and potted plants were toppling.

Scarlet didn't feature much in the photos; she was a blurry, bright-haired figure in the background at most, but Mal had gotten several first-hand accounts of the tawdry event. The wedding had dissolved into chaos, the bride had run away with a waiter, and Scarlet had shared choice words with the mother of the bride publicly, quoted in damning detail within the article. The lawsuit that had been filed against the resort was a veritable tome of complaint; a copy of it sat on his desk next to the folder.

Mal almost felt guilty for his part in the pandemonium.

Almost.

The waiter, Breck, still worked at the resort with his runaway bride. As did the washed up mermaid, Saina, the twin sisters Jenny and Laura (who had fled here from the mob), and Wrench, the brute with the unsavory past who had tried to kidnap the wrong one of them for money.

Scarlet had shown them all utterly illogical compassion and they had returned her trust with loyalty that gave Mal considerable pause; they had denied every tempting offer he had dangled in front of them and ignored every subtle attempt to sow discord.

All because of Scarlet.

And Scarlet herself was a cypher. How had she managed to win such devotion from her staff? She had even convinced Grant Lyons to shake off his identity as Graham Long and claim his first right of refusal to buy the island itself. The staff had scrounged the exorbitant price of the sale in nickels and dimes and gifted it to her in entirety.

Mal trailed his hand across the offer that they'd sent, shaking his head in grudging admiration, and then began to get dressed. Mal had managed to keep a life insurance policy owed to Laura and Jenny tied up in paperwork for almost a year and he'd scared two buyers off from buying Conall's business—Conall was a permanent resident retiring from a life of celebrity as a classic musician who had built a business empire and given it all up to settle down on the island with his skittish mate Gizelle, one of the longest imprisoned and most damaged residents of Beehag's cruel menagerie.

But Mal hadn't counted on Magnolia, another of the resort's permanent residents, reconciling with her royal family and regaining access to her inheritance, or on a third buyer for Conall's music empire appearing out of the woodwork while he was still busy with the second.

He had no legal recourse to stop the sale.

It was downright sloppy of him to let them get this far, build this much hope.

Then there was the fact that Scarlet was, completely beyond expectation, his *mate*.

She was so beautiful, so strong, so... vulnerable.

And she was going to be *crushed* when the resort inevitably fell.

A knock at the door interrupted the unavoidable spiral of his thoughts.

He opened the door to find a curvy, dark-skinned woman holding out a key and a brochure.

"Ms. Smith," he greeted.

She smirked at him. "That's a safe guess," she said mockingly. "But it's my sister you'll be needing to see if you have any business to discuss."

This was Laura then, the wolf shifter who had married the cowboy bartender, identical twin to the lawyer Jenny. "Thank you," Mal said gravely, accepting the items. The resort hadn't upgraded to keycards; it was an actual key on a large wooden keychain.

"Breakfast is open for another few hours," Laura added. "Scarlet said you are to be treated exactly like any other guest and that you are… *welcome*… to enjoy the amenities."

Her emphasis suggested that *welcome* was not exactly what he could expect, but Mal only said, "I appreciate it."

Once she left, he was dismayed to find that he was hungry. It had been a long flight the night before and his dragon's appetite was considerable… even if food was his second choice.

The restaurant was not terribly busy, but several of the tables were in use when Mal arrived. He seated himself at the edge of the deck, overlooking the bar and the pool beyond.

The waiter, sharply dressed, plunked a glass of ice water down in front of him and gave him a distinctly unfriendly appraisal. "Chef is making custom omelets this morning. We have most ingredients you could want in stock to build your own, or you can choose from a Denver—a proper Denver, with no cheese—or a vegetable lovers that uses what's fresh with mozzarella. Do you need a moment to decide?"

He waltzed to the next table without waiting for Mal's answer and spent notably longer chatting up the guests and flirting with the matron of the group.

Breck. Mal remembered vividly his role in the recent wedding disaster and he was amused to note the dragon runes that circled one of Breck's wrists when he reached to refill a water glass. Mal fingered the long sleeves of his own light bamboo shirt thoughtfully.

The waiter took the order for the second table back to the kitchen, served a third table, refilled drinks throughout the restaurant, and finally returned to Mal's table, his slight obvious. "Have you decided?" He did not offer to refill the half-empty water glass, despite the towel-wrapped pitcher he held.

"Vegetable with a side of bacon," Mal said serenely. "Coffee."

"There's bacon at the buffet," Breck said dismissively, and he turned coldly away.

Mal did not expect his meal to come without a generous seasoning of spit and briefly considered feeding himself solely from the buffet. It was clear that the staff knew exactly who he was and had no qualms making sure that he knew exactly how little they cared for his presence.

It wasn't entirely unexpected.

He'd already tested their loyalty to Scarlet and found it impenetrable. It must look, from their narrow view, as if he had some kind of vendetta against her, or against the resort itself.

The omelet came cold and late, neither of which could quite disguise the quality of it. The vegetables were stunningly fresh and perfectly cooked and the white cheese was a good pair with the fluffy eggs. It was served, despite Breck's earlier brush-off, with a generous platter of thick, salty bacon, and a stout cup of strong, good quality coffee (also nearly cold).

Mal ate it without complaint and did not bring attention to his empty water glass, despite Breck's several circuits of the room with the pitcher.

He left his starched napkin on the table when he had finished and went to the railing that overlooked the bar and the glimmering pool below that. It was a tasteful paradise, with shining tile, perfectly groomed foliage, and grand, Greek-style columns.

It was really no wonder Scarlet didn't want to let go of it.

Mal leaned onto the railing, then shifted as he kicked off, launching from the deck on mottled golden dragon wings. Sunbathers around the sapphire pool looked up in wonder as his dragon form passed over, gleaming in the sun.

Showing off a bit? Mal asked. Mythical creatures were usually invisible to humans and regular shifters, but they could choose to be seen.

She should see and admire us, his dragon said smugly as they circled over the resort. *The light here is flattering.*

We have work to do, Mal reminded him. *Let's focus.*

CHAPTER 4

Scarlet stalked into the early afternoon senior staff meeting and glared them to silence.

They stared back, clearly dying of curiosity over the events of the night before but not quite willing to ask.

"The resort will be at just over sixty percent capacity this week," she said coolly. "We've got a request in for a whale spotting tour later this afternoon—Travis, can I put you down for that?"

Travis agreed. "Not a problem. The solar panel on cottage seven just needs to be wired in, and that's the last one."

Scarlet nodded. It had been an expensive investment and the panels were only installed at a few cottages so far, but if they could start moving away from pricey fuels that had to be imported from the mainland, it would be worth it. If she could just keep her resort long enough to see the payoff… she caught her hands curling into fists as she thought about Mal… *N. Padrikanth Moore.*

"We have two guests of particular note coming in on the morning charter," Scarlet said, consulting her notes with a scowl. "One is an elderly domestic cat shifter who has mobility issues. I've talked with her companion and will be putting her at cottage twenty-two. Liam, that's right there next to your elders, because we've got the most access infrastructure in that area and it won't involve stairs to reach the restaurant."

Liam, who was in charge of a small shifter retirement community within the resort, nodded agreeably. "I'll reach out and see if she's interested in some of the activities we've got scheduled. She can take meals with our crew, if that's convenient."

Scarlet nodded crisply. "Thank you. The other guest requiring special consideration is a fire ant shifter. I want any pest control to be extremely careful this week. I would like to maintain our good record of not having squashed any guests."

There was a cautious wave of chuckles through the room, and then expectant silence.

Scarlet, knowing what they were really dying to ask, nodded instead at the large, gray-haired man sitting at the side of the room in an apron. "Chef, if you'd like to start off our department reports."

She remained standing as he confirmed the status of inventory. He added, "I'd like to have Travis look at the grill; I feel like it's acting a little sluggish, not running quite as hot as usual. Oh! And I'm down fifty pounds of salt. I'll need to have some picked up from the mainland before the end of the week."

Scarlet furrowed her brow at him. "Fifty *pounds*?" Chef was usually excellent at inventory management and this was a significant quantity.

"An unopened bag went missing from storage yesterday. I've looked every place it might have accidentally been put, but it's just gone."

"Stolen?" Wrench asked swiftly. Scarlet had placed the tattooed panther shifter in charge of security and he was taking his new duties very seriously. There was almost no crime at the resort, and she rarely needed additional enforcement, but she suspected that it would give the guests peace of mind to know that there was someone in charge of such matters. Most of all, it made Wrench feel like he had a purpose; he refused to take his mosaic art seriously, though Scarlet was encouraging him to continue his work.

"Who would steal salt?" Travis asked, laughing. "The whole bag costs less than ten dollars, and there's not much black market use for it."

"Someone with a vendetta against snails?" Breck suggested.

Others chuckled, Scarlet made a note to order the salt, and the meeting passed to Breck, who gave an entertaining report about the service schedules, and then to Graham.

"If you're going to borrow my tools, you'd better put them back," the lion shifter growled. "I'm missing a shovel from the uphill storage room. Putting in two new beds of herbs, have a surplus of lettuce, the lower paths need raking, I'll get on that tomorrow before it's too hot."

"Salt and now a shovel! It's an out-of-control crime spree!" Breck observed drolly. "Wrench, you'd better get on this!"

Wrench gave a grunt that might have been a laugh.

"No one would steal from Grant Lyons, King of the Jungle," Travis joked. "A shovel made of pure gold wouldn't be worth that risk."

A swift smile crossed Graham's face at the sound of his previous name and fighting title; he had somehow found a sense of humor when he'd met his mate, Alice, and Scarlet caught a smile of her own briefly on her face.

Smiling managed to remind her of Mal, of his self-assured grin and the feeling of his hand at her waist.

"Lydia," she said, more sharply than she meant to. "Anything we should be aware of at the spa?"

She only caught about half of Lydia's report, stewing over the sheer gall of Mal Moore, showing up here, at her resort, under the guise of being a guest. What did he think he could accomplish in person that he couldn't over dozens of phone calls and letters? In what world did he think that he could convince her not to go forward with the offer for the resort? He must be desperate, knowing that he had no legal recourse to stop her.

Or maybe he thought that his charms could persuade her in person where they'd failed over distance?

Scarlet didn't realize how angry she had gotten until she

snapped the pen she was holding and everyone went silent and stared at her.

"Thank you, Lydia," she said as mildly as she could manage. "Tex?"

Tex drawled a bar report, requesting some mixers and reporting a broken tap for Travis to look into.

"Is there any other business?" Scarlet finally asked, finishing her notes with half a pen.

There was a brief moment of anticipatory silence, then Breck asked boldly, "I don't know… *is* there any other business?"

Scarlet glowered at him. "I think we're done here," she said dismissively.

She left the room swiftly and heard the conversation lift into gossip and speculation behind her.

~

"Thank you for playing last night," Scarlet said to Conall sincerely, gravely accepting his offer of a glass of water. "Performing has never been a part of your contract and I don't want to take advantage of your kindness."

Conall poured them each a glass of water from the icy pitcher at the small kitchenette. "I don't feel taken advantage of," he assured Scarlet as he turned back and gave her the glass. "It's a pleasure to be able to play again." He gave the young woman in the living room a quick, amused smile, but she didn't notice.

Gizelle was lying on her belly on the couch, engrossed in something on her tablet. Her bare legs were up in the air behind her, ankles crossed, and there were headphones over her ears. The cord, Scarlet noticed, had been chewed on, probably by Gizelle's kitten, Sweet One. The young gray cat was on the back of the sofa just above Gizelle, curled up asleep.

Scarlet smiled as they sat across from each other at the dining room table. "They were extremely excited to have played with you." Conall, as a young musician, had been on a skyrocket to success. He produced several bestselling albums and garnered several awards before a car accident stole his hearing.

He had come to Shifting Sands a bitter, angry man, resentful of his loss and disenchanted with the fast-paced, highly successful business life he had tried to use to replace music.

Gizelle had changed everything for him.

Shy and frightened, his mate had lived all of her life imprisoned by a madman, trapped in her gazelle form. She had no memory of the time before her rescue and few social skills. Neal Byrne, one of her fellow prisoners who had been key in releasing the inmates of the zoo, had helped coax her back to human shape, but it was Conall's love that had made her truly bloom.

Her greatest gift to him in return was arguably the ability to hear again; when she touched him, particularly skin to skin, he could hear again, using her ears.

But Scarlet was fairly sure that his ability to smile again was actually the most precious thing that Gizelle had given him.

He was smiling now and he put his hand across the table to take the paperwork that Scarlet had put down. He had to scoot the papers around a curious centerpiece: a heavy lump of unattractive metal that had once been a lock on one of the cages of the zoo where Gizelle had been imprisoned. It had been a gift from her, the most precious item of her possession. Conall sometimes carried it with him, despite its awkwardness, and it had been fitted with a carabiner to hang off his belt.

"These are the revisions to the lease, provisional to the purchase of the island." Scarlet let herself feel a moment of grateful wonder and anticipation. The idea that she would own the island and never have to worry about it being taken from her again was still fresh and new.

"Beehag hasn't accepted the offer yet?" Conall said, glancing through the paperwork.

"He has thirty days to accept per the contract," Scarlet said as serenely as she could manage, remembering the feeling of Mal's hand at her waist as they danced instead of how he had tried to weasel the resort away from her. "Jenny says there's no reason they shouldn't simply accept, but I suspect Beehag's lawyer will wait the full window just to be a jerk about it." An unexpectedly *hot* jerk, it turned out.

"How is she?" Scarlet asked, lowering her voice. She didn't have to worry about Conall hearing her; without Gizelle's touch he couldn't hear her at all and was relying on his ability to read her lips.

"She's nervous about something," Conall said honestly in return.

"Neal…?" Gizelle had been anxious about Neal's return to the resort to marry his mate Mary; she had changed so much since he had left and come so far from the gazelle who wouldn't shift to human.

Conall shook his head firmly. "She talked with him before their wedding and as far as I can tell, that's all fine now. No, this is…" he shrugged, looking over at the couch where Gizelle's bare feet suggested she couldn't hear anything outside of her earphones. "It's getting hard to hear," he said thoughtfully. "The background noises she hears are getting worse. It's like being surrounded by a hundred radios playing different stations that are mostly tuned to static, and they've all gone up a notch lately."

"The voices of more shifter animals," Scarlet suggested. It had been a surprise to the staff when Conall revealed that Gizelle could hear their animals. Conall had been quick to explain that it wasn't anything that could be considered eavesdropping—only when she touched a shifter did their animal's voice come into focus.

"Sometimes I think it's more than that," he said reluctantly. "It's been getting… louder? Clearer? There are more voices, even though there are no more guests? It's hard to pinpoint. And…" Conall looked uncomfortable. "She's been talking about the end."

"Death?" Scarlet glanced at Gizelle's feet, her fragile toes flexing. "It's a concept she may only be starting to understand. There are so many things that she's never faced before." She had a pang of empathy. "It's a big world and there's so much I wish she could be sheltered from."

Conall frowned at her mouth and Scarlet wondered if she would need to repeat herself until Conall shook his head. "She doesn't seem to be fixated on death, she seems very matter-of-fact that the end—her end—is coming, and she talks about things that are her fault, and how she's got to figure out how to fix things. Her fugue states are happening more often lately, like they're getting harder for her to ignore."

Scarlet frowned in sympathy. "There's so much we don't understand about her." She finished her water. "Is there anything I can do to help?"

Conall shook his head and stood to gather their glasses. "I will read over the revisions and let you know if I have any changes after I've conferred with my lawyer," he promised.

Theirs was an efficient friendship, Scarlet thought with amusement as she stood. They didn't tend to waste words, but their mutual affection for Gizelle gave them a broad common ground that they had built a sturdy companionship upon. She was grateful for that friendship, even as it left her craving for something deeper.

Her thoughts returned without bidding to Mal—Mr. Moore.

She stood, dismissing her thoughts fiercely. Mal Moore was a thorn in her side, a problem to be dealt with, not danced with. "Thank you. Let me know if you have any concerns."

As she walked past the couch, Gizelle suddenly slipped off her headphones and fixed her with a wide-eyed look as she righted herself. "Do you know about sonic booms?" There was a physics lesson paused on her tablet.

"A little," Scarlet said. Physics had never been a topic of particular interest, but she had slogged through a few years of study. "It was a long time ago."

Gizelle was happy to explain, bouncing to her feet. "All the sounds want to go fast but they can only go one speed, the speed of sound, and they get all backed up in one wave that hits you at once and it's like a great big explosion."

"It really is fascinating," Scarlet agreed. Gizelle's enthusiasm was contagious.

"Can people make sonic booms? They're all trying to go so fast, but can only go the one speed through time. Will they get all backed up and explode, too?"

Scarlet looked at Conall helplessly, but Gizelle was speaking obliquely and he couldn't read her lips.

"I have no idea," Scarlet said. "But it certainly paints a vivid picture."

"No," Gizelle said thoughtfully. "Not a picture, a song." Then she scolded, "Oh, Sweet One, no!" because the kitten, startled out of sleep, had slipped down onto the couch and was extending a paw at the headphone cable. "Conall has already bought me three of those!"

Scarlet chuckled as she slipped out of the door; she had already gone through at least a half dozen of her own various cables thanks to Sweet One's sister, Tyrant. It had amused everyone when the cream-colored cat had attached herself to Scarlet instead of Gizelle, and Scarlet was grateful for the companionship, even while she sometimes found herself frustrated by the creature's destructiveness.

Outside of Conall and Gizelle's cottage, Scarlet turned her feet to the central path running up the resort and she allowed herself a moment of pride looking up over the resort. White columns and glossy tiles graced the gorgeous central buildings of the resort and everywhere, verdant green trees and flowering bushes cast cooling shadows and provided pockets of privacy.

She'd done well, she thought.

The resort was finally thriving, and—her heart squeezed—it was finally almost *hers*, outright. It was a safe place, the haven for shifters that she'd always imagined it could be. It was just the right touch of luxury and practicality, beauty and durability.

Mal's presence here... surely that was just some final bluster before the sale was finalized. He couldn't stop her, he didn't have any legal leg left. And if he was hoping to come win her with his admittedly considerable masculine charms, he was about to find out exactly how practiced she was in ignoring the desires of her body.

CHAPTER 5

Mal pivoted on a wingtip and flew over the crescent of golden sand beach, then followed the edge of the sea on the west coast of the island.

He extended his senses, the runes etched into his scales momentarily flaring with light.

The flow of power was as bad as he'd feared coming in the night before. It was like looking at a bad light ballast in a dark room, dim and flickering. The spell he had come to renew—a spell that should be steady for decades more—was *failing*.

Another little white beach opened up, a tiny half-circle bisected by a river that snaked from a beautiful waterfall. Cliffs on all sides isolated it. Under other circumstances, Mal might have been tempted to stop and bask in the warm sunlight.

But worry drew him on, the island rising to his right, the ocean stretching to his left, as he flew north. The dock for Beehag's compound appeared and Mal swung inland and rose into the air with powerful wingbeats, following the steep, winding road.

The compound was half-destroyed; the Phoenix had done his work well, and the zoo had been scorched to the earth in many places; no full cages remained. The arboretum was crumbling. The lawns that had been so tidy and well-groomed when Mal had last been here, many years ago, were overgrown.

There was a beaten-down area in the center of the zoo, the grass trampled to brown.

Mal circled it curiously, then reconciled it with the Civil Guard report he'd intercepted the week before; this would be where the fighting ring had operated, pitting Grant Lyons in a handicapped revenge match.

With wingbeats that raised dust, Mal found the sturdiest of the remaining walls and perched.

He shifted back to human.

From his vantage point, he could see the encroaching rainforest. The rain must not be as frequent here; it seemed less vividly green than the jungle that ringed the resort.

He gave a casual murmur and gestured. Energy overlaid his sight once again.

This was a passive spell; he didn't wish to further muddy the evidence, or cause more damage inadvertently. He paced to one end of the wall and stared down at the burned zoo.

It hadn't been long since a great battle had taken place here. Mal already knew the story behind it: the Eternal Phoenix had fought a human wizard here, and Mal's mouth curled in fury to think of it.

Corbin, the wizard, had wielded a perverted kind of enchantment. Because he was human and had no magical reserves of his own, he had captured and bound shifters, draining them to collapse for his own evil purposes. His attempt to bind the Phoenix had ultimately backfired on him.

Traces of the Phoenix's magic teased at the edges of his vision, and Corbin's contaminated power was like a distasteful oily smear over the entire area, rainbow hued with the flavors of the mythic shifters he and his followers had been draining.

Corbin, Mal thought in disgust. Corbin could be the cause of this disruption. With his ham-handed, stolen shreds of magic, he might have disturbed the spell that was carefully laid so far below.

Mal could tell, just from the evidence left, that Corbin had been loud, unconstrained, unrefined. But it didn't feel… focused. He'd been a child with a canon, so self-absorbed and noisy that he probably hadn't even *realized* there was anything beneath the island.

Beneath him, the ground suddenly rumbled, and the trees shuddered. The wall he was on even swayed for a moment. Then, as quickly as it had come, the earthquake was over, leaving Mal coursing with adrenaline.

He centered himself, once the earth stopped moving and he was sure the danger had passed.

Curious, his dragon said as an understatement. His voice had a current of worry, which was itself worrisome. Mal's dragon was a well of confidence; apprehension rarely intruded from that quarter.

Mal gathered himself and shifted as he leaped from the wall, a strong downbeat of his wings bringing him into the air over the compound.

He flew back to the resort following the east coast, over the primitive airstrip, along the winding road to the resort.

After the abandoned and destroyed Beehag property, the resort was like a gleaming jewel, beautiful and perfect. But Mal's dragon, for once, was not interested in beauty; he was focused on the low building at the top of the resort with the open courtyard.

Our mate, he insisted. *We have to get her away from here.*

With effort, Mal kept him from landing at Scarlet's office and trying to force her into fleeing with them. *We have some time*, he reminded his dragon. And he already knew that trying to force Scarlet to do anything was a losing game.

Not much time, his dragon countered unhappily. *She is our treasure. We must get her off this island.*

CHAPTER 6

Scarlet glared out over the resort through her office window after she righted the pots that had toppled in the brief earthquake. Tyrant jumped up on the pillow she kept there and Scarlet petted her absently.

She couldn't feel Mal, which meant he wasn't at the resort, or anywhere on her half of the island.

That should be a good thing, she reminded herself. Maybe he'd packed his bags and flown home, knowing a losing battle when he faced it.

But she'd seen the amusement in his eyes, and the determination. She already knew he wasn't going to give up that easily.

Her traitor body still remembered the feeling of his hand at her waist and her fingers remembered the muscles under his dress coat.

Mal…

That was her problem. She was thinking of Mal, when she should be thinking of Mr. Moore. *Mr. Moore* was a voice on the phone that never came with good news. *Mr. Moore* was the lawyer who tried to buy the resort out from under her with drug dealers and mercenaries. *Mr. Moore* was the one making offers too good to be true for whatever nefarious purpose he clearly needed the resort for.

Mal was a different kind of problem altogether.

Tyrant reached a paw up for Scarlet's hand and extended her claws just enough to prick skin.

Scarlet obediently resumed petting her.

"I'm an idiot," Scarlet told her fiercely, then turned away. If Mal—Mr. Moore—wasn't at the resort right now, she could conduct her usual business without fear of—

Scarlet stopped herself furiously. She *wasn't* afraid.

What on earth was there to be afraid of? Mal—Mr. Moore—had no power over her. That he was here at all was an admission that all of his usual ways had failed him. The island would be hers, the resort would be hers, all of her dreams were on the brink of happening.

All of her dreams except…

Scarlet scowled and went at once to the back entrance of the kitchen, startling Darla with her approach.

The once-heiress was emptying trash into the bin, sorting out reusables, recyclables, and compost from what little would actually have to be taken to the mainland for disposal. She had a handkerchief around her strawberry-blond hair and she looked up in surprise. "I didn't hear you coming," she said, visibly alarmed and a little afraid.

Scarlet tempered her furious expression. She wasn't angry with Darla and the young woman already felt responsible for the lawsuit hanging over the resort. "I'm sorry to alarm you," she said politely. "Is Chef still in?"

"He is. They're doing some prep work for dinner." Darla looked like she was resisting the urge to curtsy, despite being covered in trash, and Scarlet strode past to go inside.

The kitchen was relatively empty; it was always busy for the catered breakfast and dinner, but midday was often quiet, with minimal wait staff attending the buffet.

Breck and Chef were merrily discussing the dinner menu.

"I don't suppose he's allergic to anything," Breck was proposing.

"I wouldn't mind watching him get all puffy-faced and choke a little."

Scarlet didn't have to ask who they were talking about. "I am quite certain you are not discussing how best to poison a *guest*," she said in utterly icy tones.

They both turned and looked at her. From the way they blanched, she realized she was glowering again and she forced herself to resume a serene expression.

"I'm sure I don't need to remind you that we are here to accommodate our guests, and that we will *uniformly* treat them with respect and cater to their various needs." She kept her voice level and reasonable.

Breck, who was never terribly good at hiding his feelings, looked like she'd just kicked him and she knew that she'd struck a nerve. She smothered the satisfaction it gave her to think of Mal—*Mr. Moore*—getting Breck's cold shoulder.

"I expect to receive no complaints about our level of service or the quality of our product," Scarlet said firmly, including Chef in her statement.

Even he looked chagrined.

"I assure you—" he began.

"Don't mind me," Tex sang out from the door. "I'm just going to be up here 'getting ingredients' for about an hour while Mr. Asshole Lawyer cools his heels by the—" He spotted Scarlet at that moment, and Scarlet realized that she could sense Mal—*Mr. Moore, dammit*—on the bar deck.

That he'd gotten there without her noticing bothered her almost as much noticing him now did. Scarlet slammed a fist onto the counter hard enough to make the plates rattle, but not hard enough to dent it. "You are not to harass the man!" she snarled. "I should not have to remind any of you how to be professionals!"

The kitchen, which had been quiet, went utterly silent.

Tex finally cleared his throat and someone began noisily washing dishes near the back of the kitchen. "Yes, Ma'am," the bartender said sheepishly.

"The dinner we serve him will be beyond reproach," Chef assured her.

"He shall not lack for a clean napkin or fresh water," Breck promised meekly.

Scarlet drew in a careful breath and unclenched her fist.

She was clearly overreacting.

They were all not quite looking at her and they had to recognize how unreasonable she was being. Did they think this was just because his presence meant some new bid to take the resort from her? Or did they know that she couldn't stop thinking about how he had danced with her and how his hand had felt in hers?

Scarlet kept herself from blushing with effort and cleared her throat. "Chef, I came to ask about your breakfast plans the next few days. A few of Liam's elders would like access to the kitchen one morning when the workload isn't high in order to do some baking. Mrs. Salvator's 100th birthday is coming up and they were hoping to make cupcakes."

"We can do a pancake day the day after tomorrow," Chef suggested. "That's fairly simple and will leave the ovens free."

"Very well," Scarlet said, as if she weren't helplessly imagining Mal's—Mr. Moore's—hand at her waist and the way he had smiled at her. A smug smile, she reminded herself. Which meant he thought he had the upper hand.

Which meant…

Which meant…?

Scarlet couldn't make sense of it. Why come here? What did he know that she didn't? She was scowling at Chef, she realized. "I'll inform Liam," she said, trying to pull herself together.

Everyone returned to their work and Scarlet wandered out to the restaurant before she recognized that she was unconsciously heading towards Mal like she was being drawn on a string.

She turned on her heel to leave and was caught instead by a guest who wanted to share suggestions for the amenities provided in their shower.

CHAPTER 7

Mal was not really expecting service at the bar when he landed there. After his experience at breakfast, he knew better than to hope for the friendly welcome that Shifting Sands had cultivated a reputation for. He was a *persona non grata* and until he had a chance to explain himself to Scarlet, he didn't expect that to change.

He wanted to find her and get this conversation out of the way, but he had to admit that he'd been shaken by his findings at Beehag's compound. A drink to settle him, and then he'd make a plan of attack. He took a beer from the cooler after the bartender's brush-off and settled into a chair near the railing that looked down over the pool.

Two giggling young women were standing near the top of the steps holding diet sodas and a short man full of attitude was trying to hold a conversation with them.

"That dragon thinks he's impressive," he was saying, nodding at the glistening green dragon acting as a lifeguard on the beach. "But pound for pound, I've got him beat with my ability to cause pain." He flexed a muscle at the nearest woman and she looked embarrassed for him. "Can you guess what I am?"

"No?" said one of the women, clearly not wanting to guess.

"Give it a shot," the man coaxed. "First one's free."

"Snake?" the other guessed with a shrug.

"Not even close," he scoffed.

"Scorpion?" the first one guessed with an ill-concealed eyeroll.

"Closer…" the man teased. When neither woman seemed interested in further speculation, he added, "People are much more terrified of me than either of those."

The women made non-committal noises and looked around for escape. Mal considered stepping in, but they only looked uncomfortable, not afraid, and now he was curious.

He didn't have to wait long.

"Fire ant," the man said smugly. "Most painful sting of any animal in the world."

The women stared.

"Do you turn into a whole swarm of them?" one asked in morbid curiosity.

The man looked confused. "Er, no."

The women exchanged amused looks and Mal could not help chuckling. While the man shot him an unappreciative look, the women escaped down the steps to the pool, their whispers and giggles trailing behind them.

Passing them on her way up was Gizelle, her hair in two untidy braids.

The fire ant shifter gave her a speculative look, but when the woman shot him a wary look and skirted along the far railing away from him in a very obvious fashion, he shrugged and went to the bar.

Mal watched Gizelle make a wide circuit of the bar, then creep around behind him. He was keenly aware of her as she circled him and finally came to stand tentatively at the table beside him. Her hands were shaking just a little.

"I remember you from the end," she said, her silky voice exactly as Mal had imagined it.

The cryptic statement cemented a suspicion that Mal had been nursing, but it didn't make him feel any better.

"You're Gizelle," Mal said gently. He was careful to keep his motions slow as he gestured to the chair. "Would you like to sit with me?"

She considered him so long that Mal was sure she was going to refuse, then, to his delight, slipped into the chair and folded herself cross-legged upon it. He had expected that it would take several tries before she trusted him enough to have a conversation.

"You're the one who sent the photographs," she said. "Tex said bad words about you and Scarlet was very angry."

She was staring hard at him and Mal thoughtfully returned her unsettling regard. "I did send the photographs," Mal admitted. "And I've discovered more about your parents since then."

Her breath caught in her throat, all of her longing bare upon her face. "Tell me…" she whispered.

Mal broke their gaze to glance around. The bartender who had gone to 'get ingredients' from the kitchen was still gone and the fire ant shifter had wandered down to the pool to try his luck with one of the sunbathers. They were, for the moment, alone on the bar deck.

"Your mother…"

"... Janine…" Gizelle sighed. "I read everything you sent. I can read now."

"Janine," Mal agreed. "She was a cockatrice shifter."

"I don't know what that is," Gizelle admitted.

"The cockatrice is a great dragon-like creature shaped a little like a bird. It has withering breath in its mythical shape, and in either form it can metaphorically turn a person to stone."

"Metaphorically?" Gizelle said sharply.

"That's when something is similar to something else, but not…" Mal started to explain.

"I know what a metaphor is," Gizelle said dismissively. "How did she turn people to stone?"

Mal found himself re-evaluating the young woman; it would be easy to assume she was simple, especially given the shy way she moved, but her gaze was sharp and knowing, if unnervingly unwavering.

"Her glance would make people afraid," Mal told her. "And with a gaze, she could trap them in their own mind, lock them away in a single memory of her choosing. Their hair would turn white and they would be like a statue, lost forever in a moment of time."

Gizelle drew in a breath, and reached for her temple, twisting her finger into one of the ivory-streaked locks.

"What was she like?" she asked plaintively.

Mal wanted to be honest with her. He wished he could reward her desperate desire for the memory of a mother to love with stories of goodness and heroism.

He thought about the lab reports he'd uncovered, the dozens of people she had destroyed in her escape, the trail of victims she'd left behind. "She was kept a long time in a laboratory, where they studied her."

"In a cage?" Gizelle said in alarm. "Like me?"

"It might as well have been a cage," Mal said carefully. "She escaped, but they chased her. And when you were young, she knew they were going to catch you."

She hadn't blinked in a long while, her brown eyes wide. "The car accident," she guessed.

"Yes. She wanted to protect you, but she wasn't able to, so she did the best thing she could for you."

"My *place*," Gizelle said knowingly, making the leap that had taken Mal months of research and dozens of spy reports to put together.

"She built a fold of time for you, so that you wouldn't have to *be* in a cage… even if she couldn't keep them from capturing you."

"Why am I not stone? Metaphorically."

Mal shrugged, and she startled back in her chair because he moved too abruptly. "I don't know how you work," he said soothingly. "I… might learn more if you showed it to me."

Gizelle knit her eyebrows together and regarded him, if possible, more intensely than before.

Was Gizelle the reason that things beneath the island were in such disrepair? Mal didn't want to believe it and certainly didn't want to think it was deliberate. But something was working at cross-purposes to him and it was possible that Gizelle's fractured magic was to blame.

He could force her to take him to that place in her mind, a few words of power and she would have to do what he told her. She was strong-willed and smart, but he was older, stronger... and wise enough to know that overpowering her would shatter the amazing progress she had made since her rescue.

Even if she was the cause of the damage he had discovered, that damage was done. Breaking her further would have only been heaping indignity on top of tragedy. Mal didn't consider the option more than the time it took to occur to him.

"I'll show you," Gizelle said at last. Before Mal could brace himself, he was falling into her eyes.

Descriptions had not prepared him.

A field of tall grass stretched in every direction, thigh-high and moving gently in a wind he couldn't feel on his skin. Everything was bright and beautiful, every blade of grass was brilliant and whispered in songs against its neighbor. Mal felt like he was bathed in sunlight, but when he looked up, squinting automatically, there was no sun and the sky was velvet black above him.

At his side, fractured from him like beams of color through a prism, was his dragon.

How curious, his dragon said, sitting up and spreading wings that cast no shadows.

Gizelle was standing before them, her hair in long, loose curls. "I made this," she said proudly. Her gazelle pranced at her side.

"Your mother made this," Mal corrected absently. "But it is from your memory." A child's memory. Incomplete.

Gizelle didn't take offense. "It is safe here, always," she said. "And I can run forever."

Mal didn't have to run for a horizon to know it would never come.

"How much time will pass, outside of here?" he asked, bending to run his fingers through the grass. He could feel each blade, but it was somehow different than physical touch.

"It depends on how wide the door is open."

"Ah…" Mal stared up at the sky. He felt like he had the pieces to several different puzzles in his hands. Puzzles with no boxes or pictures. "The door was never meant to be left open." Time was something even he didn't trifle with.

Gizelle stared. "But if the door isn't open, I can't get out."

"Your mother did that for you," Mal said, feeling as if he was on the verge of understanding something profound. "I don't know how. She wanted you to have a chance at a life outside. But *time* isn't meant to be wedged open like that. It could have… consequences."

"The rain of blood…" Gizelle murmured. "The storm… This is all my fault."

Mal scowled up at the featureless blackness above. He didn't know how things fit together yet.

"It doesn't feel right," he said, frustrated.

"I never meant to be trouble," Gizelle said as she raised her tearful gaze to Mal. She was trembling. They were sitting at the table by the bar again as all the noises of the world returned and Mal's dragon had only a moment to hiss in warning before a fist was connecting to Mal's jaw.

CHAPTER 8

Scarlet was beginning to suspect that the guest had a financial interest in the soaps they were trying to convince her to stock when she heard a wordless roar of rage, the sound of a punch, and then there was the crashing music of toppling chairs and tables and breaking glass.

"You must excuse me!" she called back to the guest, fleeing for the stairs.

She knew that Mal was in the thick of it, but there were people all along the way and she was concentrating so hard on getting there swiftly using her feet that she was utterly unprepared for the scene she found.

Mal was lying in the middle of a tumble of chairs and tables and broken glasses, one arm flung up over his bloodied face. Conall was holding a hysterically crying Gizelle in his arms, snarling defensively at everyone nearby. Tex was looming over Mal with a baseball bat, demanding, "What did you do to her?!" Graham, hands curled into fists, was at the far side blocking any escape and Travis was sprinting up the stairs from the pool deck.

Scarlet waded in with a snarl, flinging Tex aside with more force than she meant to. "Did I not *just* finish instructing you not to harass him? Now what the hell is going on here?"

"He wasn't hurting me," Gizelle sobbed. "He was *explaining* me."

Conall, arms wrapped firmly around her, glared at Scarlet. "She was crying," he growled without apology.

Tex, rubbing the arm that Scarlet had grabbed, sheepishly lowered his baseball bat. "I got here as Conall was landing a punch, I just assumed that Gizelle had been hassled…"

Scarlet turned to where Mal was lowering his arm. The bloody lip did not make him any less handsome, to her irritation. "*Were* you bothering Gizelle?"

"I swear I was not," he said gravely, appearing barely ruffled for all that he was looking up at her from the floor. "We were merely having… a conversation."

Scarlet glared at him, trying to assess his part in this. She had no doubts that he could have countered any attack he received; his human form was a strong as Conall or Tex's and Scarlet could not miss the dragon power that simmered beneath the surface. But he hadn't hurt either of them.

She had a chance to slight him, to make him struggle to his own feet amid the toppled furniture, and Scarlet was sorely tempted.

But she was trying to set an example of dignity, dammit, so she extended a hand to help him up.

She meant it to be just a polite assistance, quickly done, but she'd forgotten what the touch of Mal's hand did to her.

"*Mr. Moore,*" she reminded herself, accidentally out loud.

"*Ms. Stanson,*" he replied with an insufferable smile as he flowed to his feet and refused to let go of her hand.

"Do you require medical assistance?" she asked shortly. Tex and Travis were righting the table and chairs and sweeping up the broken bottle, but she was keenly aware of their listening ears. Graham had vanished again, at least.

Mal touched his bloody lip gingerly with his free hand and worked his jaw. "I do not," he said formally. "It should be healed in very short order. Mr. Wright has an excellent right hook." He nodded towards Conall, but the Irish elk shifter was focused entirely on Gizelle, who was beginning to calm.

Scarlet wondered if she was going to have to extract her hand using force just as he let go of it and she ground her teeth in frustration at the feeling of loss it left her with. She detested everything about this man and the way he effortlessly left her feeling like a swooning schoolgirl was the absolute worst of it.

Conall gathered Gizelle up in his arms and carried her away, murmuring to her. He shot one look of pure hatred back at Mal that made Scarlet prickle irrationally.

"I'm afraid that Mr. Wright does not appreciate my interference," Mal said regretfully.

"I'm not sure anyone appreciates your interference," Scarlet said tartly. His lip was still bloody, if not actually bleeding, and it was distracting. "You have… oh here." She stepped smartly behind the bar for a clean bar towel and wet it at the sink. "You have blood on your face," she said, holding it out to Mal, who had followed her.

He unhelpfully did not offer to take the towel and left her standing with the damp towel extended until she finally snapped, "Fine," and stepped forward to dab his jaw as efficiently as she could manage.

The worst part of it was that he knew exactly what he was doing, Scarlet thought, hating how close she had to get. She could smell his faint, heady musk, see the slight little smile at his mouth, and feel his breath against her skin. It took all of her self-control not to linger over the task.

"Thank you," Mal said quietly as she stepped back and went to rinse the towel in the sink.

He made no move to leave as she cleaned his blood from the towel and hung it to dry. "Sit with me and talk a moment," he told her, not making it a question. "I won't take much of your time."

Scarlet didn't want to give him any of her time. She only wanted him to leave her in peace and stop looking so carelessly handsome.

But he had just been *assaulted* at her resort and she was keenly aware of the curious eyes pretending not to watch them. As satisfying as giving him a cold shoulder would be, it would reflect poorly on the resort and give the staff mixed messages after her lecture about professionalism. She could have a civilized conversation with him, reiterate the uselessness of trying to talk her out of the purchase of the island, and then wash her hands of the man when he realized that his trip had been pointless.

She nodded crisply. Tex handed Mal a beer to replace the one that had been shattered and the dragon shifter took it gravely.

Scarlet led him to the far side of the bar level, above the pool, where the noise from the water features would keep their conversation private.

"I'm not sure what you hope to accomplish here," she said as they settled across the small table from each other.

"I'm hoping to convince you that the island is a poor investment choice and reconsider your offer."

"I appreciate your candor, but I am resolved to make the purchase," Scarlet replied, every bit as formally. "I have the money," she added. "And the contract dictates…"

"It's not about contracts," Mal said.

Scarlet was surprised by how passionately he said it.

He took a deep swig of his beer and looked away over the big pool. A polar bear was paddling around in the deep end and several guests in human form were lounging on pool floats at the other end. An otter was frolicking cheerfully at the base of one of the falls.

"Three hundred and fifty million dollars would buy you an island just as good," Mal said thoughtfully. "Something off of Mexico that doesn't require as much air travel, maybe. There are some properties in the Bahamas that you could get for a song compared to this."

"I think you grossly overestimate your powers of persuasion," Scarlet said coolly. "Why would I shop for another resort when I've already built exactly what I wanted?"

Mal leaned forward and looked at her intensely. His brown eyes were flecked with gold, Scarlet realized, and it took a moment for his words to register: "Because your resort isn't *safe*."

CHAPTER 9

If Scarlet had not been his mate, and if he had not been half in love with her before he first set eyes on her, Mal was still sure this would have been a difficult conversation.

He was used to delivering bad news and had no qualms giving hard truths to people. It was second nature to steel himself against emotional investment before all such meetings.

But Scarlet…

It wasn't just the threat of her sizzling power and it wasn't just her beauty, though both of those complicated things more than he liked to admit. He wondered if she knew exactly what she did to his body when she tucked a loose lock of hair behind her ear. The curve of her neck, the grace of her fingers, the line of her collarbone, just visible at the open neck of her blouse; it was enough to make him adjust his seat… and Mal never brought his libido to a negotiation.

It wasn't even his desire that was making it so hard to speak.

It was the vulnerability he'd glimpsed behind those flinty green eyes, the aching longing he doubted anyone else saw. He wanted to be her safety... he had never desired anything in the world so much as to be someone she could trust. He desperately wished he could tell her what she wanted to hear.

Instead, she thought he was her enemy, and he was bringing her news that would break her heart.

Scarlet narrowed her eyes. "Is this the point in our negotiations where you start threatening me?"

"No," he promised. "It's out of my hands, I swear to you. This island… it was an unfortunate place to build. It was never meant to be developed and you can't stay here much longer. I didn't realize how close to the end it was, before I came and saw for myself."

"I'm going to need more than a vague statement of doom to convince me cancel the purchase," Scarlet told him flatly. Then she gave a devastating smile, shook her head, and added, "Though I have to admit, that's a more creative angle than I was expecting."

"It's not creative," Mal protested. "I promise. Just hear me out, because benea—"

"Scarlet, I'm sorry to bother you…"

They both looked around to find Breck, looking very sorry indeed to bother them. "The cruise ship is in early with our new guests," he said apologetically. He looked at Mal warily, his tray clutched like he feared he'd have to use it as a shield.

More guests, Mal thought, his hands clenching around the beer. *More innocent shifters.*

Scarlet was standing. "We'll have to continue this conversation later," she said dismissively to Mal.

Mal stood as well. "Today," he insisted. "It's important, and we're running out of time."

For a moment, he thought she was going to refuse.

"Please," he added as an afterthought.

She pursed her lips and said reluctantly, "I should be free later this afternoon, after four."

Mal extended a hand. "At four," he said firmly.

She eyed his hand a moment before gingerly taking it and Mal savored the feeling of hers in his own. "At four, Mr. Moore," she agreed faintly, and there was that spark of uncertainty in her gaze that made him want to fold her into his arms and protect her from anything.

"Mal," he corrected. "Call me Mal."

She scowled and her eyes shuttered. "Mr. Moore," she repeated coldly and her hand was simply not in his any longer.

Her low heels clicked away over the hard tiles with a sound that Mal was already able to distinguish from anyone else and he watched her go with a smile of amusement.

Did she feel it? Did she already know that she was his mate, that he was hers, completely and utterly? Was she being coy, or simply defensive?

Alice had sworn that Scarlet wasn't a shifter; was it possible that she honestly didn't know about the bond they had? Humans supposedly felt overwhelming attraction when they met their mate, but she certainly wasn't human. Mal had seen warmth and interest in her eyes when they danced, but little of either since then. Was she denying their connection because she was angry with him, or was she truly not aware of it?

Mal realized that Breck was still standing there, watching him watch Scarlet walk away.

The waiter cleared his throat. "I owe you an apology," he said stiffly.

Mal refrained from smiling. "If you feel it necessary, I will accept your apology." Scarlet must have given him an earful. Mal sat back down.

But Breck didn't simply take his statement and go. Instead, he crossed his arms and adapted a wide-legged stance that would have looked more natural on Wrench or Graham. "Look, we all know you want the resort. But *you* should know that you won't get it without a fight. And we're all going to take it very poorly if you hurt Scarlet."

We would never hurt her, his dragon said with a hint of righteous anger. *We will protect her. At all costs.*

"I have no desire to harm Scarlet," Mal said. "And I'm sorry for the resort. I can only promise that I am not doing anything vindictively."

Breck gave a scowl that didn't suit his laughing features. "This is our home," he said fiercely. "We're not just leaving so you can make an easy buck."

Mal stared. "You think this is about money?" He gave a helpless chuckle. "If this was about money, I would not have offered Scarlet a buyout worth many times the value of the entire island."

"You offered her a buyout?" Breck looked confused.

"Several now," Mal said. "Worth millions more than your purchase offer. Didn't she tell you? She could have left the resort and bought a new place twice the size, with more amenities, or retired you all as millionaires and lived a life of luxury on some beach sipping tequila."

"*Millions* more?" Breck's look of confusion had turned to suspicion.

"All of my offers were very generous," Mal assured him. "And completely fair. No strings, no hidden agendas."

"Well you and Beehag have got some kind of agenda," Breck said, clearly not convinced. "Or you wouldn't be here, and you wouldn't have trotted those so-called businessmen through here like a slap in the face."

Mal winced. He'd begun things by trying to convince Benedict Beehag that a sale was necessary, and finding buyers he wouldn't mind watching slide into the ocean. He had hoped it would help scare Scarlet off, but she was made of sterner stuff... and once she had Jenny's help in identifying the protections set out in her contract, he realized that even an unsavory sale of the island wasn't going to convince her to break the lease.

"I can promise you that Benedict Beehag has no interest in the island whatsoever," Mal said honestly. He'd been working independently since Benedict had come whining back from one of the purchase attempts about how dangerous everything was and how crazy Scarlet was. He was currently spending his inheritance at breakneck speed through Europe on all the tail and alcohol that money could buy.

"Then why not just accept the purchase?" Breck said. "Why not just leave us in peace?"

For all of the worldliness that Breck pretended to have, he was painfully innocent.

"There are bigger things at stake," Mal said, carefully vague. He didn't want to send rumors through the staff before he was able to tell Scarlet the details himself. "Congratulations, by the way."

Breck was eyeing Mal's empty beer bottle, clearly just keeping himself from sweeping to collect it out of habit. "Congratulations for what, now?"

"Your recent nuptials," Mal reminded him. "It made waves in shifter society."

Breck gave a helpless smile. "Thank you," he said, and he rubbed his left wrist self-consciously.

"I'm pleased that my gift got to the right people," Mal couldn't help adding. "Eventually."

It didn't take Breck long to figure out what he was talking about; he was naive, but not stupid. "You gave the engagement bracelets to Darla and Liam?" Breck said in astonishment. "They were from *you*?"

"More accurately, they were from her father, who commissioned me to make them before his death."

"Why?" Breck asked avidly.

"Her father wanted her to be happy. He hoped that they would help show her the way to her own heart." Mal did not have to add that Darla's father had been desperately unhappy with his own marriage; Breck had met Darla's mother. "How are you liking the fringe benefits of my gift?"

Breck tried unsuccessfully to smother his grin. "It can be *very* entertaining."

Mal couldn't help but chuckle. "Of all the people on this island, I imagine you would be the one who could get the most enjoyment out of it."

Breck's curiosity had clearly overcome his dislike. "Did you know? When you sent these, did you know that Darla and I were mates?"

"No," Mal said with a brisk shake of his head. "I had no idea.

But I knew that Liam wasn't, and I knew that Darla would somehow get to where she needed to be to meet her destiny."

"You actually believe in destiny?" Breck sounded dubious.

Mal was quiet, thoughtful. "We're all called to be in certain places, to face certain tasks. Sometimes it's not clear to us when or where or what, but shifters in particular are tuned to patterns in the world." He eyed Breck. "Would you have *chosen* to fall in love with Darla, if you'd been given a choice in the matter?"

Breck looked taken aback. "Of course not," he said, deeply reluctant. "She was promised to another. She was out of my league. She broke all my rules."

"And yet now, with her…?"

"There's no other life without her, no possible path. I never dreamed I could be so happy."

Mal nodded. "I have a theory that our animal selves can see our best possible outcome, instinctively. They recognize the pieces that take us there, even if we don't understand all the rules and can't see the full pattern."

Breck studied him. "But you think *you* do. Understand the rules. See the whole picture." His voice was full of challenge.

"More than most people, maybe," Mal said, thinking of Scarlet. He hadn't seen Scarlet coming.

We have always known that our destiny was at this island, his dragon assured him confidently.

But Mal's vision of that destiny had been glorious battle, victory over a terrible threat to the world. It hadn't involved a woman with eyes that looked straight into his soul, or the ferocious desire that rose in him every time he caught sight of her. His whole understanding of his fate had been turned on its head.

He finished the last swig of his beer and handed the bottle to Breck, who put it on his tray with a practiced flair.

"Shifting Sands might surprise you," the waiter said in unexpected echo to his own thoughts. "It might even teach you something about yourself. It has a habit of doing that."

Mal thought it just might.

CHAPTER 10

Scarlet checked in the new guests personally, as she usually did. It was the usual mix: dilettantes who spent money like water, couples who were celebrating anniversaries or honeymoons, middle class people who had carefully saved up for the vacation of a lifetime. She confirmed the rules with each of them, gathered signatures for all the various forms, and gave them keys.

Usually, this was one of her favorite things to do. It was pleasant to meet new people, to see the shining anticipation in their faces, to watch how they reacted to the amenities and activities she described to them. They took deep breaths of the island air and marveled at the smells and delighted in the architecture and Scarlet felt a sense of deep accomplishment and pride.

But today she could not help but think of Mal's statement: *Your resort isn't safe.*

What did he mean by that? Was this just lawyer talk? He seemed sincere. Insufferably smug, yes, but when he'd talked to her, he seemed genuinely concerned.

Concerned and… interested.

His eyes haunted her, so warm and fearless.

Their conversations on the phone had prepared her for someone cool and logical. But Mal—Mr. Moore—had an expressive face and Scarlet had caught a dozen emotions there in the space of a conversation. She found this very unnerving.

That, and she had expected someone old. Jenny said he'd been practicing law since the sixties, which meant he had to be at least eighty.

"Which room number?"

"Eighty…" Scarlet said, distracted. She shook herself. "I mean, that will be 215 in the hotel. You have a lovely view from that floor."

The guest smiled gratefully and Scarlet made herself concentrate on the transaction and show her the map. "My staff has already delivered your luggage, no need to worry."

"Thank you so much!"

Scarlet shut down the computer after the guest took their oversized purse and left the courtyard and stared at her dark reflection in the screen for a moment. It wasn't like she should judge Mal for looking younger than he was. She closed the laptop firmly.

The resort outside the courtyard was filled with the noises of new guests, people exclaiming over the beauty and thoughtfulness of the layout, loudly asking for directions, greeting the people they'd gotten to know on the cruise. Some of them went directly for the bar, where there was already happy chatter despite the early hour.

Your resort isn't safe.

Scarlet scowled over her domain. *Mr. Moore* had some explaining to do.

She stalked to the spa, where several guests were already gathered around the board that described the various services available.

"Oh, I'm definitely up for a massage," a young woman was saying.

"But what kind?" the older woman with her asked eagerly. "I don't even know what some of these *are*!"

Scarlet slipped past them to catch Lydia settling clean sheets over the massage tables.

"I wanted to give you heads up about a guest with a coconut allergy, a Mrs. Orainda Santaga."

Lydia finished tucking the corners under and went to write

down the allergy on her scheduling sheet. "Thank you, Scarlet. Did we get many guests from the cruise ship?"

"About a dozen," Scarlet said.

"Oh good, we should be set for hands in the spa for today without calling Laura in." Lydia suddenly looked very cagey, an unnatural look for her, and added, "She wasn't feeling well earlier today, poor thing."

Scarlet, who already knew about Laura's pregnant condition but was letting everyone think she didn't, had to keep an amused smile from her face with effort as Lydia bustled to find an alternate oil for the woman with the coconut allergy.

She caught sight of her reflection in one of the many mirrors and gave her serene face some thoughtful consideration.

Was she looking dated? Her clothing was the type generally called *timeless*, but maybe it was *past* time to try something new. And her hair, was it too severe? She touched the bun that always pulled her bright hair back from her face and wondered if it seemed uninviting.

A scowl reflected back at her. She didn't want to look inviting and she was certainly not going to change her look because some stuck up, big-shot lawyer from the city had come to her resort and danced with her.

Scarlet was furious with herself.

She rolled her shoulders back firmly and went to the kitchen to deliver the coconut allergy warning to Chef personally as well.

She *hated* Mal Moore, she reminded herself. He was her *enemy*.

CHAPTER 11

There was a young cat on Scarlet's windowsill, grooming itself with one green eye firmly on Mal.

Mal had never considered that Scarlet would be the kind of person to have a pet and the creature was rather confounding.

He should probably attempt to win it over; the best way to exert influence was sometimes sideways. He stood on the far side of Scarlet's desk trying to figure out how to achieve this goal. "Nice, kitty," he attempted. "Come."

The cat continued to twist itself in an impressive display of flexibility and run its tongue over its short, plush fur vigorously. It clearly had no intention of obeying.

It is very… small, his dragon observed. *What purpose does it serve? Is she raising it to eat?*

Don't eat it, Mal said firmly. He was sure that would not improve his relationship with Scarlet.

He went around the desk to stand near it, since it was clearly not well-trained. Food was not the worst idea that his dragon had ever had. Perhaps it could be tempted with a treat. "What do cats eat?" He knew a little about dogs, but his exposure to cats was limited to media, and *limited* was the appropriate word for it.

His dragon gave a mental shrug. *Mice?*

Mal was strongly dubious that Scarlet would allow roaming mice at the resort. Unless they were guests.

The cat appeared to have finished its licking and now stared up at him, unblinking. After a moment of contemplation, it gave a trilling half-purr. Mal extended a hand to pet it and, alarmingly, it fell over on its side and rolled to its back.

Had he frightened it? It extended its legs, four limbs in each direction, and writhed in place as it made more of its trilling noises. Its belly was soft-looking and fluffy. Clearly this was an invitation for affection.

"It's a trap," Scarlet said from behind him.

Mal, alarmed that he hadn't heard her approach, let his hand fall carelessly to the young cat's belly.

The cat instantly curled into itself and reached up with all four paws, wrapping itself around Mal's forearm with suddenly extended claws. Sharp teeth gnawed at his wrist, hard enough that he felt the prick through his shirt sleeve, but not quite hard enough to draw blood.

Mal bit back a yelp of surprise and forced himself not to fling the little monster; it was clearly young and just as clearly playing; once he'd gotten past the shock of the attack he recognized that it hadn't caused any real pain, even when it kicked out with its rear feet.

Ah, his dragon said. *Our mate is raising it as a guardian.*

Mal was pretty sure she didn't need one.

"Hsst, Tyrant," Scarlet said, sounding amused. "She's only playing," she explained to Mal.

Tyrant—fittingly named—gave Mal one final gnaw and then let go. Ears back against her head, she leapt for the floor, raced under the desk, and streaked out into the courtyard, nearly crashing into the door frame as her paws scrabbled on the hard tile.

"She's a feisty thing," Mal observed.

"You were going to explain why my resort is in terrible peril," Scarlet reminded him. "And I was going to decide if I should believe you."

Mal came around the desk so that he was standing close to her, breathing in the green scent of her, enraptured by the marble perfection of her pale skin and the fiery strands of her gleaming hair. Her eyelashes were coal black over her endless eyes.

"Scarlet Stanson," he said after a moment. "Aaric Lyons' secretary."

"That was a long time ago," Scarlet said coldly.

"Do you know, there was a while I suspected you were an impersonator. I thought you'd hacked the Lyons' account, found the lease contract, and decided it would be convenient to pretend to be the only person with the power to re-open the resort. For a short time, I even thought you might be working with Alistair Beehag, to supply him with rare shifters for his zoo."

Her cool mask cracked to hot fury. "I would *never*—"

"I know," Mal said swiftly. "That theory didn't last much longer than the others that I had. But it *was* a surprise to find out you weren't a shifter," he said softly. "It raised so many questions."

"Alice might have been lying," Scarlet suggested, confirming that she knew about Alice's deal with Mal. "Or maybe she just got the wrong information. Perhaps even on purpose..."

Mal laughed. Her misdirection was convincing, but: "I know you're not a shifter."

"How can you be so sure?" Scarlet asked.

"If you were a shifter, you would have recognized me as your mate when we met."

Her entire face changed, melting into astonishment and wonder as her lips parted in shock. "Your… mate?" Her voice was full of longing, and she seemed to hear herself and drew back a step. "I don't know what kind of joke this is..."

"That's not something I would joke about," he told her. He closed the distance between them with a decisive step. "Scarlet…"

She tipped her face up to gaze at him in confusion and desire and didn't pull back as he cupped her jaw and bent to kiss her.

For a moment, she was stone against his lips, then he tasted a wistful sigh and she was opening her mouth to kiss him back.

Her arms slipped up around him and he pulled her close against him, twining fingers into her upswept hair. He didn't feel any pins, but he must have dislodged them, because her hair was suddenly alive around them.

She was all the wildness and strength she promised, all the untamed passion he'd known lurked behind her icy control. She was desperate and hungry and she was his.

She was *his*.

Mal had never felt such joy and satisfaction and aching need. She would come safely away from the island with him and he would worship her for the rest of their long lives.

He would never be alone again...

He lifted her to the top of her desk, hands at her waist, and a pile of papers tilted and slipped off the back of the desk.

Scarlet didn't seem to care.

She was pushing his shirt off his shoulders, hands caressing down his arms as she bared them. The cuffs were buttoned too tight to slip from his wrists so she was thwarted above his elbows, but she was busy using her fingers to explore, wandering across his chest as they kissed again, desperately and deeply.

He had one hand up under her skirt exploring the plane of her thigh, one at her neck, and her skin was every bit as silky as he'd imagined it must be. He needed her, like he'd never needed anything, and triumph rose in his chest because finally, *finally*… The months they'd sparred, the phone calls, the letters… it was like the longest foreplay in the world.

And now they would have forever.

Forever, he thought, then he realized in shock that his hand had reached her hip and not found the line of underwear he was expecting. He laughed into her kiss, delighted and amused as his fingers walked over her perfect thigh to verify the shocking truth: she wasn't wearing undergarments.

Conservatively dressed, fiercely independent, perfectly put together Scarlet Stanson was completely naked under her modest skirt. And when he touched her clit, carefully and gently, she gave a whimper of desire and spread her legs for him, tearing at his shirt, desperately seeking his skin.

Yes, his dragon purred. *Ours…*

Mal had only a split second to recognize Scarlet's hand, flat on his chest, before he was smashing into the opposite wall, hard enough to rattle every book on the shelves.

He was confused, blinking at Scarlet, and his dragon mantled his wings in surprise. Hadn't he managed to get a few of her buttons undone? But she was fully dressed again, bearing down on him from across the room, and even her hair was neatly back in its bun. She was somehow larger and the air in the room felt hard to breathe.

"How dare you!" she snarled. "Was this your plan all along? Did you think you could bind my people? Did you think you could *seduce* me into complacency and steal them from under my nose? Is this why you wanted the resort so *badly*?"

Mal stared, still not making sense of how everything had changed so completely in so little time. This felt like much more than just moving too fast… then he realized that Scarlet had gotten one of his sleeves off—who knows where the buttons had gone—and the runic tattoos that swirled down his left forearm were clearly visible.

Her sole experience with warlock tattoos would have been Corbin, who stole shifters and bound them to drain their magical energy.

"Scarlet—"

"You won't get a single one of them without going through me," she hissed. "And good luck with that!"

The vines that were draped around the room had come to life and were snaking down from every direction to twist around his wrists and ankles and neck. He tore free from one to find another, and another, swiftly unfurling new growth at him.

"I'm not here for them," he protested.

"Me, then?" Scarlet was standing at arm's length, and Mal didn't think he imagined the fact that she was taller now, looking him straight in the eyes with blazing anger. "Did you think you could bind *me*?"

"Scarlet, wait—" Mal was trying to unbutton his remaining sleeve, but the vines and the pressure of magic in the room were making it a struggle. He muttered a quick incantation and the buttons burst from the sleeve so that he could slip it off. "I don't need to bind anyone," he insisted, holding up his right forearm. "I'm a dragon shifter, my own power is more than sufficient."

Scarlet paused as the runes on both of his arms, now exposed, flared with brief light, and the air seemed a little less thick.

Mal used her moment of hesitation to rip free of the vines and close the distance between them.

"Corbin and his cronies used a terrible perversion of ancient dragon magic. If the Phoenix had not taken care of them, I would have done so personally. Your guests—*your* people—have nothing to fear from me."

"So it's only *me* that you've got some sort of vendetta against," Scarlet hissed.

Mal drew a deep breath for patience and it seemed less dense. The vines still whispered threateningly behind and above him, but didn't move to try to restrain him again. "I don't have a vendetta," he said firmly. "But I can explain, if you'd just *listen*."

"I'm not leaving the island," Scarlet insisted. "You can't frighten me, and you can't fool me."

"Dammit, Scarlet," Mal said, letting all of his frustration show. "Stop being so stubborn. Listen and judge for yourself. Sit down with me and let me tell you what I know. Please."

The anger seemed to have leaked out of her, leaving only wariness. "Fine," she said, after a moment of silence. "*Outside*."

A door from her office led to a tidy, sparsely decorated bedroom with sliding glass doors that opened onto a small, private lawn with a round table and two chairs. Mal took one sideways look at the bed as they passed through, wishing things had gone a different way.

Soon, his dragon growled. *She cannot resist us long, and we will take her safely from this place.*

CHAPTER 12

The sun was still high in the sky, a blazing coin above them in a bright blue sky. It was baking hot on Scarlet's lawn, though the worst of the afternoon heat was past.

She should have made him put his shirt back on, missing buttons or not, Scarlet thought as she settled into one of the chairs. His chest was terribly distracting and she scowled to think how easily he had weaseled his way through her defenses.

He *wasn't* her mate. That could only be another half-truth to wear her down. He hadn't actually said he was her mate, had he? Only that if she were a shifter she'd have known he *was* her mate… there was surely some sort of lawyer loophole there. She'd been a fool to let him kiss her, too surprised, too full of longing and desire to be sensible.

He clearly knew her greatest weakness. She needed to keep more distance, be more careful, and shut down her instincts more thoroughly.

And his bare chest was suggesting that the table between them was not nearly wide enough for the distance she needed. She couldn't stop replaying his kiss, his words, the feeling of his hands over her skin...

"What do you have to tell me?" she demanded, furious with herself for continuing to let him bait her with his sexual appeal.

"I'm a dragon shifter," Mal said, and he raised his arms to her in demonstration. "A warlock dragon from a long proud line going back for thousands of years. Our magic has quietly been keeping order between shifters and humans… and other things… for centuries."

"Other things…" Scarlet said suspiciously.

"There are old things in the world. Older than people. Older than dragons. And one of those things sleeps beneath this island."

Did he think she would be surprised by this revelation? "I know of this creature," she said cautiously. "It has never bothered me or mine." She could not help adding, "Which is more than I can say about you."

"I have never tried to destroy the world," Mal retorted. "And if—when—it wakes, it will attempt to take a vengeance that will drown not just this island, but all islands, and all continents, and it will not rest until the world has been ravaged."

Scarlet scowled at him skeptically, but she was listening carefully. "What *is* it?"

"It is a great wyrm with two heads, covered in deadly sharp feathers. It can appear as a human, but don't be deceived. It is not a *shifter*, it is a powerful, old creature of air and water and it is wrathful. It is instinct and anger, not reason. It is wild, and vicious… and it's going to be really pissed off when it wakes up."

"You're saying this thing is just... napping beneath my island?"

"Not just sleeping, but imprisoned as well; my family is thorough. Eleven hundred years ago, my great-grandfather battled him into submission and built a cage around him deep beneath the island."

"Why not just kill him?" Scarlet asked. "Wouldn't that have been simpler?"

"It is immortal. There is no way to *kill* it because it's not really alive. Imprisonment was the only choice. Every three hundred years, the spells are renewed, the cage is rebuilt, and the wyrm is cast down again. My grandfather did so the second time, and then my father, almost two hundred years ago."

"And now it's your turn?" Scarlet wrenched her eyes up from his damned chest and scowled, trying to make herself focus. "That math doesn't add up."

Mal's eyes were no less distracting than his muscle-knotted shoulders. "We should have decades more, but we don't. I don't understand what has happened, but the cage is crumbling, and its slumber has been disturbed."

"Corbin?" Scarlet proposed. "Gizelle said he was... noisy."

"He might have precipitated the creature waking, but I don't understand the damage to the cage that I've seen. It's less recent, more insidious. It's as if it has slowly rusted… the magic feels old and weak, and it's leaked into all of the rock around it." If Mal full of confidence was devastating to Scarlet's peace of mind, Mal admitting that he didn't know something was even more unsettling. He raked a hand through his hair and gave a confused shrug. "I checked the wyrm's prison myself when Rupert Beehag began construction and it was as strong and impenetrable as ever at that time. There's been some change, something new since then. I thought it might be Gizelle's broken magic… but it could just as easily be *you*."

Scarlet drew in her breath with a hiss. "You think *I* did this?"

Mal met her gaze without flinching. "I don't know what you are," he reminded her. "I don't know how you work. But since *you* came here, a spell that previously withstood hundreds of years containing the power of creature older than the continents has crumbled to almost nothing in the span of a few decades."

Scarlet stared back at him, more dismayed than she wanted him to know.

"I don't think you necessarily did anything on purpose," Mal added swiftly. "I know you well enough to know that you aren't trying to release an old thing to destroy or rule the world. Maybe this has happened because of some aspect of what you are. Or some side effect of something you're *doing* here. If I knew more about your nature..."

This could be *her* fault? Scarlet almost drowned in the guilt that rose in her throat.

Mal leaned forward onto his elbows, which made all the planes of his shoulders change in a terribly distracting way.

"You were never my enemy, Scarlet," he said.

"You certainly never treated me like an ally," Scarlet retorted sharply. "If you needed me to leave so badly, why didn't you come tell me all this in the first place?"

"Would you have gone? Would you have believed me?" Mal countered. "Until I saw the radar maps of the storms this week, I thought I had plenty of time to solve this puzzle—years if not decades. I had no idea that Corbin would do anything so stupid as start to wake the creature up, and I didn't realize that the cage was failing until I got here. I thought I could play the long game, and I could apply just enough pressure that you would do what was best… best for *you*… without having to step in and force your hand."

"Is that what this is to you?" Scarlet asked scathingly. "A *game*? Where *you* are the superior chessmaster sitting back in his throne dictating the lives of those less worthy?"

"No," Mal said at once. Then, hesitantly, "Maybe." He raked his hand through his hair again and Scarlet had to glare at her hands to stop herself from staring at his chest. She really should have made him put that shirt back on.

"I'm sorry," he said, so unexpectedly that Scarlet had to look at him again. She nearly drowned in his intense golden-brown eyes. "I played this whole situation poorly and if I had it to do over, I would have done things very differently. I made assumptions I never should have made. I expected you to…"

"...Roll over and take gobs of money to move somewhere else like a good little game piece." Scarlet laughed humorlessly. "And I was having none of that."

She tried to focus on the larger problem. "Can you make the cage again, from scratch? Can you set the spell again, but early? Do you have that power?"

"Of course," Mal said with maddening confidence. "I have

trained all of my life for it, and have all the power and knowledge necessary. But doing so will wake the wyrm. I will have to fight him into submission to build the cage around him and that will raze the island. There was not a tree left standing here after the last battle."

Scarlet could not quite keep the noise of dismay from escaping her pursed lips.

"That, *that,* is why I have been trying to get you to release the resort. I thought I had plenty of time until I got here, but the end result was always going to be the same. The island will certainly be destroyed and everyone still on it will die."

The look of sympathy in his eyes was both unwelcome and unnerving. "I understand that you built this place with Aaric Lyons and that you have some debt to him that you feel compels you to continue his dream. I know that this resort is your calling and that your hard work and perseverance has seen it to fruition. And I admire that, Scarlet. I admire *you.* This place you've built is impressive, and you've done it against incredible odds… myself included. You don't want my charity, that's fine, I more than respect that. So take the three-hundred-fifty million you raised by yourself. Go buy a beautiful new island and build a better resort. I'll fight my fight, recast the spells, and the last of Beehag's terrible zoo will crumble to dust and slide into the sea. Everyone will live happily ever after. You have to see why this is the only path ahead."

Scarlet stood and paced away to the edge of the lawn, staring over the resort to the ocean with her arms wrapped around herself.

She didn't want to believe him, and she didn't want to trust him. But everything Mal said rang true, and everything matched the things she already knew. She'd felt the creature below the island, and knew its wild power, even if she didn't understand what it was or where it had come from. She had always known, instinctively, that to wake it would spell disaster.

And Mal…

She'd spent so long hating him that she had a hollow place in her chest where that anger had burned, and it felt raw and tender inside… and that frightened her more than her fury ever had.

Was he really her mate? Yearning threatened to swamp her logical thought and she forced the question away. It had no bearing here.

What mattered were the people who trusted her, all the shifters at the resort who didn't know the danger they were in: her guests, her staff… her friends.

"How long?" she asked, not turning. "How long do we have?"

She heard Mal rise and cross the lawn to her. "Not long. The storms that will make landfall in a few days are his doing. He has control over wind and water and my gut says that they aren't a coincidence. His method of destruction will be storms and floods of a scope humans have never seen and have no defense against. He will make our category fives look like child's play. Storm surge will reach your office."

She looked down the long, steep slope over the roofs of the cottages, the waving treetops, and the glittering pool. The ocean looked peaceful, far below.

"When he wakes, the cage won't be able to withstand him in its current state." Mal hesitated. "Scarlet, I have to stop him if that happens. I *have* to battle him down and reset the spell *at that moment,* before he breaks free… it wouldn't matter who was here, who got killed in the crossfire. I can fight him in his resting place, but if he breaks free, he's in his element of strength and I'm at a disadvantage. And if he gets loose on the world, it would be so much worse. I don't know who could stop him, or how long it would take, and how many he would kill first. You have to believe me, Scarlet. You have to leave. You have to leave *now*."

Scarlet turned to him. "I believe you," she said quietly. "I don't *want* to believe you, but I do."

His eyes were full of sympathy she didn't want... and he didn't even understand the scope of what he was telling her.

"It's late and the storms are a few days out. I'll start the evacuation tomorrow morning. I need to make some phone calls, we'll get the air charter out here as many times as they can schedule. The storms at least are real, we can use them as our reason for the exodus." She paced to the table and pushed the chairs in neatly, as if arranging the furniture would somehow make everything better.

"I know someone who can put a few news articles up to support the story," Mal offered. "A general widespread evacuation warning of the coast in this area might look more likely than just a single island."

"I'll have Jenny cancel the purchase and return the funds they raised. But…" Scarlet looked at Mal and swallowed her pride with effort. "You offered me a buyout. I know I refused it. But if it's still on the table, I want it. I want the staff to be able to retire comfortably. They deserve that."

"I offered you three buyouts," Mal said dryly. "Every one of them generous by any measure. But why not start the resort again somewhere else? Your people would follow you anywhere and you *have* the funds."

Scarlet smiled at him, a slow, sad smile. "*I* can't leave the island."

"I know it means a lot to you…"

She reached out and touched his face, because he was standing so close, and because he was so handsome that she couldn't resist it. "I *can't* leave the island," she repeated with emphasis. She took her hand back before she was tempted to do more. "It didn't matter how much money you offered me, or how much pressure you put on me… leaving the island was never an *option* for me."

Mal scowled at her. "I don't understand. Is it a magical compulsion? I can break those."

Scarlet shook her head slowly.

"A contract?" Mal's voice took on a hint of alarm as the ramifications of what she was telling him sunk in. "I'm arguably one of the best lawyers in the world. I could get you out of anything."

"Modest, too," Scarlet observed wryly. "The only contracts binding me are the ones you already know about."

"Then *what*? Scarlet, you *can't* be here when this goes down!" He sounded angry, but Scarlet heard the note of panic in his voice.

Scarlet lifted her chin and smoothed down her skirt. "I'll show you," she decided finally. "Come with me."

"Show me what?" Mal scrambled to follow.

Scarlet shot him a look over her shoulder as she led him back through her office. "What I really am." She pointed to his shirt, slumped on the floor. "Put your shirt on."

CHAPTER 13

Mal suspected he'd appreciate Scarlet's suggestion to wear his shirt; the buttons at the wrists were gone, but he solved this indignity by rolling up his sleeves, walking fast to catch Scarlet. To his surprise, she did not pause at her office door, or head down into the resort, but led him out of the courtyard, past the entrance, along the low stone wall, and then plunged into the jungle before him.

Scarlet moved swiftly through the trees before him, flitting ahead as easily as if she was on a paved walk. Mal had glimpses of her ahead, as he clamored over roots and pushed aside leaves the size of tables to follow. Her skirt, which had seemed so conservative in her office—lack of undergarments aside—was hiked up above her knees and her long, pale legs flashed in the deepening green shadows.

At one point, Mal was astonished to realize that she was still wearing her modestly-heeled shoes, over ground that even he found challenging in flat dress shoes… and that he still seemed to hear the distinctive click that they made over tile.

Before he could reconcile this oddity, he was breaking out of the clinging shadows into an unexpected clearing. The sun was beginning to set; the sky above them was stained purple and gold in the hole of the jungle canopy above.

For a moment, Mal thought that Scarlet's true form was too big to show him in a constrained space and she'd brought him here for privacy.

Then he realized that the clearing wasn't empty.

In the center of the jungle-ringed space was a tree.

Mal was no arborist, but even he could tell at once that this was no ordinary tree. It wasn't that impressive in size, compared to the gigantic trees of the jungle surrounding them, but it was still grand, as big as a house, with thick fern-like leaves and a heavy crown of brilliant red flowers.

Mal didn't have to cast his power sight to know that it sizzled with power: power like Scarlet's.

And it had brilliant red flowers: red like Scarlet's hair.

She was watching him with something that might have been anxiousness in a lesser person.

"This is me," she said needlessly, because Mal had put all the pieces of this puzzle together at last. "This is why I can never leave the island."

"You're a dryad," he said in wonder.

Dryads were a Greek myth, but similar stories existed in many cultures: a powerful nature spirit who was anchored to a single tree, guardian of her forest and land.

"This is my tree," she said simply. "This is my forest. This is my island."

They had closed the distance to the tree and the branches bent down in greeting.

Mal reached up and ran his fingers through the feathery leaves. They curled around his fingers and stroked his arms curiously.

Scarlet gave a little sigh, and Mal turned to see her eyes half-closed in pleasure.

"It has been a long time since anyone really touched me," she said achingly.

Questions crowded in Mal's mouth: how did she grow here?

What was her connection with the Lyons? How did her stunning power *work*?

And most critical: how could he protect her from the devastation of rebuilding the wyrm's prison? Letting the island become a battleground was no longer a palatable option… but it had always been the *only* option.

We cannot let her come to harm, his dragon wailed. *But we cannot fail our destiny!*

"I have photographs of you in England, from the sixties," Mal said, confused. "You had brown hair."

"Royal poinciana doesn't bloom in England," Scarlet said, as if it made perfect sense. She reached up and caressed some of the leaves; they twined around her fingers. "It only thrives in the tropics."

"But… you were *in* England. How…?"

"I woke up there. Probably a traveler brought a seed pod back from a vacation; I only know that I woke up when I was a sapling in a pot. I was root bound, starting to die, so I picked up my pot and went looking for someone to help me. I found the lot with the happiest trees and went to ask them to save me."

While Scarlet spoke, she sat down in the thick moss beneath her tree, and the ground beneath her raised into a mossy root chair that conformed to her shape and cradled her like a throne. Apparently, she was done hiding her abilities from him and the analyst in him desperately wanted to test what she could do.

He didn't doubt she could raise the entire jungle onto its roots and march it forward in battle, if it came down to it. Could she use her power to protect the island while he battled the wyrm? Already, his mind was churning through possible solutions.

Mal sat carefully across from her, mimicking her motion, and was unnerved by the sensation of the roots beneath the springy moss rearranging themselves and lifting him into a chair.

"That lot, as you've probably guessed, belonged to Aaric Lyons, who was in the midst of preparing for his wedding."

"To Coral Jennings," Mal said, recalling his research.

"No, actually," Scarlet gave a tiny, conflicted smile. "He was engaged to Rupert Beehag's daughter, Anna. Coral was a landscaper who was there to do the finishing touches on the grounds for the ceremony. He took me to find her for advice on my tree… and met his mate. He had hired her by phone, and that was the first time they'd seen each other…"

Scarlet was avoiding his gaze, finding anything else to look at. Mal wanted to reach for her, badly, and his dragon was grumbling impatiently inside. He waited.

"They were very kind to me. I had nothing but a pot with a dying tropical tree in it and Aaric had me re-potted, took me into his household, taught me how to blend in, educated me, and eventually built a glass greenhouse where I lived for nearly twenty years. Then, he bought half of a tropical island and paid an exorbitant amount of money to have me freighted across the world and planted here."

She pursed her lips, then went on evenly. "It wasn't an easy road for them. She was from a poor area where shifters were being harassed and he was a young lord who was expected to make a brilliant match with an influential businessman's daughter. Aaric chose to break off the engagement at the last moment and marry Coral."

She shook her head. "It was messy. Anna was already pregnant —not by Aaric, but I think her father was hoping that her marriage to him would hide the shame, and instead, it became very public and ugly. I thought that Rupert Beehag took the disgrace very well; they continued business arrangements, and even made the purchase of this island together. But it's clear he never forgave Aaric and, it appears, grew to hate shifters."

Scarlet balled fists at her side.

"When Aaric vanished, the resort was almost finished, but it was discovered that he had been in financial straits. I wonder now, if Rupert didn't play a large role in that, as well. The workers all quit and left, and Coral… Coral was devastated. She knew that Aaric was dead, even if she didn't have any proof. She wanted to take their son to England, where she thought they would be safe, and *Rupert,* her good friend *Rupert,* made a very generous offer to buy her half of the island, leaving the option open to buy it back whenever she, or her heirs, could. It was quicker than a loan, and the contract looked ironclad. Rupert didn't know what I was, of course… I was just Aaric's secretary on paper, he had no idea I was tethered to the island. Coral… she thought she'd come back quickly, that it would take a few years at the most to figure out what had gone wrong with the bookkeeping and get it all fixed. A few years isn't so long for a dryad."

"She never came back," Mal finished for her.

"I found out, decades later, that she died in a car accident, shortly after returning to England. Her son received a life insurance settlement that got him on his feet again, but he was just a kid, and he only knew me as an eccentric aunt. He had problems of his own, without wondering what had happened to me or worrying about some island he barely remembered. He got married, had a son… died a pauper. I didn't know any of that… I was just… waiting."

"For almost forty years."

"Until cell phone coverage reached the island and I could communicate with the rest of the world again."

"*That's* why you were missing for so long." Mal whistled. "You were actually *here* the whole time." *Alone*, Mal thought. *Alone on an island of your broken hopes.*

"If you tell me I look good for my age, I will throw you off my island, reservation or not." That was the Scarlet he knew so well, full of spice.

"I wouldn't dream of it," Mal said honestly. "My compliments are much more clever than that."

"I wouldn't know," Scarlet said dryly. "The last time we spoke on the phone, I believe you called me a stubborn harpy who wouldn't understand a smart deal if it bit me in the ass."

For a moment Mal could only smile at her, bemused. "I had offered you twice the value of the island and a reasonable settlement on Jubilee Grant's lawsuit simply to sever the lease. What else was I supposed to assume?"

"Maybe you shouldn't make assumptions," Scarlet said sharply.

She rose from her chair and paced away. The moss chair melted back into the earth. Mal rose and followed her.

The tree above them shuddered and Scarlet shut her eyes. "I found Aaric's hide in Alistair's study, after we freed the zoo. There was a short time there, after his death, where the contract hadn't been passed to Benedict yet and I could go there."

"You were there when the zoo was freed," Mal remembered.

"I made Jimmy invite me," Scarlet hissed. "I was extremely persuasive. The contract allowed me to visit, though I could feel it dampening my power."

Mal could feel her fury and helplessness. He remembered puzzling over the weirdly detailed specifications in the resort lease and the older contract that dictated rights of first sale. "The Beehags have always been very good at hiding their true nature," he growled, remembering how betrayed he'd felt when he discovered what was happening at their compound.

"I still feel like I should have known what was happening," Scarlet said quietly, bowing her head. The wind in the branches gave a sorrowful sigh.

"The contract..."

"The contract was written to protect the shifters at Shifting Sands... and to protect *me*. None of us ever dreamed that Rupert and later his grandson would use it to conceal something like... *that*."

The sun was almost down now, the sky a velvety indigo overhead. A silver moon, nearly full, cast crisp, cool light over the clearing, and in the shadows under Scarlet's tree it was growing dark. Mal could see in the dark, thanks to his dragon, but it was almost colorless sight; Scarlet's hair, and the flowers in the tree, had lost their red hue.

Her eyes were still emerald when she turned to look at him, luminescent to his sight, and Mal felt like he was looking straight down to the center of her, to all of her years of loneliness, all of her strength, and every regret.

She was so beautiful, so complicated.

"I wish I had done something sooner, stopped him..."

"It wasn't your fault," Mal interjected.

"I could have..." she spread her hands helplessly.

"You did everything you could. More than you had to." Mal had kept his hands from her longer than he'd thought possible and he failed to resist the urge to comfort her where he'd been able to resist touching her for his own pleasure. She didn't pull away when he took her hands, and when he drew her close, she didn't protest, merely looked at him with those glowing eyes.

He didn't kiss her, though he desperately wanted to, only opened his arms and gathered her into a tight embrace. He held her close and, after a moment, she sighed and put her arms around him.

CHAPTER 14

Scarlet leaned into Mal's body, trying to absorb his strength and comfort. She was so filled with yearning and emotion that she didn't know what to do with any of it. She hadn't spoken of Aaric or her guilt over Beehag's zoo to anyone, bottling it up as deeply as she could manage.

Her trust of Mal was alarming in its intensity. His motives were clear now and all of their past strife had logical, if misguided, explanations once they'd bothered to sit down and untangle the underlying confusion.

It felt amazing not to have secrets, for the first time in such a long time… almost as amazing as it felt to have strong arms around her, holding her close.

Scarlet could not help but remember his gaze—amused and full of wonder—as he told her why he knew she wasn't a shifter.

Her *mate*. Was it true?

It was impossible not to realize he wanted her; he was trying not to press his erection against her, but Scarlet was not oblivious to its hardness between them, or the way his fingers kept caressing her and stopping as if the desire was rising in him like it was in her and he wasn't sure what to do with it.

"We never finished our dance," he murmured near her ear.

"That's a shame," she whispered back. "But I suppose we still could..."

With small adjustments, one hand was in hers and one was at the small of her back, and they were no less close as Scarlet walked her fingers to his shoulder, wishing now that she *hadn't* encouraged him to put his shirt back on. The runes on his forearms gleamed slightly in the darkness below his rolled-up sleeves.

She smoothed the mossy ground to a seamless flat dance floor and when he led her out into a slow, sensual salsa set to the sounds of the jungle at night, she let herself close her eyes and melt into him the way she had been dying to when he first danced with her.

This time, he did dip her, and she rose back up to the unheard music that they were dancing to and pressed her mouth against his, too hungry to resist any longer.

They made love slowly this time, the frantic need they felt tempered with the will to prolong every touch, every caress, every discovery they made of each other.

Scarlet drew a fingernail curiously along his runes as she pulled his shirt off of him for a second time and he hissed and yanked too hard on one of her blouse buttons. She forced herself to be patient and let him remove every piece of clothing and was rewarded with careful kisses that made her whimper in anticipation.

Mal slipped off his shoes without untying them and when they were finally naked together, he kissed her again and again, and it was even more glorious without anything keeping their moonlit skin apart.

He laid her down onto the moss—she made a thick, moss-soft bed for them without more than a thought for it—and she spread her legs for him eagerly.

Mal teased her, pressing but not entering, until she was begging him without words, scratching his shoulder and tugging at his strong arms and arching up to thrust herself at him in desperation.

When he finally slid into her, she was wet and more than ready and her world exploded into light. He brought her wave after wave of pleasure, every thrust a crest, every kiss a surrender, and Scarlet felt as if her heart would give out from sheer joy.

He finally gave a cry of release and cradled her through their aftershocks as he succumbed to his own need at last.

They lay tangled together as Scarlet remembered to breathe again and Mal's heartbeat returned to something more normal against her ear.

"Do you always do this?" he gasped suddenly.

Scarlet opened her eyes and realized that they were surrounded by flowers. Where there had been soft moss and short grass, there were now riots of knee-high flowers. Even day-bloomers were reaching for the weak moonlight, filling the entire clearing.

Scarlet laughed helplessly. "I've *never* done this," she admitted as she sat up. She held a hand to an orchid that bobbed to touch her and unfurled a happy new leaf. "It's beautiful."

"*You're* beautiful," Mal said, rising on one elbow. He traced the line of her leg with a finger that promised more of what they had just enjoyed and Scarlet had to keep herself from falling upon him once again.

"It's vanity," Scarlet confessed. "I could look my age, if I wanted. Or… if there was something you liked..." she added shyly.

Mal sat the rest of the way up. "You are perfect just this way. I want nothing else. You are exactly the Scarlet I fell in love with… the beautiful pain in my ass that told me where to shove it the very first time we talked."

Scarlet had to smile and when Mal reached to kiss her, she flowed into his arms.

When he ran out of air, she held his face in her hands for a long moment. "Did you mean it?"

"That you're beautiful?"

"That you're my… my mate." Scarlet almost didn't dare to say it.

"Can't you tell?" Mal traced the line of her neck with one finger and his breath stirred the hair that was loose around her face. "Don't you feel it?"

His touch raised fire in Scarlet's veins, but she hesitated. "If you will recall your Greek mythology, dryads are regularly described as lusty," she said primly. "I run hot, and it has been a long, long time. Maybe I'm confusing need with… with…"

"With love?" Mal asked intensely.

Scarlet took her hands back from his face and then didn't know what to do with them. "We just met," she chided.

"We've known each other for more than a year," Mal pointed out, taking one of her hands in his own and kissing it. He looked insufferably pleased with himself.

"A year that you were a complete ass to me," Scarlet pointed out.

"Did I ever actually do you wrong?" Mal still had her hand, and he turned it over to lay a second kiss on her palm.

"You tried to sell my island to horrible people. You attempted to steal my staff," Scarlet reminded him, trying to dampen the desire he was igniting. She rallied. "You wanted to have Gizelle committed to a mental institution."

"I couldn't let that poor woman stay here and be destroyed," Mal said firmly. "And I gave you as many carrots as sticks. You never admitted to your staff how much I offered to pay you if you broke the lease."

It was hard to think with her hand captured in his, with his shoulders and chest bare, with the warmth of him so close it made her skin prickle. "You could have told me the truth," she pointed out faintly.

"It didn't occur to me that I needed to," Mal said. "But I'm sorry that I didn't, if that helps."

It did, somehow. "We still have a problem," Scarlet pointed out. "I would also like to not be destroyed and you said that we were running out of time."

Mal sobered.

"So tell me how you plan to battle this creature, and how I might help."

"I'll do better," Mal said, pulling away from her seriously. "I'll show you."

CHAPTER 15

It was full night now and the silver moon was no longer above the clearing. But they didn't need light where Mal planned to take them.

He stepped away from Scarlet, wading through knee-deep flowers that whispered against his legs and smelled like paradise. When he had enough space, he shifted and his dragon arched his neck in pleasure at his mate's admiring eyes.

He was a large dragon, in shimmering golden earth colors muted by the darkness. In sunlight, he was like tiger's eye gemstone.

I'm an earth dragon, he told Scarlet, and he felt her delight in the brush of his mind.

You're beautiful. Her mental voice had layers that spoken voices couldn't hold: admiration, wonder, curiosity.

His dragon spread his wings and sat up to turn and share a new angle.

Don't let it go to your head, Mal snorted privately. To Scarlet, he cautioned, *I cannot go deep without risking waking the wyrm. But I can take you under.*

Under the island? Scarlet looked down curiously. *Is there a cave?*

I don't need caves, Mal scoffed. He regarded her form thoughtfully.

She was standing now, her pale, lithe form dressed only in her wild hair. *Your form, it is solid?*

You tell me, Scarlet teased, brushing her hair back over her shoulder.

Certainly she had been plenty to hold onto just moments before. Mal gave a huff of a dragon laugh and vowed to do further experimentation with the solidity of her form at the first available opportunity.

He crouched. *Hold onto me and don't let go. I can take you with me, but I cannot protect you if I lose contact. It's a little like Saina's ability to allow others to breathe underwater when she's touching them, but it would be much more painful than drowning.*

Where are you taking me? Scarlet asked, walking fearlessly between his forelegs and putting her hand on one of his front feet. Mal closed his claws around her waist gently and then folded his wings around them both.

Down.

He fell forward into the earth, keeping his dive shallow and quiet. Even so, the island trembled as he passed the top levels of the dirt, sliding into the bedrock that lay below. He could feel it flow through him as he sank, carefully, not too far. He could sense the creature further down and he stayed well away, near the surface. They were near the peak of the island; hundreds of feet of rock separated them.

Scarlet was alarmed at first, then Mal felt her curiosity and wonder blossom.

It's not dark, she observed in surprise.

It's not really sight, Mal tried to explain. *Not with eyes.*

The different kinds of rock were rainbows of colors, patterns of earth energy. The soil at the top was a soup of mineral hues. The stone roots of the world stretched below them in glowing tones, and the surface of the earth was like the surface of water, reflecting back a distorted view.

The threads of rock snagged and caught on him as he swam through the slabs and they made a ringing song that wasn't really sound as they dove.

Mal moved carefully, slipping through the rock gently. Even so, the resort would be getting a good tremor; Scarlet would undoubtedly bill him for the broken glassware.

He drew them back up into the clearing and as they approached the surface, they caught a glimpse of Scarlet's roots, gleaming with life and power.

You are as beautiful from below as you are from above, Mal told her.

Her laughter was flattered.

Then, not wanting to disrupt more than he had to, or risk disturbing the wyrm's slumber, Mal reluctantly returned to the air.

The ground was still resettling as he broke the surface and Scarlet nearly lost her balance on the heaving moss as he set her down again, shifting to catch her.

He needn't have bothered; it steadied at once, but the feeling of her in his arms was intoxicating, so he didn't let go.

"Did you… like it?"

Scarlet regarded him seriously. "I can't say it was comfortable," she confessed. "But it was beautiful."

"There aren't many places I can go deep without risking innocent surface casualties," Mal said regretfully. "Only a few of the stronger seams of the earth, or land where no one lives."

"You planned to fight the wyrm like that, from inside the rock?" Scarlet didn't seem to be in a hurry to be free of his embrace, letting her hands wander up his arms to his shoulders.

"We would be evenly matched on neutral ground," Mal conceded, trying to concentrate on problems that didn't involve her clever fingers and their dearth of clothing. "And if he gains the sky, my chances of success start to plummet. I don't particularly want to give up my advantage… but that was just a skim into upper bedrock. Our battle will shake the pillars of the island itself. There may not even be an island at the end of it." He did not have to add that with no island, there would be no Scarlet.

We cannot let her be destroyed, his dragon creeled.

There's a way, Mal insisted. He didn't know what it was, yet, but he was used to solving insurmountable problems and they had time before the storms crept in.

"You don't seem all that worried," Scarlet observed skeptically.

"We've got days before the storms arrive," Mal pointed out. "And your power is not to be discounted. I cannot believe that I will not be able to figure out a way to either protect your clearing from an underground battle, or fight the creature above. I'll fix this," he said confidently. "I will protect you, and I *will* fulfill my destiny."

Scarlet shook her head at him. "I want you to try another word in that sentence."

Mal was puzzled. "Fate?" he suggested, wondering if she had a problem with the word *destiny*.

"*We*," Scarlet corrected. "*We'll* fix it, *we'll* figure it out. It's my life at risk and I have no intention of sitting aside wringing my hands while you try to save me."

Mal felt something in his chest shift unexpectedly.

He'd never had a partner. He'd always relied on his own cleverness, his dragon, and his power. He had clients, and business associates, and plenty of people who were desperate to claim him as a friend to their own advantage. But wealth and magic were better allies and he'd never acknowledged the empty place that lay like a cave in the stone of his heart, or the walls that he'd built to protect it after the last of his family had died.

Those walls had cracked at the first sight of Scarlet... or maybe even before, as he had investigated her and built an impression of who she was from her selfless actions. And now she was here, with him: his soulmate, his partner.

He traced the edge of her face in wonder. "Scarlet…"

"Mal," she said warmly, and it was a thousand times more beautiful than *Mr. Moore* had ever been. Her arms were around his neck and her slim, strong body was against his. "Did I warn you about the lusty part?" she purred, her mouth near his. "We have a few hours before I can do anything about the evacuation… and I don't need sleep."

Mal could only growl in reply and catch her in his arms and kiss her. He laid her down in the mossy flowers of the clearing and the earth rose up to meet them. They were two of a kind, isolated by their strength, sharing powers of earth. He felt like every moment of loneliness was swept away at the touch of her mouth and the stroke of her fingers.

Show her, his dragon begged. *Show her that she is our mate, that there is no room for doubt between us, that we are hers.*

Mal could feel it, that bright, unbreakable bond, streaked with need and longing and joy. "I love you," he murmured between kisses, knowing that it was pitiful compared to the strength and the beauty of what they shared. "I will love you to the end of the world and I give you everything that I am and everything I have and everything I will ever be."

She gave a small wordless keen of pleasure and surrender and Mal set himself to satisfying the needs of her nature.

CHAPTER 16

Scarlet met Graham at the entrance to the courtyard, her phone with the text she'd just sent in her hand. Sunrise was staining the sky.

"Graham, thank you for coming so quickly. I need an emergency staff meeting. All the senior and secondary staff, please, within the hour. We'll meet at the event hall; there isn't space for everyone in our usual room."

Graham cleared his throat. "Ah, Scarlet?" he asked, gesturing behind her.

Scarlet turned, to find that the courtyard behind her had erupted into bloom. Every plant that ever put out a flower had done so, and in many cases, glorious clusters of them. Some of the plants had changed colors, showing off their most flamboyant hues, regardless of the season.

"Oh, hmm," Scarlet said, looking over the blossom-crowded room. *Oops.*

A swollen bud gave an audible little pop as it burst into flower and a vine unfurled a whole flurry of folded up leaves and fresh buds.

"This is new," Graham observed.

Scarlet blushed.

Graham's eyes narrowed suspiciously.

"I'll keep it under control," Scarlet promised. Another flower unfolded petals and the hedge leading down into the resort was rather suddenly peppered with white blossoms.

"This have to do with Beehag's lawyer?" Graham guessed.

My mate, Scarlet thought, for a moment so giddy and full of tangled emotion that she almost forgot he had come to destroy her resort.

Graham was still looking at her dubiously and Scarlet realized that she was smiling foolishly at him. "It's complicated," she said, in vast understatement. "Please get everyone ready as quickly as you can."

After he left, Scarlet closed her eyes and tried to center herself. It felt so unreal, to feel so happy, to know that so much was at risk.

Mal seemed confident he—that *they*—could find a solution to the wyrm problem that didn't involve the destruction of her tree, but she could see the fear and worry beneath that.

Together, *together,* they would be able to make it work. They were both strong and clever, and with their combined might, there must be a way to overcome the wyrm.

She went into her office to see if the printer needed more paper and to gather the rest of the notes she had taken.

First, she had to make certain that the people who trusted her with their safety were taken care of. She knew they weren't going to like what she had to tell them.

~

Scarlet didn't have to wait for the staff to grow quiet; they were already poised in anxious expectation. So many dear faces, so many people she had come to consider friends and closer.

She didn't try to soften the blow. "The island has come under an emergency storm evacuation warning. We will be closing indefinitely. We need to safely and calmly evacuate all guests and staff as quickly as possible."

There was stunned silence. Whatever they had expected, this was not it.

"I have already contacted the charter and they will be able to get a plane here three times today in total, which should be sufficient to clear out the guests and about two-thirds of the staff in coordination with using our boat to take trips to the mainland; Travis, that will be your focus today. I've started negotiations with hotels along the coast to take our clients. The restaurant will remain open with full services as long as possible, if you are willing, Chef. The spa is to be closed and all activities will be canceled. We'll leave the bar open unless it proves problematic. Tex, please use your best judgment."

She calmly called off the remainder of the assignments:

"Lydia, I'd like your staff to assist with letting the guests know about our predicament and prioritizing the ones who should be evacuated first." Lydia had a quiet manner suited to keeping people from panic and her beauty team was well-trained in deflecting drama. "I have printed out a letter of explanation to be distributed that should answer most of their questions and explain the evacuation procedure."

"Liam, I want you and the elders on the first flight out. I've got housing reserved for you in San Jose. It's just a warehouse with some bunk beds, I'm afraid. There wasn't time to find anything more suitable but I hope to have something more long term in place by the end of today so you shouldn't have to stay there long." Liam ran a modest shifter retirement home and, among other complications, needed a place where an elderly mammoth shifter with poor shifting control could have 'accidents.'

"Wrench, Graham, I'm not expecting any major trouble, but I'd like you to keep order. The perceived pinch point will be the shuttle to the airstrip, so I'd like you to maintain a presence there and respond to other incidents as needed. You'll want to keep an eye on the dock as well, keep in touch with Travis about his schedule."

She put down her clipboard. "Please pack everything you need and do not assume that return to the resort will be possible. This is not a drill. The storm shouldn't hit for several days yet, so anyone willing to stay through to tomorrow and help buckle down the resort will be very appreciated; the last group will go by boat to the mainland. There are sign up sheets by the kitchen for each of the charters."

Whispers of speculation and surprise rose as she paused. Scarlet watched some of them surreptitiously check with their smartphones, muttering about the poor data connection. They swiftly found the confirmation that Mal had promised in dire articles with splashy, threatening headlines.

She cleared her throat and they all fell silent again. "Jenny, I would like you to cancel the resort sale, return any collected funds, and sever outstanding contracts. You will each be receiving a severance package based on longevity that I hope you will find an ample cushion for this blow. Please double-check the contact address I have on file so that follow-up paperwork can be sent to you in a timely way. I have enjoyed working with every one of you and am grateful for your efforts and work ethic. That is all."

She didn't linger, but she wasn't surprised when she heard urgent footsteps behind her as she left the hall to start in on the list of guests she wanted to inform personally.

"What the hell?"

She turned to find that Graham had beat the others out. She could hear loud conversation in the event hall behind them and kept walking.

"Between the return of Alice's money and your severance pay, you should be able to retire to your own private island if you wanted to," she said conversationally. "Find a place with good soil and plant a new garden. Take some starts, if you want. We have some plants you can't find elsewhere."

Graham took her boldly by the arm. "I don't give a damn about the money," he growled, pulling her to a stop. "Or the plants. What the hell is going on with the island? What about *you*? If the storm is severe enough to evacuate the resort, what happens to your… to *you*?"

Sometimes she saw more of his grandfather in him than she should. "I will be fine," she said, resisting the urge to pat his cheek.

"But I can't protect myself and everyone else who is here at the same time."

"This has everything to do with that *lawyer*," Graham snarled. "What has he done? What lies is he telling you now?"

"Mal is not our enemy," Scarlet said firmly.

"You're certainly on a first name basis now." Graham's eyes were narrow and accusatory.

Scarlet wanted to explain, badly. She wanted to tell Graham every part of it, from the heady dawning certainty that Mal really, truly was her mate, to the danger that lurked beneath the island. "You have to trust me," she said simply. "I will tell you everything when I have a moment to breathe. But we have to get the innocent people off of this island as soon as possible, now. We don't have much time, and I need your help with that."

Graham opened his mouth to continue his protest, then snapped it shut as there was a sudden, rolling rumble and the ground beneath them gave a wild leap. Graham staggered, while Scarlet swayed in place. Someone screamed and there was the sound of shattering glass from the bar. Gravel danced at their feet and finally—after much longer than most of their usual small quakes—the earth stilled again.

Scarlet stared down, wondering if she should be concerned. Had the wyrm woken? But it was quiet now and the upheaval she was braced for never happened. She raised her gaze to Graham's concerned blue eyes. "That may make our evacuation job a little easier. Please go help Tex clean up the bar. I'm going to see Conall and work on getting Gizelle to safety."

He didn't follow her again when she resumed her swift travel across the resort.

CHAPTER 17

Mal picked up the masks that had fallen from the walls and straightened the artwork. The wyrm was restless, which wasn't unexpected, given the storms that were just days away. This was the light sleep before he woke, the slow stirring of a waking beast.

He had a problem in front of him.

This wasn't unusual. His entire life, both his law career and his pursuit of magic, had involved solving one problem after another, in calculated order.

Distilled to the bones, he had two choices: battle the wyrm beneath the island, or above it.

He had prepared—for decades—to fight it in his own element, deep in the earth, knowing that the resort, the compound, every living thing on the surface might be a casualty of their fight, but confident in his ability to win easily in this manner.

That was before he had realized that his mate was an irrevocable *part* of that island, and that she was, if not a certain, at least a very probable casualty of a pitched underground battle.

He only had to think of her, the flash of her hair, the silky touch of her skin, the stubborn set of her smile, to know that it wasn't a risk he was willing to take.

He had already all but eliminated the possibility of removing Scarlet's tree to safe location. It would require a larger portal than he had ever created and he was doubtful of the safety of transplanting a tree of that age and size even if he could manage it. Could she even leave the rest of her forest behind? He made a note to do more research and to consult with Scarlet on the topic, but he didn't consider it a likely avenue. Not in the few days that they had available.

Everything pointed to fighting the wyrm above the island.

Mal was a capable flyer and a more than competent warrior in air, just as he was in earth.

But with the wyrm in the air, came the wyrm's powers of air and water. He would be fighting in a powerful storm, at a difficult disadvantage. And he would have to win swiftly, decisively, before the storm damaged the island—and Scarlet's tree—effectively undermining his attempt to keep her safe in the first place.

He could construct a magical shield. That would protect her from flying debris and falling trees, but it wouldn't do anything to stabilize the earth beneath her. And it would be a challenge to maintain a shield larger than any he'd ever made around her while in the midst of a fight.

We have to protect her, his dragon fretted, like a dog on a bone.

There is a way, Mal insisted. *We are neglecting one thing: Scarlet herself.*

She had a sizzling power of her own. There was a way to use that, there had to be.

If he could teach her to stabilize her own piece of land, perhaps she would be able to survive the upheaval that his underground battle would cause. She was a creature of earth like he was; perhaps he could show her how to strengthen the stone beneath her.

Her magic felt raw, elemental. It wasn't anything like his ordered arsenal of spells. It wasn't shifter magic, and he didn't know if his techniques would be the slightest bit effective with her kind of power.

He rolled his shoulders back and sighed. He could almost hear his father's voice in his ear. *What's the first thing you do when you have a problem to solve?*

Mal had resented his destiny, as a boy who wanted nothing more than to be a boy. But his life had never had time for games or play.

From the time he could walk, he was learning how to control magic; his earliest runes were tattooed to his forearm when he was still barely speaking. He clearly remembered his father's arms around him. *It's good that it hurts*, he'd said, while Mal tried desperately not to cry. *Magic always has a price. Remember that.*

From the time he could shift, Mal was learning to fight, flung into hopeless battles with older, stronger dragons and shifters. He had lost repeatedly, failing over and over… until suddenly he didn't.

You don't have to be stronger than your enemy if you are smarter and faster, his father pointed out. *And there is one edge you should always have.*

Magic? eleven-year-old Mal had guessed.

Even that can be taken, his father explained patiently. *Knowledge*, knowledge *is your greatest advantage. Know your enemy, know their weaknesses, and better yet, know how to prevent having to battle them altogether. Not all fights are claws and spells.*

It had taken Mal years to understand that, years alone, spent honing magic, fighting, and later learning law.

The first step was always research. *Know your enemy… and know your allies.* Mal looked at his phone and frowned at the weak WiFi signal. He stood, gameplan firmly in mind, and traced a doorway in the air ahead of him. The air sizzled, and his library opened up before him. Two more destinations, and several armfuls of books, and he settled in to learn as much about Scarlet and her curious power as possible.

A fierce knock at the door startled him. "Come!" he called.

Graham didn't look like he'd come for a social call, a scowl across his face as angry as his knock. He opened the door, then paused in the doorway, hands balling into fists at his side.

Mal was amused. "I assure you, force won't be necessary. Come in, Grant Lyons, I have questions for you."

"I'm not here to answer your questions," Graham growled as he stepped into the cottage. "I'm here to find out what you've done to Scarlet."

In a moment of pure mischief, Mal nearly told him *exactly* what he'd done to Scarlet, laying her back in the moss with her hair loose, kissing her neck, coaxing those noises of pleasure from her parted lips… he managed to keep himself from speaking, but Graham seemed to take the grin he wasn't able to smother quite personally.

"You keep your hands off of her and your nose out of her business," Graham snarled. "I don't know what you've said to her, but you can't stop the sale of the resort and this evacuation is *bullshit.*"

Mal sobered. "I assure you, it isn't."

Graham closed the distance between them. "This is Scarlet's resort. You can't take it from her without going through *me.*"

We can go through him easily, Mal's dragon hissed, suggesting that they do exactly that.

But Mal restrained himself from rising to the gardener's threat, choosing instead to sit and gesture Graham to a free chair. Graham crossed his arms over his chest and remained standing. "Suit yourself," Mal said mildly. "Can you tell me what her powers entail? That pressure in the room when she's angry, do you know how she causes that? I presume it's an instinctive power; she doesn't have any of the usual trappings of structured magic."

Graham's expression of confusion and mistrust only deepened. "I'm not telling you *anything*," he said shortly.

Mal sighed. "I understand that you have no reason to believe me, but I am actually pursuing Scarlet's best interests here."

Graham snorted, but his initial bluster had muted as Mal continued to maintain his composure, to his dragon's disappointment.

"A terrible battle is coming to this island," Mal said frankly. "And the more I know about Scarlet, the better I'll be able to protect her." He gestured to the books: a selection of mythology and magic.

"Scarlet doesn't need protecting," Graham growled. "What kind of battle?" he added.

"The kind of battle that isn't yours to fight," Mal said cuttingly. "This is my fight, and I'm sorry that it had to happen here of all places, but I don't have the time or energy to watch over a bunch of misfit shifters who aren't smart enough to get out of the way. My first goal is making sure that my mate and I get out of this alive and if you aren't going to be helpful to *me*, I suggest that you go help Scarlet with the evacuation."

Graham's whole body changed, reflecting his astonishment. "Your *mate*?"

"Scarlet is my mate," Mal said. It was an unexpected new thrill to say it out loud, even if the audience was looking more distrustful than impressed.

"If you're pretending… if this is some kind of game..."

Mal flowed to his feet. "I don't have time to convince you and I don't care if you believe me." He was as tall as Graham and as powerfully built. "All you need to know is that I will do everything I can to save her."

Graham looked back at him with challenge and didn't say anything, clearly not convinced… and not ready to back off. They stared at each other for a long, silent moment.

"I don't trust you," Graham said frankly. "You act like you're better than everyone, like you know more, like that gives you the right to make decisions for the rest of us. I don't know what you're trying to do here, but if you hurt Scarlet, you'll be sorry you ever set foot here."

"I have no desire to hurt Scarlet. I want to save her."

"Do you love her?"

The question stole Mal's breath. "More than I ever thought possible," he admitted.

"Then why are you making her give up everything she's worked so hard for?" Graham demanded.

"I'm not," Mal said as calmly as he could manage. "It's complicated. There's a fight coming—"

"We'd fight for *Scarlet*," Graham growled, his emphasis implying that he'd rather leave Mal to defend himself.

"This isn't a fight for fists," Mal said impatiently. "This is a fight far beyond anything you could possibly imagine and you'd only be in the way."

Graham took that about as well as Mal expected him to, turning red and growling before he turned and stomped away.

CHAPTER 18

Conall's cottage had been fitted with a visual door alert; when Scarlet pushed the doorbell, the lights inside flashed so that Conall would know someone was there even if he didn't have the assistance of Gizelle's touch.

"Come!" he called gruffly.

Several items of artwork had fallen off of the wall in the rumbling earthquake, and one of the kitchen table chairs was on its side.

Gizelle was at one end of the couch, curled into a tight shivering ball and Conall was standing beside her. "She doesn't like the earthquakes," he said to Scarlet. "And that was one of the worst yet."

Scarlet took a gentle seat next to her but didn't touch her. "Gizelle, I've come to talk about going away." Though her words were pitched for the young woman, she was carefully facing Conall.

Conall scowled at her, glancing at Gizelle. Her face was still buried in her knees, her hair tangled loose around her, and she was trembling violently. "What's this about?" he hissed. "Who's going away?"

"You two," Scarlet said serenely. "We're evacuating the resort…"

Conall's face grew alarmed. "You can't just spring this on us," he growled angrily. "What's happening? Is it the earthquakes?"

For a moment, Scarlet thought she would tell him the same story that she was giving the guests, that there was a terrible storm coming, that it wouldn't be safe for anyone on the island… it was the truth and she could keep the details vague.

Instead, she bowed her head and touched Gizelle gently on the shoulder. The young woman startled, but didn't pull away. Scarlet thought her shivering was a little less.

"There is a battle coming," she said carefully, looking up at Conall. "A battle that may not leave the resort in one piece. This earthquake was just a hint of what's to come."

Conall stared at her. "A battle that *what*? With *who*?"

Scarlet chuckled humorlessly. "An ancient two-headed monster who has been asleep beneath the island for hundreds of years."

Conall squinted at her mouth dubiously. "A what?"

"An ancient two-headed wyrm," Scarlet said, then shook her head. That might be nonsense if Conall didn't have context. What could she say that be easy to lipread?

Conall put his hand tentatively on Gizelle and flinched at the contact.

"A great, feathered, two-headed wyrm that has been imprisoned underneath the island, hellbent on the destruction of the world."

"Feathers…" Gizelle moaned. "Rain and wind. I don't want to, don't make me..."

"No one is going to make you do *anything*," Conall said fiercely, glaring at Scarlet. "I'm going to need a hell of a lot more information than that."

"We're evacuating the resort today, but there will be a few days before the danger is imminent," Scarlet said as calmly as she could. Gizelle leaned into Conall's hand, and he rubbed her cheek with his thumb. His touch had calmed her, but she was still shivering. "We can arrange private transport for you, of course. I presume you'll want to take her to Boston, and if you want to talk about sedation…"

"No, no sedation," Conall said firmly. "I'll handle the details." He seemed inclined to believe her, at least.

"I'm canceling the lease, of course, and the purchase of the island altogether. I'm having Jenny see what I need to do to return everyone's payments."

"You're treating this as a pretty final thing," Conall observed.

Scarlet met his eyes without flinching. "I don't want any loose ends in case I'm not around to tie them up later."

Conall's nostrils flared in alarm and his eyebrows knit. "Is that likely?"

Scarlet didn't have an answer for him. Mal seemed confident that he could find a way to protect her, but she could feel his underlying thread of doubt and worry.

"I'm not going," Gizelle said quietly. "The end was *here*." Then she lifted her head. "Is Chef still making cherry chocolate cake tonight?"

"To the best of my knowledge, yes," Scarlet said, glad to see Gizelle perk up. It wasn't often that Conall's touch couldn't calm her.

"I should wear red." The young woman slipped off the couch and padded across the cottage towards the bedroom. "So that I match the rain."

"I'll let you know what I arrange," Conall said quietly, watching her go. "I'll probably have a private jet come tomorrow afternoon."

"Conall," Scarlet said, and she wondered if he would be able to tell that her voice had cracked. "I have a favor to ask."

Conall frowned at her. "Anything," he said, his tone at cautious odds with his statement.

Scarlet had not expected it to be so difficult to make the request. "Will you take Tyrant with you?" She hastily added, "She should be with her sister, they grew up together, it's not safe here and I don't want her to get hurt…"

Conall, to Scarlet's astonishment, stepped gently forward, took her by the shoulders, and gave her one swift, utterly unexpected hug before stepping back again. "I will do anything I can to help," he said, voice clipped with embarrassment. "Anything you need." He didn't have the luxury of looking away, but he did look rather fixedly at her mouth rather than her eyes.

"Keep Gizelle safe," Scarlet said quietly. "Gizelle and Tyrant."

"You have my word," Conall promised.

Scarlet left, feeling relieved, and stepped out into an ants' nest of angry guests and flabbergasted staff members, all of whom needed reassurance and explanations that she couldn't give them. The earthquake, at least, seemed to be an extra bit of motivation to convince them that leaving really was in their best interests.

CHAPTER 19

Mal felt Scarlet behind the door as she raised her hand to knock. He opened it with a spell as he rose to his feet and met her with a hungry kiss.

"How's the evacuation going?" Mal asked, when he had his lips back.

"As smoothly as possible," Scarlet said with great serenity, straightening her skirt as if she had not just made love to his face. "I think the timing of the earthquake was actually excellent, since it frightened a lot of people. The first flight has come and gone. Liam's elders are safely off, and the most problematic of the guests."

"Mr. scarier-than-a-dragon fire ant shifter?" Mal suggested wryly.

Scarlet rolled her eyes. "Demanded to be on the very first flight out," she scoffed. "Wanted a full refund of his expenses."

She looked around, puzzled. "You did not come with this much luggage," she said, observing the piles of books that Mal was cross-referencing.

"Portals," Mal said dismissively. "This stack is from a library in London, these are from my personal collection."

"Portals?" Scarlet looked at him in surprise. "You can do that?"

Mal took no small amount of pleasure in being able to impress her. "It's fairly straightforward, if I've been somewhere before," he said with a modest shrug. "The power required depends on the distance." He wouldn't need to start conserving energy for a few more days.

Scarlet gave him a narrow-eyed look. "That… would be very convenient. Guests would pay a great deal to bypass the hassle of traveling by airline and it would solve probably half of our new-guest complaints. Something about crowding people into tin rockets for several hours makes everyone very grouchy." She looked excited about the idea. "Everyone says traveling would be more fun without that traveling part… could you teach *me* to do that?"

Mal smiled at her. Even now she was finding clever ways to improve her business.

They both sobered at the same moment, remembering the impending ruin of that business.

"I don't know about your capitalistic goals for it," Mal said carefully. "But I would like to do a little experimentation with your magic. I hesitate to try moving your tree, and that would take a larger portal than I've ever even heard of anyone making… but I think I can show you how to harden the earth beneath you, so that it doesn't move when I battle the wyrm below the surface. You're undeniably powerful, and you are a creature of earth like I am, so it should be simple for you to learn.

Scarlet gave him a quick glance, then looked down at the clipboard she was holding, the paper thick with notes. "We have about an hour before the next charter gets in for the next wave of evacuations. My people have things well in hand, for now." She put down the clipboard and spread her hands. "Where do we start?"

Mal began by trying to get her to transform dirt to sturdy stone.

"How?" Scarlet asked.

Mal turned his forearms, showing her the runes. "Each of these has meaning, and a spoken word that accompanies it. Corbin's acolytes—" he snarled the name "—only memorized chants and never understood a word of them, but there are layers of meaning, and a decent warlock can modify a spell on the fly, simply by changing the order of the runes." He touched the symbols one by one. "Sleep, *nurl*. Help, *ashenad*. Build, *yawen*. Hinder, break, go, see..."

Scarlet touched one of them curiously and Mal had to tamp down the desire that even a casual a touch caused. "This one is on Breck's wrist, from the engagement bracelet he shares with Darla."

"Join, *sheln*," Mal said and he said it more intensely than he intended. Scarlet's eyes were hot and mirrored his own need. It would be entirely too easy to get distracted.

But as much as he wanted to lay her down and kiss her into filling the room with flowers, he needed to save her much more. "I made those bracelets with the purpose of helping soulmates find each other, at the request of Darla's father, who very much hoped that she would find true love."

Scarlet's needy look turned instantly to irritation. "Do I have you to thank for that nightmare of a wedding, as well?" she asked in exasperation.

Mal grimaced. "I'm afraid so, at least in some small part. Though I am sure that Darla's *charming* mother would have found something else to sue over even if everything else had gone to plan. You do not need to worry about the lawsuit," he was quick to assure her. "The case will be settled quietly out of court. My treat."

Scarlet didn't look terribly mollified. She only frowned and touched one of the runes he had already pointed out. "*Ashenad*," she said firmly, and she held out her opposite arm.

A gleaming rune, a perfect duplicate of Mal's, appeared on both her arms.

He scowled to cover his surprise as she turned her arms to inspect her work. "It's meant to be a painful ordeal. You have to suffer for every rune and gain understanding through trial."

Scarlet raised an eyebrow at him. "*Yawen*," she said, and a second shimmering rune appeared at her wrist. "Is there one for protect?"

Mal showed it to her and told her the word. "You're *supposed* to spend a week or more meditating over the order for your rune tattoos, because they will define you as a warlock forever." He sounded sulky to his own ears.

"Do we *have* a week for meditation?" Scarlet asked scathingly as a third rune appeared on her fair skin.

"Probably not," Mal admitted.

"I can rearrange them anyway," Scarlet said, demonstrating by switching two of them and Mal couldn't quite keep from sputtering in protest. "Is there a rune for turn-dirt-into-stone?"

"There is no single rune for that. You would build that out of words, like writing a sentence."

"What other runes will I need to do this, then?"

Mal shook his head in wonder. "This one," he said, rolling his arm over. "It translates as roots, though it can also mean ancestors. I think that's particularly appropriate for you."

They added protect, *djek*, and strength, *rawen*.

And at the very end, she whispered, "*Sheln*," and when the join rune was on her skin, completing a circlet of her wrist, Mal felt a jolt of power settling into place.

This could work, he thought, full of optimism.

CHAPTER 20

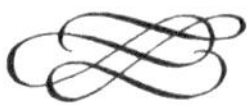

It didn't work.

Scarlet spoke the runes perfectly, touching each one, and… nothing happened.

"Is it because I'm touching them?" she asked, disappointed. "You just gesture a bit, should I also?"

"That usually comes with practice," Mal explained. "I don't have to touch them to activate them anymore, but I did when I was first learning."

Mal walked through a simple shield spell that he'd started with as a young man and brought a flaring egg of glittering power around him to life. Scarlet tossed a pen at him curiously and it snapped and fell, charred, to the ground without touching him.

Scarlet rearranged her runes, followed his steps, and mimicked his chant, with and without touching the runes directly… and still nothing happened. She couldn't alter dirt, or move it at all, and she couldn't bring up a simple shield.

Mal sighed in frustration. "I can feel the power," he said, peering at her inert runes and stroking them with his thumbs, agitated. They were sitting together on his porch; they'd already set off the fire alarm once experimenting with Mal's shields. "I can sense it. You're saying the words correctly, I can even feel your will. By rights, this ought to work."

"Who taught you?" Scarlet asked, putting her free hand on his shoulder. "How old were you?"

Mal's strokes on her skin slowed. "My father taught me, when I was very young. He knew that I would be the next in line to battle the wyrm, and I spent my childhood learning to tap into my shifter power and fight."

"You were close with your father," Scarlet guessed.

Mal's head bowed. "Yes," he said simply. Scarlet gave him space and after a moment he went on. "I was a mage before I was a man, and I lost him shortly after that," he said grimly, standing and walking to the porch railing. "But he taught me everything he… thought I needed to know. He was a brilliant teacher."

"Don't think for a moment that you aren't, just because I can't seem to wield power the way you do," Scarlet said, aching to see him doubting himself.

Scarlet looked at the silhouette of him, gloomy against the brilliant sunset sky. When she'd imagined Mr. Moore, the lawyer, she'd pictured him as a shallow old man, set in his ways and stubborn, not willing to take her seriously as a woman.

Instead, he'd proved to be complicated, appealingly *good*, and dazzling handsome, with just a trace of silver in his hair to hint at his wisdom. And he listened to her, his brown eyes unexpectedly gentle, his hands warm and strong, his skin…

Scarlet shook her head and reminded herself to focus.

"Mal…" The idea had come to her some time earlier, but it was a wild gamble, a terrible risk.

"I've been looking at shield spells," he said, voice determined. "Something I could set beforehand and don't have to feed with magic while I'm fighting. I've done hoard locks before, and they're complicated, they require a lot of setup. We still have a few days, so I could probably work something out."

If she was wrong about him... If she was only blinded by her attraction, fooled by his flattery…

"Mal," she repeated more firmly.

"I could solidify the earth below your tree myself, I think, too," Mal said, thumbing absently through the book in his hand. "Make a safe place that wouldn't be damaged. But it would take months to do it so that I don't have to hold it together while I fight, and we have days, not months." He had clearly hoped that she would be able to hold the spell herself and Scarlet felt guilty that she couldn't manage something so simple.

She closed the distance between them and put her hands on his broad back, letting her head lean between his shoulders. "You could bind me."

Mal went rigid. "Scarlet…" He shrugged from her embrace and turned to face her, shaking his head.

"I know what I'm asking."

"You have no *idea* what you're asking."

"I'm asking you to save me," Scarlet reminded him. "I have a certain amount at stake here, too."

Mal's mouth worked silently a moment and he stalked away, to the end of his porch. The book was tossed carelessly to his table. "What Corbin and his acolytes did, that was unconscionable. I couldn't do that."

Scarlet followed him. "But if you had my power at your command, you could meet the wyrm in his own domain, battle and defeat him."

"At what cost?" Mal asked the porch railing tightly. "You'd lose yourself."

"It wouldn't be like that," Scarlet reminded him. "I would be *willing*."

"You might go into it thinking you were," Mal said, turning to face her. "But that spell, that spell was made to control, to sap will and drain humanity. It wasn't designed to let you retain your own self-awareness."

"I'm not a shifter," Scarlet pointed out. "There's no reason to think it would affect me the same way."

"It's not worth the risk," Mal said ferociously.

"It's my risk to take," she answered just as fiercely.

Mal gazed at her stubbornly and she glared back.

The cautious part of her wanted to claim that what she felt for him was mere attraction, a simple physical reaction to a smart, sexy man who checked off all her feature requests and had hands that could make her body sing.

But it wasn't her body that was singing, she was reluctant to admit.

It was her soul.

Deep within her own chest, she could feel the mate-bond, like a shy bird fluttering in the cage of her ribs.

Mal, for all of his arrogance and irritating confidence, for every one of his flaws, was a kindred spirit. He was lonely beneath his beautiful veneer, isolated by power and position, and his heart was filled with a yearning so familiar that Scarlet could barely tell where her desire ended and where his began.

"Scarlet…"

"You *are* my mate," she said, savoring the words as she faced them at last. "And I am already bound to you."

Saying it aloud unleashed every last reservation. Scarlet closed her eyes and brought her hand to his chest, letting her power flow into him.

Mal made a strangled noise. She found her center and pulled back. "Did I hurt you?" she asked anxiously, but she knew she hadn't.

He stared at her in wonder.

"You are more than I ever imagined…" he breathed. "I cannot fail—"

He stopped himself, then stepped closer. "*We* cannot fail," he corrected himself, and when he brought his mouth to Scarlet's, every tree within a hundred feet burst into bloom.

CHAPTER 21

Mal would have liked to spend more time experimenting with Scarlet's power… or exploring her kisses with the new strength of their mate-bond.

But time was one thing they didn't have.

She drew back reluctantly. "I have to go. There are angry guests gathering, and I can't leave Graham and Wrench to deal with them alone."

"Do you always know what is going on, everywhere at the resort?" Mal had to ask.

Scarlet, leaving one last kiss along his jaw that he knew was going to burn for hours after she left, shook her head. "Not always, everywhere. I have to think about someone to know where they are, or think about a place and know what is happening there."

She closed her eyes and showed him, and it was a weird and dissociated feeling, like he was looking down at the courtyard by her office using some kind of heat vision. Someone was snapping with anger and fear, another was a tangle of anxiousness, another frustrated and confused. What he saw was much more about what they were feeling than what they looked like.

"I have to go," she said apologetically. Before he could ask when she would be back, or any of the hundreds of questions that were crowding his mind, she vanished from his arms.

Mal wondered if he'd ever get used to the sense of loss when she did that, but was comforted by the feel of her inside his chest. He would never lose her, they would never truly be apart.

Our mate, his dragon sighed happily. *Forever.*

He looked at the book he had tossed on the table and narrowed his eyes thoughtfully. Trying to very specifically draw only on the power through the gleaming mate-bond inside, he muttered a short spell and gestured.

The book shot open, flipped through every page like a crazed fan, and violently shut again, nearly bouncing off the table.

What are you doing? Scarlet demanded in his head.

Sorry, Mal laughed helplessly. *I was experimenting, did I bother you?*

I'm trying to evacuate my resort and that's very distracting, Scarlet said impatiently. Then she softened. *It tickles.*

I'll keep it to a minimum, Mal promised.

She gave him a parting caress of her mind, like a kiss on the cheek, and Mal refrained from disturbing the mate-bond again.

He cleaned up the books he'd brought in, returning the stacks to the library through a portal that he had to consciously not draw from Scarlet's abundant energy. If the library was alarmed by the swift return, they were professional enough not to comment by his unexpected arrival.

As full as he was, with her bright power, and the warm presence of her, Mal became aware that his body was hungry. He considered using a portal to obtain a meal, but steeled himself to have dinner at the restaurant instead. He was, after all, paying a considerable amount for gourmet food, and whatever else he was, he was not too cowardly to face Scarlet's staff again.

The glow of Scarlet's mate-bond also helped him admit to himself that he also wanted the companionship of the restaurant. He was tired of solitary meals and isolated studies.

Breck gave him a curious look when he arrived at the restaurant, but led him to a table without comment. It was the same table that

Mal had seated himself in the morning before, and he guessed that wasn't a coincidence.

Breck poured him a tall glass of cold water. "Our dinner menu tonight is your choice of a halibut with cream sauce and dill, served with either a baked or mashed potato side, or a Mediterranean lamb roast with young root vegetables and a reduced olive glaze."

"Lamb," Mal selected mildly, and both of them pretended that there was not any more important conversation they could possibly have than the choice of drink to accompany it, even though Breck was clearly dying for more information.

It was quiet; most of the guests had already been evacuated, and several members of the staff were murmuring and watching him not at all surreptitiously as they helped themselves from the buffet.

Mal was not unaware of the entrance of Alice, Amber, and Mary, but he was surprised when Alice led them in a beeline directly to his table.

"Mind if we sit with you?"

Alice, her head cocked in challenge, towered over Mal where he was seated. Mary and Amber looked dubious, but when Mal graciously gestured at the empty chairs, they all took seats. Alice was brave enough to sit beside him, while Mary timidly took the seat across from him and Amber awkwardly lowered herself into the remaining chair.

Breck returned to pour everyone water and give the dinner choices, a distinct lack of flirtation in his service.

"I am surprised to see you two here still," Mal observed across the table, once the waiter had returned to the kitchen with their choices.

Alice snorted. "Neither Neal nor Tony are particularly happy with it," she observed frankly. "But you try telling Amber to do anything. She looks all sweet and pliable, but good luck getting her to comply."

Amber looked abashed by the honest assessment and Alice cleared her throat. "I mean… you're leaving on the boat first thing tomorrow morning, right Amber?"

"Yes," Amber said shortly, taking a sip of her water.

Mal, following Alice's blunt example, gathered himself. "Amber, I'd like a moment to speak with you alone, if you're willing."

Amber stared at him with alarmed golden eyes.

Mary squirmed. "We could get salads from the buffet…" she started to suggest politely.

"No," Alice said flatly. "Look, no one knows what you're up to here, or what you've done to Scarlet, but I'm not real excited to leave my pregnant friend in your clutches for a conversation."

Mal protested, "I assure you—"

"Your *pregnant* friend?" Amber exclaimed in disgust. "*Really*, Alice?"

Alice still had her baleful gaze fixed on Mal. "I promised Tony I wouldn't let you out of my sight for a second."

"I think you could see anything that was going to go wrong from across the restaurant full of shifters," Amber pointed out.

"I want to be in hitting distance," Alice declared.

"I wish I were in hitting distance," Amber muttered, glaring across the table at her.

Mary looked like she wanted to fold into her chair and die.

"It can wait," Mal said peacefully.

Amber gave him a piercing look. "You can say anything you have to say to me in front of them," she said firmly.

"I was sorry to miss your mother's visit," Mal said gently. "I would have preferred to tell her what I found out about your father in person."

Everyone at the table stiffened and Mal steeled himself.

"My… father?" Amber said numbly, with a hand to her belly.

"If you'd prefer to..."

"What do you know about my father?" Amber demanded, bringing a fist down on the table that made all the glasses jump.

Mal kept his voice low. "You're aware of the warlock Corbin and his… use of shifters."

Amber's face went white.

"Your father's sole goal was to keep you from Corbin's clutches," Mal said gently. "I don't believe he would have given you up for any other reason. My guess is that he knew he was close to capture."

Amber was staring down at the surface of the table, taking careful breaths. Alice swore quietly. Mal was surprised by his own sympathy. He usually maintained a professional detachment from this sort of thing, but the look on Amber's face cut deeper than it should.

"I've… there's a fund set up for victims of the warlock and his—"

Amber surged to her feet, shoving her chair back hard. "Maybe it's hard for you to understand, but money doesn't *fix* everything," she snarled at him.

Mal took her outburst without comment. "I'm sorry for your—"

"I'm not hungry," Amber growled and she stormed as gracefully as she possibly could for the entrance to the restaurant.

Alice rose to follow her, shooting Mal a baleful look over her shoulder as she called to Amber to wait for her.

Mary remained behind. Her look was thoughtful and measuring. Mal remembered that she was the timid one of the bunch and was surprised that she didn't flee at the first opportunity.

Instead, they sat for a long moment in silence, regarding each other.

"Are you the one who set up the anonymous trust for the victims of Beehag's zoo?" she finally asked.

"Yes," Mal said simply.

"You did that for Benedict Beehag, as his lawyer, because of the horrible things that his uncle had done?"

"No," Mal said shortly. He had tried to convince Benedict to set something up, but the heir to the Beehag fortune had proved to be as self-centered and shallow as Mal had come to expect of billionaires; even the promise of a tax shelter had not strong-armed generosity from him.

"You made secrecy about the payment a condition of the allotment," Mary observed. "Neal almost didn't take it."

"I'm glad he did," Mal said.

"I'm trying to decide if I should thank you," Mary said honestly. "On the one hand, that money made it much easier for him to change careers and get his life back. On the other… it feels like dirty money."

Mal was having to reconsider Mary; though she was quiet and unsure compared to the forward, forthright Alice, the deer shifter was no coward. He sighed. "Because I've been trying to get Scarlet to sell out her lease?"

"She loves the resort. This is her home. Why would you try to take that from her? I take a dim view of anyone who can't take no for an answer."

Mal wasn't used to justifying himself to anyone, let alone *wanting* to. He made the best choices with the information he had, and he almost always had *more* information than anyone. He never felt the need to waste time seeking approval for the choices he made, and his ego didn't need stroking.

But he found himself wanting to explain himself to Mary… to the entire staff of Shifting Sands and all the people who cared for Scarlet.

"I'm willing to admit I made a mistake with Scarlet," he said honestly. "I made assumptions I should not have." He did not add that it was a very reasonable expectation that Scarlet could have rebuilt elsewhere. It had never even occurred to him that she would be literally incapable of leaving the island.

He wondered what other assumptions would prove false.

"I have the lamb for the lawyer," Breck said, clearing his throat. He looked askance at the chairs Alice and Amber had vacated; their meals were balanced on his tray. "And halibut for the *deer* Mary?" He paused a moment before putting Mary's down, giving her a chance to declare her intention to switch seats.

But Mary only smiled. "Thank you, Breck."

The waiter spread a napkin into her lap as Mal laid out his own.

The food—hot and fresh this time—was everything that he had hoped for, with balanced spice and perfectly cooked vegetables.

They ate quietly for a while after Breck refilled their water and left, with minimal conversation about the food. Then Mary abruptly asked, "Is it true you're Scarlet's mate?"

Mal wasn't the slightest bit surprised that she had already heard;

Alice was Graham's mate, and Alice was Mary's closest friend. Honestly, Mal would not have been surprised if the entire resort knew.

"I am," he said simply.

"And you're a warlock like Corbin?"

Any warm, companionable feelings that had started to bloom in Mal's chest turned to ash. "I am *nothing* like Corbin," he said fiercely.

Mary gave his forearm tattoos a long measured look.

For a second time, Mal desperately wanted to explain, to make her hear his side of the story. "I'm not like Corbin," he reasserted. "I'm..." He paused.

"A good guy?" Mary guessed.

Mal met her gaze appraisingly. "I was going to say that I was trying to save the world, not rule it."

"Noble goal," Mary said, mopping up a last of her sauce with a piece of bread. "But goals don't define someone, their actions do."

Mal gravely replied, "Then I hope that my actions prove to you my sincerity." And he meant it with his whole heart.

CHAPTER 22

Scarlet hesitated on Mal's front step, her hand lifted to knock. Should she just go in? Should she simply materialize inside? She didn't know the rules of engagement for having a mate.

Just as she decided to knock, the door opened and she sucked in a breath. Mal was wearing pants, and nothing else, the broad expanse of his chest like a landscape of toned muscle.

"I wasn't sure if you needed to sleep," she said apologetically, lowering her hand.

Mal was gazing back at her. "You are so beautiful," he said in awe. "I keep thinking I've imagined you more gorgeous in my mind than you could possibly be, and then I see you again and you are so much *more*."

Scarlet hadn't thought a compliment could undo her so completely. She felt her cheeks heat and felt like a trembling sapling all over again. "I… I…" His bare chest didn't do much to help her keep her thoughts together.

Then he closed the distance between them and Scarlet was eagerly meeting him.

To her shock, he lifted her up into his arms, kissing her as he carried her into his cottage. She felt his hand make a gesture behind her and the door swung shut behind them. No one had ever carried her anywhere, and Scarlet savored the unexpected delight of it, wrapping her legs eagerly around him.

He laughed against her lips. "You weren't kidding about that whole *lusty* business, were you?"

"Let's find out together," Scarlet suggested, moving to nibble his ear.

Mal's arms tightened and he hissed in pleasure as he navigated them to his bedroom and laid her down on the broad bed. A stack of books was swept carelessly to the floor to clear space for them.

It was like being offered a buffet with too many delicious options: she wanted to kiss his amazing lips, and she wanted to spread her hands over his strong shoulders, and she wanted to wrap herself around him, and she wanted to run her fingers through his silver-touched hair, all at the same time.

And most of all, she wanted him in her, filling her physically as well as emotionally. She craved his warmth inside of her, his skin against hers, his weight… she was whimpering, tugging at the closure of his pants.

But he pressed her down onto the bed with gentle, slow kisses, thwarting her desperate efforts. "Shhh," he said, putting first one of her hands, then the other, above her head. "Shhh," he repeated, kissing sweetly down her neck.

Scarlet squirmed, but left her hands above her head obediently as he reached for the buttons of her blouse.

He unbuttoned her so slowly that Scarlet had to force herself not to hasten the process by simply unmaking her clothing out of impatience. His hands caressed everything he uncovered, in slow, unhurried worship. He followed his fingers with kisses and nibbles as he finished with the buttons and pulled her into a seated position so he could slip the blouse off her arms.

They kissed there a long moment and Mal unclasped the bra and slid the straps from her shoulders. Scarlet could not help gasping as he cupped her breasts in his hands, growling against her lips.

"Mal," she begged, clawing at his gorgeous shoulders. "Mal…" He was still wearing pants, and Scarlet was beginning to think this was a desperate injustice.

"Shhh…" he said again, leaving a trail of butterfly kisses across her cheek. Then he was pressing her back down into the bed and kissing down her belly to unzip her skirt. Scarlet lifted her hips to let him slide it down off of her, hopeful, longing, waiting for the sound of his zipper, and she was disappointed when he threw aside her skirt but returned to the bed still clothed.

Then his mouth met her nethers and Scarlet gave a cry of surprised pleasure as she took double-handfuls of the quilt beneath her. His tongue teased her, licking and probing gently, slowly, drawing out the orgasm that washed over her.

When she could see again, Mal was once again straddling her and she could feel how hard he was through his now-hated pants. "Mal…" she begged. "Mal…"

He bent to kiss her, and she tasted herself, tangy and salty, on his lips. She wrapped one leg around him and pushed him over on his back, rolling over to straddle him confidently.

"Scarlet," he started to say.

"Shhh…" she told him with a smile. Then she kissed the base of his throat, drawing a groan from his lips as he tipped his head back.

She kissed slowly down his chest, then unbuttoned his pants with her teeth, nibbling at the muscles that tensed in his stomach as she used her fingers to unzip him at last.

He sprang into her hand as she wrestled the pants down around his hips and she teased him and bent to kiss him, to draw him into her mouth as slowly as she could manage. His hips squirmed as she licked and sucked and her own desire was mounting to a new pitch as he growled her name.

When he was reduced to fragments of sentences—*please, you have to, Scarlet, wait!*—she crawled up his intoxicating body and lowered herself onto him in one smooth motion that made them both cry out. The orgasm was only the first of several, as Mal managed to hold off his own pleasure by sheer force of will and bring her again and again to climax. Scarlet wondered if he was using a spell to prolong things, he was so keyed up, and then decided to stop overthinking it and let herself enjoy the pulsing waves of bliss that he woke in her body.

At last, he joined her in one final release, desperately holding her hips as he thrust into her. Still coupled, Scarlet sank down and they lay together as their bodies shivered off the last spasms of their lovemaking.

"Scarlet," Mal said breathlessly, leaving little kisses on her forehead. "My mate."

"I… love you," Scarlet confessed.

Mal's entire body stiffened and Scarlet wondered if she'd said the wrong thing. Was it tainted by the overwhelming rush from such incredible sex? Should she have waited for the afterglow to pass?

But it wasn't the sex that made her say it; her body was already humming comfortably, but there was new need beneath it. She loved the sex, but this was more. This was his arms around her, his gentle mouth on her brow. It was the way she wanted to tell him everything and discover everything about him. It was the way she was dying to find out what his favorite food was and feed it to him, figure out where he was ticklish, learn all his habits and quirks and shyly show him hers.

It was the way she recognized herself in his eyes: all the isolation and buried desire for connection.

He made a noise that Scarlet couldn't interpret and drew her closer. "I love you," he replied, and Scarlet hadn't known that the feelings inside her could swell further.

They continued to lazily touch and caress for what might have been moments or hours, unwilling to move apart.

"You never did answer the question about whether or not you needed sleep," Scarlet reminded him, when he bent to draw the displaced quilt over them against the late night chill. He had fascinating goosebumps all along his arm. She stroked them as he folded her back into his arms.

"I have a better idea," he said, and Scarlet was delighted to feel him stir in interest against her leg.

CHAPTER 23

Mal fell into inevitable sleep after a second round with the fiery, insatiable dryad.

No, not insatiable, he thought, laying in his bed as he woke. He could bring her to pleasure and leave her flatteringly limp with contentment. Just… how had she put it? She ran *hot*. Every time he touched her, she was instantly interested, responsive to his touch. He smiled, still not ready to open his eyes.

Scarlet wasn't in bed with him, wasn't in his cottage at all. She was in her office, he knew, by the singing mate-bond in his heart, and when he *reached*, she answered.

You dreamed, she observed.

Of you? Mal didn't remember his dreams often.

Of deep places, Scarlet told him. She was distracted.

What are you doing?

Paperwork, Scarlet said wryly. *It's incredible how much paperwork is involved in the end of the world. I'll need your buyout offer in writing before Jenny and Travis leave. They're taking the boat to the mainland with the last of the staff once the private jet has left with Conall and Gizelle.*

All business. Focused. Mal was still half-asleep, and he tried to figure out why she felt a little different than usual, why things felt a little off. He dismissed the niggling worry as lingering concern about the looming battle.

We are ready, his dragon said confidently. *It is a good plan, and we are strong together.*

They had a few days left to perfect their synchronicity, but Mal already knew that with Scarlet's power behind his magic, there was little chance of failure. His fate felt like it was easily in hand.

Also, he was hungry.

We worked up an appetite, his dragon said smugly.

Mal threw off the sheet he'd slept under, pausing to press his face into a tangle of it and inhale Scarlet's intoxicating scent of earth and growing things.

Our mate, he thought with triumph.

He had to drag himself out of the bed with effort and after a quick shower, he dressed and decided to get a quick snack from the bar cooler.

The resort was weirdly quiet.

All the usual birds and insects were chirping, but there was no one splashing in the pool, no loud chatter at the bar, no music anywhere. The restaurant and kitchen were still; Mal had not realized what a constant Chef's singing was until it was gone.

The last of the staff would be packing, he realized with a pang. This was the end. They would leave on the boat and Conall and Gizelle would take a private jet away to a new life.

If—when—he and Scarlet were triumphant over the wyrm, the resort would still be battered by their battle. It would take time to get repairs facilitated.

He would build her a new resort, Mal thought. A better one, if she wanted. But would it ever be the same? Would the staff return, or would they take their severances and settle into new lives of luxury? He'd never seen such a close-knit found family, hadn't even realized it was possible. Was this really the end of it, as they scattered across the globe?

His thoughts took him into the back entrance of the bar, where he was startled to find exactly the staff he'd been pondering quietly sitting in a loose circle around a cluster of tables.

"I`'m sorry," he said, realizing he was disrupting a private moment. "I can get something from the kitchen."

"I don't think so."

Graham was looming behind him.

Mal gave him an amused look. "Do you have to get to the point of fisticuffs with everyone, Grant?"

Lydia stood to pull up another chair, and she gave Graham a chiding look. "Please join us," she invited gently. "We all have a lot of questions."

The audience he faced would have intimidated greater men than Mal but he squared his shoulders and took the seat Lydia indicated.

Laura looked like she had been crying, her mouth a firm line in her face. Amber had clearly not forgiven him for the news he had delivered the night before and Tony looked like he would have gleefully crossed the table that separated them to claw his eyes out. Mary's expression was thoughtful, Alice looked like she'd just had a bad cup of coffee. Neal was frowning at Graham as he took a seat at the fringe of the group and Wrench looked like he was trying to figure out how to switch chairs with Lydia, who was patting Mal on the knee.

"This has come as quite a shock to everyone," Lydia said in a smashing understatement.

"Whatever you've done to Scarlet, we're not going to let you get away with it." That was Travis, crossing his arms and glaring at Mal suspiciously.

"Graham says there's a *battle* coming," Alice said, sitting forward to lean on the table towards him. "Did you mean a *legal* battle?"

"Was the evacuation really necessary?" Magnolia and Chef were even there, sitting close together in creaking chairs. Chef had clearly been cooking and there was a platter of miscellaneous leftovers that no one seemed to have touched.

The sound of a throat clearing drew them all up short and Scarlet was coming in through the back entrance to the bar, Jenny at her side with a pile of papers. Mal had to make himself scowl not to smile foolishly at her and it took him a moment to realize why she looked so different.

Her hair was down, loose over her shoulders and in thick waves down her back. Mal dearly wanted to bury his fingers in that mane, to kiss her neck… he wrenched himself back to the moment with effort.

To Mal she said, "They deserve to know the whole story. This was their home, too."

She walked into the bar like she owned it, which... she almost did. "I'm not enspelled," she assured the rest of them as she picked up a tray and began to gather abandoned glassware; everyone had undoubtedly been busy with the evacuation the night before. "I'm not being blackmailed, I'm not being paid off, Mal hasn't hypnotized me, and this isn't his fault. It's an unfortunate set of circumstances, and there are no fingers to be pointed."

"It's not because of the storms," Graham growled.

"No one believes that for a moment," Travis agreed.

"If there's some way we can help..." Lydia offered.

"Anything, darling," Magnolia added.

"Anything," Chef agreed firmly.

Scarlet gave a warm smile around the room and Mal half-expected flowers to start sprouting out from between the tiles. How had he ever thought of her as chilly?

"You have been good friends," Scarlet said. "Like family to me in all the *best* meanings of the word,"—Darla chuckled wryly—"and I have been touched and honored by your trust in me over the years, and your loyalty and your generosity."

Her voice became firm. "But this is not your fight. Beneath the island is a monster, a sleeping wyrm from prehistory. The storms that are coming are a sign that it is waking, and if it does, it will break free and destroy everything he can reach."

"The resort?" Tex asked.

"The resort," Mal interjected. "The island. The mainland towns. The nearby cities, the farms, every ship on the ocean. He is destructive and strong, and if I fail to cage him, I don't know who or what could stop him, but I know that the death toll would be unconscionable."

Graham gave him a suspicious look. "And you think *you* can cage him? By yourself."

"I know I can," Mal said confidentially. "This has always been my destiny: to fight him and win."

"What kind of monster is it?" Laura asked.

"How are you going to fight it?" Saina demanded.

"That's the rub," Mal explained. "The battle... there's going to be a lot of collateral damage. It could level the resort. Or even the whole island." He nodded at Bastian. "You've witnessed dragon battles. They banned them in Europe because of the damage they could cause. Now take that and amplify it by a creature ten times the size, with powers of water and wind and no care at all for bystanders. I cannot promise that anyone—or anything—on this island will be standing at the end of it."

Graham froze. "You can't do that."

"Oh," Lydia said with a sigh. "How terrible. The whole resort?"

"We could rebuild," Travis suggested. "On another island if this one was too wrecked up."

"The sale hasn't been accepted yet," Jenny said, eyeing Mal. "We've still got all that money we raised..."

"What about *Scarlet*?" Graham demanded.

"What *about* Scarlet?" Lydia asked. "She's evacuating too, aren't you, Scarlet? We're *all* leaving."

There was a moment of silence and everyone craned around to look at Scarlet where she was piling her tray full of glasses.

"I can't leave the island," Scarlet said with a wry little smile. "It's impossible for me to evacuate with you. I'm—"

A sudden keen and the sound of slapping footsteps preceded Gizelle's headlong race up the stairs and into the bar. She skidded to a barefooted stop at the edge of the tables. "Sweet One!" she said in alarm. "I can't find Sweet One! We can't leave without her! I won't go!" She rubbed her head and moaned. "I can't go. I haven't gone. *It's my fault.*"

Conall followed at a brisk pace. "The jet's coming in an hour and we can't find the kitten," he explained patiently, trying to comfort her. "Has anyone seen her? Gizelle, why are your hands dirty, sweetheart?"

Scarlet offered, "Tyrant was sleeping on my bed earlier, perhaps she's there?" She gave a curious expression of concentration which faded to confusion. "I… I can't…" She lifted the tray of glassware and abruptly dropped it. Glasses and bottles shattered around her.

"Scarlet…" Mal surged to his feet in alarm. Several of the others stood as well and there was a murmur of surprise and speculation.

"It was… *heavy*," she said in astonishment, staring down at the broken glass around her. "I can't remember the last time something was *heavy*…"

Then she raised her eyes to Mal and he watched shock and fear fill her face and felt his heart stop in his chest. "Something is wrong," she whispered. "Something is very, very wrong."

She vanished.

Gizelle gave a shriek and everyone else gasped.

"Scarlet!" Mal roared. "Graham, what's happened?"

Graham was already in motion. "Amber! Amber, I'm going to need your help! Now!"

Chaos ensued as he bolted for the tool shed behind the bar.

"What do you need Amber for?" Tony demanded protectively as Amber stood in confusion.

"What is going on?" "Where did she go?" "What is happening?" "Is it the monster?"

Gizelle sobbed, "It's my fault, it's all my fault," and Conall tried to comfort her.

Mal blistered the air and ripped a portal through to Scarlet's clearing without a second thought for protecting her secret.

A gasp went through the staff, but Mal didn't wait to watch their reactions before he was bolting through the glimmering doorway.

Mal was no expert on trees, but he could recognize a dying plant when he saw one.

Already, more than half of the flowers had fallen off, and the leaves were limp and curled, with alarming brown, burnt tips. The moss was carpeted in red petals.

Scarlet stood at the base of the tree, arms around the trunk. "No…" she moaned. "No…"

Mal went to her, but when he tried to take her into his arms, there was nothing *to* her. The sensation of her power was notably missing. "Scarlet…?"

She sank to her knees, forehead pressed against the bark, and Mal couldn't touch her to lift her up. "Scarlet!"

Red petals fell around them like rain.

"Grant Lyons, get your ass over here!" he shouted back through the portal. Half the staff had already come through, blinking around at the jungle glade in wonder and alarm.

Bastian followed him to Scarlet, threw his first aid kit down beside him and drew his fingers wonderingly through her. As they watched, she slowly vanished, writhing in pain.

"Scarlet's… a tree?" Saina was at his heels.

"A dryad…" Laura breathed.

"What's going on?"

"Oh, Scarlet…" Lydia murmured. "She's beautiful…"

Graham was finally there, Amber at his heels. He was holding a bucket of tools and Tony had a shovel that he clearly wasn't going to let his mate carry.

"What happened to her?" Mal demanded, just resisting the urge to take Graham by the throat. "What's wrong with her?"

"Graham, it's your missing shovel!" Travis called from the far side of the tree. "And an... empty bag of salt?"

Mal's mood changed from panicked to enraged. "What did you *do* to her?" he hissed at the gardener.

"I didn't do anything!" Graham snarled in return. "I should be asking what you've done. She was just *fine* until you got here."

"The tree has been salted!" Amber exclaimed. "Someone has dug up the roots and salted them! Oh, Scarlet!"

"Can you save her?" Mal raged. He didn't have a spell for this, and didn't have the tools to face a life without the woman who'd gone from a thorn in his side to the air that he breathed. "You have to. You have to save her."

"We can dig out the contaminated soil, but she's already absorbed so much of it…" Amber fingered a wilted leaf and shook her head. "I… don't know. This should have taken weeks to happen..."

"Out of my way," Mal warned. That was one thing he could do. The soil around Scarlet's tree boiled like water and rose up in a wave away from the trunk of the tree.

Not sure how far was far enough, Mal spun a second portal into existence and dumped the contaminated soil out into the ocean.

Amber stared at him in boggled astonishment. "Well, that's one way to do it," she squeaked.

"What now?" Mal snarled.

"Fresh dirt," Graham growled. "If it's not too late."

Amber added, "Water. Lots of water. Flush the poison out of her."

It was not too late. It could not be too late.

The other side of the clearing provided a clean source of earth, and everyone danced a moment as Mal moved the ground beneath their feet and tenderly filled in the holes he'd created.

Her red flowers continued to fall, carpeting the earth in crimson.

"It's like it's raining blood," Lydia murmured.

Gizelle, who had crept through the portal with Conall at her heels, gave a whimper of fear, trembling and weeping.

Mal barely noticed them, too consumed with anger and fear. He needed water, fresh water, and he was deeply alarmed to find it within easy reach above. The storms that should have been a few days away were already touching the far side of the island and it was a simple matter to pull in a cloud of rain that drenched the new soil and soaked everyone to the skin.

"You can stop!" Graham finally shouted, when the dirt around Scarlet's tree was churned to mud. "Stop!"

Mal released the tendril of cloud with effort and the rain slowed; water was not easy for him to control.

He staggered over the mud to fall at the base of Scarlet's tree. He leaned against the trunk of her tree.

"Scarlet," he begged. "Scarlet, you have to fight, you can't give up. I'm nothing without you, I'm no one. I may as well let the wyrm drown the world if I lose you because there will be nothing left for me here. Dammit, Scarlet, you stubborn pain in my ass, if you don't shake this off, I'll… I'll…"

Mal ran out of words, something that hadn't happened in recent memory, and he pressed his face into her bark and felt tears prick behind his eyes.

At first he thought that the song he heard was the ache of his own heart. Then he realized it was a voice, and he looked up to find the mermaid, Saina, standing with her legs planted, singing, and there was an unexpected tickle of magic as her voice soared.

CHAPTER 24

Scarlet was floating.

Pain was a concept she had never understood. She sympathized with it, saw what it did to humans and shifters, but it had always been an abstract; it was a thing that happened to other people, not to her.

Now, she was *all* pain. Pain and poison and darkness. She could feel the salt in her veins, biting into her power, sucking it away.

She wasn't floating, she was sinking, sinking through the earth as she had when Mal had taken her into the depths of the island.

But this time, she was alone and adrift, without Mal's wings folded protectively around her, and she wasn't sure which way was up.

All around her was laughter and a whisper like silk against silk.

Mal? she tried to call. He was so far away.

And someone else answered.

Ah… the tree.

There was a malevolence with her: a terrible, powerful presence that had always been safely below, safely slumbering.

Scarlet could not see, but she could sense great eyes on her, half-lidded. *You were one of the ones who could stop me,* a silvery voice whispered. *The tree and the song. Together with the stone dragon, you could have kept me in my prison, rebuilt my cage around me.*

The song? Scarlet felt like her mind was moving sluggishly, like she was on the verge of understanding something just out of her capability. Everything *hurt.*

She could hear… singing.

Of course! He meant Saina.

Saina was trying to sing the salt from her… but Scarlet knew it was too late, the damage was too deep and it had already hurt her tree too badly. Even if Saina could draw every crystal from her veins, her tree was dying; Scarlet's power was already drained.

She could feel the wyrm grin and suddenly recognized its plan.

You did this on purpose! You're trying to get her to exhaust herself saving me! It had neutralized the two of them in one simple move.

Behind her, there was another set of eyes opening in the darkness.

I don't take chances, the feathered wyrm chuckled from its second head.

This was our third try, the first head admitted. *She resisted the first attempt.*

The second snapped, *You pushed too far, too fast, promised too much.*

The broken mind should have done her job the second time. The first one whined.

It's been undone, somehow. I think the broken mind went back, but we don't know when, the second speculated.

The first head growled. *It's too bright between the broken mind and the stag. We can't always see there.*

Broken mind? *Gizelle!*

The second head smirked, hearing Scarlet's sudden realization. *Such a sweet thing, so trusting. And you did most of the work for me, winning her faith and affection, drawing her out of her safe place. All I had to do was give her your own words, push her to the edge, and then tell her exactly how to fix everything.*

A chorus of voices rose like a storm all around Scarlet, drowning out Saina's far-off song. The dryad would have covered her ears if she'd been able to. It was impossible to pick individual phrases from the chaos.

For you, perhaps, the wyrm scoffed. *I have much more sophisticated minds.*

Scarlet could feel its self satisfaction, its pride.

The broken one merely needed a little direction, a little focus… the wyrm demonstrated, pulling a few of the voices forward, insistent and emotional. Mal's dragon: *She is our treasure. We must get her off this island.* Scarlet heard her own voice: *It's all my fault.*

And the wyrm's voice, thick with kindness and sorrow as its heads circled her: *If you kill the tree, Scarlet will be free... she can go to safety with everyone else... release her from the tree.* You *can fix everything! You can help!*

Scarlet, even knowing what the monster was and the lies it told, was dazzled by the promise in its words.

I have to be careful when the stag can hear us, one of the heads hissed.

Fortunately, he is not always *there,* the other head chuckled.

But when he is... we do not understand why she stops listening, the things she feels, the first pouted.

It is too bright, between them, the second agreed.

How could this all happen so quickly?

Scarlet hadn't meant to ask the question out loud, but the wyrm plucked it effortlessly from her mind.

The broken one can wedge cracks in time. Speed things up, slow them down… It is a curious side effect of her mother's gift, and because she trusts me, she trusts me to control it for her.

Scarlet felt anger rise in her throat. Gentle Gizelle, whose trust was so hard to win, had been fooled into believing that this voice was her friend. How long had it been whispering to the poor young woman, feeding her out-of-context voices, convincing her of its friendship, and using her to its own purpose?

That's what happened to the cage, she realized. *You* aged *it, using Gizelle's magic.*

One of the heads—Scarlet had lost track of which was which—laughed triumphantly. *The spell that trapped me made two foolish assump-*

tions, it sneered. *The first was that time would flow uniformly, that it was an immutable constant.*

The second? Scarlet asked, afraid of its answer.

That I have been asleep.

Whatever of Scarlet wasn't pain was now fear and she would have flung herself away if she had possessed a body to control.

The wyrm's voice filled the rock around her as both heads spoke. *I have watched, and I have waited, and I have learned, and I have stolen, and the world shall fall before me and know my wrath and I will not rest until I have cleansed the surface of the blight of man and taken back my kingdom.*

Mal will end you, Scarlet cried desperately. *Above the ground or below, he* will *stop you.*

He cannot end me, I am immortal! No one can best me. The wyrm sound more amused than intimidated.

Immortal is not infallible. You've been caged before, Scarlet pointed out. *You can be caged again!*

The wyrm grinned with both of its dire mouths.

But I won't be. The song will end, the tree will fall, and I will be free at last...

Scarlet could hear the desperation in Saina's distant song, the strength bleeding from it as she sang her heart out.

Saina, no...

The music trailed off.

You are alone now, the wyrm told her with hissing satisfaction. *You are powerless and I am all but free and the world will fall before me.*

But he was wrong—at least about one thing.

She *wasn't* alone. She was never truly alone, even in her greatest loneliness.

Trees didn't speak in words.

They spoke in slow impressions of sunlight and rain, in memories of cool earth and whispers of wind. Their words were bright flowers and dark shadows and deep roots and tall, grasping branches.

Scarlet knew them, like humans knew the steady thrum of their own heartbeats and the regular breaths of their own lungs.

If the wyrm had been made of anger and false promise, her trees were made of trust and selfless love.

And as she had devoted herself to them, they repaid it now, giving their own life energy to purge the last of the poison from her tree and reinstate her there.

The wyrm snarled, trying to keep her as her rainforest pulled her gently back.

But it was not in its element, and her trees were patient and strong.

The stone dragon does not have enough power to stop me without you! the wyrm hissed, releasing her contemptuously. *I have still won!*

Scarlet had an impression of a great force, coiling to strike, and then she was standing in a rain of her own petals.

CHAPTER 25

Mal raged helplessly. "What is the siren doing?" he demanded of no one in particular. He could feel the pull of Saina's magic song, but couldn't figure out what was happening, and it made him feel useless and on edge. It wasn't like his own healing spells, and Scarlet's tree looked worse than ever.

"She's drawing the poison from the tree," Bastian said, watching her almost as anxiously as Mal was. "She did this with me once, with goldshot, and with Wrench, after a snakebite. But this… it's more than she's ever tried to do before."

The dying leaves were starting to shimmer and, after a moment of alarm, Mal realized that they were covered in crystals. Confusion resolved into understanding: they were crystals of salt that Saina was pulling out of the tree through the leaves.

"We're losing her!" Mal said in despair.

"I don't understand," Amber said, shaking her head. Tony had his arms around her. "I don't understand how it could happen so fast. This soil was just disturbed, but it can take weeks for a tree to leech salt up from its roots. It shouldn't have hurt her so badly so quickly."

Graham grunted what Mal assumed was an agreement.

Mal stared at the tree, which was starting to look frosted in the salt crystals, like a great, gorgeous chandelier. It was possible that Scarlet's magic just moved at a faster pace than a normal tree… but the storm had arrived much faster than it ought to as well; the air was already thick with moisture and pressure and the wind was making the crystalized leaves chime together. Red petals were swirling through the air.

When there were problems with time, he knew where to look.

In three swift steps, he closed the distance to Gizelle and took her face in his hand. "What did you do?" he snarled. "What did you do to her?"

Gizelle gave a wordless cry of fear and despair. Mal saw Conall gather himself to attack and locked the Irish elk shifter into stasis with a few quick words and a gesture.

His focus was still on Gizelle. "You *salted* her! You tried to *kill* her! Why would you do this?"

The rest of the staff started to surge forward to protect her but Mal froze them all with a flick of his wrist.

"You told me we had to!" Gizelle wailed. "Your dragon said, *She is our treasure. We must get her off the island*!"

Mal went as rigid as the frozen staff as he recognized his dragon's exact words.

"My friend told me I had to free her from the tree so she wouldn't get hurt!" Gizelle buried her face in her hands. "So many voices, so many places! One of them said this was the only way! Over and over, this was the only way, and there are so many voices and it's *all my fault*!"

"What voice told you this?" Mal demanded in icy suspicion. "This specifically, with the salt and the shovel. What did it sound like?"

"So many voices…" Gizelle moaned. "Gathered up at the end like a sonic wave."

"The voice that told you to put salt on Scarlet," Mal roared at her. "What did it sound like?"

Gizelle looked at him with terror and misery in her eyes. "Rustling feathers…"

Conall, somehow, furiously, was fighting his way forward as if he was moving through honey, his mate-bond overcoming even Mal's spell.

Mal released the spell with a sweep of his hand and let go of the woman. Conall went not for Mal, but for Gizelle, sweeping her into his arms protectively. The rest of the staff staggered in place, not sure what to do with their new freedom and new information.

"So many voices," Gizelle wept hysterically into Conall's shoulder, trembling violently. "Too many! I don't understand how to make sense of it! I want them to end!"

"You gave me sound, beloved," he murmured gently, cradling her close. "Let me give you silence." He closed his eyes and concentrated.

Relief spread over Gizelle's face like a sunrise and she went limp in his arms. "It is quiet at the end, past the wave where voices can't reach," she said, exhausted and she touched her mouth in wonder. Mal guessed she couldn't hear her own spoken words.

He met Conall's angry gaze over Gizelle's head. "If she's been hearing the wyrm…"

A gasp made him turn, just in time to see Saina crumple into Bastian's arms… and Scarlet was suddenly standing among them.

She was solid again, but she was not the Scarlet that Mal knew. Gone were the heels and the timeless business clothes. Her bright hair was loose and wild around her, and her bare feet were a few inches above the moss. She stood for a moment like this, her eyes like feral emeralds, and Mal climbed to his feet.

"Scarlet," he said helplessly. His dragon seized his heart in careless claws and squeezed the breath from him.

She lives.

Mal knew that he could never lose her again, that he would trade the entire world to save her if that's what it took, and his chest felt like it would crack from the conflict he faced.

She looked at him, her gaze like a million miles, then blinked. She took a breath—her first—and bent her head with great effort, stepping out of the air and back to the earth. As she took that small step, she was somehow smaller, more Scarlet and less elemental. Her hair twisted itself back and she was dressed again, with short heels and a narrow skirt.

The effort it took was palpable and the Scarlet that remained looked tired and weak. Mal did not need to cast power sight to know that her energy had been drained to almost nothing.

"I didn't do that," Saina said hoarsely from Bastian's arms. "I was losing her. I tried, but I couldn't save her. There was… something else."

For a moment, the only sound was the wind, and the chime of salt-heavy leaves falling; Scarlet's tree was nearly bare and the jungle was weirdly still.

"My forest," Scarlet said, swaying in place. "My forest gave itself… there's almost nothing left."

"Scarlet…" Mal was at her side, catching her desperately into his embrace.

She was alarmingly frail in his grasp, a shadow of her former self as she clung to his arms. "Mal," she whispered. "Mal, it's awake. It's been awake. You have to stop it, *now*. This is your chance. I can't help you."

Mal's stomach clenched. "If I go down to fight him now, everyone here on the surface dies."

He had to shout, because the wind was suddenly howling. Scarlet winced as there was a crash in the jungle and one of the huge trees toppled slowly towards into the clearing. It ripped branches from its neighbors and Mal thought the tearing sounds as it fell seemed like screams.

The ground trembled at its fall, though it came down well away from Scarlet's tree. Everyone clung to each other, staring with wide eyes, but the earth didn't stop its growling and shaking as the fallen tree settled.

"More earthquakes?" Jenny said in alarm.

"I don't think this is an earthquake," Travis said, with none of his usual light humor.

"If you don't go down to fight him, far more people die," Scarlet reminded him. "I've met him, Mal. You can't let him go free."

"This is just the edge of the storm," Mal said in despair. "And much worse is to come."

"Can you make one of those fancy portals to somewhere a little safer?" Breck yelled over the whipping wind.

Mal hesitated. The safe places he was familiar with and could portal to were halfway around the world. He should be conserving his magic for the fight that was galloping down on them, but he couldn't leave them here to die. He hadn't realized how much he'd relied on the promise of having Scarlet's magic to draw on.

"You have to save your strength for the fight," Scarlet said miserably, guessing his train of thought. "Can you portal them just to the dock? They can escape on the boat…"

Mal hadn't been to the dock, but he'd been to the pool deck, and he sketched as big a doorway as he dared into the air and brought it to sizzling life. Everyone dashed through, just as a great boom shook the island and Mal felt the cage below the surface explode into shards of broken magic.

They staggered from Scarlet's clearing to a pool deck that was shaking and buckling, tiles popping out as great cracks appeared. Glass everywhere was shattering, furniture from the pool was picked up by wild winds and smashed to the far walls. As they fought to stand on the swaying ground, against the wind, a storm surge rolled in from the angered ocean and buried the dock and the entire beach in swirling foam and crashing waves.

The boat docked there was flung as if it was a child's toy, right into the railing of the pool deck, and it broke into chunks. Some of the pieces bounced back into the roiling water and some flew up to skid over the tiles and splash into the churning pool. One of the motors struck a palm tree that gave a shudder and upended.

"Or not!" Travis said wryly, shouting over the wind.

Laura lost her footing on the heaving ground and Tex caught her before she fell. Mates clung to each other. Several shifted to find better steadiness on four paws, including Chef and Magnolia, who sheltered others from the wind behind their massive bears.

For a moment, the earth stilled slightly and the wind was a little less, but Mal knew that it was only a matter of time before the wyrm fought his way to the surface.

"You have to get out of here now," he said in despair. He couldn't save Scarlet, but he could save the people who were loyal to her. Scarlet stepped back from him, swaying weakly in place. He started to sketch a new doorway, focusing on his stronghold in New York. It would take a reckless amount of energy, but he knew he had to do it. The earth was starting to rumble again as the wyrm crawled for the surface; they didn't have more than a few minutes.

"Wait!" It was Graham, stepping forward with Alice's hand in his own. "You could have beat it with Scarlet's power, right?"

"I don't have anything left," Scarlet said helplessly.

The gardener ignored her, glaring at Mal in challenge. "Corbin... he could use a shifter's energy to do magic. Could you do that with us?"

Mal stared at him. "Bind *you*? You're just..."

"All of us. If you could tap all of our power, would it be enough?" Graham looked aside at Alice, and she set her jaw and stepped closer to him, nodding in agreement.

"I've never had a chance to save the world before," she said merrily.

Mal swept his gaze over the assembled shifters and gestured carefully. They all glowed with power—if not the scope of Scarlet's single-handed energy, each with their own unique strength—and strongest of all were the mate-bonds between them, a curious glow of magic and love. "I could do that," he realized in astonishment. Graham and Alice both stood open to him, the simple act of their offer putting their potential in his hands.

This wasn't magic the way that he had studied it, with spells and structure and study. This was something more elemental, like his innate ability to slip through rock, or Scarlet's ability to make things grow. "This could work," he said, with something painfully like hope growing in his gut.

Bastian, just behind Alice, exchanged a look with Saina and moved to stand beside Graham with her. "I'm not Scarlet's caliber, but I *am* a dragon," he said proudly.

Mal hadn't banished his energy sight and it was as if a veil had fallen away from Bastian's source.

Scarlet put a trembling hand to her mouth, tears shining in her eyes.

"I'm nearly tapped," Saina said, coming to Bastian's side. "But what I've got, I'd give." She was a gentle light, even exhausted.

Darla and Breck came forward, hand in hand. "We're not going to let you have all that fun without us," Breck called over a gust of wind.

"I got a debt to pay back," Wrench said to Lydia, and she lifted her chin proudly and met Mal's gaze with a firm nod.

Magnolia and Chef, still in bear form, bowed their great heads in agreement.

It was Mary who dragged Neal forward. "We're in."

Tony gave Scarlet a conflicted look and Amber spoke his concerns aloud. "Could this hurt our child?"

Mal felt like he'd been sideswiped by the offers, his power sight nearly overwhelmed. "I don't think so," he said, dazedly. "The data I've seen suggests that *in vitro* exposure to magic may cause children to shift earlier, but I've never seen evidence of harm. I would not take enough to hurt any of you."

"Then I'm in," Amber said with a lift of her chin.

"*Pura vida*," Tony said. *Pure life*, the Costa Rican motto. Their magic was suddenly at his fingertips.

"Us, too," Tex and Laura said in unison.

Jenny shifted from the otter form she'd taken shelter in. "Is it a conflict of interest if we have to face each other in the courtroom later?"

"I will preemptively concede every case to you," Mal said, a hint of a smile at his mouth.

The smile died as the subtle rumble of the earth beneath them intensified.

"We're with you," Jenny said swiftly. "Do you need something more than that?"

"You'd all do this?" Mal said in astonishment, looking at the assembled shifters who had gathered forward. "You'd take this risk?"

"Not for *you*," Graham growled. "And maybe not for the world. But we'd do it for Scarlet."

CHAPTER 26

Scarlet was the only one of the group who wasn't soaking wet, so nothing could hide the tears tracking down her face. She didn't try to wipe them away.

She understood the depth of what each of them was offering, she knew the trust it took, and it left her awed and honored.

Conall had been standing back with Gizelle curled in his arms. Scarlet wasn't sure whether he could hear any of what was happening, or if he understood it, until he stepped forward, glaring at Mal.

"What do you have to do?" he asked.

Gizelle rolled out of his embrace and landed on her feet, nearly falling to her knees on the unsteady tile. "I can't run," she said in alarm, looking up at Conall.

"And I won't run without you," Conall told her firmly.

"You have us," Gizelle said to Mal gravely. Then she looked up at Conall. "But I have to do something first!" she said wildly, and she bolted to stand in front of Saina and stare into her eyes for a long moment.

Saina shook her head in confusion and then Gizelle was dashing back to hold onto Conall's hand and nod at Mal.

Scarlet remembered the wyrm's cryptic talk: *It was undone, somehow. I don't know when.*

Mal closed his eyes and everyone gave a sudden intake of breath. Scarlet, her own power cold and banked inside, could still sense the swell of magic in her mate. It was a muddier magic than her own, or even than Mal's innate earth dragon magic, but it was as solid.

I can do this, she heard him say in a sudden burst of hope. Then she felt his laughter like a caress. We *can do this*, he corrected.

It wasn't any too soon; the long, low growl of the ground beneath them was a crescendo and they were having to dance in place for balance. Gravel rattled and some of the remaining glass shattered in place as the earth began to shake in earnest.

Mal fixed his eyes on the ground and Scarlet touched his arm, knowing he wanted to dive into the earth and stop the monster now, while he still had some advantage. He turned and pulled her into a last, damp embrace.

Whatever you have to do... Scarlet started sincerely, thinking of her helpless tree.

I won't drain them, Mal said fiercely. *I will be able to release them before the end, if it comes to that.*

He kissed her once, briefly and hard, then pushed her away. "Take what shelter you can," he commanded over the sound of the rising wind. "The bar may stand."

The shifters gathered themselves and fled up the shivering stairs, just as the gathering clouds opened up and rain began to pelt down on them.

The rain changed to hail before they were all under the overhanging restaurant deck, first pebble-sized, then fist-sized, then chunks of ice the size of small melons were hurtling towards them at impossible speeds. Tex and Travis toppled the cooler onto its side to act as a defense against the onslaught while some of them hid behind of the bar. Magnolia and Chef, still in their bear forms, protected others, thick fur ruffled in the wind.

Unable to help them, barely able to keep her physical form, Scarlet stood at the edge of the bar deck, watching her resort tremble as Mal began to chant in earnest. The runes on his forearms were bright in the gathering darkness.

The hail gave way to rain, heavy and driving. Scarlet stared through the gloom to where Mal was beginning to weave the tools he needed to subdue the monster long enough to cage it.

Shimmering ropes appeared, looping around the cottages and across the pool deck, and Scarlet wasn't sure if they were shivering with energy, or from the endless shaking of the earth. It was starting to feel almost normal, the earthquake had gone on so long.

Then, as if challenging that idea, it intensified and someone screamed as one of the columns cracked and a portion of the restaurant deck collapsed. Further away, Scarlet could hear buildings and trees groan in protest, and more glass was shattering.

Mal leaped into the air, spreading tiger's eye wings, just as the wyrm emerged from beneath one of Scarlet's cottages, throwing rock and earth out of its path.

Each of its heads was a wedge nearly the size of Mal's entire dragon, its great eyes lightning white above a snarling mouth full of shining teeth. Coils of its legless body flattened another cottage, and its tail sent white gravel spitting in all directions as it sliced up through the resort paths.

Scarlet had expected the wyrm's size, but she hadn't expected the creature's unearthly beauty. The serpentine body was most similar to a snake, but moved in ways that no snake could ever manage, flowing and pulsing in shimmering waves. Its gleaming body was covered from face to tail-tip in razor-tipped iridescent blue and green feathers, each one reflective and flexible enough to move like a leaf. They sang like tuned windchimes with every sinuous movement.

It was like watching music, shimmering waves of color blazing from its feathered hide.

Mal rose up into the storm and fell down upon him like a sparrow on an alligator, the runes on his dragon's forelegs glowing as he folded his wings and dropped. Magic-strengthened, he hit the wyrm right behind the nearest head, driving it down to the earth as the ropes whipped up to capture one of its long necks.

The second head dove for the golden dragon, snapping down… on a brilliant blue shield that flared to life. Through the driving, pounding sound of the storm, Scarlet could hear the teeth screech off of the barrier. The first head was ripping up from the ropes holding it, straining and pulling as the second head changed its tactic and rammed into Mal with all of its strength.

A portal opened behind him, another opening directly above him with the same sweep of his tail, and then Mal was dropping into one and out of the other to dive onto the head flailing through empty space. Claws that gleamed blue light drove through the slithering feathers. The first head had fought its way free of the magical rope and was snapping at Mal in fury.

The wyrm, now free, twisted in a corkscrew into the air like it was climbing an invisible ladder and scraped along Mal's hide with a sound like metal on stone.

That was when Scarlet realized that the plumage wasn't merely decorative. Every gleaming blue-green feather was knife-edged, and strong enough that she felt scale slice beneath it.

Mal, she whispered, staggered by his pain.

She could feel the spell that healed the cuts, and see the runes flare briefly on the dragon's forearms. Flexible as a cat, he twisted away, vanished through a portal, and reappeared above the wyrm once again.

One of its heads turned to snap at him, the other ducked to come up behind him, but Mal dove between them, then made a mid-air turn that no bird would have attempted and came up under one of the chins, digging in with magic-hardened claws as he hauled it back down toward the magical ropes wriggling above the resort below.

The other head screamed and came crashing in against Mal's blazing shield.

CHAPTER 27

This isn't anything we haven't trained for, Mal told his dragon as they tumbled through another portal to get behind the wyrm again. They both knew he was desperately lying.

The magic from the Shifting Sands staff was nearly as strong as Scarlet's had been. But it was incoherent, competitive, and using magic that wasn't his was just different enough than using his own that he was sometimes scrambling to understand what he was doing. His shields were a moment slower than they needed to be, his portals just a little sloppier. His concentration was broken between smoothing the lines of power and setting the spells, all while he fought an angry, razor-feathered, two-headed wyrm who had everything to lose and vengeance to gain... in the middle of a raging storm.

He felt like a boy again, a dragon who could barely fly, in the air being pitted against experienced warriors with the advantage of fire.

We won those battles, his dragon reminded him, dodging a head followed by a swirling blender of sharp feathers. *Sometimes.*

Mal could hear his father's voice. *What edge do you always have? Knowledge.* What did he know that could possibly help him?

You know nothing, a voice intruded scornfully.

Less than nothing, a second voice chimed.

Then, together, W*e have all the* edgesssssss.

The wyrm cackled in unison at its own joke as it sent the tail that Mal had lost track of to twist around him in a swirl of dark, iridescent feathers. Mal gave a roar of pain, failing in surprise to raise a shield before they sliced into the scales along his side, through the magic-hardening spell altogether. He was poorly positioned for a portal. The driving rain and wind made it difficult to stay steady long enough to accurately dive through a small one and a large one took more power.

A swift healing spell kept the cuts from being deadly, but Mal was keenly aware that he was burning through the magical reserves at an unsustainable rate.

He steeled himself for a phased attack, dropping through a portal just a little above from one of the great heads as he escaped snapping jaws. He took hold of the huge wedge head and used a jolt of magic that burned like acid through his veins to drag the wyrm with him back to where the ropes waited to capture it. The other head and the tail twisted to batter against his gleaming shield.

They fought, teeth shrieking over shield, claws digging through feathers, magic will against brute strength and fury.

Harder and deeper, Mal poured the magic that had been given to him into all of the spells he was keeping alive: the shield, the force dragging them towards the shining ropes he was keeping alive and waiting, the magic reinforcement of his claws and scales.

For one bright moment, he thought he could do it; one strong push and he could force the wyrm down to his destiny.

But then the wyrm flared every feather in braking power and the free head opened its toothy jaws to roar a command into the storm. Furious wind tore through the shield to Mal's wings, ripping the membrane. The rain was so dense that it blinded him and Mal, unable to divert any magic to healing, shivered in pain.

The wyrm took advantage of his distraction and crashed into his shield with its tail, overpowering it with sheer force. Mal clung to the head under his claws desperately; he couldn't portal in this kind of wind, and he didn't dare let go, even as the spell pulling the wyrm back to be caged unraveled in the air and the wyrm slithered back up into the clouds.

Then the second head bit into him and ripped him loose, tossing him end over end into the storm.

For a moment, Mal only tumbled, helpless and stunned. Then he cast a swift healing spell to stem the worst of the bleeding and he tried to make sense of where he was and where the wyrm was.

Out of the cloud and rain, a grinning head came sweeping with jaws wide to snap at his ravaged wings. Mal dived for a portal, missed it in the driving wind, and slammed into the body of the wyrm beyond.

Landing in feathers was somehow less comfortable than it sounded when the feathers were tipped in knives.

Mal kicked off and fell backwards through the clouds until he could spread his wings and fly again with his damaged wings.

Think! he berated himself. *Act! Fight!* His magic stores were draining too quickly, and he couldn't risk harming the shifters who had so selflessly given it to him.

The wyrm spiraled down towards him, lazily, and batted at him with a playful tail.

It was a game, Mal realized as he dodged the tail with effort and feathers skidded off a hasty shield when he wasn't quite fast enough. The wyrm was toying with him, confident in its victory now.

Their battle, swiftly becoming one-sided, was taking them out over the storm-raged jungle and Mal had a sudden cold moment of terror. Was the wyrm deliberately taking them to Scarlet's grove?

The tree… one of the heads hissed dismissively, as if it felt his thought. *We stopped the tree.*

She is powerless, the other smirked.

To Mal's horror, the storm was effortlessly flattening the giant trees of the rain forest below them, ripping them up by their roots and tossing them aside as if they were tiny saplings. He had a glimpse of the clearing, just beyond.

Scarlet…

Mal closed his eyes and dug as deep into the magic as he dared, waiting until the two baleful heads were close together and then casting a shield not over himself, but over the wyrm's two heads, like throwing a bag over two squirming snakes.

He had only a heartbeat of optimism before the two heads, growling, moved in opposite directions and ripped the shield into a spray of sparks.

Before we take the world back, we will make you suffer, the wyrm snarled in harmony. *We will make you pay the sins of your forefathers in the blood we draw from your sides and the pain we will make you scream.*

But when Mal expected the feathered creature to rip his heart out by upending Scarlet's tree, it only growled into the storm and the wind sent him tumbling as the wyrm chased him like a cat chasing a crippled mouse.

Mal spread badly injured wings, breathing what he knew was his last healing spell into them as he fled back towards the ocean, hoping only to draw the monster and the storm it was making from Scarlet's unprotected grove.

CHAPTER 28

Scarlet had never felt so helpless. Not as a new dryad, not wandering the streets in England with her dying tree. Not when she was most sure she would lose her resort. Not even feeling her tree's life slip away after she had been salted.

Her forest was tapped, the life energy that they had shared with her so selflessly drained to nothing. Even if they survived the storm and captured the wyrm, she didn't know if the jungle would ever thrive again.

And there was nothing she could do for her mate.

She stood at the edge of the bar deck, as if she could do anything to protect the staff hiding there. They were crouched behind whatever shelter they could find—toppled tables, chunks of rubble from the restaurant deck above.

And above them was the terrible aerial battle, half obscured by charcoal clouds and blowing debris.

The wyrm tore chunks from Mal's hide, ripped at the webbing of his wings, batting him out of the sky like he was nothing more than a minor inconvenience. Every time, Mal returned to try to drag it back, every time more slowly. Bright shields flared more briefly with each hit.

He was being idly savaged, Scarlet realized. The only reason that the wyrm hadn't left the island for its freedom yet was to exact painful revenge from Mal himself, playing with him like a cat with its helpless prey. Mal's magic was finite, his ability to heal was slowing and his protections were failing.

Bastian was suddenly standing beside her. "He's released us," he said, sounding weary.

Scarlet felt her chest seize with pain. Mal had only his own magical reserves remaining, and she knew they would not last long.

It was still raining, still windy, but the worst of it was away over the jungle, beating on her forest and battering Mal.

Bastian went to the edge of the deck; the railing was drunken on the cracked concrete.

Saina staggered to him against the wind. "What are you doing?"

"I'm going to go fight with him," Bastian said matter-of-factly. "He isn't going to save the world alone."

Saina gave a low keen of misery and dragged his face down to hers for a long kiss. Then she released him. "I will sing for you," she said. "As long as I have voice."

Then Bastian was rising on his green wings into the buffeting wind.

"I wish there was something we could do," Jenny said, shifting from otter to woman at Scarlet's side.

"He could have used more of our magic," Travis said, soaking wet at her side.

"He didn't want to drain you too far," Scarlet said miserably.

Mal and Bastian looked like tiny songbirds trying to harass a great roc. A great, angry, confident roc.

Saina was singing what little power she had left into her mate with a hoarse voice against the grasping wind.

Scarlet cringed. Even that was her fault. If Saina had not exhausted herself saving the dryad... If she had not *been* a dryad, Mal would have been able to evacuate everyone and fight the battle where he could beat it.

Scarlet thought bitterly. *It's all my fault*!

Gizelle, crouching behind a table near Conall, looked up at her abruptly, as if she'd heard Scarlet's thought. Her white-streaked hair was dripping wet and tangled, and Scarlet wondered how many ways she had failed the young woman. She should have persuaded Conall to take her off the island earlier. She should have taken the threat that slept—didn't sleep—below them more seriously.

Scarlet dragged her eyes up to the storm.

Mal and Bastian gamely fought, but no one on the ground had any illusions that they had a chance against the beast.

Jenny couldn't watch after only a few moments, turning to bury her face in Travis' chest.

"It's just toying with them," Travis said quietly.

Jenny looked up. "If it really wanted to hurt Mal, why hasn't it gone for Scarlet's tree?" she asked quietly.

"It doesn't think I'm important anymore," Scarlet guessed, remembering the wyrm's confusion over the bond that Gizelle and Conall shared. "It doesn't understand love, or loyalty. Because I have no power, it thinks Mal doesn't care for me any further."

She knew love. And loyalty… she only had to think about the staff of Shifting Sands and everything they'd done for her. They'd offered up their own shifter energy. They'd even pooled their resources to *buy* her the island.

Scarlet froze.

Mal! she cried, knowing the risk of distracting him. *Mal, you have to sell me the island!*

The wyrm twisted beneath him, the razor edges of his feathers slicing up into Mal's claws. Mal roared in pain, but pressed his assault, futilely trying to drive the wyrm back down with Bastian's help. *I'm a little busy for a real estate transaction,* he pointed out. His voice was not defeated, though he must surely recognize his inevitable loss of this game.

There was no time to explain. *Trust me,* Scarlet begged. *Shift and accept my offer for the island so I can help you. Aloud, with witnesses. There can be no doubts.*

She could feel his hesitation as he considered. The storm was rising to an impossible tenor, the wyrm was driving him back up into the clouds. He'd be more vulnerable yet in his human form.

But he *trusted* her.

The jaws of one of the heads snapped in air as Mal unexpectedly streaked away from the battle, retreating to the battered resort.

Bastian swooped down at the creature's tail, sending a blast of flame over the wyrm that simply rolled off its shimmering feathers. But the attack made the wyrm hesitate, and that was enough time for Mal to fly over the jungle, drop from the sky and shift to human long enough to shout over the wind, "I accept your offer for the island before these witnesses with no exceptions or refusals!"

He gave Scarlet a piercing look. "I hope you know what you're doing," he told her, then he was launching into the violent air again just as the wyrm got its teeth around one of Bastian's rear legs midair and Saina screamed helplessly.

It was enough.

Scarlet felt the contract that had walled her from the far half of the island dissolve with Mal's words, and all that had been there was suddenly *hers*.

She could feel every inch of the island, every ridge and rock and beach.

The forest there was not as vital as her half of the island had been, not nurtured as hers had been by a dryad of great power for many decades, but it was thick and *alive*, and when she reached out for it, it answered.

Wild jungle covered most of the island, and even the blades of grass where tame lawn had been gave her a little tickle of awareness. The arboretum at Beehag's compound had housed dozens of rare trees, their dormant energy buzzing awake as she caressed them with her greeting.

You are my forest now, she told them lovingly, and from the smallest sapling to the greatest giant kapok, they answered with devotion and delight.

Power coursed through her once more, nearly as strong as it had ever been, filling all the empty corners of her tree.

And she knew exactly what to do with it.

As Mal battled against the wind to rejoin the fight, he went incandescent with the magic that Scarlet abruptly flung at him. His golden claws struck fast and true, magic-strengthened. The wyrm gave a cry of rage and pain as the claws managed to penetrate its armor-like feathers, dropping its hold on Bastian's leg.

The green dragon fell away from the battle with a final jet of flame and tumbled into a shallow glide to land in the turbulent pool, shifting into human form as he hit the surface and sank.

Saina left the questionable shelter of the rubble of the bar, scrambled down the broken steps and dived fearlessly after him, nearly falling as the wind howled against her.

Scarlet had no attention to spare for them, or for any of the people she loved as dearly. All of her focus was on the battle above as she coiled in wait.

CHAPTER 29

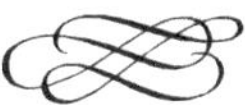

Mal felt his exhaustion burn away as Scarlet—his amazing, brilliant Scarlet—re-filled his wells of magic with her pure, elemental power. He was going to pay for this soon enough, he knew, but the important thing was that he had it *now*. He had a chance again to fulfill his destiny.

The wyrm was not convinced of that truth, snarling and fighting with all its considerable strength against Mal's claws.

You cannot beat me, one of the heads snarled.

I do not have to beat you, Mal retorted. Not by himself.

They were in the belly of the storm now, and Mal's wings could not keep him steady in the raging winds. But he wasn't trying to fly, he wasn't even trying to fight. He wrapped a strong tail around the wyrm's throat and let himself tumble towards the ground with sudden, enchanted mass, dragging his adversary with him as the feathers scraped uselessly on Mal's magic-hardened scales.

They didn't fall for long; the wyrm was stronger than Mal's dead weight, and its surprise at Mal's action didn't last.

But they didn't have to fall far.

They had been fighting high over the tops of the whipping trees of the island, Mal trying hard not to think of Scarlet's tree and the damage it must be taking as huge branches and whole trees were pulled up into the maelstrom.

Now they were just brushing those treetops and as the wyrm gathered itself to spring higher and unleash his anger from above, the rainforest itself came to life.

Green vines whipped up into the storm and wrapped themselves around the sinuous feathered creature. He broke them easily at first, verdant leaves spiraling up into his storm, but more followed, and more, and more, folding down his feathers, dragging him down into the upper canopy, where thick branches stretched and grew into giant, grasping fingers.

The wyrm thrashed, uprooting entire trees and snapping branches, but the sheer number of trees against him saw him pinned, utterly unable to break free. His wind howled, and his rain drove hard against them, but the jungle was unified against him, and Mal set himself into a dive from above.

Ignoring the wind that tore at his scales, Mal set himself upon the wyrm, driving it further down towards the earth. He roared the names of the runes into the storm and the marks on his front legs flared with power as the bars of the new cage rose from the earth to meet them.

The wyrm, thrashing now like a pinned snake, gave a cry of desperate fury. His wind raged, ripping trees from their roots and smashing them down in every direction. His feathers sliced into thick trunks and severed branches.

Mal wasn't sure where they were, how close they were to Scarlet's vulnerable tree, but he made a split-second hesitation at the thought of it.

The hesitation broke his concentration and, for a moment, the wyrm was free. It slipped between the half-formed bars to slither towards the resort itself.

Mal wasn't sure if it was seeking a place with fewer trees to hold it, or if he knew the value of the shifters huddled in the ruins to the combatants and hoped to use them as hostages. Mal was after him again in a heartbeat as he coiled out of the jungle and smashed through the cottages that were still standing. Broken glass and roof tiles swirled up into the wind, bouncing harmlessly off of Mal as he blocked the wyrm's escape to the sky with a shield more vast than any he had ever managed before.

Trees exploded up from the ground and potted plants burst their vessels as they instantly grew and grasped at the two-headed wyrm, tying it to the ground.

Mal spoke the words of power again and dropped down onto the wyrm, pressing it down into the earth again as the glimmering bars rose up around them.

The wyrm thrashed and the ground shook and rumbled from the force of its struggle.

A scream made Mal realize that the battered restaurant was beginning to groan and collapse and Scarlet's ragged staff fled from the bar where they'd been sheltered.

The wyrm, in one final, vindictive effort, chose the most helpless of the creatures before it, and sucked in breath for a last blast of wind.

"Get down!" Scarlet cried in a great voice. "Hold on!" All of them automatically dropped to the shivering ground to cover their heads from the flying debris…

...All of them except Conall, who was not touching Gizelle and could not hear the warning.

Scarlet's shroud of greenery rose moments too late; the wyrm's gust caught the musician square in the chest and swept him backwards into the crumbling building.

The musician hit one of the columns, so hard that the terrible crunch of his breaking bones was louder than the storm. Jagged pieces of the restaurant deck rained down like hail over his still form.

Mal did not have to wonder if he had survived the impact; Gizelle's scream of agony and loss would haunt his dreams forever: a thin wail of despair that threaded the music of the storm like a harmony.

The wyrm, mistakenly thinking that this distraction had bought it escape, made another bid for freedom, to face Mal bristling in new rage.

We will cage you again and bury you deep! his dragon swore. *We will fulfill our destiny!*

You are nothing! the wyrm snarled.

You cannot defeat us! the other head protested.

The feathered wyrm struck out with its tail, and the earth shuddered and groaned, but when it tried to lift it for a second strike, there were new trees and bushes pinning it, its entire body and both necks were being wrapped in leaves and branches like a great green cast as Scarlet unleashed her forest on him.

The storm continued to rage, but the monster was caught.

Mal landed and shifted to human form to perform the final stages of the cage.

CHAPTER 30

The wyrm snarled, struggling against the vines that were rising from the island. The gleaming bars Mal was building around it were semi-transparent and too far apart to hold it in, but as he chanted, the cage began to solidify and condense upon the captured monster.

Scarlet, concentrating fiercely on keeping the creature subdued and already distracted by another task, was suddenly surprised as something small dashed beside her down the steps to where Mal was facing the feathered heads.

"Gizelle, no!"

Scarlet's first thought was that Gizelle was mad with grief and wanted revenge on the creature that had killed Conall. "Gizelle, wait!"

But the slight woman wasn't trying to get through the bars of the cage to the wyrm in some fit of rage, she was leaping at Mal.

"No!" the gazelle shifter cried, clinging to his arm and covering his runes. "Stop! You have to stop!"

"I have to do this," Mal said, trying to pull away from her without harming her. His teeth were gritted and Scarlet could feel the strain he was under; already he had burned through too much of the magical stores she'd refilled, and she could feel the underlying exhaustion. "Gizelle, it's not a person, it's a creature of destruction!"

The bars of the cage wavered with his distraction.

Scarlet had half her mind on the forest wrapping the wyrm, regrowing vines and grasping trees as fast as his sharp-edged feathers could cut through them. She flickered to Gizelle's side, prepared to try to draw her away. "Gizelle…"

"You can't do this!" Gizelle's voice was big compared to her little frame, wavering but firm.

"I don't have a choice," Mal said between gritted teeth. The runes on his forearms flared, his concentration divided.

"No!" Gizelle wept. "No one deserves to be in a cage!"

She gave up trying to stop Mal and before Scarlet realized what she was doing, Gizelle had darted between the big bars of the cage to face the wyrm.

Scarlet cried out as the wyrm twisted and opened two sets of giant jaws in Gizelle's direction, tearing from her trees. "Gizelle, no!" She lost her grip on the vines she was controlling and was suddenly… somewhere else.

She was standing in knee-deep grass, brilliantly lit by nothing at all. Above her, the sky was featureless black: no stars, no sun, no color.

Gizelle stood with her back straight, her slim gazelle shivering at her side. Mal was here, too, his golden dragon towering above his human form, both of them looking around in curious wonder.

And the wyrm was with them, fluttering its blue and green feathers in confusion. It had no human self beside it.

Mal gestured, and spoke a few words that Scarlet didn't catch, but nothing happened. The wyrm opened its mouths as if it would spit wind at them… but the grass continued to wave peacefully.

Suspiciously, Scarlet reached out with her own power, calling on the grass to grow… and found that nothing answered.

Gizelle was walking fearlessly forward towards it. "You can run here, always," she said to it, sounding weary and worn down. It thrashed in fury but, despite its great size, seemed incapable of harm. When it screamed, even the sound seemed powerless.

Gizelle turned her back on it, facing Mal and Scarlet. "No one belongs in a cage," she repeated. "Not even that. Better that it stay here, forever and never, until the sky goes dark."

The wyrm suddenly shifted forms and was a human, with silky, rainbow-dark hair, dressed in soft feathers in peacock blues and greens. "Gizelle," it said coaxingly. "I have always been your friend. Free me and I will make you a queen! We will make the whole world a place to run and you will rule at my side."

Scarlet made a small noise of anger and dismay and Mal said flatly, "Don't listen to it, Gizelle. It was never your friend."

Gizelle turned to regard the wyrm again, ignoring both of them.

"I was Conall's queen," she said mournfully.

"I can bring him back," the wyrm whispered temptingly in a new voice, stepping close to Gizelle. "I brought him down, and I can bring him back, but only if you free me. Let me go from this place and you will be together again."

Scarlet could see the quiver in Gizelle's frame, the hesitation. "No…" she whispered.

"He lies," Mal told Gizelle firmly. "No one can do that."

Scarlet bit her lip.

Gizelle turned and looked at them each in turn and then faced the wyrm again. "You've always spoken nicely to me, and for a long time, I thought that *nice* meant *good*. But you would hurt so many people, and cause so much pain. Even Conall isn't worth that price. I couldn't be that selfish." She stepped closer to it, trembling and fearless at once. "I'm sorry for your hatred and your hunger for destruction. I'm sorry for all your time in a cage, awake and angry. I don't know if you are capable of happiness, but here there will be no time and you will not suffer."

The wyrm seemed to gather itself and Scarlet took a step forward to protect Gizelle—if she even needed protecting in this place—and saw Mal do the same.

Then they were suddenly outside again, the storm still whipping around them as they faced the monstrous form of the half-caged wyrm.

The creature was weirdly still, every feather frozen in space; it was the only thing not moving in the wind. Even small rocks skidded across the tiles in the gale.

"We will have to close the door completely," Mal said, looking at Gizelle in awe. "He will find a way out, if we leave even the tiniest crack. You'll never be able to go back."

Gizelle's shoulders drooped, but she nodded. "I knew that," she said simply. "But I am done running. Nothing matters that much anymore." The tearless grief in her face was like a great weight and Scarlet hurt for her.

"He is immortal and can never die," Mal said gravely. "He will be locked in your place forever in that single moment and I will bury his earthly body. Close the door, Gizelle."

She looked up at him with trusting eyes. "I don't know how."

CHAPTER 31

Mal gazed down at Gizelle. So much of what she did was instinct, in sharp contrast to his own carefully learned, orderly methods. "I think I can help you," he offered. "I need a physical anchor. Something that means a lot to you would be best, but anything will do."

Gizelle's glance flickered up to the bar deck, where Conall's body lay half-covered in rubble.

"What about this?"

Mal turned to find that Bastian and Saina had climbed from the crumbling pool, and the dragon shifter, looking rather worse for the wear and leaning heavily on his mate, was holding out an ugly, battered piece of metal.

"I found it when we were fleeing back from Scarlet's tree," the lifeguard explained. "My treasure sense went nuts and I had to pick it up."

Gizelle gave a sigh. "Yes," she said.

Mal took it, hefting it in his hand. It was a big chunk of metal, clearly a mechanical lock of some kind that had been badly damaged. A hole had been drilled in it, and a carabiner was looped through that hole. A lock had good symbolism, and when he cast his power sight on it—wincing at the effort it took—he was stunned by the emotions it had captured: Neal's years of anger and helplessness, Gizelle's fears and confusion… and Conall's deep love.

"This is perfect," he agreed. He put it in Gizelle's hands. "I want you to picture a large door."

She closed her eyes obediently.

"Now imagine a deadbolt—do you know what that is?"

Gizelle nodded.

"Good. Imagine that you've closed the door, and now you're locking it. The lock is heavy, like this, and you can hear it shooting home. You might have to press on the door to make the lock fit. And then nothing can get in or out, forever."

"It's the end," Gizelle said quietly.

Mal didn't need to cast his power sight to confirm her success; Gizelle's hair suddenly shimmered to pure white and the feathered wyrm bleached of color as if it had turned into pale marble.

Forever.

"You did it," Mal murmured to Gizelle.

Scarlet, the same exhaustion in her shoulders that Mal felt on his own, let the vines and trees wrapping the creature go slack and turned to account for the rest of her staff. They began to emerge from the rubble they had used as cover as the storm, no longer powered by the wyrm's wrath, began to die. It was still raining, but it was a gentle rain now, warm and apologetic.

Two bears, one white and one golden brown, rose to four feet and shook rubble and rain off of them as staff who had sheltered behind them dazedly dusted themselves off.

Gizelle lifted a face tracked with raindrops to look at Mal. "Why am I still here? I don't remember this..."

"The door is closed," Mal said wearily. "You're locked to one time now, like all of us. No more whispers from the future, only memories of the past."

She made a wordless noise of agony and turned away. "I don't want to be here. I thought it would *end* when the door shut."

She slipped around Mal and climbed up the shattered stairs to where Conall's body lay crumpled, her white hair a tangled cloak behind her. Jenny let go of Travis to follow her, and after a moment, Lydia gave Wrench a squeeze and trailed after.

Slowly, weary and battered, they all picked their way one by one and two by two through the rubble, standing in a stunned group on the broken tile to gather around Conall.

Mal, feeling empty and exhausted as never before, stood alone for a moment on the bar level.

"Can you heal him?" Scarlet demanded quietly, suddenly at his side.

"He's dead," Mal told her. "I can't do anything about that."

"I know *that*," Scarlet said impatiently. "Can you *heal* him?"

"It wouldn't do any good," Mal said gently. Should he be flattered that she thought him capable of that? He was too *tired* to feel flattered.

"You have got to stop making assumptions," she replied with a sigh. "I do not have dominion over earth, Mal."

"You're a dryad…" he started.

"And do you see me throwing rocks around or making mountains move?" Scarlet asked scathingly. "Was I even slightly comfortable underground? Did I have any luck controlling dirt? Just because my roots are in earth doesn't mean I don't need air, or fire from the sun, or water from the rain. I don't have any power over dirt or rocks, I make things *grow*."

Mal scowled at her in confusion, trying to make sense of what she was trying to tell him.

"My dominion is *life*, Mal. I can bring Conall back, but it won't do more than make him suffer needlessly and die again if he can't also be healed."

"You can…"

"I can bring him back to life," she said calmly, as if she was not offering the impossible.

"You're sure?"

"I caught him as he died," Scarlet explained. "And I have only been able to hold him here this long because of his bond with Gizelle. We have to hurry, or I will lose him entirely."

"I can heal him," Mal said, testing his wells of power cautiously.

They were badly drained, and his ability to control it was nearly burned out completely. He had never strained himself like this before, never even dreamed of controlling so much energy. There were a few swirls of magic left and just enough strength in his mind. "I can do that much."

"Do it then." Scarlet took his hand and they walked slowly up to where Gizelle was lying curled against Conall's still side. Lydia and Jenny were sitting on either side of her, offering mute comfort and the rest of the staff was in a loose, grieving semi-circle around them. They had pulled most of the rubble off of Conall, and tried to lay him out in a less unnatural position.

Scarlet took her hand back, but didn't gesture or chant. She only looked at the fallen shifter and Mal didn't understand that she was using her power until Conall suddenly took a shuddering breath, groaned, and began to die from his injuries once more.

Gizelle gave a frightened squeak of alarm, shrinking away. "Conall!"

Jenny stood and stepped back, nearly colliding with Scarlet, and Lydia reached for Gizelle and clasped her hand, murmuring a prayer.

The rest of the staff gasped and whispered and swore in surprise.

Mal cursed and brought his scattered thoughts to bear, naming the runes as he gestured to them. Conall's body arched as the last tattered remains of Mal's magic knit his bones back together and mended crushed organs. He had underestimated the amount of damage the man had taken, and for a bad moment he feared he wouldn't be able to do as he'd promised.

Then Scarlet's pure power was bolstering him again, flowing into him like water after terrible thirst.

Life, her power was *life*.

Her entire forest, now both sides of the island, gave her a deep wellspring of energy without even trying.

Mal would have laughed, if he had the energy left for it. It all made so much sense.

Then Conall began to cough and rolled to one side with a moan of pain. Gizelle reached for him, weeping and shaking.

"I can't… hear…" he said breathlessly, when her hands were on him. "No, I can… but it's so *quiet.*"

"The door is shut," Gizelle said simply, laying her head on his shoulder. "I only hear things that are *now.*"

Mal couldn't stand any longer, every muscle in his body trembled as badly as Gizelle ever had, and he felt like he had worked his brain into the same kind of weak exhaustion. He could not have managed the most basic of portals or simplest of power sights. He could barely handle the effort of his own thoughts.

He sat down in his tracks, and he might have fallen over on his side, but Scarlet was suddenly behind him, holding him cradled in her arms. The scent of her damp hair swirling around him made him feel utterly, completely safe.

We are *safe*, his dragon told him, feeling equally stretched thin. *We are safe and we have fulfilled our destiny and our mate will protect us while we rest.*

It wasn't the destiny that Mal had come to Shifting Sands expecting, and he didn't have answers for their future: Would he move his hoard from New York? Would she agree to marry him, or was she too independent to accept such an earthly conceit? Would there be children? *Could* there be? Would her staff ever accept him as one of them? Wasn't there something else he had to tell her…?

Blackness darker than the sky of Gizelle's place took him at last.

CHAPTER 32

Scarlet could feel the tiny flicker of life in Mal's chest, the slow, tired sparkle of it, just as she could feel the soul-deep weariness that had driven his body to collapse. For a long moment, she only held him, while the warm rain slowed to nothing as the wyrm's power dissipated.

She had expected victory to feel... like victory.

But there was no sense of celebration to the scene.

The wyrm, frozen out of time, was stretched from the edge of her battered rain forest, across dozens of crushed cottages, to the cracked, tiled expanse of the pool deck. Columns lay scattered in coins of concrete, as if she had gone for Greek *ruins* in her architecture aesthetic.

She did not need to be an engineer to know that the central buildings were a complete loss. What wasn't caved in had been badly shaken, wind-damaged, and nearly washed away in the torrential rains. The pool had cracked; the water features were silent for the first time in years. The slopes were eroded, her trees—her precious, life-giving trees—had been toppled. The event hall appeared to have collapsed. Hedges had been stripped of flowers and leaves, leaving only bare sticks.

It was weirdly quiet, except for the sound of running water. All of the bugs and frogs and birds had been driven to ground by the rain and wind.

Scarlet closed her eyes, looking further. Mudslides showed dark scars through the green forest. Water still ran in rivulets all down the slopes of the island. Great swathes of jungle had been ripped up by the roots, washed away, or shredded in place.

Graham's garden and greenhouse had been flattened. The Den was still standing, but all of the windows had been shattered and half the roof ripped off; the interior was drenched and Bastian's hoard was scattered across the island. The other manors along the cliff were in similar shape. Half of the hotel had collapsed in on itself. Her office and her courtyard were sodden; the entire outside wall of her bedroom had fallen down, leaving the bones of the roof over an open room.

Tyrant…

She found him at once, safely—if not happily—huddled with Sweet One under the dumpster behind the kitchen, and relief flooded through her.

Tyrant was safe. They had evacuated in time. Everyone trapped here had survived. Her tree still stood. That was all that mattered.

But she couldn't quite keep tears from tracking down her face.

"Is he… *dead*?"

Scarlet looked up in alarm, to find Conall standing above them, Gizelle plastered against his side. The rest of the staff was picking through the rubble, clinging to their mates and assessing their wounds; no one was unscathed.

"No," she said swiftly, her arms tightening around Mal. "Only… tired."

She had never been so exhausted, either. Not even after Gizelle had tried to poison her.

"He… saved me," Conall said numbly. "But… *you* brought me back."

"Gizelle made it possible," Scarlet said wearily. "If your mate-bond had not kept you here a little while, I would not have been able to help you."

Slowly, painfully, Conall knelt beside her, hampered by Gizelle's iron grip on his side and his own obvious pain. "I am in your debt."

Scarlet laughed humorlessly. "That's probably good, because your share of the island doesn't have a lot of resale value right now. I'm afraid it has depreciated greatly over the last few hours."

Conall put his head down and for a moment Scarlet thought he was shaking in pain. Then he began to laugh, a halting, hesitant chuckle that bloomed into a great guffaw of humor.

Gizelle stared at him in alarm for a moment, then began to giggle helplessly.

Scarlet couldn't help herself, joining them in hysterical merriment, and soon everyone was in stages of shocky laughter, interspersed with tears and chatter.

"I'm fine," Amber assured Tony. "I promise, I'm *fine*."

"The baby…" Tony insisted. "We should get to the mainland and have you both checked. Does anyone have a working phone?"

No one did.

"I barely have working clothing," Breck pointed out, lifting the drenched shreds of his shirt.

"The baby is fine," Scarlet could tell Tony, at least. "A healthy, happy life spark." A sense of mischief overcame her. "And so is Laura's, and Lydia's."

"You knew?" Laura exclaimed over her mate's arm as Tex enfolded her in a protective hug.

Wrench was staring at his mate in surprise. "You… you're…"

Lydia's smile was slow and stunning. "I only knew I might be," she said, shaking her head. She gave Scarlet a sly, sideways look. "It was going to be a surprise!"

"He looks surprised to me," Travis pointed out.

Wrench was still standing with his arms limp at his side and his mouth open, unable to form complete sentences, or even, apparently, full words.

"What about me?" Breck joked irrepressibly. "Am *I* pregnant?"

Darla punched him in the arm and said, "Ouch! We have a bruise there." She twisted her arm to inspect her purpling flesh.

Scarlet gave a sigh, and felt it ripple through the island.

The clouds overhead were beginning to thin, with shafts of sunlight burning through. Mist clouded over the ground, and gradually the surviving insects started to sing. The breeze from the ocean was friendly again and Scarlet could feel her trees getting down to the business of growing again, slowly putting out new branches and sprouting new leaves to replace the ravaged canopy.

They were all *alive.*

Scarlet carried Mal to her room and salvaged enough of a bed to make him comfortable while he regained consciousness.

Chef insisted on feeding everyone, and somehow managed to make a hot meal from the ruins of his powerless kitchen; Travis assembled a working grill from broken parts and Graham and Alice scavenged fruit and vegetables from the destroyed greenhouse. Bastian bandaged up anyone who needed it, though no one was in worse shape than he was... except Mal.

They found enough tables and working chairs to put together a makeshift feast. The mood was light, and still a little stunned.

Tyrant and Sweet One, desperately offended by the day's events, made an appearance as Chef brought out dessert. Gizelle tried to cuddle with Sweet One, but the young cat had no interest in the gazelle shifter's comfort and yowled her way out of Gizelle's arms after only a few moments.

Tyrant, by contrast, wanted nothing more than to attach herself to Scarlet's ankles, constantly underfoot as Scarlet investigated the debris for anything that could be salvaged.

She was standing at the back of the restaurant deck holding a dented soup ladle when Gizelle found her.

"Be careful, Gizelle," Scarlet warned. "The deck isn't sound here."

Sweet One was being groomed vigorously by Tyrant on a broken table that was starting to dry in the baking sun.

Gizelle crept forward carefully to stand next to Scarlet.

"I didn't want to hurt you," she said mournfully.

"I know you didn't," Scarlet said. "I don't blame you."

"It was…"

"It wasn't your fault."

"But I…"

Scarlet turned to face her. "Good people blame themselves, Gizelle. Because good people take responsibility for what they do. I can only guess what it was like with that wyrm in your head, and you did the very best you could and I would never hold that against you."

"Am I a *good* person?" Gizelle asked plaintively.

"The very best," Scarlet assured her. "You are braver and better than anyone I know. And you are merciful, which is much, much harder than being merely good."

Gizelle stood still a moment and the loudest sounds were Sweet One's trilling protests as Tyrant held her down and licked her ears.

"It's quieter now," she observed. "In my head, I mean." She cocked her head at Scarlet curiously. "Does this mean I'll be normal?"

"I am not sure any of us are normal," Scarlet said dryly. "But that's not something you should aspire to anyway."

Gizelle gave her a swift, grateful hug. "I can hear your forest," she said, while her head was leaning against Scarlet's collarbone. "It sounds like *growing*."

Scarlet squeezed her back and let her go gather Sweet One into her arms. The kitten decided that Gizelle's attention was preferable to being further mauled by Tyrant and purred as she was picked up.

Scarlet collected Tyrant into her own arms and was given purring head-butts and vocal complaints. "Let's go see if your cat food survived," Scarlet suggested.

CHAPTER 33

Mal jerked awake at the attack, blindly reaching for his magic and finding that his stores were still empty.

It was just as well; the ferocious assailant was only Tyrant, who had decided that Mal's toes beneath the light quilt were clearly prey.

Mal sat up, precipitating a strategic retreat on the part of the kitten, and tried to figure out why Scarlet's room felt so odd.

He finally realized that it was missing an entire wall.

Where there had been tall windows and French doors, there was now… nothing. There was still a roof above, but the rest of the room was in ruins.

Ruins seemed an apt description for the entire resort, Mal decided. He hauled himself from the bed, which was only an air mattress on a sodden box spring; the original mattress, soaked, was standing on end in a pile of broken glass.

His muscles were reluctant to answer his demands, and he was glad to find a column that had survived the damage to lean against, looking out over the resort.

All that remained of the storm were tatters of dark clouds reflecting sunset colors across the deepening sky.

"It would be nice if we could take care of that before the civil guard got here," Scarlet said.

The doorway she stood in didn't hold a door any longer, and the jamb was splintered.

She, of course, looked perfectly put together in the midst of all the chaos: her hair swept back, her expression unruffled. Tyrant twined around her ankles, purring.

"Take care of what, now?" The sight of her drove every thought from his mind but one.

"The giant, frozen, feathered, two-headed beast that is crushing half of my resort. Most of the damage can be attributed to the storm and the earthquakes… but it's a little hard to explain that part."

"You know, you aren't supposed to disturb things until the insurance adjuster has had a chance to see the site," Mal said lightly. "You can get ugly lawsuits doing that."

"I'm pretty sure my insurance doesn't cover attack by angry ancient creatures, anyway," Scarlet said dryly. "And I'm vastly under-insured for this anyway."

"Insurance policies are put together by amateurs," Mal scoffed. He started to step towards her, and decided that holding onto the column was a better choice.

In a blink, Scarlet was at his side, her arm up under his. "It can wait," she said softly. "You should rest more."

As she led him back to the bed, giving him no choice in the matter, Mal had to ask, "Everyone? Everyone is okay?"

"Bruised and battered," Scarlet said gravely. "But no injuries that won't heal after a few shifts and some good meals."

"Your tree?" Mal asked reluctantly. Visions of the great rainforest trees being sucked into the raging storm had been firmly placed into his collection of nightmare fodder.

"A few fallen branches," Scarlet said calmly, helping him settle back into the bed. "But my leaves will grow back. I'll flower again."

"What happens now?" Mal asked, not releasing her.

Scarlet gazed at him. "I… don't know."

"Do you want to rebuild?"

Scarlet sighed and sat beside him. "I… I want to. But…"

"Money's no object," Mal reminded her.

Scarlet regarded him thoughtfully. "That doesn't feel right," she admitted.

"Would it feel better if it came through your staff?"

Scarlet smiled faintly. "It might. But they've already tapped everything they had just to buy this place." She looked wryly through the missing wall over the savaged resort. "For all the good it will do them. I bankrupted us all when I asked you to accept the offer."

"But you saved the world," Mal pointed out. "Oh, and they haven't begun to tap their resources." He had remembered the other thing he needed to tell Scarlet.

She looked at him suspiciously. "What are you on about now?"

Mal didn't have the energy to bait her further, though his dragon wearily admitted it might have been fun. "Darla's hoard. It's not locked."

Scarlet blinked at him and furrowed her brow. "What?"

Mal chuckled. "It's not locked. Those bracelets that were sent for Darla's engagement? Those were a gift commissioned by her father. That they were activated shows his blessing; she never needed her mother's. The hoard is hers. She has wealth that pales even mine, and she could give you enough to rebuild the entire island, pay off your debt, pave the road from the airstrip, put in an amusement park, and hire celebrity musicians every night without even noticing the difference."

Scarlet's face went from astonished, through amazed, to angry in the blink of an eye. "You're telling me that you've let Darla and Breck believe that they gave up the hoard to be together and this *whole time* they've had access to it?"

"Resources hold amazing bargaining power," Mal said apologetically. "I knew I'd lose that advantage over you if I told them because they would already give you the shirts from their backs if you asked."

Scarlet opened and closed her mouth several times, then sighed and laughed helplessly. "I suppose I understand that," she admitted, shaking her head. "It doesn't mean I entirely forgive it," she added threateningly. "They suffered so needlessly!"

Mal took her hand. "I shall endeavor to earn your absolution in the future," he promised. "And I will tell Darla and Breck myself and fall upon their mercy."

"I think that they are feeling fairly merciful," Scarlet said, amused. "Given that you've just saved the world and healed Conall."

"*We've* saved the world," Mal reminded her. "And *you* are the one who brought Conall back."

"We make a good team," Scarlet murmured, leaning her forehead against his.

Mal kissed her, and ran out of air long before he wanted to.

"I have a question for you," he said, when Scarlet released him.

"Ask," Scarlet said gently.

"Will you marry me, Scarlet Stanson? Will you be my partner as well as my mate? Will you allow me to bring my hoard here and give you half of it as my wife? You can fund your own rebuild, with your own money, and keep your pride as well as your resort."

Scarlet wiped her eyes. "Are you trying to offer me a buyout in order to get me to marry you?" she demanded.

"Dammit," Mal said with a laugh. "Old habits die hard."

She was smiling like the sun behind her tears and surely, somewhere, there were riots of rainbows from the combination.

"Yes," she said. "I will marry you. I will take half of your hoard and give you half of my island and all of my heart and the rest of my life. I love you, Mal Padrikanth Moore."

Mal gathered her into his aching arms and kissed her until the resort burst into bloom around them.

A WILL AND A WEDDING

In a lot of ways, the entire series was actually Gizelle's story: her rescue, her struggle back to human form, making friends…and eventually finding her mate and all the answers to who she was and where she came from. She was pivotal in saving the resort in Tropical Dragon's Destiny, and it was her betrayal and sacrifice that brought the series full circle.

I ***owed*** *this story to Gizelle.*

Conall remembered being dead.

Most of the time, he didn't think about it too hard.

There was too much to do, in those first days after the fight, to really stop and process.

His first care was for Gizelle, who was a seesaw of raw emotions in the wake of everything that had happened. Even if the voices in her head were considerably less now, she had been through a wringer of guilt and fear and despair. She had watched him die, let go of the safest place she knew, and saved the world, whether she really *understood* it or not.

His second thoughts were for rebuilding, sorting through the rubble of his cottage, organizing his finances and methodically working to get a *home* back in order.

Mal, drained from his exertions, had to wait several fraught days before he was able to lower the great two-headed wyrm into the earth, and it was several days after that before he could even think of something as complex as a portal to reconnect them to the world.

They spent those first days staring at the monolithic white wyrm, its coils in high arches, every knife-edged feather looking like it might move at any moment. They wandered through the necessities of life, trying to make sense of what their lives had become.

There was still work to do regarding the sale of his business, and the vast destruction involved insurance companies and lawyers. Conall, now officially a major shareholder of the island, spent the hours he wasn't comforting Gizelle with Mal and Scarlet, poring over paperwork and arguing with tight-collared beancounters.

He was plenty busy enough not to stop and dwell on things.

But sometimes, clawing back from sleep, or reminded by some sight or smell, Conall would be jolted back to that moment when he'd escaped the pain of dying into death itself.

Death had not been unpleasant.

Before it had been unpleasant, hearing bones snap and feeling all of his strength pour out of him in a wave of agony, Gizelle in his mind full of panic and pain.

But death itself had been...peaceful.

It wasn't blackness or silence, because those relied on senses he didn't have anymore. It was like floating in a sea of *new* senses, of being stretched like taffy to almost nothing...and then burned back into excruciating life at Scarlet's inexorable command.

Mal's healing had been as wracking as dying had been in the first place, but more drawn out, and only the bright flame of Gizelle's hope had kept him from begging for release.

They both tried to talk about it, with one another and with others, and in the end, the most comfort was from clinging wordlessly to each other.

Contact was more than simply sensual, more than a conduit for him to hear. It was an anchor—a reminder of senses he'd never imagined losing...of senses he'd never imagined having.

"I miss your music," Gizelle said, one evening, after Chef had served them the remaining perishable food from storage, on broken plates and battered cookware.

Conall was curled together with her on a broken wicker couch with mis-matched cushions.

"The frogs have no sense of rhythm," Gizelle complained. They were on what was left of the bar deck, a blue tarp strung up over a few cobbled-together tables and some makeshift chairs and surviving couches. This was where the staff gathered a few times a day, staggering towards some kind of normalcy as they camped in the ruins.

All of his instruments had been destroyed in the wreckage of his cottage, and Conall couldn't quite bring himself to order a new guitar, even if he thought it was worth asking Mal for assistance. He'd bought every one of his instruments when he could *hear*, had spent hours finding the ones with the perfect mellow tone, just the right richness, a light touch on the frets. He'd collaborated with master craftsmen to get instruments that exactly fit him. It wasn't the kind of thing he could just order online.

"You could play mine," Tex offered unexpectedly, getting up from his seat next to Laura.

Conall shot him a look of surprise. "It survived?"

"It was in a hard case under the bar," Tex said, fishing it out of the crooked bar. "Not even scratched."

"It's the only thing in this place that can say that," Conall said wryly.

Everyone's injuries had healed, but they were still all walking around in shock. Scarlet spoke of sending them all out on a cruise while they rebuilt in earnest, and was already working with Travis and a selection of architects on new plans. She alone seemed as serene as ever.

Conall took Tex's guitar with a nod of appreciation and tuned it patiently, Gizelle's hand on his shoulder allowing him to hear the sounds.

When he played at last, he was gratified to watch everyone seem to relax. It was a breath of normalcy, the smallest hint of familiarity and safety, and he played until his hands reminded him that he had let his calluses grow soft.

Tex took the guitar back, saying with laughter, "You're a hard act to follow!" But follow he did, with slower, simpler chords of increasingly absurd country music that they ended up all singing along with, even Conall and Gizelle. Saina, her voice still recovering, was able to give them just a faint feeling of peace and Conall could feel Gizelle relax beside him and eventually fall asleep. He exchanged a grateful look with the mermaid, and gathered Gizelle up to take her to the cot that they had salvaged from storage and set up in their makeshift tent.

~

He woke up, reaching for Gizelle, and had a moment of sheer panic when she wasn't nearby.

It didn't take long to find her, picking through the debris of their cottage as they had done every day, finding new pieces and parts, very little of it intact.

She was sitting where their living room might have been, now a tortured, twisted skeleton with broken wood and glass and roof tile in drifts filling every corner, and she looked up at Conall's approach with tears in her eyes.

She spoke, but looked down, and he was not touching her so that he could hear.

"Are you hurt?" he asked, scrambling through the wreckage. There were shards of glass everywhere, and they had both been cut more than once moving carelessly.

She shook her head, and held up her latest find. It took Conall a moment to recognize it, a portfolio he'd given her, that she had filled with her artwork. It was soaked, and the clasp was broken. Only a few pages remained.

"These were…" he couldn't identify the word on her lips, but he was close enough to touch her now, and he could hear the grief-stricken catch to her breath when he did.

"What is it?" he asked, gathering her carefully close. It was not a good place to settle; there were shards and broken timbers and tangled exposed wires.

"These were our wedding invitations," she sobbed. "I made them. But the lawn isn't there any more. It's gone and even Scarlet can't grow it back the way it was and now we can't get *married.*"

"We can still marry," Conall insisted.

Gizelle stilled in his arms, then looked up at him, bumping her nose against his chin. "Why? What is it for?"

"Getting married?"

"Jenny said that it was a legal issue, that people do it to protect each other." Gizelle shook her head against Conall's collarbone. "I didn't understand it."

Conall picked her up and carried her out of the hazardous building to a place on the collapsed deck that was free of rubble. It was tilted, and not the most comfortable place to sit, with his foot wedged against the broken railing, but it beat crouching in a pile of broken glass.

"Legally, when you marry, if you...die...everything that you have goes to your spouse. This can be done other ways. I have something called a will, and everything I have is already yours." It had been complicated to set up, with Gizelle's legal identity assumed dead for so long, but Conall had hired the best lawyers.

"Then why marry?" Gizelle wanted to know. "I don't have anything."

"It's more about...celebrating our promise to each other."

"What promise?"

"To love each other, and care for each other forever," Conall said slowly.

"I promise that," Gizelle said earnestly. "Are we married, now?"

Conall had to laugh. "Not technically. We have to fill out paperwork that gets filed with the appropriate departments. There have to be witnesses, it usually involves a ceremony."

"Like Darla, when she was going to marry Liam?"

"There is a whole wide world of marriage ceremonies," Conall explained. "That was a traditional dragon wedding. Laura and Jenny had a modern American wedding. Darla and Breck drew on a whole host of traditions and made up their own. But it isn't as much about the flowers and the march down the aisle and the exchange of rings as it is about the people who are there with you. The best weddings are about the people who come to see it, people who want to be there to celebrate with you when you make your promise official."

Gizelle was quiet for a long moment. "Will your mother come?"

"Only if you want her there," Conall said firmly.

Gizelle curled tighter, and shivered. "It's so *much*," she said plaintively.

"It doesn't have to be," Conall told her. "It can be exactly what you want. We can do it now, here, with just what we have. Scarlet can perform these ceremonies and we'll sign some paperwork, and it can just be done. Or we can wait, and do something fancier. Whatever you want."

"Can I have flowers?"

"Flowers, rings, whatever you want."

"No ring," Gizelle said swiftly. "I might forget to take it off before I shift. Or lose it when I do."

They sat in silence for a moment, Conall trying not to think about death.

"You're trembling," Gizelle said unexpectedly.

He'd done a very poor job of not thinking about it, and he pulled her tighter into his arms and buried his face in her wild white hair. "I don't want to wait," he confessed. "I don't want to wait for anything, ever again."

Gizelle squirmed in his arms until she could wrap her arms around him. "I don't, either," she said warmly. "You are my best friend and it would make you feel better."

It wasn't often that Gizelle was the one offering comfort, but Conall accepted it without question, letting all of his grief and fear and confusion flow away in the strength of her embrace.

"I want to get married," Gizelle declared. "I want to get married with flowers and our friends. I want *everyone* to feel better."

~

"Nervous?" Wrench asked, giving Conall's tie one last adjustment.

Conall was looking right at his mouth because of their proximity, so he couldn't easily ignore the question. "Not terribly," he conceded. *Not at all* would have been a lie, but not much of one.

"Lydia says that Gizelle is doing fine. Almost ready."

It was more than Wrench usually bothered saying, which was one of the reasons they got along so well. Theirs had been an unexpected friendship, but the Boston billionaire and the ex-con had spent many silent evenings drinking beer together at the bar, and he had been the obvious choice to be Conall's not-official best man.

They had decided against a formal wedding party when Gizelle had nearly melted down trying to decide who would be a maid of honor, so they didn't give anyone titles, only jobs. Lydia did her hair, Laura did her nails, and Travis made her a dress out of salvaged lace curtains. Jenny would hold her bouquet during the ceremony, and Neal would give her away.

Chef, Darla, and Breck were providing and serving the reception meal. Tex had coordinated the supplies and set up a bar, working with Mal, who was slowly recovering his magical abilities, to provide portals, and money, because the rest of their funds were so knotted up in paperwork.

Scarlet would perform the ceremony, and Magnolia said she would make the speech at the reception, while Saina agreed to sing.

There were no invitations, no carefully orchestrated seating charts, no rings, and no mothers-in-law.

It was a beautiful day, the sky a cloudless blue. At the beach it was probably oppressively hot, but here, near the peak of the steep island, in Scarlet's shaded grove, it was perfectly warm and delightful. The air was filled with the scent of flowers and moss, and sunlight sparkled through the leaves.

Scarlet had grown them a perfect setup for a small, quiet wedding, with a dais covered in bell-like flowers and twined with vines in a rainbow of colors.

Conall waited, patiently, for Neal to bring Gizelle.

And waited.

"She'll come," Wrench promised.

And she did.

Lydia and Laura slipped into the audience, standing with the others because they hadn't planned a ceremony long enough to require chairs.

Gizelle stood at the start of the aisle, trembling on Neal's arm, and clutching her flowers so hard that her knuckles were white.

Conall had never seen anything so beautiful as his bride, her ice-white hair around her the only veil she needed. Lydia had braided part of it up and left most of it loose over her bare shoulders, tucking flowers of every color into it. The lace curtain dress that Travis had concocted was smooth over her slim torso and flared loose to her calves. Her feet beneath were bare, and for a long moment, she only stood at the far end of the aisle, visibly shaking.

She took a hesitant step, then another, slowly, gazing to where Conall waited.

The next step was faster, and the next even faster, until Neal was having to lengthen his stride to keep up and finally he let her go because she was running, running joyously for Conall, who could not keep himself from leaving the dais to meet her and sweep her up into his waiting arms and kiss her in a blast of sound.

"I promise," she said eagerly. "I promise to run only *to* you, forever, for always. I promise to love you forever, and to be your ears and your song *forever*."

If anyone knew forever, it was Gizelle.

"I promise," he replied. "I promise to always be your shelter and your safety and your heart, forever."

He did not mention death, because even that could clearly not part them, and put her gently back down on her toes.

They walked together, more sedately, to face Scarlet, who smiled fondly at them. "It appears that you have exchanged your vows," she observed. "And I believe that everyone knows why we have gathered here today. And so by the power vested in me by the country of Costa Rica, I now declare you man and wife. You've already had your kiss, but I won't stop you from having another."

Conall wasn't sure that even *she* could have.

Gizelle tipped her face up to meet him, and he gathered his wife into his arms and kissed her gently, deeply, until the cheers of the audience penetrated his haze of joy.

"I forgot about the flowers," Gizelle confessed near his ear as he set her carefully down once more. The bouquet was rather worse for the wear, having been carelessly battered against his back as they kissed, and petals and leaves were strewn around them.

Saina began to sing, then, but she needed no magic to influence the joy that was all around them in the little grove. Each of them was embraced, and Conall shook so many hands that he was pretty sure that everyone there had started over with him. Chef served a masterful spread of mostly island-grown food, and Tex plied everyone with custom-mixed drinks as the ceremony devolved directly into happy chaos.

They danced, Saina sang, Tex played guitar, and Conall took the instrument himself to play a song he had composed to Gizelle, with chords like a gazelle springing through tall grass. Magnolia gave a rousing toast that left them all in happy tears.

Through it all, every song and hug, Gizelle held doggedly to her bouquet, and as much as possible, to Conall's hand, until the sun was setting into the jungle treetops and the sky was turning purple. As they were beginning to gather up everything to return to the tents set up at the ruined resort, she went to Scarlet, dragging Conall willingly with her.

If it had been somewhat crushed at the beginning of the ceremony, there was little of the flower arrangement left after the dancing and cavorting. She pressed it into Scarlet's hand anyway.

"I'm supposed to throw it," she said shyly, "but I want *you* to be next." She frowned at the sad collection of bare stems and bruised flowers. "It was prettier, before. You could probably make something better."

"It wouldn't mean as much," Scarlet told her, accepting the battered bouquet as if it was the finest collection.

Gizelle smiled like the sun. "Yes," she agreed. "Like a song means more if you dance."

Conall met Mal's gaze over Scarlet's crimson crown, and recognized the look in his golden eyes. None of them had cxpected to survive the terrible battle for the island, and had been wandering around in a daze ever since, grateful for life, but not quite living it, until now.

Now, like Scarlet's grove, they were all filled with new life and anticipation.

"You gave them this," he told Gizelle, as they walked back to the resort, hand-in-hand. "Your joy gives us a place to start again."

"Your joy, too," Gizelle reminded him.

"Mine, too," Conall agreed. "I promise." And for Gizelle, only for Gizelle, it was a promise he thought he could keep.

A HOARD OF THEIR OWN

I absolutely ***love*** *Darla and Breck. This story was written completely for my own indulgence.*

"Oh," Breck said, and then he added, "Wow." He took another step, and stopped. "Wow," he repeated.

Darla could feel his astonishment and the chill of awe that raised goosebumps all over his arms. She stepped beside him so that she could twine her fingers into his.

"I told you," she couldn't resist saying. She had gone to great effort to prepare him. Even Liam had tried, since he had actually seen the hoard, but descriptions always fell short, and nothing compared to actually standing in the arched subterranean rooms.

Breck squeezed her hand. They were finally starting to get a handle on their curious magic bond, so that they weren't constantly feeling the sensations of two separate bodies. But when emotions ran particularly high, it was harder to tamp it down, and Darla could feel the shocky adrenaline that Breck was swimming in, mixed with her own dread.

"My imagination failed," he admitted. "I mean, I thought I could picture it, I figured...it couldn't *really* be..."

"It is a hoard beyond imagining," Darla said dryly. "The culmination of dozens of generations of greed from two powerful dragon lines that ended with me."

"If you put this out on the market, you'd glut it," Breck said, still sounding stunned. "The price of gold would nosedive." He picked up a glittering cup before Darla could warn him not to touch anything, and she was relieved to see the shimmering web of the hoard protection spell dissolve before him.

Breck seemed to recognize the danger of what he'd done and he looked at Darla with his golden eyes wide. "It's really...ours."

"Are you two going to be long?"

Darla turned politely to Mal, who was holding a portal open. Scarlet's mate looked rather crabby about the whole affair, but Darla thought it must be masking exhaustion. It hadn't been that long since he had battled a giant, two-headed monster to protect Scarlet and the resort, and though he wasn't the type to admit weakness, Darla suspected that he was still pretty tapped.

"Is this going to be like one of those shopping sprees where you try to fill up a shopping cart in five minutes?" Breck wanted to know, eyeing the nearest heap of golden coins.

Mal, unexpectedly, chuckled. "I don't want to rush you," he said wearily. "Maybe I can come back for you. Tell me when."

"An hour?" Darla suggested. "We'll want to select for things that will be simple to sell." That would eliminate most of the antiques, the artwork, and the more ancient coins. But there were plenty of other treasures.

"An hour," Mal agreed, and he stepped back through the portal that had brought them there and vanished with a gesture.

The light went away when the portal closed, but there were modern fixtures all along the walls and Darla used the flashlight she'd thought to bring to find the switch that turned them on.

Breck whistled, as further chambers flickered into view. "How far does it go?" he asked in stunned wonder.

"There are approximately ten thousand square feet," Darla said, and she heard the careful coolness of her voice.

Breck did not miss it. "What's wrong?"

Darla closed her eyes. Training told her to deny that anything was amiss. *Don't acknowledge weakness, maintain your image, stay aloof.*

But Breck was her mate, her husband, her *everything*, and it was a relief to admit, "I *hate* it. I hate every jewel and coin and chain in this place. It's tacky, and greedy, and *gross*. It represents everything I hated about my privilege." She sucked in her air and barely kept it from being a sob by sheer force of will. She hated the power that this place had over her.

Breck took her outburst without judgement, nodding thoughtfully. "It definitely has that...*gaudy* feeling to it. I mean...this guy!" He gestured at a nude statue plated in gold, its erection draped in jeweled necklaces. "Why would you look so grim when you've got literal family jewels hanging from your junk?"

Darla had to giggle. "Maybe the same reason she looks positively bored?" A matching female statue reclined suggestively nearby.

"You know what I see?" Breck asked, taking her by the shoulders and turning her to a jeweled goblet on a marble column.

"Obscene excess and terrible taste?" Darla ventured.

Breck lifted the goblet. "I see food for Liam's elders, for a year." He knelt and ran his fingers through a pile of coins, and when he stood, he poured them from his hand into the goblet. "You know what that is? One of those imaging machines for the new clinic Liam wants to build." He pulled a necklace off of a silver hat rack. "This? This is a whole row of washing machines that don't need new motors." It went into the goblet.

He tugged a diamond-studded dog collar from a hook on a jade cabinet. "A scholarship for an underprivileged kid. Hell, a whole *school*. You look around and see your mother's shallow greed. I look around and see the possibilities, the good we could do with it."

"I wish I could see it that way," Darla said wistfully. "It's all so ugly and *tainted* to me."

"Hmm," Breck said thoughtfully.

"What are you thinking?" Darla asked suspiciously.

"I'm thinking about how to make it yours," he said innocently.

"Ours," Darla corrected. "It's all *ours*. If I have to be saddled with Mr. Midas Dangly Jewels, so do you."

Breck snapped his fingers. "I know exactly how to fix this," he said in triumph. He put the goblet down on a nearby dais and scrambled up a heap of coins that shifted under his feet like sand dunes. There were a series of silk-embroidered tapestries hanging on the far wall, and he climbed up the heap of coins and tore one recklessly down, slinging it across his shoulders and sliding down like he was a superhero.

"What are you going to do with that?" Darla wanted to know. "I would think that would be hard to sell, especially since you just ripped it…"

"We're not going to sell this one," Breck assured her, unfurling it with flair and laying it out over a heap of silver coins. "It...ah...may not be in good enough shape to sell when we're done with it."

"What are we going to do with it?" Darla asked suspiciously, a smile starting to curve up the corner of her mouth as Breck came staggering down the loose coins to take her hand

"There are some...traditional ways to *claim* things," Breck told her, drawing her close and kissing her nose as his fingers managed to find a way up under her hair.

"You want me to have *sex* in the *hoard*?" Darla thought she ought to feel outraged, but she couldn't help giggling.

Breck smiled, and lowered his mouth to hers for a kiss that stole her resistance. "Why not?" he asked when he drew away. "Mal won't be back for almost an hour. We've got plenty of time to stuff quarters into socks and still give this place a few memories that I *guarantee* will be happy."

"Mm," Darla said, sounding as skeptical as she could manage. "You *guarantee* that? In writing?"

Breck drew a finger down her collarbone and unbuttoned her shirt. "I p-r-o-m-i-s-e," he said, writing with his fingertip across her breast bone.

Then he took her hand and clambered with her up the slipping pile of coins.

It was a little like making love on a crooked, half-full waterbed, and a little like making love on a beach. A clinking beach that sounded like chimes and was constantly slipping and sliding away underneath them.

They shimmied out of their clothing and reached for each other eagerly. Darla forgot to think about the hoard at the first touch of skin on skin, and was hungry only for Breck's fingers and mouth and the length of his cock as he lay her back and teased her mercilessly.

"Say my name," Breck whispered near her ear, and she obediently whispered it back to him. She didn't have to look at her wrist to know that their bracelet runes would be glowing slightly.

Then he was entering her, torturously slowly, and she was crying it louder, echoing back from the high, vaulted ceiling above them. "Breck, oh, *yes*..."

They made love as long as they dared, then lay panting in release as they waited for their heartbeats to slow.

"I think I have a scepter in my backside," Darla said, laughing and trying to shift on the pile of coins. The tapestry wasn't thick enough to pad everything, and the pile of coins apparently hid some less comfortable items that were exposed as they shook it down.

"Maybe the hoard is just happy to see you," Breck said, sitting up and grinning down at her. "Feeling better?"

Darla sat up and caught him in her arms. "You know just how to fix things," she said. "Flat tires, moods, tainted hoards..."

They cuddled together in blissful afterglow until Darla caught a glimpse of a grandfather clock. "How much time do we have left?" she asked, reaching for her clothing in a flash of panic.

"Probably not long enough to do that again," Breck said with an exaggerated sigh.

They dressed awkwardly on the lumpy tapestry, and began collecting items that would be easy to sell—gold nuggets and loose jewels, simple chains of precious metal, and the less garish jewelry.

By the time Mal returned in a slash of space-time, looking more weary and disgruntled than ever, they had collected enough that Darla thought they could probably fund the entire resort. Their bags were heavy, and Breck had insisted on piling necklaces around her neck. He was wearing several fetching bracelets and a tiara, himself.

"What about Mr. Goldencock McJewelnuts?" Breck asked as they passed him.

"What, you think someone would actually pay money for Goldfinger here?" Darla scoffed.

"We could keep him," Breck said merrily. "Put him above our bed to hang our own jewelry on."

Darla gave a dramatic shudder. "Please tell me you're kidding!"

"No, no, you're right," Breck agreed, pulling on his chin thoughtfully. "We should have a statue of *me* made. Solid gold, none of this plating nonsense. And it should be bigger. Much, *much* bigger."

"The whole thing?" Darla giggled. "Or just certain parts?"

"Are we bringing that with us or not?" Mal asked crossly, not at all amused by their banter.

"No!" Darla said at once, and she walked briskly to the portal.

She paused on the other side and looked back at the hoard that had featured in her nightmares since she was a child. It looked...harmless now. Its sparkle was only glitter and potential, and she knew that it would never have power over her again.

OF COURSE

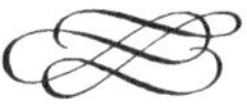

This takes place somewhat after the series concludes and was basically an excuse to go back and visit with some of my favorite characters a little.

"Being filthy rich is unexpectedly boring," Breck said, lounging back in one of the deck chairs pulled up close next to Darla so that he could reach over and caress the length of her thigh any time he wished.

His feet were up on the railing opposite, and the ocean was rolling away behind them. The swirl of their wake was mesmerizing, but the appeal of simply sitting and watching it was beginning to wane after several weeks.

"You don't have to tell *me*," Darla said wryly. She was smoothing a last layer of suntan lotion over the pale, faintly-freckled skin on her arms, and Breck watched admiringly from behind his sunglasses.

"Of course," Wrench said thoughtfully from beyond her, "it beats bein' poor." He was drinking a beer and had a ridiculously large straw hat shading his face.

"Of course," Breck agreed.

"I'll be glad to go home to Shifting Sands," Lydia said peacefully from beneath a hat that was even larger than Wrench's, but somehow half as ridiculous. "I don't think any of us were meant to be idle."

"Graham, maybe," Breck groused. "All those years we thought he was one of the hardest workers at the resort, and the whole time, Scarlet was the one pulling the landscaping miracles. Graham was probably napping or drinking every time he was out of sight."

"Hey!" Alice protested for her mate as she sat up from her lounge.

"Still had to cut the grass," Graham said, not at all offended as he took a long swig from his own bottle. "She couldn't un-grow things."

"And the strawberries and tomatoes were always yours," Alice said defensively. "The entire upper gardens were."

Graham made a sorrowful grunt. The gardens had been utterly wiped out in the battle with the two-headed wyrm, and although Scarlet would be able to make everything grow back after the greenhouses were rebuilt, Breck strongly suspected that it wouldn't be the *same* as the plants that Graham had nurtured from seeds.

"What do you think they're doing with all our money?" Breck mused lazily.

"It isn't even close to *all* our money," Darla reminded him, because she would always keep him honest as well as happy. "And I'm sure Scarlet is spending it very well."

"She sent photos of the construction," Tex drawled. "So you could keep tabs on her."

Breck hadn't been very impressed with the photos of half-built structures sprouting rebar amid great piles of tiles and steel beams, but the buildings were definitely starting to take shape.

"Poor Travis," Darla said, because she had a heart of absolute gold. "It doesn't seem fair that we're all here while he had to stay behind."

"His choice," Breck reminded her. "He's the one who wanted to have his fingers in on the ground floor, so to speak."

"Poor *Jenny*," her twin sister, Laura, teased. "She's the one having to suffer a luxury cruise on a giant private yacht while her mate works his fingers to the bone."

"You jest," Jenny said firmly, "but I'm thinking about heading back early. I was going to see if I could get a charter out of Antofagasta when we stopped there."

Everyone was quiet at that idea, and Breck found himself sorely tempted. Darla's hand slipped into his as if she guessed what he was thinking about.

"Of course, Scarlet said the bay community won't be ready for residents for a few more months," Laura said sorrowfully. She rubbed her round belly and made a grimace of discomfort.

"The hotel at the resort is nearly complete," Tex said thoughtfully. "It wouldn't be The Den, but we lived in a hotel once before."

"They won't need us underfoot," Lydia said chidingly. "Surely we'd only be in the way."

"I can lug building supplies from one place to another," Wrench offered.

Graham grunted thoughtfully and Alice, proving that mates grew even more like each other, gave an equally pensive grunt in reply.

"Workers get thirsty," Tex said. "And it would be a shame if Scarlet stocked substandard liquor because I wasn't there to steer her right."

"I'm sure they're doing fine," Lydia protested, but she laughed her giving-up laugh and Breck knew that she was no happier than any of the rest of them there.

Breck put his feet down on the deck and sat forward. "Well, there it is, then," he said firmly. "Let's turn this creaky thing around and head back home."

"You can't do that," Laura laughed.

"Why not?" Breck demanded. "It's my boat. I bought it."

"Scarlet said we should go out on a *several month* cruise," Jenny protested, but her eyes were full of longing. "It's only been a few weeks."

Breck made a rude noise through his lips. "Scarlet's not here. She can't boss me around from there."

Graham's noise was not so much a grunt as it was a snort.

"Okay, maybe she can, but will she stop us? We don't need a tropical cruise, we have a tropical island. I don't mind tenting it at Shifting Sands, or sleeping on the beach."

"The bay dock is deep enough for a boat this big," Tex suggested. "We could just stay in *it.*"

"I'll be happier to have ground underneath me that isn't swaying," Laura suggested. "I can't tell what is morning sickness and what is sea sickness anymore. I'm tired of being constantly queasy."

"A tent sounds just fine," Tex swiftly amended.

No one said a word about *not* wanting to go back.

"I'll go talk to the captain," Breck announced, getting to his feet.

"Didn't *Scarlet* hire the captain?" Tex reminded him. "He might have other plans."

"It's my boat!" Breck repeated. "I bought it!"

Darla laughingly rose and followed him as Breck walked around to the starboard side. She scampered to catch up with him and slip her hand into his.

"I should have asked you," Breck said apologetically, with a smiling sideways look. "It's your boat, too."

"They call it a ship, at this size," Darla teased him. "Three full decks above the waterline." Then she sobered. "And you already knew I was ready to go home. I miss the elders, and baking in the kitchen with Chef."

"Chef and Magnolia won't be back yet," Breck reminded her. "Probably they're bringing bread in from the mainland instead of baking it there. We'll be roughing it for a while."

"Oh yes," Darla drawled. "So rough. Only everything that money can buy at our fingertips thanks to magical portals."

"You get to ask Mal for the portals," Breck said with a dramatic shudder. "He's scary." Breck's fear was mostly feigned, but it was hard not to notice how powerful Mal was. And although he'd proved a valuable ally, Breck hadn't forgotten that he'd been an enemy of the island for longer than he'd been a friend.

They stopped near the stairs that went up to the captain's bridge and Breck drew Darla into his arms. "We could go anywhere, you know," he reminded her. "Anywhere in the world, wherever you wanted. Paris? Moscow? We could buy a city, if you picked one."

Darla smiled up at him, the waves of her strawberry blonde hair glowing around her in the low evening light. "I'd be happy enough anywhere I was with you," she reminded him. "But I think you're right. It's time to go back to Shifting Sands. It's time to go *home*."

Home was Darla's lips, and his fingers tangled in her hair. Home was lost in her blue eyes, and feeling her close to him and knowing she was his.

But home was also warm breezes over restaurant decks, and finding satisfaction in good service. It was banter with the other staff, and flattering the customers. It was singing with Chef in the kitchen and knowing that he was part of something better, something greater, making people happy.

"Let's go home," he agreed, kissing her nose. Then he let go of her and dashed to the stairs going up. "Captain," he called, "we have a change of course!"

PERFECT MATCH

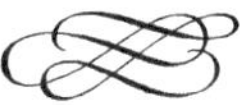

This was another accidental story.

But let me back up! While I was writing Tropical Dragon's Destiny, someone posted a funny meme to my Facebook readers group about a fire ant who thought they were the tiniest dragon. I accepted the challenge, and said that I'd write a fire ant shifter into my current book. He ended up being a pompous, self-absorbed jerk, and I thought that was the end of him…until one of my readers suggested a redemption arc.

I couldn't resist! Like Her Hellhound Bodyguard, I had to make an April Fool's cover for this one, and eventually even write it, although I've changed the title and many details from that first ridiculous premise.

"I can't *believe* you invited *him* back," Mal observed, standing at the railing of the restaurant with Scarlet.

The new resort was laid out much as the old resort had been, but everything was just a little *more.* The trim was fancier. There were more columns, more colorful mosaics. The bar deck was a little larger, with a big outdoor grill, and more covered seating. The pool deck, below, was sprawling, and the pool itself was no longer just a simple rectangle, but a tangled collection of ponds and lagoons attached to a longer pool suitable for laps. Some of them were on separate levels, with waterfalls connecting them.

Beyond the main pool deck was the beach, and even *its* shape was slightly different after the great storm had battered it into submission. It was still pale golden sand, and the jungle around it was all in perfect order. Cottages, uncrowded but cozy, dotted the north slope and tidy, white gravel paths wound everywhere.

It wasn't all entirely finished, but it certainly didn't look as though an epic battle had ever taken place there.

"I couldn't very well invite everyone else and *not* him," Scarlet pointed out, not at all confused about who Mal was referencing. "How would that look?"

"Like he was a conceited, self-serving, narcissistic asshole who all but pushed old women out of the way to get on the airplane off this island in an emergency?" The man in question was standing below them at the bar; Mal had passed him on the stairs to the restaurant and recognized him at once as a fire ant shifter who had completely failed to impress him shortly before the fall of the resort.

He thought he was more feared than a dragon, Mal's own dragon added derisively.

Scarlet smothered a laugh. "You didn't mention the Yelp review."

"Nor did I mention his desire to compensate for his shift size. I'm not questioning your business choices," Mal said, glowering down to where the man was waiting at the bar, "but I don't think anyone would have blamed you for leaving him off the guest list."

"I did book his ticket on the smallest and most inconvenient flight," Scarlet said, with a sideways look of mischief.

Mal grinned back and caught himself chuckling.

If anyone had told him, three years ago, that he would be snickering with his then-nemesis on the deck of a restaurant that they'd painstakingly rebuilt, he...well, he wouldn't have laughed. He didn't laugh as much then.

"Besides, doesn't he seem...nicer?"

Mal watched, skeptically.

From above, the man's nervousness was obvious. He'd gotten his drink from the bar, and was approaching a woman reading at a table near the railing. Mal started to frown, anticipating the unwelcome pushy pass he was about to witness.

But the fire ant shifter seemed uncharacteristically hesitant. His previous bluster and flexing was noticeably missing. He was approaching with what could only be called shyness, and Mal desperately wished he could hear their conversation from the deck above as the woman looked up from her book. It would probably be a terrible breach of privacy to cast a spell to listen in, but Mal was still tempted.

Then they locked eyes, and Mal didn't need to eavesdrop because they didn't exchange a single word.

They must have stared at each other for several minutes before Scarlet gave a sigh and dropped her head into her hands. "I swear, this island is cursed. Do you know that there's a rumor going around that this resort is the place to go to meet your mate? I do *not* want this resort to become a pick-up destination for lonely hearts. Mates are *nothing* but trouble."

"*Nothing?*" Mal asked leadingly.

"*You* were the most trouble of all," Scarlet pointed out.

"Should we save her?" Mal asked, looking back at the drama unfolding below. The fire ant shifter had dropped to his knees at the woman's feet and she was holding her book to her chest.

"From her *mate?*" Scarlet scoffed. "Good luck with that. Besides, she'll be just fine."

"Even though he's a scary fire ant? Their bites sting like fire! He's clearly more dangerous than a dragon!" Mal was sure he should not be having this much fun at the man's expense.

Scarlet gave him a sudden grin. "I remember her from the guest list," she said reassuringly. "She's an anteater. They're immune to fire ant venom."

Then Mal really did laugh, until he was leaning against the railing for support and people were staring at them. "Mates really are perfect for each other, aren't they?"

Scarlet threaded an arm into his. "They really are."

ALL IN THE TIMING

I introduced Liam in Tropical Leopard's Longing as a jilted groom and promptly knew I would have to write him his own happy ending. A longing for connection is not always sexual, and doesn't always have to follow the usual established conventions. Asexual (ace) doesn't have to mean alone…

This story takes place several months after the end of the series, but before the epilogue of Tropical Dragon's Destiny.

~

Caroline knew she had terrible timing, but this was *ridiculous.*

She was at the job interview of her life, a chance to be exactly the kind of small town doctor she'd always dreamed of being. They even already knew she was a shifter, so there were no awkward secrets to keep.

What's more, it was in *paradise.*

The interview was supposed to be in New York City, and that was where she'd arrived, gulping over the cost of the taxi from the airport. But after the gleaming elevator took her to a lush penthouse office, the lawyer who met her there witnessed her non-disclosure contract and ripped a doorway into thin air with a few spoken words and a brief gesture.

"Regular means of travel are inconvenient to our schedule and of considerable unwarranted cost," the lawyer told her casually, as if he had not just revealed that he was a wizard and upended Caroline's entire life view. "Scarlet cannot conduct interviews here, so we shall go there."

There, it turned out, was a tropical island off the coast of Costa Rica, a place that smelled intoxicatingly of spices and green growing things, warm and humid after the biting wind and slushy snow of New York City in December. There was a tiny town being built on a jeweled bay, buildings of stone and warm wood being actively constructed as the lawyer led Caroline down a winding street to a small, quaint building.

It was obvious that the community was just being started—there were more blank spaces along the streets than buildings, and it was clear that many of the buildings were little more than basic shells. There were makeshift kitchens out back of some of the houses, and trenches where plumbing hadn't been laid yet.

She tried not to stare at the massive green dragon who was lowering great ceiling beams onto walls with ease while a man gave him directions and scrambled along the walls to tack down the huge timbers.

The lawyer left her at the doorway of one of the only finished-looking little buildings. "I'll return in an hour and a half to take you back," he said. He didn't offer her luck, and Caroline wondered—not for the first time—how many applicants had made it to this stage of consideration. She was determined to nail this interview, to give it everything she had, to convince them of her competency. It wasn't just that she needed this job, she needed the life it could give her son.

She stared at the Christmas garland, which seemed glaringly out of place in the heat and humidity. It could be the greatest Christmas present in the world, to get them out of their dank, poorly insulated apartment. When the advertisement had said 'must prepare to relocate,' she would have honestly taken *anything*, but this was beyond the scope of her imagination.

"May I take your jacket?"

The woman who greeted her was tall and intimidating, and Caroline guessed at once that this was Scarlet by her brilliant—almost certainly not natural-colored—red hair, pulled professionally up in a bun. She was the owner of the island, in charge of the entire town. She had an easy sense of power and confidence.

"Yes, please," Caroline said, shedding the suit jacket willingly. She had dressed for an interview in winter in New York, and was already perspiring uncomfortably from both nerves and heat.

"It is cooler inside," Scarlet said kindly, and led her within. "My name is Scarlet, welcome to Shifting Sands."

Caroline found herself invited into a pleasant room filled with potted plants, but otherwise undecorated. Her heels were loud over the tile floor, louder than Scarlet's. Three comfortable wicker chairs were arranged subtly facing a fourth over a small glass coffee table. Caroline swallowed her nerves and settled herself into the solo chair as she gave herself a last minute instant pep talk. She could do this interview, she would be on top of her game. She would be clever and gentle and convince them entirely that she was the best for this job. She'd practiced what to say for hours in front of the mirror. She knew her answers. She could *do* this.

Scarlet took the center chair opposite from her. A moment later, a strawberry-blonde woman came in. "Mrs. Henderson! I am delighted to meet you. I'm Darla Grant. Liam will be here in just a moment. We lost the mouse shifter Mrs. Asher down a drain and had to get Travis to help fish her out."

Caroline stood to shake her hand and smile, hoping it didn't look nervous. "Caroline, please!"

Darla smiled warmly at her with beautiful blue eyes and they sat.

"I hope you had a good trip," Darla said conversationally.

"It was a little surprising, to be frank," Caroline said. "But it certainly beats the commute by plane. This place is absolutely beautiful, thank you so much for having me."

That sounded polite and professional, didn't it? Not too nervous and overwhelmed? Hopefully it was the right blend of confident and humble.

"Ah, here's Liam," Scarlet said, as a tall, elegant man of Asian descent entered the room.

"I'm sorry for the delay," he said smoothly, as Caroline rose to her feet again. She lifted her gaze to his as she offered her hand politely…and every perfectly planned speech and careful phrase vanished from her head, overwhelmed by her red panda's sudden overwhelming rush of joy and recognition.

She was looking into the eyes of her mate.

~

Liam was lost.

Utterly, entirely, lost.

Caroline Henderson had excelled at every stage of the hiring process, beating out her competitors neatly with her experience, her glowing references, and her measured responses to unexpected questions. There were no other candidates at this point; this interview was only meant to be a chance for Scarlet in particular to vet her as a new member of the community and to make sure that Darla and Liam thought she would suit their elderly charges, since that was who she would most frequently be serving.

Liam had expected to like her, from her application, and from their phone interview.

He had not at all expected to look into her face and fall into her dark blue eyes, or to feel a jolt like lightning when he took her hand. She was so lovely, with her brown hair in a short pixie-cut. The hair at her ears was dyed blue, like her eyes. She wasn't tall and she wasn't short, and she was slim and fit under her modest, off-the-rack pantsuit.

Her oval face and button nose were the dearest thing that Liam had ever seen, burned into his memory at only the briefest of glances.

They staggered apart from each other as quickly as they could, and all but fell into their chairs.

Darla gave him a puzzled sideways look as he looked fixedly back at her, not daring to look again at Caroline.

"I understand that you have family that you would bring to Shifting Sands with you," Scarlet said invitingly.

Caroline stared at Scarlet with blind panic. Finally, she squeaked, "Yes."

"Can you tell us about them?" Darla encouraged kindly, when Caroline seemed incapable of going on.

"Him," Caroline said. "Not them. My son, James." She seemed to find some steadiness in looking only at Darla and Scarlet. Liam could not help watching her from the corner of his eyes. "My husband died five years ago."

She is ours now, Liam's dragon said possessively. *Ours forever. Ours completely.*

Darla and Scarlet both made vague noises of sympathy and Caroline swallowed hard. "It was just as I was finishing my residency, and...J-James was in second grade. It was...a challenge. We...got through it."

She sounded rattled and Liam, because he was watching them instead of Caroline, saw Scarlet and Darla exchange quick, concerned glances. They must assume that she was struggling with grief, and Liam could confirm that she did feel some sorrow, but it was round-edged with time and acceptance, not at all the source of her fluster.

Probably, her animal was jabbering in her ear like Liam's was in his, a constant song of joy and recognition and annoying insistence that made it extremely hard to *think.*

"We don't have many children here yet," Darla said gently. "There will only be a few others anywhere near his age, though you know we are expecting some babies soon."

Caroline blinked at her. "I don't think that will b-bother him," she said. "And if you don't have a school established, I was prep-p-p—ready to—homeschool. The advertisement did say isolated, and I was prep-p-pared for that."

"We'll have a school in the village," Scarlet said evenly. "But it won't be operational for some time. Possibly years."

"That's fine. I mean...that's fine. Yes. Of course." She must look tremendously nervous to Darla and Scarlet, Liam realized, and his heart ached for her, even as he was distracted wrestling his dragon back.

Our greatest treasure! he sang in Liam's head in an unending chorus. *Our other half! Our destiny! Forever!*

Will you hush and let me figure this out?

Brilliant joy! Dancing and singing and never alone and yearning and loving and longing and holding and being and everything good in the world! It wasn't even all words that Liam could parse, just a tumbling, endless, emotional onslaught.

Liam couldn't continue to stare only at Darla and Scarlet indefinitely and transferred his gaze to the coffee table between them. Out of the edge of his vision, he saw Caroline look at her lap and take a deep breath.

Scarlet asked her a few questions about the kinds of supplies and equipment she would require. Caroline answered haltingly, second-guessing her own requests, and Liam wanted to throw himself between them when Scarlet frowned, unimpressed.

Darla, skilled at making people feel at ease, turned the topic to the elders, asking sweetly about Caroline's experience with geriatric problems specific to shifters.

"Only my own grandparents," Caroline explained, and there was another wave of gentle sorrow, worn even more smooth than her last. "They are a large part of the reason that I chose to p-p-pursue both veterinary and human medical studies. Shifters don't often need doctors, but...but...when they do, it's very difficult to find the special help they need. If I could be...I wanted to be...to be there…for anyone else in that place."

As speeches went, it was poorly executed, but the feeling behind it was beautiful, and Liam knew the selflessness and brilliant soul that had pushed her to such a challenging occupation.

"Did you have any questions to add, Liam?" Scarlet asked, her eyes narrow.

Liam had prepared several. "No!" he said, now panicked and blank-minded. "I'm…no!"

"Darla, why don't you show Caroline what we've completed of the medical center and the housing for the retirement home," Scarlet suggested in her not-really-a-suggestion voice. "It's a little while before Mal comes back to escort her home. Thank you for joining us, we'll be in touch regarding your application."

It was unquestionably a dismissal. And not an encouraging one.

Everyone stood and Caroline thanked them all and shook hands with Scarlet and Darla and faced Liam breathlessly and there were no less than three false starts between them. Finally, she swept in, gave his hand one swift, professional shake and fled the room without even waiting for Darla.

Liam sank back into his chair as Darla scampered after her and Scarlet more sedately resumed her seat.

"That was the worst interview we've had at this stage," Scarlet observed. "Perhaps she really isn't suited for Shifting Sands after all."

Liam defensively snarled, "It's not her fault," then realized that Scarlet's eyes were dancing and full of speculation.

"Your mate," Scarlet surmised.

"My mate," Liam agreed, over the fireworks his whiskered dragon was setting off in his head.

Scarlet's look was long and thoughtful. "Is it going to be a problem?" she asked frankly.

"No," Liam said. "Of course not. We're both mature people and I assure you that we can behave professionally."

Scarlet continued to regard him. "I had no doubts about your professionalism," she said, absolutely neutral.

And that was when the whole idea of mates came crashing down around his head.

His dragon, and his mate's presence, had kept anything as mundane as a worry from his mind, but now that she was gone and his dragon was more quietly composing poetry to her in some corner of his soul, he remembered all the *things* that came with having a mate.

One thing in particular.

She was going to want *sex*.

To his surprise, and a pang of dismay, his yearning for her wasn't the slightest bit carnal. He wanted her, and it was both emotional and cerebral, but the physical manifestation was only a desire to be close, a longing for her presence. He wanted to hold her in his arms...but nothing more.

There had never been anything more.

It was hard not to feel the social pressure for desire. Advertisements, movies, literature, even *history* itself, all were shaped by a baseline assumption that everyone was driven by their basic fleshly instincts. He'd thought it was a gross exaggeration when he was young, a conspiracy of adulthood...then found that everyone around him really did think almost constantly about pleasure and sensual satisfaction. Even sensible people shocked him by reacting exactly as society predicted to attractive specimens of their gender of choice, to stimulus of calculated sexuality.

Slowly, he realized that they weren't the odd ones out. *He* was.

He made peace with his lack of appetite and his failure to feel attraction. It was no odder, at the end of the day, than a dozen other things that made him an individual. He even found a certain amount of superiority in knowing that he couldn't be manipulated by the same puppet strings of advertisers, that he could see things with a cool head that people tangled in lust would never be able to.

But he didn't feel cool-headed now.

The chance that she was asexual like he was...it was just so entirely unlikely. She would want him in the *usual* mate ways. And the idea that he might disappoint her was a gut punch. His dragon abandoned his poetry and swirled in dismay at even the idea of it.

He was still staring at Scarlet, who was patiently letting him untangle his thoughts without prodding.

"It's not going to be a problem," he said, drawing his mouth into a determined frown.

He wasn't going to borrow trouble before he knew he had it. He was going to find solutions. The safest way forward was to ask her questions, to swallow his pride and tell her, straight up, everything about him. He wasn't going to go sideways into this.

And if it came to it, he would even have sex for this woman.

Somehow.

~

Darla absolutely oozed money. She was kind and sweet, but everything, from her polished manners to the cut of her clothing, screamed of privilege. The way she automatically checked her appearance in reflective surfaces, even the way she walked, suggested years of finishing school and specialized tutors.

It immediately put Caroline, who'd come from nothing and knew it well, on edge.

It didn't help that Darla was absolutely bubbling over with curiosity. Her eyes were dancing, and as she showed Caroline the blossoming little community, she kept casting excited sideways glances that weren't nearly as hidden as she seemed to think they were.

Was it because she was glad to have a doctor and confident of Caroline's hire—which Caroline was not at all convinced of at the moment—or did she guess at the cause of Caroline's disaster of an interview?

The elders, just more than half a dozen of them, were a cast of indisputable characters, and Caroline, able to gradually get herself and her red panda back under some semblance of control, greeted them cordially.

When they found out she was under consideration as a doctor for the little community, they plied her with questions about their every injury and illness, imagined or otherwise, and grilled her about her experience.

"I don't know if I'm hired yet," Caroline was frank with them, and patient. "But I can leave the name of a steroid cream that should help that rash. Even shifters can develop sensitivities, especially as they age."

Mrs. Asher insisted she have a cup of tea, and Mrs. Shandy

plied her with delicious cookies. Mr. Danby was clearly non-verbal, and quite crabby about being woken from his nap by one of the old ladies, but he brightened at the attention of Caroline and Darla, and patted their hands absently.

Darla herself was as gracious and kind with the elders as if they were of the same social status that she was, not penniless pensioners, and Caroline found herself warming up to the young woman despite her best intentions to stay aloof.

The medical facility was nothing more than an empty building still, just a few steps from the housing for the retirees. There weren't even counters yet, though their locations were marked off on the floor in chalk. The rooms were cool, built of thick concrete walls and tiled in dark blue. The living quarters were small, but there were two rooms. The second would have been a perfect personal office for a single doctor, but would suffice as a room for James. It was smaller than he was used to, but considerably better in quality.

"Mr. Moore—Mal—will be back for Caroline soon," Darla said, to the disappointment of the elderly ladies and Mr. Danby. "We don't want to keep him waiting."

Caroline checked her phone for the time; they still had twenty minutes or so before she had agreed to meet him, but perhaps there was more to do first. She tried not to think too longingly about signing paperwork. Or Liam.

Darla sighed happily and slipped her arm into Caroline's as they left the building and climbed the winding road towards the place where Mal had created the doorway that brought her here.

Caroline caught herself waiting to see Liam around every corner and hedge. Her red panda was excited and impatient, and still maintaining a constant, if quieter, chorus of anticipation.

"Is he your mate?" Darla finally asked, as Caroline could tell she'd been dying to. "Liam, I mean? I don't want to pry, but it just seemed like you two…had a moment."

A *moment*. Like it had been only a flash of lightning, not the sun rising in her soul. It was so much more than a *moment*.

Caroline didn't answer, but she did stumble and flush and Darla drew her aside on the empty road and gazed into her face. What she saw there must have been the answer she'd been hoping for, and her mouth curved into a wide, delighted smile. "I am so happy for you," she said in pure joy that Caroline didn't think any acting class or etiquette class could have taught. "Liam is dear to my heart," Darla said warmly. "And I like you already. I have wanted this for him, so much."

"H-how do you know him?" Caroline stammered. It was the least of the questions she wanted to ask.

"We met through the retirement home," Darla said eagerly. "Before it was here at Shifting Sands, I mean. We were engaged to be married for a time…before I met my own mate."

Caroline swirled through a lagoon of jealousy at the idea of Liam engaged to this beautiful, bubbly woman, however briefly, and tried to soothe her red panda's possessiveness. It was inevitable that they both already had pasts. She was a widow and had a son, so it was obvious *she* hadn't waited chastely for *him*.

"There is so much I want to tell you," Darla said, taking her by the hands and drawing her around in a half-circle. "But I think Liam should tell you most of it himself."

And there he was, standing behind them, looking as dazed and eager as she was.

"Caroline," he breathed.

Caroline barely noticed Darla's laughing departure, walking to Liam with her hands irresistibly outstretched.

He met her halfway, and his touch was like *home* as their fingers twined together.

For a long moment, they only stood, gazing at each other with yearning and recognition. His smile was the most beautiful thing that Caroline had ever seen in her life.

"You're my mate," he said in wonder.

"You're *my* mate," she echoed.

She should kiss him, she thought. That was where this went next, wasn't it? She felt like everything was new and unknown again.

"We don't have long," Liam said apologetically. "It's not a good idea to make Mal wait."

"Oh, no," Caroline agreed. "I wouldn't want to be rude."

Make him wait, her red panda suggested. *We should be here.*

"There are…things you should know," he said, and Caroline could feel his sudden hesitation to the very bottom of his soul and she wanted to reassure him that nothing he could tell her could possibly make her love him any less.

"I have things I want to tell you, too," she told him. "Maybe I can do a little better than I managed in my interview…"

"You were amazing," Liam said swiftly. "I couldn't keep a thought in my head and you pushed right through, utterly professional."

Caroline smiled. "Oh, wow, you really are sweet," she teased him. "I was a disaster."

They were grinning at each other, and Caroline felt like she was on the brink of laughing, or singing, or dancing.

"When you come back…" Liam started, as if that was a completely done deal.

Maybe it was. Caroline wasn't sure she could imagine a life without this man at her side, whether she got the job or not.

"I can't wait to introduce you to James," she said. "He's a good kid, and I think he'll like you."

All of us together, her red panda sighed.

"About that…sort of..."

"Ah, Mrs. Henderson. Are you ready to go?"

The lawyer, Mal Moore, had worse timing than Caroline did, she decided. "At your convenience, of course," she said politely.

Either oblivious to anything occurring between Liam and Caroline, or choosing to ignore it, Mal nodded briskly. "Excellent."

"Wait," Liam said desperately, clinging to her hands. "Give us just a moment, please."

Mal frowned and walked a little ways up the hill out of earshot, irritation in every line of his impeccable silk suit.

It was the kiss moment, Caroline thought, and she realized that her hands were trembling. She started to move into him, lifting her face to his, but he stopped her.

"There's something I have to ask you," he said reluctantly.

“Anything,” she told him.

Liam swallowed. “Do you like sex?”

The question was almost absurd.

Almost.

He must have read something about it through the mate bond that was already humming, so strong, between them.

“Yes,” she said promptly, and the wave of dismay from him was unmistakable. Did he think she was *lying*? Caroline was confused by the tangled emotions she was feeling, not sure what was him and what was her.

“Liam…” she started, reaching for him. “What is it?”

“I’ll make it work,” he said to her, taking her by the shoulders. “I will. I promise.”

“I don’t understand,” Caroline said, hopelessly lost.

He cupped her face in his hands...and still didn’t kiss her, only leaned his forehead against hers. “It’s going to take time to explain. Time I don’t have right now. Please, trust me. Come back to me.”

“Yes,” Caroline promised, baffled. “Of course.”

Then he walked away, determination in his stride.

Caroline watched him go, admiring his graceful lope even as it took him away from her, then turned numbly to where Mal was impatiently waiting. He had created the magic doorway by the time she got to him, and she was whisked through efficiently. It closed behind her and she was back in New York City. There were Christmas carols playing in the elevator as she descended from the office, and a notification about long-distance International roaming charges on her phone.

She was halfway back to the airport in another expensive taxi before she realized that she’d never gotten a definite answer about whether or not she’d gotten the job.

“iam, you *dog*! I hear you met your mate today!”

Darla had clearly spared no time in letting Breck know

the news. The waiter opened the door to his cottage and welcomed Liam in. "Can I get you a celebratory drink?"

I'm not a dog, Liam's literal-minded dragon said haughtily.

Liam ignored the dragon, who was already sulking because their mate was so far away. Half a world, or a lifetime, according to his dramatic woe at the moment.

"I need your help," Liam said to Breck.

"Believe me, you are in the right place for all forms of romantic assistance," Breck said, grinning broadly. "Looking for the right poem? Fashion advice? Wine selection? Some people go with champagne, but a light blush works as well and actually tastes—"

"I need to know how to have sex," Liam blurted.

Breck sobered, finally noticing how distraught Liam actually was. "And finding a mate…"

"Didn't fix me," Liam said in despair.

Breck frowned. "You aren't broken," he said defensively. "You never were."

For all of Breck's flamboyant, sometimes outrageous sexuality, he had never once made Liam feel like less of a man for his own preference towards nothing.

But it didn't matter what his *preference* was. "She…she wants it. I *have* to."

Breck looked as confused as Liam felt. "But she's your mate. It shouldn't *be* like that."

"I *asked*," Liam said. "I asked because I didn't want to assume anything, and she *likes* it, and I could never forgive myself for not being what she needs." He gritted his teeth. "So here I am. Teach me your ways."

Breck's expression was conflicted, and he hesitated.

"She's my mate, Breck," Liam pressed. "There is nothing that I want in this world more than to bring her pleasure. It doesn't matter what I have to do."

Breck shook his head slowly. "Well, the first item of business is not looking like you're about to walk a plank. Sex is not about giving pleasure, it's about *sharing* pleasure. Want to know the absolute secret to making sure your partner has fun? It's having fun *with* them. I've always said that sex is like a good joke."

"This is not a joke," Liam protested.

Breck smiled at him. "No, but it's *like* a joke. The success of it is all in the timing, and everyone should be smiling at the end." He cracked his knuckles. "Okay, let's start at the beginning. What kind of experiences have you had?"

"I can never remember the bases," Liam moaned. "I hate baseball."

"You've kissed?"

"Badly."

"You've…er…fondled?"

"That was worse."

"You've seen a woman naked."

"It's hard to avoid." Liam was beginning to wish he'd accepted the drink. "Especially after a few months at a clothing-optional resort."

"Pick an instance. What did it do for you?"

"She was beautiful, but it was very...aesthetic. I didn't mind...ah...touching. Like petting a cat, or feeling a soft cloth. But the rubbing seemed...crude. Repetitive. And I had no interest in doing more. None."

"Actively repulsed?" Breck asked, absolutely neutral.

Liam considered. "Not entirely. More like baffled that anyone would want to do something so absurd."

"You aren't reading the right poetry," Breck suggested. "I'll have some homework for you. Now, am I correct in assuming that there's no...shwing?" He mimed a hard-on.

Liam groaned, but shook his head. "No shwing," he said honestly. "Maybe a little...swell...with...er...dedicated attention...but nothing that survives contact with the…ah…enemy."

"And kissing? How was that?"

"It was okay up to the tongue part. Not exciting, like it's supposed to be, but comfortable enough. But then...well, it seems really unsanitary, and I already have my own tongue taking up space in there. It was just awkward and…yeah, maybe a little repulsive."

Breck stifled a laugh.

"That's not useful, is it?" Liam despaired.

"It's absolutely useful," Breck said frankly. "Knowing what your own boundaries are is the first step towards figuring out how to work within them." He tipped his head back and narrowed his eyes. "Now, do you want to stimulate with your fingers, your tongue, or a tool?"

"A...tool?" Liam squawked.

"Something you wear, or something you don't, there are options. But you can accomplish everything you need to without them, if you'd prefer."

"Fingers," Liam said weakly, wishing he was having any other conversation.

"Good choice," Breck approved. "You have finer control. You can graduate to something else later. Now, I assume you have a basic working knowledge of the anatomy in question?"

Liam nodded numbly. "I do have *some* medical background," he said. "And I've read books."

"Oo!" Breck seemed excited by the prospect. "Which ones?"

"Introduction to Anatomy."

Breck groaned. "I'll have some other homework for you. Do you know what a clitoris is?"

"In theory," Liam conceded.

"You can usually tell by the reaction if you've found the right place, but I'll draw you a diagram. It's not as hard to find as some men claim. The g-spot, ah, that's a little trickier." Breck said it with relish; this was the kind of challenge he loved. He rubbed his hands together. "But you don't just start there directly; that would be amateur. We're going to start at the top, work our way down. Do you need anything before we get started?"

Liam gave him a steady look. "I think I'll take that drink you offered."

~

The official job offer arrived in Caroline's inbox before her plane from New York touched down.

She sat in her seat, staring at the phone, while the plane emptied around her and they began to clean it.

A new life. A new start. A new *mate.*

It was dark out; she had only been in New York for a few hours, most of it spent commuting. And a blissful, confusing, utterly insane hour and a half an entire world away.

"Can I help you with something?" the attendant asked.

Caroline looked around at the empty plane. "No, I'm sorry, thank you. I'll get out of your way."

"Take your time," the attendant replied kindly, bustling away.

Caroline rose, and pulled her small day pack from the overhead bin, dazedly wandering out into the airport and to the lot where she'd parked her car.

She could not recall the actual drive later, only the emotions as she navigated the familiar roads: confusion, elation, and bone-deep longing. She knew her destiny, now, and it filled her with hope and anticipation.

Now, she just had to get James to buy off on it.

He was awake, and Caroline knocked on his door. "Hey, Jamie?"

She had to knock again; he was wearing headphones, playing a game, but he put the console down when he saw her and slipped off the headset. "Hey, Mom." He was past the age of running to greet her with a hug, to Caroline's disappointment, but he was unfailingly polite, a rarity at his age, she thought. "How'd the interview go?"

"I got the job," Caroline said, and it seemed like the least of her news. Saying it made it feel real for the first time.

"Awesome!" That did, apparently warrant a hug, and James untangled himself from his gaming chair and came to dispense it.

"It will mean moving," Caroline cautioned, wrapping him into her arms. "And you won't believe *where.*"

"Just tell me it has WiFi," James begged.

Caroline paused. "I honestly don't know," she said. "It...might not."

"Oh, my God, Mom. That's like the one thing I need. Where is it? Timbuktu?" James let go of her and retreated back to his chair.

"Costa Rica. A private island off of Central America, where there are only shifters."

James stared at her.

"There won't be a lot of other kids," Caroline told him. "And we'll probably have to homeschool, at least for a few years."

"A tropical *island*?" James sounded deeply skeptical.

"It's beautiful," Caroline said coaxingly. "White sand beaches, palm trees, turquoise seas."

"Yeah, *that* sounds like me," James said in that sharply sarcastic tone that only teenagers could manage. He was thirteen, and sometimes seemed like a very *old* thirteen.

"Will you give it a try?" Caroline asked. "If you hate it…" her voice wavered and she caught herself twisting the hem of her jacket. She couldn't voice a promise to turn her back on her mate and *leave*. But she couldn't take her son to a place that he wouldn't be *happy*.

Her face must have betrayed her conflict. James frowned at her. "You really want this job, don't you."

"It's not just the job," Caroline said, and she moved a pile of dirty clothes to sit on his bed.

James sat beside her. "What's up?" he asked cautiously.

Caroline drew in a breath. Some parts of parenting were harder than others. "There are some things I never told you, about being a shifter."

James was unhelpfully quiet.

"A shifter can have...a mate. And our animals recognize that person, and there's this...connection." Longing. Yearning. Knowing that he was the one, the person who could make her happier than any other...she looked at James, who was looking back quizzically. "It's physical, and emotional, and basically undeniable."

"Was Dad your *mate*?"

Caroline dropped her gaze. "No," she said reluctantly. "I loved him, but he wasn't. Some shifters go their whole lives without meeting their mates."

"So you're telling me this now—you *met* someone!"

Not just someone, *him. Liam.* Caroline felt like her chest was filled with swirling pressure and her red panda was purring in eagerness.

James punched her in the shoulder. "That's awesome."

Caroline looked up at him sharply. "You're okay with this?"

"You don't have to be a nun, Mom," James scoffed. "Dad's been gone a long time."

Do you like sex? It was still the weirdest question Liam could have asked, and Caroline shoved it back.

"I want you to meet him," she said. "I hope that you'll like him."

"What kind of shifter is he?" James quizzed her. "Is he nice? Does he have a job?"

"He's...I don't know what kind of shifter he is," Caroline admitted. "We just met and we only had a few moments to talk. He works with the elders at the island, and he's...*nice*." *So* nice. She wanted to curl up in his lap and stay there forever *nice*.

James frowned. "That doesn't seem like much to go on."

Caroline flapped her hands uselessly. "It's hard to explain," she said. "But I know him, I can *feel* him, it's like he's a part of me I never realized was missing. My red panda recognized him and honestly won't shut up about how *amazing* he is and I can't stop thinking about him."

To her surprise, James put his arm around her and squeezed. "You don't have to justify it to me, Mom," he said kindly. "I'll go to the island and I'll try to like it."

"If you don't…"

"Don't make promises you can't keep," James reminded her.

"I want you to be happy," Caroline said firmly.

"I want you to be happy, too," James said. "You deserve a good job and a good guy. We'll make it work."

Caroline wrapped him into a hug, marveling over how big he was getting, and how smart and good-hearted. "Thank you, James."

James squirmed out of the embrace. "Ew, Mom, you're crying. You're not allowed to do that except on alternating Tuesdays."

Caroline let him go and stood up as she wiped her eyes. "I'm starving," she admitted. "Did you eat?"

"Oven corn dogs and a bag of chips," James told her with shrug.

Caroline groaned. "I buy vegetables, you know."

"What do I look like, a rabbit?"

"Red pandas eat plants," Caroline teased him.

"My panda and I are in agreement that corn dogs are the superior source of protein." James sat back down in his gaming chair and started to put his headphones back on. "That island better have WiFi," he told her as Caroline started to leave. "And Mom…"

She paused in the doorway.

"Merry Christmas!"

~

It was excruciating, waiting for Caroline's return to the island.

Liam read every book that Breck assigned him, from elegant collections of poetry that he appreciated for their quality, to novels so trashy and explicit that Liam was surprised that they'd been put in print. Maybe not terribly surprised.

"This is really how it works?" he asked Breck skeptically. "I mean...heaving? Thrusting? She *gushes*?"

"It varies delightfully," Breck said cheerfully. "Every specimen is completely different, every encounter entirely new."

"Then how do you know what to do?"

"You read the room," Breck told him. "You try things and pay attention, ask, and listen. If she's having fun, and you're having fun, you're doing it right; there's no one way."

He lent Liam videos that were not so much educational as they were grueling.

Why are we doing this? his dragon asked, as bored as Liam.

We're going to figure out how to be what she needs, Liam insisted. He winced and hoped she wouldn't want what was happening on the screen at that moment. His dragon was surprisingly unconcerned about the issue.

The only thing that got him through it all were the emails.

It started with a very brief, professional email asking her about supplies. He agonized over the correct tone, and right measure of friendliness, and finally ended with "I can't wait to see you again."

She responded with an email exactly as efficient, and finished, "I'm looking forward to seeing you, too."

Liam fabricated another reason to email her, signing his letter, "I am delighted to hear you may be back by Christmas. Do you do anything to celebrate?"

And that unleashed a delightful, warm email exchange about how Caroline was regretting that they wouldn't have a tree that year because they were in the throes of packing, and stories about favorite presents and singing carols and candlelight services at church.

Holiday food was the next topic, and general food from there, until they were sharing recipes, and then comparing music and media and somehow that turned into childhood stories and long, rambling exchanges about their ambitions and regrets.

Every word felt like a promise, every little red flag on his laptop or phone was a moment of anticipation and eagerness. He was a disaster at duties, constantly distracted, desperate to escape to read her messages over and over, to carefully compose his replies.

His sign-offs gradually moved from 'Regards, Liam' to 'Yours most truly, Liam' and he agonized over committing to 'Love, Liam.' Would that assume too much?

Hers were always simply, 'Caroline.'

But sometimes they had sideways text hearts.

He was baffled that he could crave something so completely…to miss being able to see her, to hunger for touching her...and still not want her in the ways that were *expected*. Dozens of times, as their emails grew more intimate, he wanted to tell her what he was, how he was different. Each time, he deleted the confession. It should be done in person, he convinced himself.

But he knew he was simply afraid of disappointing her.

So he read every book Breck handed him, and watched every movie, and tried to make sense of the sex by sheer force of will.

Finally, there was a date set: she was coming a few days before Christmas. There were several babies due early in the new year, and Scarlet suggested that it would be a nice treat to attend the big staff dinner; the restaurant was the only part of the resort that had been completed. Caroline assured her that wouldn't disrupt any existing plans. Liam, who had despaired of seeing her until after New Year's, felt like he was in a flurry of anticipation.

It rather suddenly occurred to him that there were important things that they *hadn't* discussed, like where she would live. Would she move in with him? Liam didn't want to presume she would want to, especially if he failed in his efforts to satisfy her, but the idea of her being several buildings away seemed like too much.

We won't fail, his dragon chided him. *We're meant to be.*

He lost sight of the actual *holiday* until the day before she was due to arrive, and was blindsided when Darla slyly asked him, "So, what are you giving her for Christmas?"

A *gift.*

He needed to get her a gift for Christmas, and now he was completely out of time to order something unless he begged a portal from the rather intimidating Mal Moore, and his mind was utterly blank.

"You could write her some poetry," Breck suggested, correctly interpreting his dumbfounded look.

They were sitting in the elder's common room, having tea with Mrs. Asher, Mrs. Shandy and Mr. Danby. By now everyone in the retirement home—probably everyone on the island—knew that the new doctor was Liam's mate, and they teased him good-heartedly.

"Bake her some cookies," Mrs. Shandy suggested. That was her answer to everything, now that she had access to the small kitchen in the retirement home.

"Give her something personal that was yours," Mrs. Asher countered. "Something that means a lot."

Mr. Danby grunted and muttered incoherently, then upset his tea.

Liam dismantled his room, trying to find anything that could serve as a gift. He'd never collected much of worth, not being the kind of dragon who hoarded things, and everything he found seemed pathetic or inappropriate. The items of *value* that he owned had come to him as presents, most of them from Darla, and re-gifting something from his former fiancée seemed tacky at best, and insulting at worst.

He frantically tried to write poetry that made even his dragon roll his eyes in disgust.

There was a tiny, half-stocked store being built in the village, and Liam wandered the shelves, staring at the practical offerings. He couldn't give his mate deodorant or drink powder. He was staring at the soap offerings when he realized that he should also find a gift for James and he gave an audible moan.

"What are you looking for?" Jenny asked, reaching past him to pick up a tube of toothpaste.

"I need a gift," Liam said. "Two gifts. I'm drawing a complete blank."

Jenny's smile was knowing. "She won't care if you don't have one," she observed.

"I'll care," Liam protested. "I want to get her something. I *have* to." His dragon was more upset by the idea of not having an expected gift than he was at the whole prospect of sex.

~

It was everything Caroline could do not to shove past Mal as soon as the portal was opened and run to find Liam, but she tightened her grip on her day pack and let the burly men in completely unseasonable short sleeves step through and unload her tiny U-Haul trailer of furniture and boxes in a few moments flat.

"Cool," James observed off-handedly, clearly trying to smother his awe.

To her disappointment, Liam wasn't waiting for her on the other side of the shimmering doorway, and when the last box had been carried through, Mal stopped her from following them. "Your possessions will be delivered to your rooms, but I've been asked to take you to Chef's. Scarlet thought that you would like refreshment, and wanted a chance to introduce you to some of her staff."

Caroline's red panda gave a growl of impatience, but she accepted as serenely as she could manage. When Mal let the doorway collapse, she felt a moment of loss, but another door was built in its place, and then she and James were being ushered through onto a wide white marble deck overlooking the Shifting Sands Resort.

Even James couldn't quite hide his amazement.

Shifting Sands Bay had been beautiful and quaint and unusual.

Shifting Sands *Resort* was astounding.

Even half-finished, with piles of building supplies scattered amid heaps of dirt and gaping holes, it was clear that this was going to be a *magnificent* resort. They were near the top, looking down, over an empty, half-tiled swimming pool and an expanse of emerald jungle peppered in beautiful private lawns, all circling down to a pristine white crescent of beach.

Caroline could see the bones of something beautiful in the chaos, and could imagine the sprawling resort finished to the same level as the restaurant, with pseudo-Greek columns and winding paths.

Mal stalked past them, to where Scarlet was standing at the railing of the restaurant and Caroline was surprised and a little embarrassed to watch his whole demeanor soften and warm as he gathered her into his arms and gave her a slow kiss in greeting.

Caroline blinked. The light made it look like buds on a potted plant behind Scarlet rather suddenly burst into bloom. But that was ridiculous, wasn't it?

They had a quiet moment of conversation, while Caroline ached to see Liam. Where was *their* kiss moment? The emails they had exchanged had been so heart-warming; if he had not been her mate, she might have fallen for him on the strength of just their correspondence. But she couldn't help but remember his moment of dismay when they had parted. Had she somehow *disappointed* him? Anticipation and anxiousness made her feel jittery.

"You must be Caroline and James." The waiter who greeted them was dashingly handsome, though not, she thought critically, as handsome as Liam. "I'm Breck, and I'll be your server, and also incidentally, your next door neighbor at the Bay, at the moment. We're all delighted to have you on staff."

She and James shook his hand and let him lead them to a table on the deck. "Chef has prepared you a welcome-to-the-island meal. Liam told us all your favorites, and he should be here shortly himself."

Chef himself came out to greet them and discuss the menu: a baked chicken and risotto for Caroline and a Salisbury steak for James. They both agreed eagerly, and then Caroline spotted Liam at the entrance of the restaurant and she forgot about food entirely.

He was everything she'd remembered: tall, beautiful, and graceful. His dark hair was cut short and stylish, and he was wearing a subtly patterned green shirt over his gorgeous broad shoulders.

He had spotted her first, and he was already hurrying towards her by the time she saw him. She stood at his approach, and it was everything she could do not to simply run forward and embrace him.

Her son stood also, and although Liam's gaze was for her initially, he swiftly turned and greeted the boy first. "You must be James." He extended a hand and James shook it gravely, looking very grown-up.

"You're Liam," James said with an exchange of uncomfortable nods.

"I've been looking forward to meeting you," Liam told him sincerely.

James mumbled something passingly polite in return and they both seemed to think that satisfied courtesy.

"Caroline." Liam took her hand, not shaking it so much as squeezing it for too brief a moment.

"Liam." She knew she was smiling foolishly, but completely incapable of doing anything else.

"I hope you won't mind if I join you for dinner," Liam said.

"Of course not," Caroline said with a sideways glance at James, who shrugged and grimaced in a way that she guessed was supposed to be encouraging.

Liam took the empty chair next to Caroline after the slightest of pauses, and Breck poured water into the glass that was already there. "Chef's got a treat for you, too," he said cheerfully. "Bacon-wrapped tenderloins with some of Graham's fresh green beans."

"Sounds wonderful," Liam agreed, spreading his napkin into his lap with hands that Caroline tried very hard not to stare at.

It was awkward to turn to look at him the way she wanted to, so mostly Caroline watched James as they all made idle small talk about the trip. His gaze flickered between both of them in return, his contributions to the conversation grudging but polite.

"It's so beautiful," Caroline said, looking out over the railing. The sun was just beginning to ease towards the ocean, and the sky was blushing in anticipation.

Breck brought their meals, and they eagerly dug in. It was the most natural thing to offer Liam a taste of her exquisite risotto, and it didn't seem strange to accept a bite of his delicious steak. Chef's food might just be the best part of moving to the island, Caroline considered, savoring her perfectly prepared chicken.

Then she caught the corner of a smile from Liam and she knew better.

Liam did a gallant job of including James in the conversation, asking about school and hobbies.

James was unhelpful, but not quite unfriendly, and Caroline could only imagine how awkward it was for him, sitting across from his long-single mother and a complete stranger who was her mate.

Her mate.

She was dizzy with unquantified joy.

Her *mate*.

"So, what kind of shifter are you?" James asked, not quite belligerent.

"Dragon," Liam said casually, and both James and Caroline really did stare at him then.

"Dragon?" James said in awe. "Do you breathe fire?"

Liam grinned at them. "I'm afraid not. I'm an Eastern dragon. With the whiskers and the coils."

James nodded in slow respect. "Cool," he said as casually as he could manage. "That's cool."

Caroline wasn't much help in the discussion herself, especially when Liam and James diverted to the topic of technical things and video games. James did seem to thaw at the assertion that there was indeed some basic WiFi, and that a better connection was being worked on.

"You heard of the Gladiator controller?" Liam asked casually.

"Oh, yeah," James said avidly. "I've read about those. Top of the line, state of the art, better connection speed, fewer drop-outs. They're sweet."

Caroline, who knew what was coming, smiled and was able to watch her son's face as Liam grinned and said, "Well, you might have a pleasant surprise, back in your room."

James stared. "What?"

"I cleared it with your mom," Liam said. "Merry Christmas."

"Get *out!*" James said in astonishment. Then, scrambling, "I mean, ah, thank you. Wow. Seriously? A *Gladiator*?"

He babbled about the device's technical specs for a while and Caroline felt a warm feeling of relief come over her at his unabashed enthusiasm. Buying an expensive gift for her son wasn't a *sure-fire* way to win him over, but Caroline thought that it certainly wouldn't hurt, and when Liam assured her that money was no issue, she had approved the purchase. She was glad, now, that she had, watching the delight in James' face and the way he relaxed with Liam.

What's more, after a delicious light dessert of toasted sugar Crème Brûlée, the waiter, Breck, came to gather their plates and casually ask, "You wouldn't happen to play Zombie Fighters Five, would you?"

Caroline looked at him as suspiciously as James did.

"Yeah..." James said slowly.

"Well, it just so happens that we're putting together a tournament this evening after I get off shift. Care to take on the island experts and an actual retired *Marine*?" Breck's tone was completely innocent, but Caroline recognized that they were being maneuvered, and she was deeply grateful.

As lovely as it was to sit next to Liam and share a meal in person, instead of emails *about* meals, she wanted him to herself. She wanted to feel those arms around her, and bury her face in his shoulder, and twine her fingers into his, without the scrutiny of anyone else.

She wanted her *kiss* moment, dammit.

"Can I, Mom?" James begged.

"We might run late," Breck said, with a smile for Caroline.

"It's not like I have school tomorrow morning," James pointed out.

"I was thinking we should start unpacking tonight," Caroline teased.

"I'm happy to help you with that tomorrow," Liam offered, as James moaned, "Come on, Mom, that can *wait*…"

"Yes," Caroline laughed. "Yes, but not *too* late."

"You're the best," James declared extravagantly.

Shifting Sands Bay was a short, delightful walk from the resort. James was enthusiastic about the apartment off the medical center, and his room, and most of all about the controller, in its glossy packaging. He immediately started setting up his computer.

The few pieces of furniture they'd brought had already been arranged in the only sensible way that it fit in the rooms, though all of their shipping boxes had politely been left unopened. Caroline wandered through the medical center, which had already been finished and stocked according to her wildest requests. The counters were all flawless stainless steel, and all of the equipment still had the clear protective film over the readouts.

"Everything was finished so quickly," she said in awe. It smelled like fresh paint and glue, but not cloyingly so. The windows were open, curtains stirring in the evening air.

Liam stood in the doorway, watching her walk around the room trailing her fingers over things in awe. This was going to be *her* clinic, she realized, and her heart gave a little trill in her chest. Her clinic, in this gorgeous place for shifters. A place where she didn't have to hide what she was. A place...with her mate.

Caroline circled the room back to Liam and wondered if this could be the moment she'd been waiting for.

But the *dismay* was back.

Everything had been so lovely over dinner, so casual and easy. Caroline had begun to wonder if she'd imagined Liam's retreat, or if she had built it up too much in her memory.

But here it was again, conflict and fear clear across features that were already dear.

Before Caroline could ask what made him look like that, there was a knock at the door.

"Doctor?"

"Caroline is fine," she corrected quickly.

The red-headed man at the doorway flashed her a brief smile. "I'm Neal, ma'am," he said politely. "Breck said your young one was interested in a gaming tournament and that it was alright with you?"

"That would be fine," Caroline said. "Try not to have him back *too* late. Let's say midnight?"

"Yes, ma'am," Neal agreed. "We'll be in the community center, I can give you the number."

Before Caroline could call to him, James was tumbling eagerly from his room, his precious new controller already unpackaged and in his hands.

He gave her the briefest of kisses on the cheeks and was gone with Neal, but not before Caroline saw Neal slip a card to Liam, who seemed to be trying hard to blend in to the paneling near the door.

He frowned at the card as the sounds of James, chattering in excitement, and Neal faded away in the night. Finally, he held it up to Caroline.

It looked like a hotel key card.

"We didn't really talk about what would happen," Liam said, his voice rich with dread. "Or...*where*. There's one finished cottage, back at the resort. They've probably gone to a lot of work…" He swallowed. "If you'd like to join me for a…nightcap?"

Was he only nervous? Caroline wondered. Well, she could appreciate the feeling. She felt like she was made of nothing *but* nerves. "Neutral ground?" she teased. Then, more warmly, "I'd *like* that."

They wandered back to the resort hand-in-hand, and Caroline could feel the reluctance in his step and in his fingers twined with hers.

What's gone wrong? she asked her red panda plaintively.

Her animal was utterly unconcerned.

~

The cottage was clearly unfinished, and had been hastily but carefully pulled together for use. Liam unlocked the door with hands that trembled, his dragon singing in his head.

He held the door for Caroline, who gave a happy intake of breath at the sight of the interior. Graham had provided flowers, to Liam's surprise, and there was even a trail of petals through the doorless frame to the bedroom. The glass for the windows out to the front porch was noticeably missing, and the bathroom was still bare plumbing. But gauze curtains had been hung, and rugs had been laid down over rough subfloor. Rudimentary power had been wired in, and there was a bluetooth radio playing low, smooth jazz.

Liam swallowed hard.

Caroline wandered in, pausing to inspect the bottle of wine that was sitting out with wine glasses, smelling the cut flowers in the vase. Then she turned to him and sighed. "What is it, Liam? Will you tell me?"

Liam realized he was still standing in the doorway, unable to make his feet carry him inside. He was such a tangle of conflict. He wanted to sweep Caroline into his arms and…just hold her.

But he knew that the moment he touched her, she'd expect more, and he quailed at the idea of the disappointment he would serve her. None of the techniques he'd studied seemed sufficient for the situation.

Was a glass of wine a coward's move? Liam wasn't sure it would help. He stared at the rose petals, heaved a great sigh, and shut the door behind him.

He ignored the trail to the bedroom and went to the framework that would be sliding glass doors leading out onto the porch. The filmy curtains stirring slightly in the breeze. He paused. "Will you...sit with me a little?"

She scampered to his side, and they sat on the little wicker loveseat, carefully leaving just a little space between them.

"Do you...know what asexual is?" he asked, not sure how else to start.

She gave a sharp, subtle intake of breath that suggested she did. "I know how some people define it," she said. Then, she turned abruptly to face him, tucking one leg underneath her. "Wait, this is why you asked me if I...*liked sex*. You knew I was ace?"

Liam stared at her. "You said you *did*. Like sex, I mean. I'm so confused."

"I *do*," she insisted. "I love to be close with someone I care about, I love that I can bring a partner to pleasure. I *enjoy* it, even if it's...not how it's all laid out in romance books." As she spoke, she touched him, a tentative hand at his shoulder first, then a stroke down his arm, and she was leaning closer to him, and Liam couldn't make sense of any of it.

His dragon was delighted, *he* was *terrified*.

"Wait," he said, warring between longing to gather her into his arms and wanting to pull away. "*You're* ace?" He felt dull and stupid. Nothing made sense.

She paused, searching his face. "Isn't that what you…?" She settled back into her own space. "I think I'm missing something here."

"I'm ace," Liam said slowly. "*I'm* ace."

She blinked at him. "Then you…"

"Have really managed to make a hash of this," Liam said in

wonder. He should have trusted his dragon, he thought. He should have trusted his *mate*.

She started to touch him and stopped herself. "Tell me what you *do* like," she begged. "Do you *want* to be touched?"

"Yes," Liam breathed around the lump in his throat, and she was reaching for him at last. "It's just that usually there's this...*expectation*."

She stopped herself again, fingers aching inches from his skin. "Tell me," she said. "I promise not to do more. Do you like kissing?"

"Yes," Liam said promptly, because he very much wanted her mouth against him. He wanted all of her against him. "Just...not tongue?"

Caroline giggled, a low, sweet sound of release, and then she was crawling into his lap, and he could put his arms around and draw her close to him, the way he'd been longing to for so long. She laid a series of light kisses on his neck and nuzzled close, and Liam thought he might burst from the pure *pleasure* of it.

She was so right in his embrace, she fit there so perfectly. Liam never wanted to let go.

"Skin?" she asked, toying with the buttons of his shirt.

Could they be *closer*? Was it possible? "Yes," Liam said, and when they pulled apart it was like losing something.

She took his hand and they stood, going together without discussion back into the cottage and following the trail of petals for the bed.

This was it, he thought with sudden fear as they undressed. This was where it would go wrong. She would ask for more, and see that he couldn't...he would fail her, it was simple human biology that had always eluded him...he was broken…

Then they were both completely unclothed and she was drawing him down onto the bed, murmuring, "Hold me, just *hold* me."

And he could do that. He *craved* that. The touch of her skin against the whole length of him, the warmth of her in his embrace, her leg just over his, her arms around his shoulders...he waited for the demands, for the awkwardness that always followed...but it didn't happen. They simply relaxed into each other, slowly and completely, until Liam could barely tell where he stopped and she started.

She sighed happily, and Liam felt it against his chest. "Do you know," she said quietly, "that the medical community hasn't settled on a concrete definition of orgasm?"

"I didn't know that," Liam admitted.

"I've always had a favorite," Caroline said. "But it's not the most widely accepted. It is 'intense pleasure resulting from the release of physical tension.' Some women have it during childbirth or exercise, completely independent of sex."

Liam could only hold her in wonder. Is that what this was? This perfect contentment as he let go of expectations and satisfied the simple yearning he'd had since he'd first laid eyes on her to hold her close?

He'd never felt so peaceful or whole, never been so in harmony with another body...or his own.

~

Caroline felt like she'd come home. Liam's arms were strong and gentle, and he held her like he never wanted to let go. She certainly never wanted him to.

She felt protected and free, all at once, completely content to lie next to her mate and simply *be*.

"Have you always known you were ace?" she asked, not wanting to disturb their tranquility, but too curious to resist.

"Since before I knew I was a dragon shifter," Liam confessed, his voice half-rumbling through his chest as she lay on him. "I thought that sexuality was a big joke for years and kept waiting for the punchline. And waiting. And waiting. Eventually I realized that I was the one out of step. I found out that ace was a thing on the Internet and finally had a name for it. You?"

"I didn't realize for a long time, not until after I was married." She made lazy patterns on his sculpted chest. "I always figured...I was just doing things wrong, that I was feeling shy, that there were other factors. My husband and I...it was challenging. I never initiated anything, and he feared it was a fault of affection. And...when we *did*, I had fun, but I rarely *came*. It was frustrating and he felt inadequate. But we loved each other, and were willing to put in the work to figure something out. And we finally realized that we didn't have to take the same things from sex."

Caroline propped herself up on one elbow and gazed down at him. "I wasn't lying. I *do* like sex. But I don't hunger for it, and I rarely come. Once we finally saw it as a pleasant thing we could do together and I stopped chasing the big O, the pressure was off and we could actually *enjoy* it together."

Liam rose to a seated position beside her, and Caroline marveled all over again at how *beautiful* he was. She couldn't resist reaching out and Liam caught her hand and held it. "You still could," he said. "I mean, I *would*...there are...tools." His whole face flushed scarlet. "I...ordered some."

He was adorably flustered, and Caroline's heart melted. "You bought me *toys*?"

"You said you liked sex!" he protested. "I was *desperate*. I watched things I can never un-watch."

Caroline wriggled closer to him and slid her arms around his neck. "You dear man," she said. "You'd do that for me?"

He captured her face in his hands. "I'd do anything for you," he vowed. He leaned down and kissed her, the barest brush of his lips against hers, and it was everything that Caroline had ever wanted.

"This is enough," she said, tangling herself against him and tipping him back onto the pillows. "This is all I need." She laid her head on his chest and curled up against him blissfully.

They cuddled together for some time, making small talk about the night sounds and the mild weather.

"Are you *out*?" she asked shyly, after a while. "Do people here know? Your family?"

"Mostly," Liam said, stroking her hair. "I was jilted at my wedding, you know, and women really go for that kind of thing. I kept having to turn them down, and it was easier just to be frank about the reason than hurt all those feelings. And my mother figured it out before I did, so I didn't have a big coming out story there. You?"

She hesitated, then shook her head. "Nobody really knows. I didn't have time or inclination to date after Jonathan died, and I never felt like I would be welcome in the ace community because I was so *complicated*. It seemed like you had to be wholly against sex in order to call yourself ace."

"Some aces even crave sex but don't feel attraction," Liam pointed out. "You should call yourself whatever you feel comfortable calling yourself. Or nothing at all."

"Yes, *exactly*," Caroline said with delight. "The infinite variety of life."

Suddenly, there was a buzz of her phone.

Caroline reluctantly untangled herself from Liam's arms and reached for their abandoned clothing. "Hello?" she answered, not recognizing the number.

"I'm very, very, *very* sorry to bother you." It was Breck's voice and Caroline had a stab of concern. Had something happened to James?

"What is it? What's wrong?" she demanded.

"Laura's having contractions. Looks like her little one has decided not to wait until the New Year to make their big entrance. Also, Tex might be having a heart attack, we're not sure." There was excited chatter in the background, and a great deal of chaotic noise. It sounded like the gaming tournament was still going on, and the groans and chainsaw noises were an odd counterpoint.

Caroline cast her thoughts back to the paperwork she'd been sent; there were several babies due, the nearest one should be just a few weeks off. She had reviewed their medical files and been relieved to find no particular concerns, but she didn't remember the particulars. "What is her due date?" she asked, slipping swiftly into her clothing. "How far apart are the contractions?"

Breck called the questions into the crowd and received an answer. Caroline did quick math in her head. "It's only two weeks ahead of schedule and she's still early in labor," she said calmly. "Nothing to fret about at all. I will be there as soon as possible just to check things out. Do you want to bring her to the clinic? Or would she prefer to be in her own quarters? It's a low risk pregnancy, our priority will be the mother's comfort."

Liam dressed as she did, pulling on pants and buttoning up his shirt. Caroline had a moment of regret; she had liked having Liam to herself for a little while. "Duty calls," she said wryly. "Babies have the worst timing."

~

They stopped by the clinic for Caroline to grab a medical bag from a neatly-marked box and the file of Laura's records from her checkups on the mainland. When Liam showed Caroline to the rooms that Laura and Tex shared, they found the bartender holding a laundry basket that he was frantically filling with scattered dirty laundry. "We weren't really ready for this yet," he drawled in his southern American accent. He paused to tip his hat to Caroline. "Ma'am."

"I won't judge," Caroline assured him with a warm smile and a handshake. "And I promise it doesn't matter to the baby."

"Baby," Tex squeaked, looking quite wild around the eyes.

Caroline turned to Liam. She was utterly unruffled by the entire thing, her blue eyes amused. "This may take a while," she warned. "It's almost never like it's shown in the movies. It is likely to be hours, possibly well into tomorrow or even the next day."

"Tomorrow?" Tex moaned. "The next day?!" Liam wasn't sure if his heart was going to last that long.

"I can…ah…wait in your apartment, make sure that James has someone to come home to?" Liam volunteered, not sure if it was an overstep. It wasn't like James wouldn't be safe here at Shifting Sands, even by himself.

"I'd appreciate that," Caroline said, and she gave Liam a brief embrace and touched her forehead to his, not offering a kiss that might have been awkward.

From within the cottage, Laura gave a muffled cry of pain. Tex turned white and Liam cringed.

"You can let it out, Mama," Caroline said briskly as she entered with confidence. "I bet you can't wait to meet your new baby."

Then the door shut and Liam was alone in the darkness. Caroline's voice was a comforting murmur, and Laura's cries seemed to calm.

After a few hours, Breck brought James back to the apartment behind the medical center. "She's still at it," the waiter reported unnecessarily. As close as the few finished core buildings were, Laura's moans carried every half an hour or so. Liam was actually considering closing the windows and losing the fresh, cooling evening air. "James did great. But Neal took the cup in the last round."

James didn't seem bothered. "It was a good game," he said casually. "Thanks for inviting me."

"Your mom might be a while," Liam said apologetically to him. "You want a snack or something?"

James went to the refrigerator. Liam had stocked a few cheese sticks, some vegetables, and a selection of condiments, but hadn't bothered to fill it further. The freezer held only ice cubes. "Nah," James said, clearly not impressed.

"Does your mom do this a lot?" Liam asked.

James shrugged. "She's not really a *baby* doctor, just general practice. The hours are usually better."

"I hope...I hope you aren't sorry you came."

"Nah," James said casually. "Whatever."

Eventually, after some halting conversation and shrugs were exchanged, they went to bed, James in his new room, Liam awkwardly sleeping with his legs dangling off one of the couches in the attached medical center because he wasn't sure if he should presume to use Caroline's bed.

Caroline hadn't been kidding about the time it would take; Laura labored through the night, and well into the next day.

Caroline returned at noon for a swift shower. James gave her a brief hug and returned to his video game. Liam plied her with questions and made sure she ate.

"I'm not really necessary at this stage," she said. "Laura is strong, and a shifter, and this is still early labor. But it seems to make them all feel better to have me around." She took a brief nap, sterilized the spotless clinic again in case Laura needed it for some reason, and returned to the house that the staff was sharing.

Liam did his own rounds at the elder's home, dodging the inevitable prying questions and drawing conversation back to speculation about Laura's pending baby, the first baby of their new home.

"No baby in the history of ever will be more spoiled," Darla warned Liam in a stage whisper.

By evening, the entire village was in a tizzy of excitement.

"How long does it *take* to have a baby?" Breck wanted to know, when he served them all a grand dinner at the restaurant for Christmas Eve. Mrs. Shandy was happy to share the grueling tales of her own labors, which, if she was to be believed, had taken several weeks apiece.

Just as Breck announced dessert, Liam saw Caroline standing at the entrance of the restaurant. He pushed his chair back and crossed the floor towards her as the others noticed her. James waved, his mouth full of food.

"Baby?" Breck asked in excitement.

"Baby!" Caroline announced, and everyone in earshot cheered. Chef, coming out from the kitchen holding a propane torch, clasped her in an impulsive hug.

"It's a boy, eight pounds and twelve ounces. Everyone's healthy and fine, they are resting now and I'm sure Tex will want to show him off to everyone in the morning."

The entire restaurant exploded into happy conversation. Liam escorted Caroline to a seat beside his and pulled out her chair as Breck brought her a plate of fresh food.

She fell upon it with shifter appetite and by the time she had finished, most of the rest of the staff had moved to celebratory drinks. Breck brought James sparkling cider with a wink.

"I didn't do the hard work," Caroline said demurely, when congratulated, but her eyes sparkled with happiness, and Liam thought that she looked very relieved.

Most of the shifters had trickled out, back to the village in groups and couples as the night grew silky and dark. Liam would have liked to linger, but Darla was starting to collect up the elders, and Mr. Danby was starting to kick up a fuss.

Caroline was watching him in concern. "He's...the mammoth shifter? Non-verbal, you said?"

Liam glanced over. "Yes. He sometimes gets frustrated—"

Caroline abandoned the last of her dessert and got to her feet. "Something's wrong…"

Mr. Danby was clutching at his neck, his breath short and shocky. There was an unusual sheen of sweat on his brow, and he was pushing with his other hand weakly at Darla, who had been helping him to his feet. Concern was just beginning to rise in Liam as Caroline swiftly closed the distance between them and pressed fingers to his pulse point. "He's having a heart attack," she said urgently. She reached to her side, for a purse she wasn't carrying. "Aspirin, does anyone have aspirin?"

"There's a first aid kit in the kitchen," Breck said, as the mood in the restaurant abruptly changed.

"What can I do?" Darla asked, in the same breath as Liam.

"Keep them back," Caroline said, holding Mr. Danby in his chair with surprising strength. "Just give us space."

Breck returned, the rest of the kitchen staff at his heels, with a bottle of aspirin. Caroline dumped half a dozen into her hands and began feeding them to the weakly resisting mammoth shifter.

"How many are you giving him?" Darla asked in shock.

"He's a shifter," Caroline said. "A normal dose won't do a thing. Chew them, don't swallow them whole!" She peered into his eyes and felt for his pulse again. "I have some better drugs at the clinic, but we'll never get him there—"

"I'll get Mal—" Breck started.

Before he could finish, there was a crackling rip in space and Mal was stepping through, grim-faced.

~

Caroline was not sure how long it would take to get used to a place where people walked around easily as shifters. It was going to take even longer to get used to a place where magic was so casual and common.

As suddenly as the portal had appeared, it sizzled into nothing behind the lawyer.

"What has happened?" Caroline hadn't seen Scarlet come through the portal, but there she was, somehow both concerned and cool-looking.

No pressure, Caroline thought, in sudden panic. It was just her first day as a doctor at her new job and here were incredibly powerful people with her entire life in their hands watching her lose her first patient. More keenly still, she was aware of Liam, watching anxiously as he comforted one of the elderly women who had been sitting next to Mr. Danby.

"Heart attack," she said briefly, returning all of her attention to what was important.

Already, he seemed calmer, his heart beat stronger. The aspirin would keep the damage from getting worse.

To her surprise, Mal stepped closer and shook back his rolled up shirt sleeves. There were rune tattoos spiraled up his forearms. "Can I help?" he offered unexpectedly. "I...know how to knit bones and repair muscle damage."

"It's a blockage of blood to his heart," Caroline said, pushing through her surprise. Why shouldn't he be able to heal? "The idea is to get the blood flowing again. But wait…"

The look of hesitation in Mal's face was some salve to Caroline's own uncertainty and she was immediately moving through all the familiar motions, focused entirely on her patient. "His heart rate is strengthening. He's already stabilizing."

The change was apparent. Mr. Danby still looked weak, but his motions were more deliberate, his eyes sharper.

There was a sag in the anxious energy around them and a low chatter of conversation rose up. Caroline looked up at Mal. "For a shifter of his age and health, I would normally just give him a treatment of thrombolytics. Stents don't always work out for shifters, and his record didn't indicate chronic problems in this...er...vein. These kinds of problems are usually caused by constriction of the arteries, exacerbated by sudden excitement or stress, of which there has been a great deal. Can you enlarge the veins?"

Mal was still for a moment, then shook his head. "It doesn't really work that precisely. It's...more like I can return a body to its recent state, not make fine adjustments to what's there. I can't leach poison out or correct existing problems, just put things back together."

Caroline nodded. As magic went, that made a certain amount of sense. She had, for a moment, hoped that it was more along the lines of precision remote surgery and been excited to think of what they might do with it, but maybe that was too much to ask of wizardry.

"If we could get him to the clinic, then…"

Almost before she had finished the request, Mal was gesturing and opening a split in space directly into her dark clinic.

It certainly beat having to call an ambulance.

Liam and Breck stepped forward, intending to lift Mr. Danby, but once his feet were under him, he brushed them aside and insisted on walking forward leaning only on Caroline. They all made their slow way to the clinic, and Darla scampered ahead of them to turn on the lights and warm up the appliances.

The clinic was equipped with a top-of-the-line imaging machine, and Caroline was reassured by what she saw in the results. Shifter healing was already at work, and it was unlikely he would need any long term treatment.

Caroline found the thrombolytics in the supply she had requested and inserted the IV in Mr. Danby's arm, keenly aware of the scrutiny of her audience. Fortunately, she got the vein on the first try, sparing her *that* embarrassment. She made him comfortable in the clinic bed and took his vitals, pleased by the numbers she was getting, and shooed everyone but Liam out.

Mr. Danby's snores were steady and even, and Liam patted his hand in an undeniably affectionate way and tucked it carefully by his side.

"It's midnight," Caroline said in astonishment, looking at her watch. "What a *day*."

"The beginning of a life, and almost the end," Liam said in wonder, coming around to her from the other side of the bed. "You saved him, you know. No one else *noticed*."

Caroline blushed and shrugged. "I gave him some aspirin and took some scans. He did the rest. He wasn't ready to say goodbye, not yet. It was good timing that I was there, but that's all."

"He's a stubborn old coot," Liam said with admiration. They were standing close, close enough that she could feel his warmth, and draw comfort from his simple nearness.

Something occurred to her. "Merry Christmas," she said, laughing wearily. "Merry Christmas."

Liam's eyes widened and he laughed with her. "Merry Christmas, my darling."

My *darling*.

It sounded like *home*, and Caroline's red panda all but rolled in delight. She closed the last distance between them, and his arms folded around her.

"I got you a present," Liam said, and she could feel his nervousness as she wrapped her arms around him.

"You didn't have to," she said contentedly into his chest.

"I wanted to. I didn't know what to get you," he admitted. "So I made you a garden. Just a windowsill garden, in the kitchen, with some herbs and little strawberry plants. They're still tiny, not much to see. And of course, if you needed anything sooner, Graham could always get them for you. But, I wanted something that would...grow. I don't know if you like plants, even. Maybe I should have gone with succulents or something harder to kill…"

Caroline chuckled, feeling the flex of his chest against her ear and let all of the tension in her body flow away. "I love it," she said sincerely. "I always wanted a window garden and I love the idea of growing things to eat." She tipped her head and looked up at him, all the angles of his face already so dear. "I got you something, too," she said gently.

"You didn't have to," Liam said automatically.

"I wanted to," she echoed him. She slipped easily from his embrace and tripped to the bedroom, where she found a wrapped package near the top of one of the boxes marked 'Important.'

Liam grinned at her when she returned, and eagerly took it.

"It's a photo album," Caroline told him as he unwrapped it and turned it over.

"It's empty," he said in surprise when he opened it. Had he expected photos of her life before this?

"It's to fill with *our* life," she explained, feeling suddenly shy. "Something...to grow."

"I can't wait to fill it up," he said gravely.

Then he drew her into his arms again, and she got her kiss moment at last, the gentlest brush of his mouth against hers, the joy of being held in his embrace, the most perfect satisfaction she could imagine.

The peace was broken by the thin wail of a newborn from the next building over and Caroline laughed into Liam's chest.

"Is it going to do that a lot?" he asked, going to close the clinic window. Mr. Danby's regular snores continued unchanged. "I mostly deal with the other end of the life cycle."

"Let's just say I hope you have a good stock of earplugs," Caroline chuckled. "There are two more babies on the way and they only get louder as they get older."

Liam groaned. "So we've got *that* to look forward to," he said lightly.

Caroline wrapped herself around him again and didn't protest when he lifted her easily into his arms. "You know what I'm looking forward to?" she asked, sighing into his shoulder.

"Tell me," Liam said.

"A good long sleep," Caroline murmured. "In your arms."

Before he could carry her to bed, there was an urgent knock on the clinic door and Tex's voice called, "Doctor? Caroline? I know that the timing is bad…"

Liam groaned in disappointment and Caroline kissed his neck, then slipped down out of his arms. "Terrible timing, indeed. Don't wait up," she told him, reminding herself that Tex and Laura were probably more tired than she was. "I might be late."

He kissed her forehead. "Your timing is never terrible," he assured her. "Merry Christmas."

Caroline caught herself smiling foolishly and humming Christmas carols as she went with Tex to do the job that she loved in the beautiful new place that she already considered her home.

~

Be sure to read on for more information about what I write, and join my mailing list so you don't miss an update…plus you'll get extra bonus epilogues and a free book! https://www.zoechant.com/join-my-mailing-list/

SCARLET'S SECRETS: SHORTS

These are stories that fit in various places throughout the timeline, but they all spoil the big secret of who and what Scarlet is, so (after some agonizing indecision) I've collected them here together at the end.

I probably won't write the entire prequel book about Coral and Auric and Scarlet as a young dryad, even though I have the plot for it firmly in my head.

…Probably.

STEPS

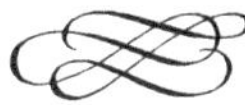

This story occurs about fifty years before Tropical Tiger Spy.

"Come and see what we've done!" Coral said, suddenly appearing at the doorway of Aaric's office.

Aaric put down the contract mimeograph, marked all over with his lawyer's notes, and had to rein his lion in at the sound of Coral's voice and the sight of her. She was smiling, her pale gold hair curly around her oval face, and her dirty gardener's coveralls hugged every perfect curve.

She is ours, his lion insisted. *Our mate.*

We can't have her, Aaric reminded him firmly. *We're getting married, remember? To someone* else.

Aaric's lion was neither convinced, nor impressed.

He'd been silent too long and Coral looked uncertain.

"If it's not a bad time, I mean…" she added hesitantly.

"It's fine," Aaric said, rising. "As good as any."

Coral smiled. "It's mostly Scarlet, of course. I just gave her a little direction."

She led him to the glass-walled hall where she had set up shop with their unexpected visitor, crowded with the budding flowers

Coral was preparing for planting outside just as soon as the weather improved.

Flowers for Aaric's wedding.

Aaric drew up in surprise as he entered the room. "Scarlet?"

The young woman at the window turned, and her smile was triumphant. "Coral said I looked too wild to pass. She showed me magazines. Is this better?"

She did a slow spin, and Aaric frowned. Her loose brown hair had been tamed into a timeless bun, and she was wearing a pea-colored skirt suit with a modest, knee-length skirt. The jacket was tailored, hugging her curves discreetly. Professional chic, Aaric suspected it would be called; Scarlet looked both business-like and seductive. She still had a cast of otherworldly beauty over her features, but it felt…domesticated now. Controlled.

Aaric might have found her distracting if he hadn't been even more keenly aware of Coral at his side, looking twice as ordinary and in every way more appealing. His lion barely noticed Scarlet, the metaphorical claws of his attention were entirely for their forbidden mate.

"It's nice," he growled.

"I like nice," Scarlet purred. She started to unbutton her shirt another hole down.

"Professional," Coral reminded her, and for a moment, Scarlet pouted.

Then she sighed, and buttoned it back up.

"Show him what you've been practicing," Coral suggested.

Scarlet drew in a breath and strolled silently across the room like she owned it, slow and deliberate in her modest heels, with her arms held elegantly at her sides. Aaric was astonished by the change. Gone was the childish scamper and the enthusiastic wild dart from place to place. Still...

"There's something a little off," he observed.

"I can't put my finger on it," Coral agreed.

Scarlet turned at the end of the hall and walked back. "Too slow?" she suggested, giving one irresistible skip at the end.

"No," Aaric said.

"Too stiff?" Coral guessed. "Maybe it's just that we have a certain expectation and we aren't used to her this way?"

Aaric shook his head, trying to concentrate on Scarlet instead of how he imagined he could feel Coral's warmth from her careful distance. "She looks right," he said. "It's something else."

Scarlet returned to her potted tree, exchanging a loving caress with it. Already, the green fronds looked less wilted. She struggled a moment figuring how to kneel in her tight skirt, and swiftly mastered the trick. Standing up was more challenging, and she frowned in concentration, then gave a triumphant trill when she succeeded. Aaric wondered if the slit up the side wasn't just a little bit higher than it needed to be.

"We'll work on formal conversation next," Coral chuckled. "Along with the reading and manners."

"Did you see the new Hepburn musical when it was the cinema?" Aaric asked, with a crooked smile. "They could take lessons from us."

"'I could have danced all night!'" Coral chorused, then she looked embarrassed. "I shouldn't sing."

"You should always sing," Aaric protested. "You have a beautiful voice!"

Coral gave a sigh of pity. "Such a shame. So good looking. So *tone deaf*."

They laughed, and Aaric marveled at the way they could pretend that all of this was perfectly normal. Like nothing was odd about suddenly "hiring" a lost dryad who couldn't even read to be his secretary. Like nothing was uncomfortable about the landscaper for his wedding turning out to be his mate and an unexpected confidant in protecting Scarlet's secret.

Like nothing was out of place...when his whole life was suddenly at odds with itself.

He was starting to lose track of where pretend stopped and real life began, it was all so surreal and everything felt mixed up and wrong. All of him wanted Coral, at his side, in his arms, and none of him could have her.

He unconsciously moved closer to her, and she gave a little

inhale of the same desire that he was feeling and stepped away, because she was stronger than he was.

Her shoe scuffed on the hardwood floor, and Aaric figured out what was bothering him about Scarlet's new illusion.

"She doesn't have audible footsteps," he realized. "She's silent when she walks."

Scarlet gazed down at her feet. "How curious!" she said. "I forgot how noisy people are." When she took her next step, it came with a loud *clomp*.

"You're right!" Coral said in delight, reaching to squeeze his arm automatically.

She realized what she was about to do just a moment before she actually touched him, and for a moment, they only stared at each other. Aaric swallowed around his desire to pull her into his arms and returned his attention to the dryad.

Scarlet strode down the hall and back, moderating the sound that her feet made striking the floor until Coral nodded in approval. "There! That's perfect."

Scarlet gave a little caper, punctuated by the distinct sound of heels on hardwood.

"Am I normal now?" she asked hopefully. "Can I pass?"

Aaric and Coral exchanged amused looks.

"It's a step in the right direction," Aaric said encouragingly.

ROOTS

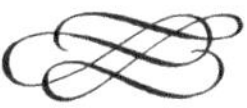

This story takes place about twenty years before Tropical Tiger Spy.

Scarlet tried not to fidget.

It has been such a long journey, so fraught. She had hated the endless ocean crossings, but the final trek to the peak of the island was worse yet. The road was steep and rutted, and she was so very *tired* of traveling. Her leaves were badly wilted, her branches felt brittle, and her roots craved peace. Peace and earth and not *moving*, after weeks and weeks of being constantly in sickening motion.

"Are you alright?" Coral asked anxiously. "We're nearly there."

The equipment was not sprung for human comfort, or for tree, and she felt rattled to pieces. Her roots could feel the dirt falling away from them, however hard she clung.

She couldn't speak, could barely make sense of Coral's words, she was so wrapped in her bark skin and failing sap.

"Did we wait too long?" Aaric wanted to know. "Will she be hurt?"

So hurt, Scarlet wanted to scream. She could scarcely feel the sunlight, her branches wrapped in landscaping cloth to protect her during this last transfer.

"I don't know," Coral confessed quietly. "It would have been easier when she was smaller."

Scarlet held her image with sheer force of will, focusing on being professional, on looking cool, collected, calm, with her brown hair all neatly restrained and her clothing free of wrinkles. It took all of her effort.

The machine operator, undoubtedly puzzled by the whole procedure, moved the machine into place by the gaping hole and swung the tree above it. Coral and Aaric dashed forward to unwrap the rootball and at last, *at last*, Scarlet's tree was lowered into place.

There was a heap of displaced soil by the hole, and while she was still held upright by the arm of the crane, Coral and Aaric shoveled it by hand into place around her.

It was like...being wrapped in blankets. Like lying down after standing for too many hours. Like taking a breath after holding it until consciousness began to fade.

"She'll need water," Coral said, and the operator unhooked the crane and switched vehicles for the full tanker truck that had been waiting for them.

Water helped. It cradled the dirt around her roots, and she drank, thirsty and desperate, as Aaric and the operator carefully pulled the cloth off her ravaged branches and Coral inspected for damage.

Sunlight again. Pure sunlight and nourishing earth, and fresh air with only a hint of salt.

Scarlet could no longer maintain her human form, retreating to her tree with a whimper of relief.

She had no sense of how much time passed before she woke again, but where the sun had been high above, it was lower now, its light dappled through the trees around. The equipment was gone, the scar of its passing still raw through the jungle.

Coral was sitting in Aaric's arms as he leaned on a tree at the far side of the little clearing, and both of them were asleep.

All around her were curious whispers.

She had always heard the forest around the Lyons estate; she could sense the gardens and lawns.

But this was new, a thousand little points of light in her mind, a rush of energy, a *connection*. She was uplifted, the sap quickening in her trunk, and when she put her human form on the mossy grass, she felt every little spark of life in a slowly expanding ring all around her.

This was *hers*, *her* forest, *her* island, *her* domain, and it was as if she were suddenly, unexpectedly, exactly where she belonged.

She closed her eyes and felt outwards, as far as she could reach in every direction, to the circle of trees around her meadow. Her tree reached hungry branches to the fractured sunlight, and her roots, free at last from the barriers of pots and concrete vessels, sank deep into the ground beneath her. It felt like freedom.

Beyond her reach, she could barely sense the island, the green rainforest, and the line to the north where Aaric's contract with Beehag was an ironclad barrier. She could just feel the resort, a bustling work zone of potential, and the village where foundations were being staked out.

It would all be hers, someday, she realized, as her power grew. She would rule it all, because this was what she was meant to be, the lynchpin of a forest of her *own.*

"Scarlet, your *hair*!"

"Your *tree*!"

With all of her attention outward, she hadn't noticed when Coral and Aaric woke. She pulled a strand of hair loose from her careful bun, only half-expecting the brilliant color that felt so right. It was exactly the hue in the photographs of the flowers she had never grown.

"You brought me home," she said in gratitude, and when she turned to follow their gaze, she found that her tree, for the very first time, had burst into bloom.

THE STORM

This story takes place at the end of Tropical Lynx's Lover where it overlaps with the beginning of Tropical Dragon Diver. I knew that Scarlet was getting a hint that things weren't quite right on the island at this point.

Scarlet had been through storms before.

She had even closed the resort for a storm, twice since it had reopened.

But this storm, driving curiously against the usual weather systems...it unnerved her.

"Does it feel...odd to you?" she asked Bastian, as they stood together at the pool deck.

But his attention was far away, wistful and strong for the rising waves.

"Is everything secure?" she asked Travis anxiously, when she found him putting the last of his tools away after boarding up vulnerable windows.

"As secure as possible," Travis assured her merrily. Everything about him was merry, now that he'd found his mate, and Scarlet scowled at him without intending to.

"You'll be missed," she told Lydia, as the black swan shifter left in the van for the last flight out.

Lydia, perhaps sensing Scarlet's unease, gave her a warm, unexpected hug that surprised and delighted her so much that she forgot to be worried for some time.

"Should I be worried?" she asked Graham later, as the wind picked up and the midday sky began to grow dark.

He gave her a skeptical look and a grunt that might have been a laugh.

But he indulged her, hiking through the dark forest to inspect her tree and assure her that everything around it would withstand the expected winds.

The storm struck as they were both still there, and the winds were so high that the high branches of the canopy trees broke, and Scarlet built a dome of vines and trees to protect them both. Graham curled as a lion at the base of her tree.

She stood outside, exposed, staring up at the hungry clouds and the whipping wind, and knew that this was an unnatural storm. Hurricanes never made it this far, and this was less a movement of moist air and more a fury of some harsher nature.

She cast her senses as far as they would go, to the edges of her side of the island, to the impenetrable boundary where her contract bound her. Her trees were in minor distress, stripped of leaves, with broken branches littering the underbrush. It was nothing she couldn't grow back.

She closed her eyes and felt her way to the resort, where the staff was hunkered down…and unexpectedly half-missing. In alarm, she searched further, and found the rest of them at the little airfield, a neutral ground, according to her contract, and a place where she had no power. She paused there a moment at the barrier, then returned to her search.

Gizelle was sheltering in the jungle as a gazelle, folded trembling into herself as the wind screamed and the branches shook above her. Scarlet comforted her, and unfurled vines all around to cushion her from the gale.

The rain was almost an afterthought, at the heels of the howling wind, driving hard and cold through the leaves.

Scarlet took it all in, all of it at once, bothered by the malevolent force, and after a moment of letting it try to soak her and tear her hair into spinning tornados, she sank down into her own roots, feeling curiously for the thing beneath the island.

The thing, impossibly far below her, was, as always, asleep, deep and far-off, like a memory and Scarlet returned to her tree in relief. It always left her feeling unnerved: it was alive but not alive, and outside of any understanding...but it was reassuringly unchanged. Still asleep.

And the storm ended, as storms always do.

She unwound the dome she'd woven and Graham emerged, shook his mane, and shifted.

He was distastefully putting his soaking clothing back on when Gizelle wandered out of the jungle, one tentative foot after another. She did not offer to shift and Scarlet sat down so that she would not seem alarming as Graham grumbled and went to inspect a broken branch on her tree.

The antelope hesitantly came to her, and cautiously bent down onto her knees and put her head in Scarlet's lap.

Scarlet stroked her soft wet hide and after a long while, Gizelle's eyes closed trustingly and her trembling stilled.

"No major damage," Graham growled quietly, when he returned from the far side of Scarlet's tree.

Gizelle startled up from the dryad's lap at Graham's words, but didn't flee, just shook herself and trotted a few paces away to graze.

Scarlet could confirm Graham's assessment. The rest of the staff was returning now, and the destruction at the resort was largely cosmetic. "No one was badly hurt," she agreed, but she still felt deeply unsettled.

"Kind of a weird storm," Graham observed.

Scarlet looked up at the scattering clouds.

The storm was a test, she thought, still feeling ruffled as the storm ebbed away. A test of her island, and she had no idea *who* was testing her, or *why*.

It was such an absurd idea that she didn't say it out loud, only suggested, "We should get back. The staff is probably wondering where we are."

And from that storm, they entered directly into another, with a trussed-up eagle shifter assassin, a hired man who seemed to think Scarlet could personally get him out of trouble with the cartel and offer him a job, and a woman with a bullet wound who had washed up into Bastian's arms...

TROPICAL DRAGON'S DESTINY: EPILOGUE

Mal looked out over the building site and had to smile.

"It's amazing what magic portals and unlimited funds can do in a few years," Scarlet observed, suddenly at his side.

"Having the ability to instantly landscape doesn't hurt anything," Mal added.

The resort was already rebuilt to its former shining glory and it was hard to tell that any trees or gardens had ever been damaged. It was, if anything, more beautiful, more luxurious, and more alive. There were new pools, a grander event hall, and the hotel had been built to effortless modern standards. Chef's kitchen had gone from good to gleaming. Solar panels shimmered from every roof, marking the resort's near independence from fuel. A broad dish near the top of the island promised better connectivity… and *mostly* delivered it.

When the last of the big work on the resort had been completed and the finishing touches were nearly done, the construction efforts had moved up the island. The resort was on the south tip, facing west for the best sunsets. Along the cliffs that went north on the east coast, where the Den had stood, there were new luxury and family cottages for month-long getaways, complete with kitchens.

They were standing further north yet, tucked away from the resort, looking out onto a bustling construction site. The center of the little village was already complete; the elders' housing, the medical center, and the school had all been priorities for the new residents, and little houses were growing around them organically, some of them still covered in blue tarps as roof work was being completed.

"Come and see the new playground," Scarlet invited. There was an unexpected sparkle to her eyes, and a mischievous quirk to her mouth. Mal was instantly suspicious.

But Scarlet only took his hand, and strolled innocently with him down the road into the village.

They passed a small sports field, and a simple community pool, Graham's second greenhouse, and the lot where Neal was running an excavator to make space for the footings for a combination restaurant and movie theater.

A tiny general store was open for business and Mal nodded to the woman sweeping in front of it.

The playground was already being broken in. Several children in a wide range of ages were playing across the metal framework of a dragon with a slide for a tail and monkey bars across its chest cavity. Swings hung from the spread wings and an older boy was gently pushing three younger children in turn.

Mal hadn't even realized that there *were* that many children on the island yet, but the little community had been slowly expanding as the infrastructure was finished and the resort was already nearly up to full capacity.

"The school will be opening up this fall," Scarlet said, with a nod to the long, low building that flanked one edge of playground. "Travis's sister has experience running an isolated, rural K-12 and I think the staff of teachers that she helped select will be a good fit here."

"I imagine this will at least be a nice change from the wilds of Alaska," Mal observed.

"It's certainly warmer," Scarlet chuckled.

One of the children on the monkey bars gave a sudden shriek and fell… only to shift midair into a black-winged panther and glide easily down onto the sand below amid the shreds of his clothing.

"Lydia's going to have words about the clothes. I think that's the third outfit this week," Scarlet said with a tolerant smile.

The children he'd been playing with scrambled down to help collect the pieces of his shirt and shorts.

"Your mom is going to be mad," a little dark-skinned girl said firmly, holding up the shorts, split along the seams.

The winged panther turned back into a little dark-haired boy. He took the shorts gravely, and attempted to put them back on. The older boy who had been pushing the swings supplied a series of safely pins from a pocket and helped him reassemble them into something that would keep him covered.

From around the corner of the community hall, there was a sudden clatter of hooves and a tiny gazelle came bolting out into the playground, pursued by a white-haired woman who was nearly as fleet on two bare feet as the foal was on four.

"You have to eat lunch before we play!" Gizelle chided, her voice full of laughter.

The little antelope darted through the metal columns of the playground dragon and drew up short against a broad, shovel-shaped pair of antlers as a giant stag suddenly appeared through the brush beyond.

The sharp stop proved too much for the gazelle in the loose sand and it tumbled over itself to bounce up as a toddler girl with a head full of dark curls. "Papa!" she burbled in glee. She grasped the antlers in two tiny hands and was lifted high into the air at the crown of the huge Irish elk that had blocked her path.

Gizelle came to a chortling stop at Conall's feet. "Clothes, Jana! We're supposed to be people right now. In clothes!"

"No clothes," Jana protested. "No clothes!"

But she let Gizelle scoop her up from Conall's lowered rack and wrapped chubby arms around her neck.

"Miss Scarlet!" The dark-skinned girl had spotted Scarlet

standing with Mal at the edge of the playground. "Miss Scarlet! Did you see the dragon? Mr. Neal made us a dragon!"

"I saw it, Amy!" Scarlet said warmly. "He made a wonderful dragon."

The other children gathered around them eagerly. "Will you do it, Miss Scarlet? Will you?"

"I wanna flower!" one of the youngest demanded.

Scarlet grinned and the hedge they were standing next to burst into bloom. She and Mal walked away to the sound of squeals and delight as the children began to gather them.

"It's almost finished," Mal observed. "Have you thought about what you want to do with Beehag's compound while we've still got all the construction equipment and workmen? Knock what's left to the ground? Build a monument?"

Scarlet's eyes crinkled into her smile. "I wanted to see what you thought about building a school there."

Mal's eyes flickered to the school in the center of the village but he immediately realized that she had something very different in mind. "What kind of school?" he asked.

"A boarding high school for shifters," Scarlet said, watching his face. "Perhaps with an emphasis on biology and pre-law; the arboretum is an amazing resource, and both you and Amber have mentioned being interested in teaching. Being a shifter in public school isn't always easy, and it would be nice if we could give kids a safe place to be themselves and learn with others who are like them while they are navigating all the problems of growing up."

An unexpected surge of interest swelled in Mal. He'd never considered teaching *seriously*, but now that it was on the table, he couldn't get the idea out of his head. "I know some professors," he said thoughtfully. "Would we do just secondary? Or post-secondary? I'd need to find some good education advisors, research the standards, find out what the legalities are in Costa Rica."

"Would you teach magic?"

Mal drew to a stop. "I… I don't know." Once, he'd thought he would have to, to train a new fighter to battle the wyrm hundreds of years in the future. But he didn't *need* to do that now.

"We'd probably have to level what's there now and build something completely new," Scarlet said, squeezing his arm. "There's a lot of time to think about it."

"It wouldn't have to be limited to shifters," Mal observed. "We could welcome other magical creatures, like mermaids… and dryads."

Scarlet's delighted smile grew smoky with secrets. "I have something to show you," she said mysteriously.

Mal stopped thinking about the school. "I love your surprises," he said honestly. The only secrets they kept from each other now were purely for the joy of it.

"Portal to my tree?" Scarlet invited, and she vanished playfully.

Mal traced a doorway in the air and murmured the words as he gestured, then stepped through to Scarlet's familiar clearing.

Scarlet wasn't by her tree. Mal looked around curiously to find her at the far edge of the clearing, kneeling in the flowers.

He could feel her pride and eagerness through their mate-bond, shimmering bright with anticipation, and her smile as she lifted her head to watch him approach was nearly as brilliant.

She stood at the last moment and took his hand.

Wordlessly, overflowing with excitement, she led him to where three saplings with feathery, fern-like leaves were growing in a little clear space together. They were knee-high and swaying in the slight breezy.

Mal had to glance back at Scarlet's scarred tree. It had the same distinctive leaves as the little sprouts.

"Are these…?"

"I don't know if they will be dryads," Scarlet confessed. "But I have never had saplings before, and they feel… more aware than other trees. Different. I don't know!"

She was looking at him with what might have been anxiousness in someone lesser and Mal realized that he was still staring in shock. He gave a great whoop of laughter and pulled Scarlet into his arms so he could twirl her around until he was dizzy and laughing. A soft bed of moss met them as he pulled her over, laughing and kissing and rolling with her.

When he could catch his breath, he took her hand and kissed the simple gold ring he'd put there. "This may be the best surprise yet," he said.

"I never knew you wanted children," Scarlet said, caressing his cheek with her other hand.

"I never did either," Mal confessed. "And to be honest, I wasn't sure how that would work. But it seems like a marvelous idea."

Scarlet pulled his mouth to hers. "I have other marvelous ideas," she said suggestively. "Did I ever warn you about that lusty nature of dryads?"

"What about the children?" Mal asked teasingly.

"They're still asleep…"

Implications of the future suddenly occurred to Mal and he sat up. "I am going to have three girls like *you*," he groaned. "If they have your lusty nature, I'm going to have to steal Graham's machete to scare off boys and beat back interested trees."

Scarlet laughed and sat up. "Or we could raise them to understand who they are, have sensible boundaries, and deal with their own boys. Maybe one of them will *be* a boy."

Mal paused. "*Are* there boy dryads?"

"I haven't the faintest idea," Scarlet confessed.

"What does all of this *mean*?" Mal felt pleased and proud and more than a little panicked.

"I haven't the faintest idea," Scarlet repeated, a slow smile blossoming on her face.

"I'm going to have to do some research," Mal said. "Start a college trust. Pick names!"

Scarlet wrapped her arms around his neck. "We have *time*," she said sweetly, kissing his ear.

It was still a strange feeling, not having a destination for his life. Mal still hadn't gotten used to the idea that there was nothing looming in his future that *had* to be done, a destiny that he had to be ready for, a task of such weight and importance that it overshadowed anything else that he did.

He got to choose now, how to spend his time—and who to be

with—without constantly thinking about how it impacted his final objective.

He put a wondering hand to Scarlet's face and she closed her eyes and leaned into it.

Mal knew what to do with *this* time and he pulled Scarlet close to kiss her deeply.

Across the island, trees burst into bloom.

UNRELIABLE SENSES

Mal felt her arrival like the first breath of spring.

Except, of course, that there was no spring here, only endless, blissful summer.

"Come to check on our progress?" he turned to ask. Scarlet had done an admirable job of leaving the school to him. The resort was hers, utterly and unquestionably, and even the little village at the Bay was very obviously under her careful management, but the school was *his* project.

"Something's…not right," she said, slipping her hand into his. The feeling she came with turned to a hint of winter, equally impossible on the season-less island. "Something's changed. Something *here*."

Mal swept his gaze over the work area. The last, charred remains of the zoo had been bulldozed over, and the estate had been leveled. The walls and gates were gone. Even the arboretum had been carefully dismantled around the living trees. Workers were building frames for new concrete footings now, swarming around the site like ants. It was hard to imagine what the final buildings would look like, no matter how many times Mal stared at the drawings.

"Did we miss a tree? Did something get lost?"

Scarlet was concentrating intensely, looking out over the space with a scowl on her face. "Something *lost*…" she echoed faintly.

"Should we stop?" Mal asked cautiously. Her disquiet was catching, and he made a gesture and spoke a few words to let his power sight rise up over his regular vision. Nothing looked out of place; the workers were all shifters, with their glow of magical strength, and there were no strands of energy that felt wrong. He had gone over the site carefully, making sure to clean all of the contamination from the terrible zoo and all of the sloppy magic that had been practiced there.

"Something alive…but not," Scarlet said, still focused somewhere else.

Mal frowned, dismissing his power sight. "Something immortal?" Scarlet's descriptions of what the wyrm had felt like to her senses had that same feeling of confusion—something alive, but with no *life*.

"No…" Scarlet said reluctantly. "Not quite."

"Should we stop?" Mal asked again.

Scarlet looked sharply at him, all of her attention back in herself. "I don't know," she confessed. "It makes me feel prickly and uncomfortable. Unsettled."

That was all Mal needed to hear. He whistled to the foreman and met him halfway between. "Have a break," he told Travis. "All of you."

"How long?" Travis asked, surprised.

Mal looked back at Scarlet, who was still scowling at nothing next to the work tents that had been set up near the entrance of the campus. "I'm not sure," he said, trusting her instincts. "Let's start with a day. Come back tomorrow after lunch."

Travis shrugged. "Well, this is a better place to stop than after we'd started mixing concrete!" he said merrily, not questioning the decision. "I'm sure the crew would appreciate an early trip back to The Bay for drinks tonight."

The lynx shifter walked back to the crew, calling out orders and coordinating the break-down. He paused to scold one of the workers good-naturedly for starting to leave behind a box of tools. Within ten minutes, the work site was buttoned up and all the shifters were cheerfully leaving in the shining new vans.

Mal paced the forms for the footings, and after a moment, Scarlet joined him. "It's quieter," she observed.

"Sometimes you sound just like Gizelle," Mal said wryly.

"Sometimes I *feel* just like Gizelle," she admitted. She slipped from his arms and knelt, running her fingers through the short, tropical grass. "A little out of step, not sure of the things I'm sensing. Do I trust my instincts? Or are they unreliable?"

Mal loved Scarlet's confidence and strength, he admired her cool professional logic. But sometimes, she let her guard down, only for him, and he loved those glimpses of her vulnerability just as much. However hard his childhood had been, he'd always had teachers, people who could show him how to use his power and give him purpose.

Scarlet had been the only one of her kind, figuring out all of her abilities by trial and error.

Mal gazed out over the field. She'd made it work for herself; she'd harnessed unbelievable power and never let it corrupt her beautiful spirit. How many children were less lucky?

Scarlet's suggestion to build a school had been planted in fertile ground, he mused. Mal loved to teach, and he never wanted a shifter to have to come into their power alone.

And now, maybe they wouldn't have to…

Scarlet stood, brushing imaginary dirt from her knees. "I don't know what was bothering me," she said. "I hear nothing out of the ordinary now. Perhaps I made you stop for nothing."

"We're not in a hurry," Mal assured her. "It's always summer here, and I'm sure that the work crew has no complaints about an unexpected break."

Scarlet twined her arms around Mal's neck. "It's not often we have the work site to ourselves," she pointed out. "And I'm in no hurry, either."

Mal kissed her waiting lips, drinking in the taste of her.

He made love to her slowly, sweetly, laying her out in the grass where his office would be, in no hurry to rush through the pleasure. The heat of the sun later drove them to the shade of the arboretum, Scarlet worrying over trivialities like his sunburnt shoulders, and they finally finished lying together in their private suite at the resort as night fell over the island.

"No more voices?" Mal asked, tracing her neck.

"No more than usual," Scarlet chuckled. "The night-bloomers are complaining about how hot it was today, and the trees are whispering poetry."

"Is it good poetry?" Mal wanted to know.

"Only if you speak in seeds and roots and reasons."

"Hmm," Mal said. "I think that may have been skipped over in my thorough education."

"Shocking oversight," Scarlet said, and when she smiled, it was its own kind of poetry.

He had to kiss her, when she smiled like that, and it was much, much later before he slept.

~

Mal woke alone.

That wasn't unusual; Scarlet didn't actually need to sleep, though sometimes she chose to, simply for the fun of waking up together. She wasn't nearby, either, Mal realized, rousing more completely.

Curiously, she was across the island, back at the site of the new school. Mal sat up in bed and stayed there for a long moment before he slipped into his clothing and portaled to the site.

He stepped through the portal into the space where the gated entrance to the compound had once been and stood looking out over the cleared area. Scarlet was not standing in the trees of the old arboretum, to his surprise, but amidst the maze of concrete forms where the compound had been, where the walls of the new school would stand.

More surprising still, she wasn't alone.

The rising sun was drawing steam in a dreamy fog up from the ground, and at first Mal thought the shape she was facing was only a whirl of thicker mist. Then it turned, and swirled, and was a maned lion so large that when Scarlet knelt before him, he could have rested his chin on her head.

They regarded each other soberly while Mal flexed his hands and wondered if he would disturb them by using his power sight. He didn't need magic to tell him that there was something supernatural afoot, but he was itching with curiosity for more details.

After a few moments, Scarlet rose gracefully back to her feet. She and the lion nodded gravely to each other and he turned on silent paws to vanish into the thinning fog. As he disappeared, Mal caught a teasing glimpse of other forms at the corners of his vision, gone again as quickly as the lion.

Scarlet walked slowly to Mal. She didn't look surprised to see him.

"Was that Aaric Lyons?" Mal guessed.

Scarlet's eyes were grim. "No," she said quietly. "But that was his lion."

Mal took her hand gently and she leaned into him willingly. "Did he speak to you?"

She shook her head against his chest. "Not in so many words. I think he could have, if he'd chosen to, but…I can already guess what happened."

"Beehag," Mal hissed.

"Most shifters, when they die, turn human. But Rupert Beehag collected their *animal* hides. He must have found some way to *anchor* them in that form when he…when he killed them."

"Magic?" Mal curled his arms tighter around his mate.

"He had dealings with Corbin," Scarlet pointed out. "But he also did a lot of other highly unethical experimentation. However he did it, something held each shifter's *animal* here, not just their skin. And now they are trapped in this place. Maybe forever."

"Ghosts." The fog had burned off in the heat of the sun already, making the idea seem almost absurd. "Should I put off building the school until I've figured out how to release them?" It didn't occur to him to doubt that he could, eventually, find a way to do so, though he wasn't even sure where to start.

Scarlet considered. "They aren't suffering," she said thoughtfully. "They're not exactly alive, even if they aren't exactly dead, but they don't seem bothered by their state. I only noticed them at all because it was so quiet here after you cleared the site. They aren't angry or bent on revenge or anything dangerous. They just feel a little *lonely*." She tipped her head up to look at him with a mischievous smile. "Will you *mind* if your school is slightly haunted?"

Mal let a laugh bubble up in his throat. "Only *slightly*?"

"You could use it in your advertising," Scarlet said drolly. "The Shifting Sands *Slightly Haunted* School for Exceptional Children."

"That may not be terribly reassuring to the parents," Mal suggested.

"You can be very persuasive," Scarlet said confidently. "On that note, I've had a few inquiries about tuition and timing of the first classes. I left a memo on your desk. I've been warning parents that we are probably still a few *years* from setting up the curriculum and being open for enrollment, but it seems like there is a lot of interest in the academy already. By the time the buildings are ready and the teachers are selected, we'll have the students to fill it."

Mal turned so that they were gazing out to where the buildings would be raised.

"Maybe, by that time, our own children will be ready for it," Mal said hopefully. He had purchased an entire bookstore worth of parenting and gardening books for his tablet, but the titles on the topic of *raising dryads* were woefully lacking.

Scarlet looked up at him and bit her lip in a gesture so genuinely excited that Mal had to kiss her. "I don't know," she cautioned, when she had reclaimed her lips. "This is as new to me as it is you."

"You're going to be an amazing mother," Mal said sincerely. "I would swear to that in any court."

"I think you're an unreliable witness," Scarlet teased him.

"Not unreliable," Mal corrected. "Biased. Terribly, terribly biased."

They stood in companionable silence for a while, looking out over the school site as they each imagined what it could become.

In a few years, it would have a whole campus of buildings: classrooms and dormitories and gymnasiums. He'd have a building dedicated to teaching magic, and there would be a pool for athletics, and climbing walls sufficiently challenging for shifters. Rooms for music, for art. It would be bustling with students and teachers, a robust place to learn and grow. Maybe his own children would be among the pupils, dryad or dragon.

That it was *slightly haunted* was the perfect touch of absurdity.

Someday, Mal thought, with perfect contentment, he would have everything he'd never even known to dream of, with Scarlet at his side.

But he was in no hurry and they had all the time in the world, on an island with no seasons.

A NOTE FROM THE AUTHOR

Shifting Sands Resort was much more than just a fictional place to me, and I want to thank all of the readers who made this amazing journey possible. This series has a really special place in my heart and I could never have made it to the boggling end without your support and encouragement.

I hope that it has been a place of escape and enchantment, and I look forward to visiting it again someday.

I would love to know what you thought—you can leave a review at Amazon or Goodreads (I read every one, and they help other readers find me, too!) or email me at elvaherself@elvabirch.com. I really enjoy hearing from my readers and I especially love finding out what your guesses for what Scarlet's true nature were before you got to the big reveal!

If you'd like to be emailed when I release my next book, please visit my webpage and sign up to be added to my mailing list at elvabirch.com, where you can find a list of all my books. You can also follow me on Facebook or join my Reader's Retreat!

Love recklessly,

Elva Birch

SHIFTING SANDS RESORT COMPLETE TIMELINE

Shifting Sands Resort shares a world with Fire and Rescue Shifters, and Shifter Kingdom. This is a complete timeline of all three series, with short stories in their appropriate order. This is not at ***all*** *the order I would recommend reading them the first time, as many of the short stories spoil the subsequent books!*

Steps (Tropical Tails)
Roots (Tropical Tails)
Run (Tropical Tails)
Treasure Sense (Tropical Tails)
A Recipe for Happiness (Tropical Holiday Tails)
Firefighter Dragon
Firefighter Pegasus
Royal Guard Lion
Royal Guard Tiger
Firefighter Griffin
Tropical Tiger Spy
Other Duties as Assigned (Tropical Tails)
Locked (Shifting Sands Omnibus Vol 1)
Tropical Wounded Wolf
Unlocked (Shifting Sands Omnibus Vol 1)

Firefighter Sea Dragon
The Master Shark's Mate
Tropical Bartender Bear
Tropical Lynx's Lover
The Storm (Tropical Tails)
Tropical Dragon Diver
Tropical Panther's Penance
A ChristMOOSE Story (Tropical Holiday Tails)
Dance Lesson (Tropical Tails)
The Betting Pool (Tropical Tails)
Firefighter Unicorn
Tropical Christmas Stag
Scarlet and the Christmas Kittens (Tropical Holiday Tails)
(the epilogue of Tropical Christmas Stag)
Lift (Shifting Sands Omnibus Vol 3)
Firefighter Phoenix
Tropical Leopard's Longing
Her Hellhound Bodyguard (Tropical Tails)
(the epilogue of Tropical Leopard's Longing)
Pregnancy Knows (Shifting Sands Omnibus Vol 3)
Tropical Lion's Legacy
Fake Fur (Tropical Tails)
Reunion (Tropical Tails)
Pickled Magnolias (Tropical Tails)
(the epilogue of Tropical Lion's Legacy)
Tropical Dragon's Destiny
A Will and a Wedding (Tropical Tails)
A Hoard of the Their Own (Tropical Tails)
Of Course (Tropical Tails)
Perfect Match (Tropical Tails)
All in the Timing (Tropical Holiday Tails)
(the epilogue of Tropical Dragon's Destiny)
Unreliable Senses (Tropical Tails)

OTHER GEMS FROM ELVA BIRCH

The Royal Dragons of Alaska (writing as Elva Birch): A fascinating alternate world where Alaska is ruled by secret dragon shifters. Adventure, romance, and humor! Reluctant royalty, relentless enemies…dogs, camping, and magic! Start with The Dragon Prince of Alaska!

Fae Shifter Knights (writing as Zoe Chant): A four-book fantasy portal romp, with cute pets and swoon-worthy knights stuck in a world of wonders like refrigerators and ham sandwiches. Start with Dragon of Glass!

A Day Care for Shifters (writing as Elva Birch): A hot new full-length series about adorable shifter kids and their struggling single parents in a town full of mystery and surprise. Start the series with Wolf's Instinct, when Addison comes to Nickel City to take a job at a very special day care and finds a family to belong to.

Green Valley Shifters (writing as Zoe Chant): A sweet, small town series with single dads, secret shifters, sweet kids, and spinsters. Standalone books where you can revisit your favorite characters. Start with Dancing Barefoot!

Suddenly Shifters (writing as Elva Birch): A hilarious series of novellas, serials, and shorts set in the small town of Anders Canyon, where something (in the water?) is making ordinary citizens turn into shifters. Start with Something in the Water!

Birch Hearts (writing as Elva Birch): An enchanting series of short stories and novellas. Unconstrained by theme or setting, each short read has romance, magic, and heart. And always, the impossible and irresistible. Start with Prompted 2 for fourteen pieces of sizzling flash fiction.

Not sure where to start? Take the quiz at elvabirch.com to find your perfect book!

www.ingramcontent.com/pod-product-compliance
Lightning Source LLC
Chambersburg PA
CBHW070551310726
48982CB00011B/1548/J

* 9 7 8 1 9 3 3 6 0 3 7 0 4 *